# THE VISITOR

"Quite a temper eh? Our Cat?" Bert was speaking to Robinson as they turned from the street containing Lomax's Club into St James's.

Robinson wiped the blood from his mouth. He could still feel the force of Catriona's knuckles. Bert was enjoying himself. It wasn't often that the Special Branch saw the Ministry get one in the laughing gear and in full view. Bert pursed his lips sententiously.

"She must feel strongly sir. To go hitting you. Our Cat?"

"Whose Cat?" said Robinson. "That's what I'd like to know."

Bert almost tut tutted. "Clean as a whistle, sir. As I told you. Even runs that club straight." He reconsidered. "Well straightish. And useful to my lot sir. Gossip, information. Background. Who's getting a bonk. Who's giving one. Who's spending too much money. It's the little things that might add up. You know that sir. You were a copper once. Although in foreign parts of course."

Robinson winced, perhaps because of his mouth. He said flatly, "That was in Hong Kong." As if it disposed of the matter.

"Yes sir," said Bert.

"Whose Cat," said Robinson. "Her birth certificate says she was Katie not CatribloodyOHna and her parents Mr and Mrs Lomax. Both by the way dead for years."

"So in the photograph. Whatsisname. That wasn't her dear old Dad?"

## About the author

Miles Donald is a university lecturer and free-lance writer. This is his third novel, after BOAST and DIPLOMACY. He lives in South London.

# THE VISITOR

## MILES DONALD

NEW ENGLISH LIBRARY
Hodder and Stoughton

First published in Great Britain in 1990 by New English Library Hardbacks

*New English Library paperback edition 1992*

**British Library C.I.P.**

Donald, Miles,
The visitor.
I. Title
823.914[F]

ISBN 0-450-55183-0

*The characters and situations in this book are entirely imaginary and bear no relation to any real person or actual happenings.*



Printed and bound in Great Britain for Hodder and Stoughton Paperbacks, a division of Hodder and Stoughton Ltd., Mill Road, Dunton Green, Sevenoaks, Kent TN13 2YA (Editorial Office: 47 Bedford Square, London WC1B 3DP) by Clays Ltd., St Ives plc.

To Barbara

# Prologue

In that part of Ireland the countryside is different.

At first the scenery is lush and almost tropical. The roads themselves are overgrown and little travelled. The population is long dead. Only its ghosts remain – an evicted village now grass high, a roofless church, a ruined National School. Nothing is farmable. Nothing to invite the return of human habitation.

Beyond the greenery lies moor, then granite mountains and finally the cold high-cliffed unwelcoming sea. This is a good country to get lost in; a country of tangled history, of ambiguous dreams, of easy disappearances.

And at the heart of it, where the lushness stops and the moor begins, at the end of an unmarked abandoned avenue, remote from any equivalent neighbour, known only to turf cutters and poachers, yet magnificent in its dilapidated grandeur stands Claremaurice House.

Here Despard died. On the fortified ground floor with its medical machinery and its team of double paid nurses flown in and out by weekly helicopter, the twilight years of senility and intermittent coma slipped at last away. Just at the end he thought he was young again in Spain, going south to Valencia carrying gold to buy the almost-lost Republic guns. He called out names but only the nurses came. All the others had forgotten or despised him.

He died and left behind the bad things. The chaos of fear and neglect; the Despard Foundation turned rotten by many-fingered Mr Schmidt; the smile on Madame Despard's face as she clicked in thousand dollar shoes across the marble New York lobby, her hand outstretched and trembling for the telegram that finally conveyed her husband's death.

And James Tar.

Above all James Tar.

It was a long time since James Tar had walked a British street. There were more cars. People looked richer. Except for the beggars. There were more beggars. The world Tar had once believed in was beggar free.

Beyond Edinburgh there was Leith. Prosperity slipped away. The docks had run down and the people with them. The streets were filthy. The unemployed stood in doorways.

He knew where he was going. He passed the Rowton House Hostel and found the corner pub. He was a small man, no longer young, but there was something in his cocky walk and bitter face that made the drunks pass to let him through.

In the bar at the back with the dirty door marked Snug there was someone waiting for him. A man, also small, but with a weak and bleary face. He lifted his glass.

"Jimmy." He said it nervously. He had a thick Scots accent.

Tar sat down. He lifted a carrier bag on to his knee.

"I've something for you, Maxwell."

The man called Maxwell looked into the bag. It contained an old fashioned suit – cheap and of a nasty violent blue.

"What's this?"

"It's time, Maxwell."

Maxwell drew back. He said, "I'm feared."

All Tar did was smile.

"Whatever you say, Jimmy," said Maxwell.

# Part I

# 1

Married men always leave.

When they do you shouldn't drink in the afternoon. She should have known better – Catriona Lomax.

The staff saw there was something wrong. They kept out of her way and fussed around the collection of well-heeled habitués who needed a legal over-priced place to lush in between the hours of three and midnight.

Normally Catriona was proud of the club – proud of its disreputable glamour – proud of the mixture of legerdemain and steadiness that running it required. Now she felt only sickened. She caught sight of herself in the pier glass. It showed a girl with fine blonde hair and pretty ankles, sublimating in drink the limited usefulness of both.

Then today of all days there had to be a Man from the Ministry. You could always tell them – Men from the Ministry. They chose tables from which they could take in the whole room . . . And watched.

Unlike every other establishment personage who patronised the club – lawyer, banker, broker, politician (she bit the rim of her glass) – Men from the Ministry didn't ogle the girls. They watched them. As they watched everything else. And waited.

Well, thought Catriona, if you can wait then so can I. God knows I've enough to think about. God knows I've waited long enough for nothing.

She had known from the beginning (two long years ago) that there could be no point to Esmond. He was a customer and that to start with was a bad idea. (Though working her hours who else could she meet?) He was a Member of Parliament. Almost by definition that made him a liar and greedy. Catriona had encountered many politicians across the haze of cigarette smoke to the accompanying clink of glasses. Each had made a private arrangement with untruth. Each was greedy for money or power or something worse. Catriona knew of no exceptions.

Esmond was a married womaniser whose wife, he claimed proudly, suspected nothing. Catriona doubted this. Esmond was too stupid. Instinct told her that the wife could see right through the man all the way to his shallow backbone. Such wives are dangerous. Especially to other women.

Then again Esmond had never attempted to understand Catriona herself, assuming cheerfully that she was as hard-boiled as her profession. In fact, lust and male vanity apart, he had not been interested in her at all.

This, all this, she had known from the beginning. From the first application of well-bred hand to well-turned thigh.

His hand. Her thigh.

So why did it hurt so much to be dumped by Esmond the Pointless whom she had *not* loved? . . . Well, not loved like that – whatever *that* was . . . She shook her head. It didn't clear. But she felt deceived; as if she had been conned by her body.

If not the pain of lost love – then what? The abruptness of his defection? The plain fact that she hadn't seen it coming, when Penelope and Louis (her best friends) had? Or just another form of vanity – this time classically female – that needs to get its rejection in first. That needs to be the one to do the leaving?

Well, there was no point in blaming Esmond for being himself. The fault lay in her own weakness for upper class men, for selfish men, for married men. A fault that originated somewhere in the past – perhaps as far back as that spruce and ugly Edinburgh bungalow in which her long dead parents tried to raise her, out of which she had somehow finally raised herself.

She might have cried if Gomez had not turned up at her shoulder and coughed. Catriona lit a cigarette and ensured, just in case, that some of the smoke got in her eyes.

Gomez was the largest quietest gentlest strongest Eurasian imaginable. Catriona had taken him on as a cellarman when he first arrived from Goa. Mr Schmidt, the club's owner, lived in Geneva and – profit permitting – left Catriona a free hand. She had made Gomez under manager. In a club where men habitually hid from their wives or girlfriends his discretion was invaluable but there were times when it got on Catriona's nerves. This was one of them. He *would* cough in times of trouble. Catriona suppressed an inclination to take things out on him. Esmond or no Esmond she should be grateful there remained a job to do; a Gomez to listen to.

"Yes, Gomez?"
"Bert's here Miss Lomax. I thought you'd want to know."
Indeed she did. Catriona looked across at the Man from the Ministry. Till now he had watched the room attentively, as if prepared to engage it in polite conversation. He checked his watch. On cue, she thought. The Ministry and the Special Branch together. Trouble. More trouble.
Bert arrived. This took time.
He greeted each of the girls to show that he was just old Bert the village bobby whom fate had unaccountably placed in the Special Branch where all that clever-Johnny business was beyond the likes of him.
Catriona knew the likes of Bert to be more than cunning. In terms of sex and alcohol her club sailed close to the wind. Bert made sure that the ordinary police minded their own business. In return Catriona provided free drinks, sporadic information and a look the other way when Bert went on his annual maudlin Christmas bender and left with a female free sample.
Bert now clumped up to her table. Most plain clothes policemen dressed like up-market yobs – suits too cheap, too tight, too modishly lapelled – with hairstyles to match. Not so Bert, who sported blue serge suits, lace up boots, starched collars and pudding basin hair. No one could have studied harder to be Uncle Bert the Lovable Anachronism.
"Cat dear," said Bert cheerily. "Business good?"
"See for yourself Bert. Sit down. Drink?"
"Only drink on duty ha ha."
"Ha ha."
"Can't have little Cat drink alone."
In other words she didn't usually drink in the afternoon. So what was wrong? He drank his whisky, rubbed his hands and asked after the off duty girls.
"Little Jacquetta all right eh?"
"Fine Bert."
"Little Tracy?"
"Fine Bert."
"Little Francesca still hanging round with that Arab?"
"That's what little Francesca's doing Bert."
Bert's expression turned extra paternal. "How's your Member Cat? Esmond Fitzwhatsisface."
Christ, thought Catriona. A man breaks up with you at

lunchtime and the Special Branch has it by late afternoon.
"Claremaurice. Severed."
"Is that right? Bloody politician. Too good for him Cat. Blonde. I always favoured blondes. Ever heard me say that Cat?"
"Yes Bert."
"Great little girl, Cat."
"I'm thirty-eight Bert."
Thirty-eight, near tears, near drunk and getting angry. Soon I'll have to dye my hair.
The Man from the Ministry bend down to open an old fashioned double clasped briefcase. He didn't look at Bert. He didn't need to.
"Time to meet a friend, Cat."
"Yours or mine?"
"Ha ha."
He rose to greet her. Catriona was used to men's stares but she didn't like the assessment in his eyes. What did he think he was about to meet – businesswoman, hostess, whore?
"Miss Catriona Lomax," Bert said, "this is Mr Robinson. He's from the Ministry."
No kidding Bert. My what a surprise. But Catriona kept silent and attempted her best managerial smile. Mr Robinson offered a dry palm and a drier smile. He was a big-boned sandy man with thick eyebrows and hair the colour of a golf bunker on a wet day. She didn't like sandy men. She looked away from his hands. She didn't want to make comparisons that would make her remember Esmond.
Esmond had beautiful hands.
"Miss Lomax. Indeed."
He had a deep voice somehow at odds with his colouring. What did he mean by indeed? Since when did her name require confirmation?
"Mr Robinson this time. Another original Ministry coinage? Not Mr Smithbrownjones?"
"Ha ha. Can't pull the wool over our Cat's eyes. Cat's eyes eh?"
"Rubbish," said Robinson in a quiet conversational tone. Bert shut up. "Do they actually call you Cat?"
"Only people like Bert. As you should have heard my name's Catriona."

Robinson thought about this. "Catri-OH-na? You pronounce it like that?"

"Yes."

"I thought," Robinson said, "that you were Scots. I thought that in Scotland they pronounced it Cat-REE-na."

"I thought you were the man of my dreams till I saw you close up."

"Now Cat . . . "

"Keep it to yourself Bert. No one else wants it. Can we get on with this."

Robinson was nodding politely. "Yes. Catri*oh*na. Your name after all. Well." He smiled as if they had just agreed about something. He laid a file on the table. "Photographs," he said.

She felt weary. More snooping on clients. What was it this time? Scandal? Identification? Blackmail? That's what you get my girl for the business you're in. So it's no use complaining when it arrives on the day your lover leaves.

Lover.

Oh God, she thought. Don't let it be Esmond. Not Esmond with his trousers down! Not Esmond with *me*.

The photographs weren't like that.

Some long ago political meeting. A platform draped with banners. A man equipped with a megaphone haranguing a sea of cloth caps.

"The second's an enlargement from the audience," said Robinson helpfully.

A tiny man in what had once been the uniform of the working class. The muffler said that if you possessed a collar and tie they were kept for best or pawned or both. A small man. One more minnow in the great river of working class poverty. Hands in his pockets to keep warm. No different from the hundreds – or was it thousands – beside him in the filth filled factory air . . . Except . . . Except that there *was* a quality that arrested her attention. An arrogance in the stance? A sneer on the face. Something hard perhaps about the eyes . . . All the same, she didn't know him.

"Sorry," she said.

"Of course," Robinson said, "that's a long time ago. During his union phase. Brief union phase?" The question was for Bert. Bert nodded. Robinson looked back at Catriona. He said, "After Spain."

"Spain?"

She must have looked adequately blank because he went on.

"This," he passed across a snapshot, "is recent. Same man."

He sat at a table covered in bottles. His face was shrunk and wizened with age. He wore a coarse ill-fitting jacket far too large for him. His mouth was open in a snarl. He might be drunk.

"Ugh," Catriona said. "I've never seen him."

"Haven't you," said Robinson, his thick red eyebrows raised. "*Haven't* you?"

Catriona stiffened. "He wouldn't be let in here."

Robinson considered this. "No." And then, "His name is James Tar. Look carefully."

"No. Never seen him. Never heard of him."

"That's odd," said Robinson. "He says he's your father."

# 2

Madame Despard no longer dared to do it in New York. She was too well known. The use of drugs complicated things. Sometimes results didn't come at all. Sometimes they were the wrong results.

You could be robbed. You could be beaten. You could be killed. Well, that had always been true. But then it would have been mixed up with the thrill of the thing itself, not for something as unsexual as drugs.

And so for those occasions when the need was desperately upon her she had made preparations. For times like these.

The need struck her at Kennedy. It came whenever it wanted to with no respect for her. It came and lived in her body till her body did something about it. Now, with age, shock brought it on. The death of Despard. The struggle with Schmidt. She began to shake. Schmidt would have to wait. And they could put Despard in the ground without her. At least that would spare her one more hypocrisy.

At the Delta desk she changed her reservation. Then from a pay phone she made the necessary arrangements. Four and a half hours later she registered at the Beau Regis on the sleazier side of New Orleans' Vieux Carré. There she kept a safe deposit box. She emptied it with trembling hands. Then she went to her hired car and drove it out of New Orleans towards the West Bayou and Busboy's place.

When she found a quiet exit on the freeway she took it, parked the car in a field and changed her clothes.

The sleek creature, preserved in raddled elegance, carrying two hundred thousand dollars on her back, her feet, her wrists, her ears, had become something else.

She wore a beehive wig, a little jewelled tank top, an imitation leather skirt riding high on her thighs. She stopped for gas and took the self serve channel. The pump boys stared as she crossed the forecourt. She needed that stare. She had not needed the gas.

Underneath she wore whore's underclothes. A cheap red brassière fringed with black, a garter belt, black stockings, split crotch panties. Panties. She made a face at the commonness of the word. Once she would not have had to use it; use them. But time had compelled her to advertise. Time. She bit her carmined lip. All the wasted time being twisted by one man or another. She thought of blackmailing Schmidt. She thought of that weak crippled wet mouthed bastard Despard who had never let go of anything, not even in paralysis. Well, he was dead. She had knelt before her last wheelchair.

Another half hour and she left the freeway.

Busboy's place stood on a patch of waste ground off a country road overlooking the Bayou.

When she first came there had been a neon sign. That had been twenty years ago when it still operated as a honky-tonk for roughnecks. Before she had bought it. Closed it down. Kept it for herself. Of course the sign had gone. It had to.

She walked up the wooden steps. A nickelodeon played. Inside Busboy was behind the bar, big and black and competent as always. He ignored her. That was part of the game.

He had worked quickly. There were dirty glasses, dirty ashtrays, jackets on chairs as if it were a normal bar.

And one notional customer.

One man.

At the bar.

Ignoring her.

She walked to the bar. Busboy looked bored.

He said, "What'll it be?"

She said, "You have quite a selection."

She moved on to a bar stool hitching her skirt as high as it would go.

The man turned. He said, "You want a drink bitch?"

Her heart sank.

Busboy had done his best. He had dirtied the guy up. His jeans and workshirt bore oil stains but they were recent. And his face was young. Far too young. A professional, she thought. Doing his obliging best to conjure up a hostility of lust. Still, he was absolutely all she had.

"You're a big one," she said.

Afterwards she lay on the floor for a while.

She could hear them talking in Busboy's office. She heard the man's voice. "Busboy," the man said, "I've turned some tricks but this is *crazy*." She could hear the intake of Busboy's breath. The man didn't notice. He continued. "Hell, Busboy, you didn't tell me she was so damned *old*." There was a thud. Busboy had the man against the wall.

"OK," the man said. "OK."

"You be mindful. She a lady."

"I *said* OK."

"You wait. I get your trash money."

Busboy came into the bar. He took the money from the drawer by the disused till. "Lady," he said, "help is hard to find."

"Don't I know it Busboy."

He left and she stayed on the floor. The disgust had started. Once love had been spontaneous and lust had not been vice. But now she had to pay for the poor recreation of her fierce past – for her one and only sexual paradigm – for that small violent body alive with an understanding of her thighs. Gone now. Long gone.

She looked up. She cried out.

Busboy was walking slowly, backwards into the room. The man held a shotgun to his stomach. Busboy looked hesitant. Busboy looked frightened. But he wasn't. Busboy knew what to do. As the man's eyes flitted to Madame Despard, Busboy did something quick with his knee. The shotgun went elsewhere then the man's neck broke.

"Too fast," said Busboy. "Should have made him talk some. Say who sends him. Then put him in the swamp."

Madame Despard tried to get up. She rose pulling down her scrap of dirty skirt. She clung to Busboy.

"Lady," he said, "Mr Tar. He say take care of you. He say be mindful."

She clung to Busboy. "Dear God," she said. "Jimmy?"

He nodded. She closed her eyes. Busboy stroked her hair.

"I'm a wreck Busboy."

"You a Lady Wreck," he said.

# 3

"Quite a temper eh? Our Cat?" Bert was speaking to Robinson as they turned from the street containing Lomax's Club into St James's.

Robinson wiped the blood from his mouth. He could still feel the force of Catriona's knuckles. Bert was enjoying himself. It wasn't often that the Special Branch saw the Ministry get one in the laughing gear and in full view. Bert pursed his lips sententiously.

"She must feel strongly sir. To go hitting you. Our Cat?"

"Whose Cat?" said Robinson. "That's what I'd like to know."

Bert almost tut tutted. "Clean as a whistle, sir. As I told you. Even runs that club straight." He reconsidered. "Well straightish. And useful to my lot sir. Gossip, information. Background. Who's getting a bonk. Who's giving one. Who's spending too much money. It's the little things that might add up. You know that sir. You were a copper once. Although in foreign parts of course."

Robinson winced, perhaps because of his mouth. He said flatly, "That was in Hong Kong." As if it disposed of the matter.

"Yes sir," said Bert.

"Whose Cat," said Robinson. "Her birth certificate says she was Katie not CatribloodyOHna and her parents Mr and Mrs Lomax. Both by the way dead for years."

"So in the photograph. Whatsisname. That wasn't her dear old Dad?"

But Robinson ignored him; he was looking for a taxi. Then he said, "What I'd like to know is what a marvellous woman like that is doing with a shit like Esmond Claremaurice."

Oy oy thought Bert. Marvellous woman! Punched him in the mouth. Hauls back and does it just like that. Then only just misses with a bleeding ashtray. I mean Cat was a looker all right but marvellous woman! Maybe he was a bit kinky Robinson. Some of those Ministry people were. Bert gave a professional older man's sigh. "To Man sir Woman is an

Enigma. And this one must have screwed a few. Men."
"What's that got to do with it," snapped Robinson. His lip bled worse now.
"Oh probably nothing sir. Nothing." Bert, accepting correction gratefully, straightened his back as if a burden of intolerable error had been lifted from him. "It wouldn't *really* . . . " Now he paused and began to frown deferentially as if attempting to bring his poor mind on to the wavelength of an immeasurably superior intellect. "Except sir . . . ?"
"Except what?"
"Except what *is it*?"
But Robinson was thinking out loud. "I don't think she recognised him. From the photographs. Or the name. Do you?"
"No I don't," said Bert. "So why then lose her temper like *that*. When you said father?"
"When I said father . . . "
A taxi pulled in. Smiling, Bert held the door open just longer than was necessary, then stooping unctuously got in next to Robinson.
"All right," said Robinson. "*It*. It begins with Tar. Once upon a time and a very long time ago he was good at something."
"And what would that be sir?"
"Killing people," said Robinson.
Bert sat back in his seat. "The old tunes are the best sir," he said contentedly.

Catriona left Gomez in charge and went home early.
Things could hardly be worse.
Her lover had left. She had punched a Man from the Ministry in the mouth in clear view of a clientele that relied upon an entire discretion. Each of her customers had a good reason for concealing his membership. Her girls might not be prostitutes in the conventional sense but they certainly didn't live on what she paid them. She might as well telephone Mr Schmidt in Geneva and ask to be fired. Maybe he wouldn't hear about it? And maybe Swiss banks would start giving their money away.
She looked despairingly out of the taxi window as four o'clock London put the crawl into rush hour. Schmidt, she

thought glumly, who had plucked her out of one of life's little reject piles and given her the unearned big chance – what would she do if he threw her back? She wasn't equipped for anything. Not one damned thing.

There was only one hope – the oddity, the mysteriousness of the man. You never knew what he would care about, bother about, show an interest in. Maybe if the membership didn't fall off . . . ? Perhaps some of them even liked it. It must have been quite a show.

Just for a moment she giggled. Then she remembered what an immense fool she had been.

Why *had* she done it? The compound interest of unhappiness and drink? Too general. It had to be more specific than that. Then she remembered – quite distinctly.

She had no idea what game they were playing – Bert and the Ministry together – but one thing was certain. Somehow, from someone they had found a way of invading her. Somehow they had dipped into her dreams. She felt again the prick of tears. Fiercely she fought them back. She would cry no more today.

The taxi turned into the Earls Court Road. The rejected produce from the shops – late night takeaways, ethnic supermarkets, sleazy liquor stores – mixed with traffic oil on the thin unstable pavements. At one corner a barrow boy sold petrol scented fruit to the gullible. Here the taxi turned, continued for a hundred yards, stopped.

The title, Chelsea Mansions, even at the very outset, must have been pretentious. Chelsea had still been a mile away, though then Earls Court had been a farm and half of Fulham open country. Still, a century ago the block must have seemed a solid modern investment of bright airy well-servanted flats.

Now the Underground alongside shook its foundations, late night visitors from the Exhibition Centre copulated against its walls. The surrounding streets had filled up with flophouse hotels. Rapacious landlords had carved the original large and lofty rooms into the maximum number of minimal units.

This is where Catriona Lomax lived. Where, at London prices, she was lucky to live. Even if the block was dilapidated, the central heating a joke, the place retained a certain vestigial charm. Snob that she was Catriona could not bear to live more than a fifteen minute taxi ride from the West End. And if the place was not what she had dreamed of in her conceited girlhood (what was?) it was not suburban; not Ealing nor Finchley nor (she shuddered to think of it) Barnet.

The lift was out of action. She took the stairs to the fourth and top floor. Louis had the flat directly beneath her. Later on, when she had calmed down, steadied herself, she would call Louis. Perhaps Penelope as well. Let her friends take care of her.

She crossed the last section of pitted rubber floor, unlocked the door of her flat and entered.

She stood in a long narrow room containing a number of oddly shaped embrasures (now bookshelves) and a huge window that stared meaninglessly out on to the four filthy walls of the building's internal well. ("My dear," Louis said, "don't think of it as a window, think of it as a picture from the Metropolitan Museum of Art.")

All the way back in the taxi she had said it to herself. Once I get home I'll be all right.

She wasn't.

She began to shake. That book – had she left it on the table? That door that opened on to the small corridor containing the bathroom and bedroom – hadn't she left it shut? Hadn't she? *Hadn't* she?

STOP IT.

She yelled the words inside herself. She'd got over this. She'd stopped being like this. It was just that photograph that had started this up. She'd got over it.

Hadn't she?

Just as if her fear was physical, just as if her fear was not mixed with expectation, just as if she believed in the possibility of an actual burglar, Catriona picked up the huge Byzantine candlestick which cheapskate Esmond had been given free in Turkey, and moved forward.

The corridor was empty. And the bedroom. The bathroom too. She went back into the main room, deposited the candlestick, picked up a high backed chair and took it into the corridor. She placed the chair against the wall and climbed up till she stood on the very top of its wooden back. This was a precarious business but she was well co-ordinated. Besides, she was used to it.

She reached up. Her fingers touched the grille of a disused

air vent. The grille came away. On tip toe she stared into the narrow hole. The dust lay thick and undisturbed. Nothing had been moved.

She got down and walked back into the main room.

One part of the ritual remained.

She knelt by the bottom row of the furthest book case. The album was where it should be, neatly in place. She took it out and turned the pages. Here she was dandled, fondled, posed, by one parent or another, against a succession of Scottish backgrounds, over a series of years. Here she was growing; here grown. Here were her parents. Old to start with, ageing beside her. Good people, as people went, with whom she had nothing in common.

And nothing had been disturbed. No displacements. No new finger marks. She turned slowly to the last page of the comedy.

Sixteen and studio posed, she stared out; that damn-you-world look that would cause her so much trouble already in her eyes.

Suddenly a wild excitement swept over her.

Someone *had* been here. The page was wet . . . There were tears on the page!

But then she realised that she was crying and the tears her own.

No one had come for those parts of her that she had hidden. No one had come for the girlhood of Catriona Lomax.

The Visitor had not come. He never did.

# 4

This is the fairy tale of the Visitor.

It belonged to Katie before Catriona, for Catriona was christened Katie. Not Catherine or even Kate but Katie. She made herself into Catriona later.

As early as she could remember her mother's voice was full of fear.

"Don't Katie . . . Katie don't."

. . . What Katie didn't do . . .

Katie didn't go anywhere alone. No, not even to the little parade of shops next door though Mother could see her from the window. Katie didn't go to school on the bus with the other children. Mother found the money for a small car though Father complained about the petrol. Mother drove her each morning and was back again each monotonous afternoon, searching the girls' faces with her anxious rapacious stare. Once Katie hid and took the bus. Although Mother screamed and, for the only time, struck her, Katie was shaken most not by the anger but by the terror in her voice.

Then at home later in the clean ugly bungalow, her mother changed tones. Wheedling, tentative, excited-fearful, she began once more the recitation that went back as far as Katie could remember.

What would Katie do if one day – unexpectedly – a Visitor arrived? Someone with a huge car and rich clothes who would come to take Katie away offering her money and houses and jewels. What would Katie say? Would she leave her poor old work worn mother for this creature of mystery? . . . No Mother no.

And yet . . .

The story invited and menaced by turns. Her mother intoned it like a ritual. Katie sensed that her mother was both frightened and fascinated by her fear. As time went by the story acquired embroidery. The Visitor would wait till Mother was out. A big car would draw up with tinted windows. A man would get out. A chauffeur. He would wear a chauffeur's cap. He would walk up the crazy paving to the bungalow door. He saluted. He brought a message. Katie would inherit a fortune, or receive a film contract, or be given a round-the-world cruise *if only she would walk away with him towards that car.*

Would she. Would? . . . Mother no. Her mother would hug her violently and swear her to secrecy. Katie felt that she had been made the celebrant at some intense mystery without the rites of initiation.

At the onset of adolescence Katie turned simultaneously against Visitor and Mother alike. This came less from distaste at her mother's perverted fantastic needs (though that distaste was real enough) than from a combination of boredom and snobbery.

The truth was that Katie's upbringing numbed with a vengeance. Her father did his garden. Her mother watched television. A great deal of tea was drunk. Nothing happened. Boredom haunted her. Boredom was worse than suffering. Boredom didn't even malform you; it didn't bother. Boredom was smug and settled and good for nothing, like the perpetually well made bed in the spare room that no one interesting would ever be fool enough to stay in.

The truth too was that she had begun to turn against her mother on class grounds, and the Visitor seemed an increasingly déclassé sort of dream. Katie's parents were the epitome of the Scots lower middle class (her father was a clerk on the railways) but they possessed a fanatical attachment to education. In Edinburgh Katie had been sent to as posh a school as her parents could afford. For Katie it was a hard school. Her accent, her clothes, her family were all wrong. Her mother's vicarious snobbery didn't help; she wanted to be told of Katie's mixing with the daughters of Miss Brodie's Edinburgh followed swiftly by her rejection of their snooty ways and her necessary preference for a humble but oh so homely home. Katie squirmed with embarrassment.

Puberty made matters worse. Heads turned. Her mother didn't like it. Her mouth grew into a hard covenanting line when Katie pleaded for clothes or unchaperoned free time. Katie stared into the mirror and dreamed hard of a world that would appreciate her – of a world worthy of her appreciation. A world in which there would be something to *do*.

And in these dreams the Visitor resumed his calls.

Perhaps her mother's disease was infectious, for now (despite herself, without thinking) Katie had taken on the Visitor as her own.

This Visitor, *her* Visitor, would be different. Not obvious like her mother's version. No top hats, cigars; no limousines. No come-on like a stupid toff from an Ealing comedy. This Visitor would be subtle.

He might announce himself at any place or time. Suddenly materialise at her elbow in a shop where she bought gloves or stockings. Stop his taxi by her bus queue on a rainy day. Rise from the shadows in the cinema or the corner table in the library or the bandstand on the beach at terrible holiday Troon.

He always wore a hat pulled down to shade his sensitive mysterious face. Sometimes he wore a double breasted suit of soft dark grey. If it was night when he came to claim her he wore a white silk dinner jacket – double breasted once again. In winter he wore an overcoat with an astrakhan collar which she had seen in a photograph of Diaghilev – and carried a silver mounted cane.

And he would speak, no matter how or where they met, with polished English diffidence. Although you may not know it . . . Although we may have not met . . . Although I may be frightening you . . . He had watched her always from afar . . . For long years he had held back his strong emotions. Years of her struggle, growth and blossoming until he came at last to claim his own.

His daughter.

The words spoken, a celebration followed . . . Those gloves – my daughter takes a hundred pairs . . . Why not a taxi all the way to London . . . *I* find your accent charming Catriona, but perhaps some elocution lessons . . . Your Majesty may I present my rather special daughter.

The fantasy upset her but she needed it. Upset her *because* she needed it. For all his polish this Visitor was nastier than her mother's version, for Katie's fantasy was the very spawn of disloyalty . . . She was denying her real parents. She was dreaming their removal, sometimes even their deaths (in one version the Visitor rescued her from the twisted metal of a parricidal car crash). She was worse than her mother, who only fantasised a loyal daughter.

She tried to stop the thing by the employment of logical self-analysis. She was not the first child to hate the drabness of life, the dullness of family, to dream of being special and so as an escape to award herself imaginary changeling status.

Then fate took a couple of turns.

Her father died first. A heart attack struck just before Katie's seventeenth birthday. Her mother unexpectedly took this death badly. Perhaps she missed having someone to ignore. Premature senility set in, as if the gods had taken revenge on unused capacity. She moved through patches of forgetfulness, aggression and self-pity.

She took to making – and leaving unfinished – cup after cup of tea. One day Katie entered the bungalow's kitchen to find her mother crouching at the table surrounded by half-filled mugs. She looked up at Katie with glazed eyes.

"Ah . . . You're very like your father," she said.

"Oh," said Katie trying to be cheerful. "Do you think so?"

Her mother began to nod with a horrible over-slow rhythm – up and down, up and down – as if the monotonous repetition of a physical movement was a proof of truth. It was a sunny winter's day. The bright hard Edinburgh light thrust itself into the room and, as Katie could see in the mirror, made her hair glow almost white.

"Mind you," Katie said, "Father was never as fair as I am."

Her mother stopped nodding. "You damned fool," she said. "I mean your real father."

Katie felt like someone in an earthquake. As if the room had moved while she stayed still. Through the beam of sunlight she made herself walk towards the woman who stared at her through a mask of recent age.

"Mother," she said, "what do you mean Mother?"

Her mother cackled slyly into a half-filled mug. "Mind your own beeswax."

Her mother's mind continued to slip. Although increasingly peculiar – she even developed an astonishing line in invective obscenity – she gave no more devastating hints. She died six months later one Wednesday, rising abruptly from her chair to point an accusing finger at a silent television set.

But although her mother left, the Visitor remained to comfort Catriona in her dreams. To comfort her on days like these when her lover left.

Except that today he couldn't. Not today. Not this evening.
For between himself and Catriona, in her tear-stained lunch-at-the-Ritz-with-Esmond dress, had come a parody – a little old drunk man in a blue proletarian suit pretending to be her father.

# 5

"A death here. A death there," said Robinson. "Back in Colonial days the French were quite unkeen on him for a while. Algeria. Cochin-China. Even Vietnam before the Americans officially arrived. Oh and other trouble spots around the globe. Anyway he picked single targets and removed them. In out and away with the money."

"So that's what he did them for? Assassinations? Money?"

"Not entirely. Claims that he only liked to kill right-wingers. He said it was easier; they were better fed; made bigger targets. He seems to have done other things too. Some gun running and general smuggling out of Tangier when it was a free port. All individual stuff. No direct allegiance to anyone."

Bert nodded slowly several times to show how seriously he was listening. Then he said, "But he's laid off for a good fifteen years during which there's no sign of him? Retired, in a manner of speaking?"

"Perhaps," said Robinson. "We don't know that much."

Robinson ticked off points on his square red fingers. "A foundling brought up in a children's home in East Kilbride. Runs away. No further mention until he's arrived in Spain to join the International Brigades. He couldn't have been more than seventeen."

"The young take easier to killing, sir. They're simpler. More practical."

Robinson looked up sharply. Bert's usual desire to irritate had been replaced by a tone that was innuendo-free, neutral, considered. Robinson reminded himself that despite the posing Bert was a shrewd and methodical policeman.

Bert promptly spoiled this good impression.

"So now he'd be sixty-seven. Shoots from the replacement hip does he?"

"Very funny."

"Yes sir," said Bert, as one complimented.

"A spell in the shipyards. A little union agitation then abroad. If he was ever in jail it must have been abroad somewhere."

"Not much to go on, eh sir?"

"No," said Robinson. "We're having to put him together rather quickly."

"To speak frankly sir I don't get it. I mean he pops up, says he's our Cat's father. Who cares?"

Robinson hesitated. Oy oy Matey, thought Bert. You're going to tell me something when you'd rather not. Now we're getting somewhere.

"I'm not sure," said Robinson. "Esmond Claremaurice might. Then there's the Despard Foundation. Ever heard of it?"

"Not had the pleasure sir." At the mention of Esmond's name Bert had begun to beam. He liked nothing more than the persecution of a Member of Parliament.

"You will," said Robinson. "Of course it all *might* be nothing."

Bert glowed with boy scout enthusiasm and did his best at looking up to someone two inches shorter.

"Ah but *you* sir. If I know you sir you have your own good reasons."

Robinson regarded Bert with exasperated distaste. Bert accepted it with pie-faced glee.

"All right," said Robinson. "It's a question of sources. I believe the source. Let me take you back a little while. To Señor Rossminster."

Señor Rossminster was enjoying one of his spells in Marrakesh. As befitted his standing – a retired gentleman of precise but slow moving habits – he followed a set, if charmingly eccentric, routine. Instead of air passage or a more proximate sea crossing he drove all the way from Marbella to Algeciras. This journey, together with lunch at the Hotel San Cristobal – same courses, same table, same tip – was, he explained, a long hallowed hangover from his wine merchant days. The subsequent stages – the filthy boat to Ceuta in Spanish Morocco, the even filthier train all the way to the foot of the Atlas Mountains – he publicly ascribed to a number of motives. Penury (offered with a little laugh), curiosity (offered with a little diffidence), boredom (offered with a little sigh). Dontcher know, said Señor Rossminster in his antiquated slang, it was cheap and the people were damned interesting if a feller only took the trouble. Besides, what else did a pensioned off old buffer have to do but kill his remaining time?

The assorted louts, crooks and tax exiles that made up Marbella's expatriate community accepted all this with a snigger. After all Señor Rossminster, at seventy something, was resolutely unmarried and wasn't Morocco the bum capital of Europe? . . . What's that? . . . Africa! . . . Anyway it was amusing to think of a nice old codger of such enduring expatriate Englishness compelled to sit upright in straw hat and MCC tie surrounded by a lot of sweaty Barbary riff-raff.

It amused Señor Rossminster to amuse them. One and a half centuries ago his forebears had left Liverpool for Seville. There they had traded in wine and Spanish wives, maintaining towards both commodities an artificial Englishness of attitude. The more Iberian blood that flowed in Rossminster veins the greater the determination to export the young "home" however briefly to the public schools of England.

So it had been with Señor Rossminster, who had seen the last of the wine and the end of the line, who was English only at a tangent, whose skin darkened suspiciously unless sheltered from the sun, who took cheap local trains because their vagaries permitted missed connections, mysterious little side journeys, and who could still kill more things than time if he really had to. This was the Señor Rossminster, toothbrush moustache neatly clipped, skin panama'd against the bright Moroccan sun, who arrived in Marrakesh to meet a man who called himself the Consul-in-Exile from Ceuta and was nothing of the kind.

As usual Señor Rossminster registered at a small local hotel behind the bus station a few strides from the extraordinary square of Djemaa-el-Fna, now taking on noon shadows cast by Kotoubia minaret. He ordered coffee and figs brought to his room, pondered a little, then had the manager send out for a whore. The manager insisted that two whores constituted the working minimum for a man in the Señor's position. The Señor knew about Moroccan rates of commission and resisted. The manager finally yielded and provided a fifteen-year-old Berber girl – cheap, hygienic, and easily silenced on the inevitable issue of procuring her brother by way of variety. True, she proposed one or two tricks with figs, but Señor

Rossminster told her to eat them instead. Cheers 'em up no end he thought, as he watched her stuff them down.

After showering in a compartment made of tin, he changed into his second linen suit, sent the first to be washed, adjusted the ribbon on his straw hat and took himself out into the marketplace.

Literally Djemaa-el-Fna means the Assembly Place of the Dead. Here in the days of the Almoravid Sultans the heads of malefactors rotted until the Jews of the Mellah ghetto, paying the dues of toleration, took them away for burning; now, even this early in the afternoon, it was crammed with more varieties of the living than any other place in Africa. Porters, cous-cous vendors, barbers, toothpullers, jewelry beaters – all yelled their wares. The professional readers had already started up, proclaiming news or crouching at the ready, quill and parchment in hand to take down the love confessions of veiled illiterate women. The beggars gave their professional all, waving stumps and poking maimed digits into sockets. Señor Rossminster moved contentedly through the smell and the clamour. Though he came here no more than three times a year, he felt sufficiently at home. He had once fought alongside these people. This might not make them comprehensible, but it made them familiar.

After two infusions of mint tea, Señor Rossminster was drifting towards the fire eaters when a small boy with a monkey on his shoulder delivered a message. Señor Rossminster followed him out of the square.

The Consul-in-Exile from Ceuta was either doing exceptionally well or expected so to do, for he was to be found at the Mammounia, the country's most expensive hotel. Señor Rossminster strode past the over-priced tourist trinkets in their gold leaf display cases, frowned as a good Englishman should at the damnable modern air-conditioning and came through the hibiscus bower into the pool garden.

The Consul-in-Exile sat under a lemon tree, spitting into the swimming pool when no one was looking. His expensive clothes were stained, his face vulpine, his eyes bagged, his skin yellowed with debauchery.

His nationality was flexible. He spoke Spanish with a Chilean accent. His English was lightly tinged with Ivy League drawl – whether self-taught or naturally acquired no one could be sure. He did, however, possess an Irish passport which he was rumoured to have made himself. Though by avocation a high class pimp, he would turn his hand to any convenient depravity. Some years previously in Ceuta he had provided well groomed young thugs for female travellers of advanced ages and peculiar tastes. There he flourished until the advent of a large client from New Jersey whose masochism he overrated. She took her breakages to the Spanish police who were going through a puritanical phase. In short order the Consul – so self-christened because he represented all sorts – found himself Morocco bound, where he had become one of Señor Rossminster's most useful informants and, inevitably, Consul-in-Exile.

Señor Rossminster sat down. The Consul shook hands. He had very dirty nails.

"Doing yourself proud eh Consul? Surprised they'll let you in here what?" The Señor gave a loud barking laugh followed by the one digit agitation of moustache bristles which, in his single distant year at Cheltenham College, had seemed to be the most English gesture of the most English master. The Consul smiled with all his yellow teeth. Señor Rossminster supposed that women must desire the man precisely because he was so disgusting.

"You'd be surprised how much of other people's money I've spent here. Besides," the Consul stretched his grin wider till it became a gash, "this is your treat."

Rossminster frowned. "I shall want receipts."

The Consul shifted irritably. He disliked records of his presence.

"Unless this is *particularly* good."

The Consul resumed his vulpine grin and crossed his legs. Like all his movements it was self-consciously graceful. Perhaps it was the Chilean blood – assuming he hadn't made that for himself too.

"Lord I believe," said the Consul, "Help thou this senior citizen's unbelief. Rosco Minster you are going to *love* this one."

He took a hefty gargle of gin fizz, checked that no one was looking, spat in the pool and began.

"Picture the scene. Your hero, myself" (he inclined his slick head) "fallen among thieves. At the Court, as it were, of

Haroun-al-Raschid . . . "

Rossminster rapped his signet ring against the table's edge. "We'll have it straightforward don't you know."

"We'll have two more gin fizzes," he waved a languid grimy hand for the waiter. "No imagination eh. That's the trouble with you Rosco. You're so damned British."

Rossminster ignored the sarcasm. "So you were in one of your regular dives in the Medina. Which one?"

"The Café Turc. A couple of American hippies." The Consul winked with a mixture of human contempt and professional pride.

Señor Rossminster wasn't surprised. Morocco in general – and Tangier and Marrakesh in particular – receives a heavy visitation from the itinerant and imbecile young. Some are rich. Some are poor. Some come to take drugs. Some come to deal in them. Some come inspired by a sham religiosity. Some come because it seems like a good idea at the time. Some come but cannot remember why, or anything else. Most are American, but all look out of date – would-be sixties dropouts who missed the sixties through being in diapers. Even the most impoverished of this number was good for some form of Consular exploitation; the theft of blue jeans or a passport; the lend-lease of a girlfriend willing to do her stuff with the swarthy gentleman for something extra in the drug direction.

The Consul, who prided himself on his knowledge of the Medina – the two square miles of impenetrable medieval street jungle that lie at the heart of Marrakesh – had a well developed line in guided tours for those who knew no better. The Café Turc was a regular port of call.

"But these hippies," said the Consul proudly, "are not quite the standard issue. They aren't the usual kind of dipshit dreamy and they look as if maybe they've done some washing around the edges. And there's none of this poor John, Mohammed can you spare a dime act. Pigtails apart they are making whoopee like the Chamber of Commerce outing. Cash money. Bundles. More than one currency. Dollars. Swiss francs. Keep pulling the stuff out the way people do who've just had a windfall or hit it big. My thought I. Dummies thought I. Lulu really is back in town."

"You are presumably going to say that if they were drug sellers to that extent they would keep quiet."

"Something like that."

"Perhaps they had rich American parents."

The Consul shook his head emphatically. "It wasn't like that. They're coming down from something and I don't mean drugs – or not just drugs. Like sailors when the fleet's in and money to burn. Kept laughing between themselves. As if they'd done something so all-fire clever. Well anyway there they are at the next table in the Café Turc where men are men and most of them are dressed as women."

"Humph," said Señor Rossminster. "And where you get a ten per cent kickback."

"Fifteen," said the Consul. "Diplomatic perks."

"Did you," said Señor Rossminster, "have any particular felony in mind?"

The Consul tried to look dignified. "The situation was generally commercial."

"D'you mind getting to the point?"

"Meanwhile back at the raunch, *ces beaux hipsteurs* are loosening the fuck up – they are becoming sufficiently stoned or pissed or maybe both and they commence tickling the sumptuous transvestites. Now Rosco I require your fullest attention for I am about to interest you strangely. Because it turns out these guys are political persons. They have political opinions for God's sake and being out of their gourds wish to air them. In addition to being dirty and stoned and off the wall affluent and generally the slobs that time forgot these guys are *intellectuals*."

"Go on," said Señor Rossminster.

"Now much of this patter your representative cannot catch. It's noisy and they keep breaking off to play tonguesy wonguesy with the boys in bombazine but most of it is pretty straightforward. America, West Germany, Israel, commercialism, capitalism. They suck. But that's not all. Russia's not so good either. Something to do with a system. Because systems *especially* suck. These people are hard to please except in respect of all that nuzzling and feeling which so far they seem to believe comes from free range farm fresh females. I mean . . . "

And the Consul took a swig, paused, smiled. "I mean they don't know what's up a skirt but they think they know all about Spain."

"Spain? What's Spain got to do with it?"

Calculated mischief drew the Consul's lips into a smile. "Not Spain mi Corazón. *Spain.* Not the country Rosco. The *war. Your* little sideshow as I recall. Boom boom. No passarán. Let's all make whoopee on the Ebro."

Señor Rossminster felt his body tighten from throat to feet.

The Consul remained in full tormenting swing. "Reading from right to left, the Spanish Civil War. You remember. The one when you were on the winning side *Señor* Rossminster."

Although a man of few principles – in themselves no more than a collection of vague and dogged loyalties – this was not a war that he liked to have joked about. Then he remembered that offence was useless; the Consul was as political as a cash register.

"And what did these intellectual hippies have to say about Spain?"

"Guess what. How the good guys – I beg your pardon Rosco, the Republic – lost because big bad Joe Stalin and his hard line Commies stabbed it in the back. How all those really cute non-totalitarian-anarcho-syndicalist-every-peasant-has-a-pig-one-man-went-down-to-mow parties that showed how gee whiz Democratic and deep down *nice* the Left was got criminally shafted by the boys from Moscow Town."

"Oh," said Señor Rossminster. "That old thing."

"Sure," said the Consul, "as the knee jerks. So they didn't know diddly shit. The usual student revolutionary garbage. A voyage round George Orwell and Joe's your wicked Stalinist uncle. But loud Rosco, very loud and it transpires in conversation with a character hitherto obscured from your hero by a pillar. A character who I suddenly realise has been winding these guys up. Anyway there he is – now in full view. Little old guy, wrinkled like a nut, wears a god-awful blue cardboard suit that maybe some Bulgarian tourist leaves behind in 1950. Speaks British English with some god-awful accent, don't ask me what. Gets out his umbrage and then some. Tells the hippies they're a pair of ignorant faggots who can't even speak Menshevik. Says that while their putative parents were pulling the puddings of the downtrodden masses he, small man in question, was in Spain fighting for la libertad el honór and a free nun for every worker. And *he* can tell them because *he* knows that this was no simple war with no simple conclusion.

Hey no offence? The nun bit?"

"I'm an Anglican," said Señor Rossminster.

"Great little church. Plenty of space. To resume. No one has told these hippies about flower power. Or maybe they've seen *Casablanca* one time too many. Or maybe Bulgarian suit is so small and old they think what the hell. Anyway, toughness ensues. Quel mistake. I tell you Rosco this old guy is good. A brief bout of martial arts and our two time travellers discover the sedentary life. The little guy gives a toast to the International Brigades. No one understands a word but they like his style so they toast right back, take his photograph, and the hippies get slung out."

"What happened to them?"

The Consul spread his grimy palms. "Rosco! Honeybunch. Carrying money. In the Medina. Maybe they're alive. Maybe not."

Rossminster sat back. "So far Consul what we have might become interesting but it's not much to write home about."

The Consul was grinning. "But Rosco *this* is?" He leaned forward. His wicked eyes gleamed with excitement. "Answer me this Señor Rossminster. When hands were laid to Bulgarian suit extra bits of the little guy appear. Why do you think his skin was blue?"

# 6

Catriona lay soaking in the bath – moodily regarding her body. First she decided that it had gone to pieces. Her breasts sagged. Her skin had coarsened. Small stretch marks had set up camp on the inside of her thighs.

No wonder Esmond had left her.

A little more drink (uncharacteristically she had taken a glass into the bath) and she started to get angry. Esmond's wife was as flat as a board. Esmond's wife was a *washboard* for Christ's sake. Esmond's wife would be lucky to have thighs that could *get* stretch marks.

Then fair-mindedness turned the anger back on herself. Why did she have to keep coming back to bloody Esmond? It just seemed to happen in spite of (to spite?) herself. Why did this decidedly inferior man have to be so important? Although Catriona hated women who hated being women there were times when she felt on their wavelength. This was one of them; it seemed that her emotions were a fifth column cunningly planted to overthrow her character.

She hadn't loved Esmond. She didn't love Esmond. That was true wasn't it? Not *really* loved. But why then was she so upset? *And what the hell was he doing not loving her?*

She threw the drink viciously against the wall. It didn't change a thing. There was the same face staring blotchily back at her from the glass shower panel that fronted the bath. The ice cubes had left little trails that fitted on to her reflection like badly painted tears.

Was this the end result of all those years of messy struggle and inflated pride? Was this after all what she had come to? A girl of diminishing assets and increasing self-pity with temper as her only outlet? A girl who (she could imagine the whispers) hadn't quite fitted in anywhere. A girl for whom there was no groove, socially or romantically. A girl who (the whispers started again) despite her looks could never get a decent man or keep a shoddy one. A girl who, since she so plainly liked men *that* way, had to have something wrong with her. A girl who had rated herself too highly, who had priced herself out of the market. Who had in front of her nothing better than an advancing middle age of more and inferior Esmonds . . . And so, back, once again, to Esmond.

Perhaps, looking back, the Visitor was to blame for her difficulties with love. From early on she had cultivated a sense of romantic specialness (honed and heightened by the nagging boredom of bungalow life) which the Visitor, descending from cloud or throne or pale grey Daimler, would confirm. Surely when love came it would come like him – magical, illicit, suave. So perhaps the psychologists were right. Perhaps her sexuality had been fixed long before the shocked whisperings of the playground had yielded up their first inaccurate secrets.

She had talked to her mother about sex only once. The woman's face had shut like a trap. "It's knowing about these things that leads folk to do them." A frigid blank wiped out any impression that Catriona/Katie might have got of her parents' sex life. She could associate her mother with nothing more physical than tea and her perhaps-father remained a pale wraith bent over in the garden giving his affection to cabbages.

But puberty confirmed her prettiness, intensified her sense of being special. Even polite men in the street attempted not to look at her and failed. All she had to do was wait and romance would come to her.

She waited. Nothing. For though the sixties might have spilled sex on to screen and turntable, genteel Edinburgh kept a tight and watchful grip on its female young.

Except for Kirstie Macrill who had DONE IT. Nobody believed her. Katie did. Katie had been there. Kirstie's "uncle", a helpful neighbourhood tutor in extra Mathematics, copulated with Kirstie between Pythagorean problems. He had made puffy childish-looking Kirstie do it in her school uniform. He never once looked at her body or in the direction of the cupboard from which Katie – puzzled yet oddly excited – watched. It was Katie's first induction into the secret service of male sexuality.

Looking back Catriona could scarcely believe what followed.

She supposed it must have been a wild gesture. Maybe Kirstie had half-dared her. Perhaps it was a way of re-establishing *her* specialness over plainish baby-fat Kirstie's early lead. And surely, whatever the oldies said, virginity was an encumbrance. Here too was the chance for an actual adventure.

Arrangements were not hard to make. Visits to the big villa in fat cat Barnton were Mother-approved; Kirstie's parents were "the right sort of people". And so one foggy afternoon Kirstie took her turn in the cupboard while the tutor of Mathematics lunged and plunged inside Katie against a bedroom wall of his choosing.

She hated it.

She blamed neither Kirstie nor the man (though she never forgot the feel of his skin; its smell). It was her own fault. What should have been a daring, independent act froze her up so that her romantic feelings remained separate from body contact. For a long time she was like a patient under local anaesthetic, observing with puzzled squeamishness the working over of her feelingless body. So tenderness stayed all the more on the dream level – the level of the Visitor.

There was one more feature to her carnal lesson. Deception. Whatever sex was or whatever sex wasn't, deceit ran through it – as omnipresent in its atmosphere as air and water. Because as far as she could see the drama, the electricity, the *movement* of sex was to do with the illicit. This applied for apparent good (Kirstie's enthusiastic panting collaboration) or ill (the coarse jigging dance of Katie's defloration). It seemed the natural product of the times embodied in the clash between the prim grey-stone mores of the middle class and the flood of easy-sleaze that it tried to wall out.

It was not until long afterwards – as the consequence of much heartache and more folly – that Catriona came to know how differently Katie might have been formed. If instead of seeing around her, emanating from the bungalow outwards, the paradigms of marriage as dull, bourgeois, immobile – if there had been one bright exception to give her hope – if she had chosen a friend other than Kirstie or realised that the girl demonstrated a promiscuous self-destructive craziness that went far beyond the stylish youthful rebellion – well then, everything might have been different.

But she hadn't. It wasn't. And that was that.

# 7

At the rear of a *souk* in the spice section of the Medina Señor Rossminster had his customary meeting with the policeman Yassin. Their relationship was well known to the Moroccan authorities. Indeed Yassin boasted of it. Not every policeman had the opportunity to extort contributions from a true English gentleman who came such distances to pay so regularly.

In reality the position was reversed; Señor Rossminster did the blackmailing. Years before he had discovered that Yassin was not as he pretended *vrai Marocain*, but Algerian, and this at a time when relationships were sourer than usual along the two countries' vast common border. The Socialist Republic of Algeria viewed the Empire of Morocco as a plague centre of fascist infection. The Emperor had responded by barring lefty Algerians (all Algerians) from government employment. So Yassin was a fake with fake papers. He was also a fake who didn't want to go home.

Exchanges between Yassin and Señor Rossminster rested on that cordial stability which only fantasy can form. Anyone who asked (and many who did not) were informed that the Señor possessed a desire *pour les très jeunes filles* – a taste fully comprehended in Morocco but not by the Señor's exalted English family. This same family, under the impetus of Yassin's professional boastings, had undergone aristocratic inflation. Yassin had long ago decided on *un chef de famille, le diable d'un milord anglais* who lived next door to *sa majesté la reine*. He now greeted Señor Rossminster in similar vein.

"Your brother the Viscount. He ails?"

"Oh absolutely," said Señor Rossminster.

"My feelings reach out to you. And your father the Milord?"

"Practically dead," said Señor Rossminster. Yassin looked expectant. "In fact," the Señor continued, "they have to feed him with a straw."

"A straw?"

"In his side."

"You will then shortly inherit the title. Both titles?"
"Bound to."
"God is great."
"See here Yassin," said Señor Rossminster, "spot of business. Involves the Consul-in-Exile from Ceuta."
"But for your presence I would expectorate."
Señor Rossminster told his tale while Yassin opened his gift – a bottle of duty-free Scotch – pouring the liquid into small virulently coloured glasses. When Rossminster finished speaking Yassin said, "The Consul is perhaps possessed by hallucinating pharmaceuticals?"
Señor Rossminster downed his thimbleful of purple Scotch and shook his head. "He is genuinely interested. He smells money."
"He genuinely smells." Yassin tittered into his handkerchief. This gesture usually meant that there was a question which he wished to avoid.
Señor Rossminster pressed on. "Blueness, Yassin. What about the bloody blueness?"
Yassin sighed dramatically. "Ah, Señor, Morocco is for fantasists."
"Come off it Yassin. Don't tell me he was painting his body for fun. The Blue People, Yassin! What about them?"
Señor Rossminster was actually on shaky ground. Like everyone else who had travelled North Africa he knew a good deal about the Tuareg, the huge nomadic warrior tribe who once controlled the Central Desert, and until less than a century ago, each vital caravan route, each item of cargo from salt to slaves. But the Blue People were a trickier matter. No one seemed sure whether they were a racial or just a cultural subdivision of the Tuareg and, gliding across the continent's face, they did not yield willingly to scrutiny. Rossminster's existing knowledge merely increased the mystery. He knew that the men were veiled but not the women. He knew that their garments were dipped in blue pigment which gradually stained the wearers' skins. He knew that they were held to be a proud vicious people now in decline who took the dregs of their culture to oasis, to town, and occasionally to city, to perform a shabby ersatz version of their native dance, the *guedra*.
"I myself," said Yassin confidentially, "would prefer the

absence of tribes. Tribes are difficult. Even one as powerful as Yassin must leave them to rot in unscathed iniquity. Once one might go about with guns and shoot them in large quantities. Alas no longer. It is all this modern liberalism."

Rossminster tut-tutted the newfangled suppression of free-lance genocide. Then he pressed on. "Fair's fair Yassin. Come clean. No traveller's tales? No white folks going native chez Tuareg? I mean this fellow's noticeable enough. Not a young blood with a pack on his back. We've got a pretty senior citizen here."

Yassin spread his hands in mock despair. "These foreign people. They come. They go. Who is to hinder them? This is a democracy."

He had another small giggling fit. Rossminster persisted.

"Nothing relevant from the Western Sahara? No British chappie cuddling up to the Blue People so he can pass as one of them – drift into the Military Zone by accident?"

Yassin shook his head. "The Blue People! What use are they? A collection of wogs who wish only to drift to steal and otherwise wogify. I say again what use are they?"

"They might be useful as a hiding place?"

Yassin shrugged. "Perhaps, but they are reclusive. Every-where they reclude. It would be a rare outsider whom they would take in."

"Yes," said Rossminster. "That's what I thought."

Yassin gave another deep sigh. "It is all most difficult."

"All right," said Rossminster, "double the usual rate."

Yassin rose promptly to his feet. "What I can do – that will I do." And then, with a sly sideways look, "The soon-to-be-Milor' has perhaps some trifling preliminary deduction for Yassin?"

Rossminster pulled at his moustache. "Looks to me as if someone's spending a lot of effort trying to get noticed."

# 8

When her mother died Catriona found herself surprisingly well off. In fact she never had so much disposable cash again. Her late father had been practically profligate in taking out insurance, her mother's main expenditure solid tasteless food, the bungalow fetched a surprisingly high price. So Catriona set off for London to find romance and adventure or, to be more exact, to create the conditions in which they might find her. After all, she believed as an article of faith that it was only a matter of time before the world discovered how special she was.

The world was in no hurry.

Its knocks came early and stayed late.

London was full of good-looking girls who believed that the possession of beauty led to the stage, the screen, the magazine cover. Unlike Kirstie (who had preceded her, who apparently could apply her acting skills), Catriona had the devil's own job in gaining admittance to the obscurest, most expensive, most conspicuously venal drama school. Even that ghastly joint possessed enough integrity to disparage Catriona's obvious lack of talent.

Gradual self-awareness began to make its bitter incursions upon her arrogance. She started to see how much she had depended on an imagination that was part overblown, part underdeveloped; a badly nurtured bloom raised in a cheap flower shop. Yet she was intrigued to realise (she had made no effort at school) that she was equipped with intelligence. As Louis said later, of the wrong kind; she had started to see through things. She had started to see through herself without the slightest idea what to do about it.

So she went on.

Her looks attracted men whom she found insufficiently interesting, and who showed no interest in staying around to be told they were callow or stupid. The more she ventured out with the usual female hope, the usual female equipment – skirts a-swish, scent behind the ear – the more usual the men, the less venturesome the venture. Yielding to these men (out of irritation, out of exhaustion, out of an overwhelming desire to escape their conversation) affected her anaesthetically. She watched the operation. She bored herself. Later she felt trivially irritated, interfered with – some clumsy oaf had tried to rearrange her internal furniture.

Once again life just didn't measure up.

Her fourth lover (she was now twenty-one and getting meaner) had more gumption than his predecessors. Instead of insults he left an uncomfortable string of semi-truths.

Catriona was provincial and conceited. She was quite possibly frigid. She had a ludicrous sense of self-importance. She wasn't even lovable. Her best chance was to find some dull uxorious business man and settle down to making him unhappy in a suburb.

After the breakages (her temper was fully formed) Catriona sat on the bed of her tiny Kilburn flat (her inheritance had gone on fees, clothes, parties) and took stock.

The boy's insults were grimly correct. In addition to everything she dressed and sounded like what she was – a member of the dullest imaginable social class. Somehow she had been unable like girls from humbler beginnings to convert her background into an advantage. And, since she was intelligent, Catriona knew precisely why. Being lower class had charm, being a petty bourgeoise had none. Slum girls had the advantage on her kind. They knew how to live on their wits. They could mutate. Because – and this was the awful thing – she still thought she was so bloody marvellous that she didn't need to do things for herself – they would somehow be done for her. As she sat over her bottle of vodka she decided that *she* was nothing more than an agglomeration of unselected dreams. The girls who succeeded dreamed, but they selected too. Each had a goal in mind. Perhaps an adjustable goal but still a goal. And the adjustment was usually a man. And in the place of a man all *she* had was the Visitor. And the Visitor was no man, all man, everyman; lover, father, star-maker, star-denier. Never there yet always in the way.

Then, for the second fateful time, Kirstie intervened.

The following evening Catriona found a plump fiftyish man weeping on the stairs outside her door. Catriona just about remembered that this was Monty Mont, Kirstie's business manager/agent/occasional lover. Catriona took him inside.

She had not seen a man cry before and the process fascinated her. He sat heavily on her bed and wept on to his big hand-painted tie until she felt that the colour must surely run. Occasionally he offered her the evening paper only to withdraw it and hug it, moaning to himself as if it were a talisman greatly to be desired, bitterly to be rendered up.

Finally Catriona got it away from him.

Kirstie had overdosed herself into death. Aspiring actress et cetera et cetera. A couple of cheesecake shots from soft porn movies that still-sobbing Monty had fixed up. There was a certain amount of chirpy moralising about the fines to be paid for living in the fast lane. Kirstie had left a note blaming no one. She hoped but doubted that her parents would understand. She just didn't see the point to it. It being life. Catriona didn't see the point either but she knew immediately that unlike Kirstie she would go on looking. And as it happened poor wrecked Monty was about to provide her with a sighting of new territories, though with inaccurate map and defective compass for the difficult journey.

"It's the strain doll," he stretched out his hands pitifully. "It's a terrible world girlie."

His kind Jewish features were twisted in pain. Her heart went out to him. Not till considerably later did she have time to feel distress and guilt at Kirstie's end. She was too busy taking care of Monty.

Monty got her out of herself. In some ways he satisfied her snobbery. At least he possessed a sleazy glamour. At least he was not commonplace.

He spoke in a mixture of pokerwork and patois. Life which BENT US TO ITS WILL had a way of PLAYING FUNNY TRICKS. At least once a day he would remind her that "Love, little girl, is what SEPARATES US FROM THE CHIMPS."

It turned out that out of guilt and/or sentimentality he had employed crazy out of work Kirstie as his entire office staff. Her death uncovered an even worse chaos than he anticipated.

Catriona went to work for him the next day. She did a good job. She was, she discovered, practical. She tidied his files, made some sense of his accounts, interviewed potential clients from child models to fruit machine operators, made sure that contracts were honoured and cash paid on the nail.

It was a liberal education. She enjoyed it. But something bothered her.

Monty was a good deal less of a wreck than he pretended. The same was true of his office. Once or twice when she got THE HANG OF THINGS it almost seemed that there might have been something contrived about the really rather exaggerated office mess. Maybe that was Kirstie's own brand of psychotic screwing around but it never quite added up. And anyway, Monty had his practical side. For all his sentimental chatter she doubted that after Kirstie he would have taken the risk of spotting hidden organisational talents in arrogant little Scottish blondes.

That left sex as a motive. Yet although a fumbler by inclination (Catriona had watched him with the nubile dumb in search of work), he treated her with circumspection as if she were, by definition, off limits. After a while she shrugged her doubts away. Perhaps, to use Monty's terminology, IT WAS JUST ONE OF THOSE THINGS.

Then she fell in love.

Monty introduced them. Apparently he had met the man at some race meeting or other; he was otherwise quite outside Monty's orbit, and Catriona's too. For this was Catriona's first upper class man, and how she liked the flavour.

It was suddenly as if the shimmering world in which she had envisaged the Visitor had come to life. She had never realised until right now – until up close now – the power of undisturbed unquestioned assumption, the pleasant effortless stylish agreeably secure world of the upper classes. The world of hand-made shoes and plain silver cuff links licked all previous competition out of sight.

Afterwards she tried to pretend that it was her fault. She had been tactless. She had been clumsy. But she knew immediately that none of that mattered. The real facts were elsewhere.

After two weeks of civilised dinners and believable compliments and the first love making she had ever enjoyed, she bent the conversation round to marriage . . . And at first she thought she had misheard him. The words made no emotional sense. He thought she knew that he was married. That was sufficiently bad. Worse followed. He had a jocular not-unkind-but-absolutely-firm way of conveying that someone like himself could never but never consider marrying the likes of Catriona Lomax.

Out of *whose* question? He made a face as if she knew very well what he meant. But Catriona, oafishly aflush with love, persisted. Why? . . . Why?

And so because she was fast developing into a nuisance and nuisances had to be got rid of, he told her the short sharp way.

She wasn't his class. Never would be. Never could be. Sorry and all that but there wasn't a thing to be done now was there.

And there wasn't. Or so it seemed then. In all his emotionally impoverished half-witted callousness the man wasn't worth loving – but that was small consolation. The fact remained that she was an inferior outsider – in class, in clothes, in accent, in manners. Across borders there might be some fraternisation, even a little sexual tourism, but in the end the frontiers would always be closed. She was second best. She was insufficient in specialness.

Which left the Visitor.

# 9

When Señor Rossminster reached Yassin at the Protestant Cemetery he was arresting grave robbers.

In one far corner a canopy had been raised. Further over in the shade of a massively pilastered shrine Yassin's men had just finished beating someone up.

Rossminster could see Yassin himself poking around under the canopy.

"Yassin," he called out.

Yassin didn't hear him. Señor Rossminster approached, stepped under the canopy. Yassin turned.

"Señor Rossminster," he pointed dramatically, "your hippies are discovered."

At the rear of the canopy Yassin's men laboured by a large mound of earth.

"Someone had buried them."

"Ah," said Señor Rossminster.

"Regrettably," said Yassin, "they were not dead at the time."

It was a mess under the canopy.

To one side lay a discarded body lightly covered in loose dirt. Beside it a hole that looked frivolously un-body shaped. Beyond that a circle of Yassin's men, bent double, pulled and scrabbled at something in the earth. From the far side of the circle came a noise like the unblocking of a drain.

Yassin took Señor Rossminster by the elbow. "Now we approach." Yassin smacked one of his men briskly on the head. The man made space, bowing. Señor Rossminster followed Yassin into the gap.

They were just getting the second hippy out of the ground. He had been buried sitting up, his head alone above ground. Someone had stuffed his ears with earth and gagged his mouth. His eyes looked as if they wanted to leave his head for some saner place. One of Yassin's men removed the gag. The hippy was so far alive, but choking. Yassin shook his head and sighed. "Why will they not stay at home?"

He might have been talking about a tourist who had shot a couple of red lights.

Rossminster gripped his stick until the knuckles were white. This was a game that had to be played by Yassin's rules or not at all. Sympathy equalled weakness. Señor Rossminster obeyed the training of a lifetime. He closed down one part of himself and put it away to be opened later.

Another of Yassin's cohorts hammered at the hippy's back. He vomited earth. An arm had been freed. It was broken. The fingers had been broken too; snapped at different angles. The hippy had been expertly tortured long before he had been placed in the ground.

Yassin rolled his eyes at the tedium of it all and turned away. "Perhaps," he said with exquisite politeness, "you would care for a cigarette?"

"Allow me," said Señor Rossminster.

"You are kind." Yassin whipped out his lighter.

"Smoking," he continued conversationally, "is an aid to tranquillity. I am unimpressed with cancer. Is it so with you?"

"Absolutely," said Señor Rossminster.

"It is possible," Yassin said slyly, "that you have noticed the absence of a doctor. Alas this is not the graveyard of the Baron your father's stately mansion where such men abound."

"Your show, Yassin," said Señor Rossminster.

Yassin sniggered. "Our police doctors are scarce. They are needed to attend upon the police. It is a bagatelle. I have seen people buried before. They do not survive. Even without antecedent torturings. For myself his death might be a great convenience. I believe however that he attempts to speak."

"Or breathe," said Rossminster grimly.

"That too," said Yassin reasonably. "Perhaps you would care to approach."

"Handsome of you."

Yassin bowed. They approached.

"You understand," said Yassin as they looked down at the horror that looked up at them, eyes staring, probably mad, "that this is a great inconvenience to my person. I must remain here to watch these lazy fellows. They might, in order to avoid vigorous digging, kill this detritus."

Yassin's men had freed the hippy and were lifting him clear.

His eyes had reached a paroxysm of agitation.

Señor Rossminster had more practice than he cared for at recognising death. He knew it hovered now over the hippy whom, pointlessly disinterred, they had propped against a stone sarcophagus in the shade of a damaged alabaster angel. Someone threw a bucket of water over him. Mud made tracks down the tee shirt, the jeans, the sneakers. His eyes had moved from madness to merciful resignation. He looked up at Rossminster as if he were the kindly family doctor. Despite Yassin Rossminster would have taken his hand but it was too cruelly broken.

He tried to speak. Then coughed but there was nothing left to cough about.

"Old boy," said Rossminster. "Something to say?"

Yassin leaned over Rossminster's shoulder. The words were indistinct. "Old son," said Rossminster. "Come again?" The hippy spoke, then died.

Yassin took Rossminster's arm and led him away.

"Faugh how he smells." Somehow Yassin made it clear that the odours attendant on live burial were no worse than those generally attendant on hippiedom.

Rossminster said, "He looks older than I expected."

"Torture, burial, these are ageing things."

"He was thirty-five at least."

"The hippies are older these days. The young believe in Reagan's America and stay at home. They remain in suburbs and salute their flag. They do not die with godlessness upon their lips saying the word shit."

"Suppose so," said Señor Rossminster.

Yassin took Rossminster's elbow and led him out away from the canopy. They walked to the corner where, at entry, Yassin's people had been engaged in beating someone up. The man in question was a local, poorly dressed, bleeding from mouth and nose, slumped against a fig tree. Three of Yassin's subordinates stood around looking sheepish. Yassin waved airily in their direction.

"These are ignorant fellows I employ. They have gone too far. I cannot be everywhere. It is a great trial upon me."

The man groaned.

"This chap here," Yassin pointed contemptuously, "was in the cemetery for what illegal purposes you may well ask. He hears terrible noises. He sees the earth move and the ground groan. He prays like his pig ancestors through all recorded time to spirits and witches and *djinns*. This is his pig story. It is of course lies."

To make his point Yassin bent and kicked the man in the knee cap. The man tried to smile. Yassin spat in his face.

"See," Yassin gestured at the sky. "His fingernails are encrusted with the dirt of the now-restless dead. His pockets he wished to fill with the treasures of your Protestant departed."

"You mean he was robbing graves," said Rossminster.

"Of course he was robbing graves." Yassin sounded disgruntled at this prosaic assessment. He switched into swift imperative Arabic which Rossminster could only just follow.

"This is a mighty English prince skilled in the art of torture beyond our ignorant understanding, brought hither by the Emperor to experiment upon the scum of the bazaars such as yourself."

"I say," said Señor Rossminster. "Steady on. Hell of a reference."

But Yassin's victim had started to babble.

Behind the infidel monument of his concealment the darkness yielded to a silver beam singly plucked from the moon's bright rays – (Christ thought Rossminster, even when you beat the bastards half to death they're still poets) – but the burial party revealed itself to his unworthy gaze.

"You don't say," said Rossminster as the man paused for effect. But somehow the information didn't surprise him.

The Blue People had come to bury their living, watched over by a small Western man. The man was old. His suit – moreover – was blue.

They walked together from the cemetery. Rossminster was glad to be out of the place. Heaven knew what horrors rested in that graveyard earth.

"Torture," said Yassin. "That means information. And no identification on the bodies. Wallet. Passport. Money. Nothing."

"In fact," said Rossminster, "easy for you to say – they never came your way. Perhaps the people who did it knew that."

"It is," said Yassin, "admirably efficient. Admirably well informed in our so primitive procedures."

"Intend to leave it old boy? All swept under the rug? That easy chum?"

Yassin gave a theatrical sigh. "Señor Rossminster. You are my friend. Although you are an Englishman of enlightened private education permit me to remind you of certain things. The Blue People are not violent. Certainly not here. But in the desert . . . " He shrugged. "This is a desert murder. To do it in a city . . . believe me Señor there would have been terrible provocation. These tribesmen are not children; they keep their own faith and pay their own debts. For them to do this you know well there was a grave provocation. See I am able in the midst of professional concerns to make your English pun. Listen to me, whatever you want, this is a form of revenge left best alone. You know well the government policy with tribes. We never interfere unless we have to. Here we do not have to."

Rossminster walked on leaning heavily on his stick. He felt sick and he felt worried but he could not afford to show either emotion. After a while he said, "Our agreement still stands. No nonsense."

Yassin pretended to look hurt. "But naturally. Let me assure you that were a man in a blue suit to be – shall we say – available, for you understand we have no charge against him only the worthless word of a grave robber . . . "

"Naturally."

"We would find a way to detain him at your lordly pleasure."

"Somehow," said Rossminster, "I don't think that'll happen."

Yassin looked sharply at Rossminster. "He is perhaps a torturing gentleman of your distinguished acquaintance?"

Rossminster stopped short. He raised his stick and pointed it at Yassin's chest. "I pay. My questions. Your answers. Just remember Yassin, there's always Algeria."

Yassin's smile turned yellow. They walked on for a while till they reached the hard covered road where a taxi was waiting. Rossminster didn't want to part on a threat. He stopped and extended his hand with all the roast beef of Old England joviality that he could summon up.

"So what do you do with our two dead pals?"

Yassin rocked from side to side with bonhomous laughter. "I tell you what we do. This is a jolly good joke."

"What's that old boy?"

"We bury them."

Señor Rossminster lay on his back in one of the private rooms in the Bath of Venus brothel. Above and beneath him two pearly breasted adolescents practised upon his old man's needs with that guiltless dexterity which the East brings regularly to sex and the West condemns as sin.

They were earning their money the hard way. All the horror which Rossminster had suppressed at the graveyard now gripped him. He had tried to vomit but the memory of the hippy's ghastly earth-filled mouth made him choke back. He now sweat and shook. The girls, who were accustomed to addicts of one kind or another, continued placidly.

Wars are dirty things. Rossminster had been to one or two and during them had developed his own defence mechanism. In peace the commonplace horror of physical mutilation became special. He had come to those broken semi-buried bodies without preparation, without defence.

It wasn't just the bodies. If he, Rossminster, had got it right the man who had tortured them was far more frightening than the shattered human shards that bore evidence to his torture. Because it was calculated. Because *he*, the man in the blue suit, had calculated.

And so he sweated and shook by turns when the Consul entered and said, "Henry?"

Although one girl was straddling his face and another was doing her polite best to achieve fellatio, Rossminster pushed them both aside. The Consul only ever used Rossminster's real first name in times of crisis. And the Consul was shaking.

The Consul-in-Exile from Ceuta was many things. A coward was not one of them. He was frightened in the way that brave men are frightened. Such fear demands respect.

Wrapped in hot towels and assisted by a jug of Moroccan wine he told his story.

"Don't tell me Henry that in the heart of the anti-Atlas the *guedra* is a genuinely moving dance of erotic whatnot whereas what we see here in Marrakesh is the faded ersatz product of a downtrodden lifeless people reduced to scrabbling for tourist pennies."

"Why not?"

"Because," said the Consul, "these fuckers have quite enough life for me. Anyway, I put the word out that I would pay for a performance of the mood indigo. Private party said I, and stuck around waiting for things to materialise. *Which* they immediately did in the shape of three downtrodden blokes as blue as a castrato's bollocks. *Peuples bleus* said I, listen here. I will pay you as much as for three performances of your tedious erotic cufuffle for some information about a Brit hanging about town who may have been consorting with you because he's got blue bits hanging out of his clothes. They pretended not to understand but they bloody well did and in receipt of a large advance away they went with a heigh and a ho and a heigh nonny no, rendered repulsively into the Moroccan. *Christ* how I hate their chanting."

He paused to drink deep.

"Back comes a message. My bale of blue cloth is waiting in the square of Djemaa-el-Fna. Off I go. I stand around watching those fucking mountain people getting their heads shaved with cut throat razors. Next thing I'm surrounded by the Blue Brothers and on my knees. Downtrodden huh! Your *Consul* was downtrodden with one of those razors behind his ears and someone speaking English. He has something for me. Well, thought I, let's hope it's an ear and not something lower down. But into my pocket it goes followed by instructions. Take contents of pocket to Henry Rossminster. Tell him it's a good likeness. And tell him that we'll meet again at the reunion."

The Consul produced the photograph with a shaking hand. A small old angry man stared across a table. An ashtray on it said Café Turc. No one he knew . . . He hesitated . . . No one he knew *now*.

The Consul seemed to be talking.

"Henry," (he was still shaken) "does that mean something? The reunion?"

The Consul had turned over the photograph. On its back, badly printed was the word MANTELETE.

Rossminster got to his feet. He took the Consul by the hand

and raised him up.

"You're safe enough. If he had wanted to kill either of us we'd be dead by now. Get dressed. We're going for a walk."

Night fell.

Señor Rossminster stood at the southern end of the great square of Djemaa-el-Fna. Next to him the Consul looked even more shaken than before; the tale of the buried hippies had done nothing to reassure him.

Stalls were dismantled to be carried away on backs and heads. Braziers were lit, food cooked over the coals on long Moroccan shovels. Animals, people, equipment – daytime life began to move off in a wedge. In the midst of them the last *guedra* danced, shuffled together, their faces wrapped in the plain blue linen; the Blue People departed.

Then Señor Rossminster heard the song. A single voice raised high above the tired murmur of humans and animals. He remembered it with a shiver. The same battle song chanted night after night half a century before, rising defiantly from the Loyalist trenches dug deep along the river bank:

*Por igual que combatimos*
*rumba la rum ba ba*
*Prometemos resistir*
*ay Carmela ay Carmela.*

In between the nonsense lines the stubborn message – just as we struggle so will we resist.

Señor Rossminster turned to the Consul. He said, "I wonder why?"

"Join the club," said the Consul. "I need a drink."

"You see," said Rossminster, "it's something I didn't mention. I wanted to think it over."

"Christ," said the Consul, "there's more?"

"Yassin was wrong. The dying hippy didn't say shit at all."

"So? He was optimistic about the next world? He said tit?"

"Actually," and for the second time that day Señor Rossminster's eyes had gone long-sighted, "what he said was Schmidt."

# 10

Schmidt, thought Catriona. Schmidt and what I owe him.

The bath water was getting cold. She ought to get out but she didn't have the energy. So she just lay there half dreaming.

Schmidt then. When you came right down to it she owed him everything – job, self-respect, even indirectly the friendship of Penelope and Louis.

One day without warning the bailiffs entered Monty's office. They took everything down to the last paper clip.

She sat in the corner on the floor while weeping guilt-stricken Monty spilled an entire cannery of beans.

It turned out that there had been another set of books kept by another girlie who'd been a bit indiscreet, not that he could really blame her. There'd been a mix up over clients' money that he'd borrowed, just temporarily of course, but then he'd dipped badly on the horses . . . After a while she stopped listening – just went on patting his damp hand.

It was only a matter of time before the police moved in and while there shouldn't be any trouble for Catriona it would be better if she got away for a bit. Right away. Out of the country. He'd kept a bit of money back . . . Here . . . No he insisted.

It was far more than she expected. It took six months of expensive wide-eyed foreign drifting before it ran out and Catriona found herself down and out in a Cairo club as part of the world's worst chorus line.

She never forgot its smell – Egyptian cigarettes and thick sweet sweat and rope soled shoes and lustful fan blown breath. It was no help either that she was absolutely useless at the routines; that even amongst this bunch of no hopers she had to be carried.

The club was run by a Marseilles Frenchman who had seen *Salad Days* at an impressionable age. The girls (all advertised as genuine English ladies) had to wear *les tea gowns.* These were mid-calf mid-fifties numbers in hard taffeta that looked as if they'd escaped from *Genevieve*. Doubtless it was an odd male fantasy but then what wasn't?

For Catriona it was rock bottom. Only out and out prostitution could be worse than the wet eyes and the damned Egyptian cigarette smoke and the big dumb tuber roses that each girl had to carry in a little straw basket hooped over her powder stained glove clad arm.

He wore a coat.

That was the first thing she noticed. Something in yellow camel hair as if the weather didn't exist. For ever after she never saw him without that coat or its sibling. She supposed he had copies made in the same material.

He came every night for a week, talking to no one, sipping chocolate or mineral water, returning from trips to the stinking lavatory with a large silk handkerchief pressed against his face. He showed no personal interest in the girls. He didn't want to buy them drinks. He didn't talk to them. He wasn't lecherous or spooky; he was – for all his distinctive sweating camel coated appearance – blank.

One of the girls in the line, the third tea gown on the right, made the most interesting guess. "He's assessing. I don't know what but mark my words he's assessing. I ought to know. My dad's an auctioneer in Bournemouth."

Then one day he wasn't there. Oddly enough she missed him. He had given her something to think about. Two shows later she was fired.

She wanted to rage out loud, to take tea gown and basket and hat, soak them in petrol and raze the place to the ground. But this was an unforgiving country – on these unyielding streets you could die for less than a tantrum.

Anyway she was exhausted. Tired all the way through. Utterly without hope.

At her just-respectable hotel between the strip joints on the Rue Bambi she found Mr Schmidt sitting on her bed. The smell had made him do his handkerchief routine. Close up he had a big square head and several necks and a fuzz of greying ex-blond hair cropped dust-close to his baby pink scalp. Before she could say anything, while her mouth stayed open in surprise, he lifted a silencing hand. It released a whiff of Parma violets.

"You don't worry. You got no worries. Not now. I do good. I make people happy. It's Monty," he said. "That's who."

"Monty? Something's wrong with Monty?"

Schmidt waved his handkerchief as if he was conducting traffic and Monty was a car to be waved on. "Monty's out. That's how Monty is. Kept out of jail. Out of the country. This is good. Monty's health is nothing to put on a postcard. I thoroughly helped Monty."

He had a thickish German accent; on top of that he sounded as if he had learnt American English at the movies.

Catriona said slowly, "I saw you once. You were leaving Monty's office as I went in. I didn't recognise you without the coat. With the coat."

"You got a memory. This is very good. Me too. Believe me. Monty tells me and I remember. That is the secret of Schmidt. That is how Schmidt is able to do good you unnerstan'. I have this girl he says. This miracle worker. He says the problem with my business Schmidt is me. He says if this girl had been in charge there would have been no problem."

She looked at him blankly. She didn't know what was going on. He appeared to want a response but she didn't have one. He waved his handkerchief in the air. He looked like a fat Morris dancer in the wrong clothes.

"He says – these you unnerstan' are Monty's very words – he says Schmidt you ever have need for such a girl I got one. You got Schmidt, an opening? You got a vacancy? But mark these words of mine Schmidtie doll – you know the funny way Monty has of speaking – this needs to be one real job. Michael Mouse is not required. Because sure this girl has ability but she has also one talent."

Girl? She almost said what girl. But she didn't and was glad. Something about Schmidt discouraged slowness – the same thing that suggested that you didn't want to risk his disapproval . . . Then she got it. That thing was power.

She said, "So what's my talent?"

He leaned forward conspiratorially. "You *move*. So now you do that, back to London. You run the club I buy. I offer you a job. You unnerstan'?"

But she never did. Still didn't.

She told herself that her luck had simply changed the way luck sometimes simply did. But she never understood why he had plucked Miss Nobody from Nowhere and given her a life.

Perhaps she didn't want to understand because understanding would have forced her to accept that this sweating pantomime-gesturing Swiss was her only authentic true blue saviour – genuine white knight.

And not the Visitor.

It took a moment before she recorded the telephone's persistent ringing. At the same time she realised that the bath water had gone cold. Shivering, half in half out of a towel but suddenly and mercifully sober, she made her way to the telephone.

It was Louis.

"My dear." She felt better already. In the whole post-Esmond world she had only two people to love. Her friends. Penelope and Louis. Of course they didn't love each other. Unless you counted what fighting cocks did as love. But she felt warmer already. Even Louis' voice did that.

"Catriona could you come down? Something odd has happened . . . Catriona?"

"Yes Louis? Oh good. Odd." Louis would have a story for her.

Then she found herself staring down, staring back at the cold water footprints trailing their way across the carpet as if to convince herself of something tangibly certain about her own existence. Because, the second time he said it, she took it in.

"Catriona? I thought you said your father was dead?"

# 11

Spain has changed, thought Señor Rossminster, and that's a fact. None of this would have happened under Franco.

The veterans had come to the battle site from every part of Spain. Grave, polite men for the most part, still half in doubt that this could happen, careful to stay out of trouble, eyeing the Guardia Civil in their tricorne hats and boastful bullies' uniforms with a long adulthood of caution.

The Guards themselves were nervous and puzzled. All they knew of the Civil War was what their fathers and grandfathers had told them. Yet they had been raised to believe that these gnarled old men and women, limping from coach and train in the best formation they could muster, Republican banners shouldered, were enemies of the State. Perhaps the Guardia had expected them to shriek anti-fascist defiance from wheel-chair and stretcher. Perhaps the Guardia were relieved to find something so old, so orderly, so Spanish.

And now the main attraction.

The whole town plus Señor Rossminster waited for those whose distant coming had memorialised the Spanish struggle far beyond the boundaries of Spain. They waited for the veterans of the International Brigades. Those people whom Señor Rossminster had fought half a century ago in what seemed another world he now came to watch.

Mantelete was built on a hill overlooking a tributary of the Guadalquivir. Like many southern towns it looked more African than Spanish. Whitewash, stone houses, stone walls, stone and dust everywhere. Before the war a place of bitter poverty. Before the war the landlords and their middle men, the *caciques* had tried to beat anarchism out of the peasantry. When the war came the peasantry settled its debts with a vicious ingenuity. Each time Mantelete was taken or retaken a fresh batch of brutal revenge was issued. Señor Rossminster knew. He had been there at the time. Even now as he walked on this fine morning towards the modern bus station he remembered how the plaza central had been filled with Republican bodies stacked three deep. They had been soaked in gasoline and burnt. A gloating corpulent monk had said Mass for the assembled Nationalist troops while the blown ashes had stuck to sweat soaked living bodies, entering their mouths and noses.

A Mass of thanksgiving, Rossminster recalled.

So what did they all make of it now, today? If the Loyalists forgave the war could they forgive the aftermath? Forgive Franco's revenge when trials lasted a minute on average and two hundred thousand more Spaniards went to their deaths?

And the Nationalists? What did *they* make of a Spain headed by a constitutional monarchy and governed by a socialist Prime Minister struggling to keep his promises? And what did either group, composed as each was of the proudest people on earth, make of the prosperity that had dampened the fires of idealism, that had taken Spain into the EEC and NATO, but which derived from something as ignoble as tourism?

Perhaps, Señor Rossminster thought, the young should light a candle at the shrine of Saint Tourism and be grateful. Few ideals were worth a square meal. The old Spain had provided too many beliefs and too few meals.

Perhaps though – he touched his moustache as a talisman – he was just too English to understand it all.

His own war had occurred by accident. Sides had been chosen for him. In his modest unsuccessful way Rossminster's father had been an exploiter, at a time when exploitation was going clean out of fashion. If Henry had not joined the Nationalists he would have burnt along with the local vineyards and the local nuns. He did not complain. There was a measure of Iberian resignation in the Rossminster bloodstream. His only real regret was in missing that small complement of English gentlemen who had enlisted in the Republican cause.

If he was right the man that he had come to meet was neither English nor a gentleman. But he was certainly someone worth meeting.

Again.

Now, turning the corner, Señor Rossminster saw the bus station below him. It was so full of people that the bus would have some difficulty in sweeping in to a safe stop. A single shout from below was taken up quickly by other voices. Arms waved. Hands pointed. Banners lifted. A mile away across the plain a cloud of dust kicked up. The bus was coming.

Señor Rossminster selected a large roadside boulder and sat on it. He extracted his binoculars from their case. He removed the handkerchief from his breast pocket and began to polish the lenses. High above the road, in his linen suit and panama hat, he made a conspicuous picture. That was his intention. He went on polishing and watching. It was, he thought, like looking down on a battlefield, watching the enemy prepare for battle – except that all this was supposed to be about peace – wasn't it?

The bus drew closer. Señor Rossminster raised the binoculars. A reception committee of old men at the front, families behind; there was a band. Comrades would meet. Most of them after almost fifty years of separation. It was a devil of a thing.

Señor Rossminster swung the binoculars round. Further back from the main crowd stood an isolated scattering of other old men – men of Señor Rossminster's own age. He knew who they were. They were like him, the victors, Franco's veterans. One bunch of old soldiers had come to look at another bunch – one that they had failed to slaughter. Nothing makes man so curious as the common avoidance of death. For a moment a huge billow of dust misted the binoculars. When it cleared Señor Rossminster saw that the bus had arrived.

The band struck up. A long disembarkation started. There was something old fashioned about these arriving travellers. They seemed to think it was socially required, a courteous necessity, to dress as if the years had not passed, in baggy trousers and dingy shapeless jackets. The locals by comparison had dressed as smartly as possible in their *ropas de pasear*. The British, but for a sprinkling of berets and trade union banners, looked as if they might have spent the entire period since the end of the war in a public library.

The wind took a turn in his direction. He could hear the wild shouts of greeting, some singing. Everywhere embraces, flowers thrown, jubilation, tears. Two men – a Brigader and a Spaniard – were even trying to dance the *carmagnole*.

Down below they formed up; International Brigaders in the centre, Spaniards on the outside. He noticed that the Spaniards, with habitual courtesy, had commandeered the two veterans in wheelchairs. For a moment they stood still together. The band broke into *El Paso del Ebro* and the Brigaders moved off, once again in step, marching down a Spanish road.

Señor Rossminster hurried after them, his binoculars bouncing inelegantly against his ribs.

It was a long road at their age and in this heat but they would not have wanted to take it any other way. It was a full twenty minutes before they stopped and there, by the ford across the river, held their commemoration.

The others, the opposition, the old enemy stood back and watched. Perhaps after all it was their commemoration also. Señor Rossminster saw that some were weeping. Perhaps, like all good Spaniards, they had come to celebrate courage.

The last post sounded and Señor Rossminster found that, like everyone else, he was standing to attention.

Long years had finally rendered it a very civil Spanish War.

By nightfall Señor Rossminster felt exhausted and despondent. Every café and bar overflowed with veterans but there was no sign of the man he sought.

The whole celebration was remarkably tame. All over town the old met up to refight the war with their only remaining weapon – rhetoric. Rossminster had actually found one bunch of Anarchists buying drinks for hard line Party members. Even the *señoritos*, the town's flashy youth, had settled in to listen to the old folks' stories. Small surprise then if his man wasn't here. Someone still fighting a private battle would hardly fit in.

For the umpteenth time Rossminster wondered if he had got his lines crossed, if he had anticipated too much. It would serve him right. His kidneys hurt from too much Spanish beer. He rose from his table and made his way out through the back door.

The pissoir consisted of a single wall open to the skies. Clouds hid the moon. He found the place by the smell. It took him a long time to urinate. He was about to curse his old man's bladder when a voice said:

"It seems funny eh comrade?"

The night was black. Señor Rossminster couldn't tell how close the speaker was to him. Had this man been waiting for him or was he just some drunk who thought an open air urinal was a good place to star gaze on an overcast night?

Rossminster cleared his throat. "Funny?"

Five or six paces distant, an arc of bright urine cut through the dark and spattered to a conclusion against the wall.

"To be back in Spain. After all this time. Eh comrade?"

"I live here. In Spain."

"Is that a fact?"

"It is."

"I walked here the first time. To the war. Over the Pyrenees. What do you think of that?"

"Ah. Longish walk."

"Longish walk. Ha ha. You're a card."

It is difficult to detect accents when you cannot see the lips move but Señor Rossminster was almost certain that the voice was Scottish. It continued in an even, pleasant tone.

"A fascist card mind you."

"Easy old boy."

"*La rum ba ba* to you laddie."

"All right," said Rossminster. "All right. What do we do next?"

"Let's take a wee walk."

A hand came up and touched Rossminster lightly on the wrist.

"That's right; take my shoulder. Just keep your hand there and follow me. I've an awful lot of practice in the dark. That's the way. Like wartime eh? Like old times eh?"

They moved off. The man was small; the shoulder gripped by Rossminster low to the ground. Once or twice they scrambled over loose stones. The man helped him. Then they seemed to be on an upward path. The man was far fitter than Rossminster, who began to breathe heavily.

Finally they stopped. The moon came out from behind the clouds. It revealed the man in the photograph. Tiny, not much above five feet – wiry, muscular, skin wrinkled brown, hair intact but grey – though younger than Señor Rossminster, an old man to be playing dangerous games.

"Well," said Rossminster. "Long time no see old boy."

"Ach," the syllable came out especially guttural, especially Scots. "Who's counting?"

"You haven't lost your accent?"

The man grinned. "Accents, languages. Don't you worry. I

can put them on or take them off."

Rossminster looked around him. They were on a patch of waste land high up. The lights of the town glittered below. Behind them ruins half stood. The locals must have plundered here for stones to rebuild their houses.

"Where the devil is this?"

"D'ye not remember? All that's left of the monastery. Where I was your prisoner. Poetic eh? Nobody'll bother us here. They're feared of ghosts. There's a lot of good dead people under here – aye and some bad ones too. Eh Enrico?"

"Henry actually. Got a name have you? Same one?"

"Oh my, Henry. We can't all go through life with the same name. That's a capitalist luxury for you. But since you ask politely I'm Jimmie Tar again."

"Not Jaime?"

The man laughed. "You're a snide bastard Rossminster under all that English flummery. Aye and a survivor like me. I like that."

"Handsome of you," said Rossminster. "Buried anyone alive lately?"

Jimmie Tar laughed some more. "You always were a grand lad for the chat."

"Old boy," said Rossminster, "it is the middle of fucking Spain and it is cold. What's on offer?"

"This," said Tar, "is going to cost."

Rossminster held up a warning hand.

"Hewer of wood carrier of water that's Henry Rossminster. Simple foot soldier. One who carries messages. *Not* in a position to pay or promise payment."

"I wasn't thinking of money."

"What then?"

But Tar seemed to have lost interest in the nature of rewards. He stood looking out over the town. Rossminster suddenly felt sorry for him. He wanted to say what are you doing here you small sad old man? What has-been's game are you playing? Then he remembered the graveyard in Marrakesh, the fingers twisted back, the earth-stuffed mouth, the bulging eyes – and kept his mouth shut.

Tar turned. He spoke quietly to Rossminster as if they were old friends going over yet again the same batch of what-has-the-world-come-to memories.

"At the siege of Madrid someone says to General Miaja – where do you retreat from here? The cemetery says he. That's what we all do sooner or later. You and me too Henry. Retreat to the cemetery."

Señor Rossminster looked around him and shivered.

Tar said, "You remember Colonel Vajas? The peasant's son. Campesino Vajas? Him that gave your lot a thing to think about at Badajoz. Him that got out to Mexico afterwards. He's back in Spain now."

"Everybody's back in Spain now. Even La Passionaria came back. You've come back for God's sake."

"You know what he's doing now – Campesino Vajas? Touring the battlefield with foreign students. Bloody Yank Japanese bourgeois riff-raff. Vajas! The war as a tourist attraction. Just like it was at the time when you think about it. Just like it was for Despard."

"Who's that old boy? Des who?"

Tar smiled. "Patience," he said. "And listen."

Half an hour later. Tar was into his second flask. A lot of fast drinking, thought Rossminster – for a *viejo*. Even if you are used to it. The moon was out. Rossminster saw the cold impassivity of Tar's expression. You may be a little mad but you are serious. You have been angry for a long time; you know how to do it. There is an age of terrible hardness in you, old man.

"Right," said Rossminster. "See if I've got this straight. Place – Switzerland. Time – just after our war in Spain. Character – Despard. Millionaire, inherited money so never done a hand's turn. Dual nationality. American and Swiss. Able to afford a nice fashionable left-wing conscience . . . "

"A tourist. That's all he ever was. A political tourist."

"Frightful fellow no doubt. Tours Spain during the war and runs out when he sees that a war can be injurious to his health. Like a number of the other *los intellectuales* of a pinko persuasion. No offence James . . . "

"I was always a working man."

"Quite, and therefore had to do the fighting. Anyway to salve his conscience and look less of a shit the aforesaid pinko starts the Despard Foundation shelling out to left-wing causes. Committee for freeing of this, journal for the radicalising of that. Yes?"

"Yes. And Spain."

"And Spain. Help for Loyalist veterans who've been interned, or whom a judicious bribe will get out of a Franco prison, or who have been otherwise shat upon by fascist swine. Long term commitment for people that everyone had forgotten. Except that there's too much talk and not enough action. Despard's no organiser. So some *compadres* get a free blanket or a passage to Mexico or an annual handout and some don't. Besides Despard likes to live in style. Needs the money to throw left-wing parties and look up left-wing actresses' skirts. Then he acquires an expensive wife and *holá* – he's in a financial mess. And so we come to Mr Schmidt?"

Tar spat.

"I thank you James. One pig-like crooked Swiss accountant who gets to run the Despard Foundation any way he likes just as long as Monsieur et Madame Despard continue to live rich. And which running is all the easier because although the Foundation sounds like a registered charity it's actually wholly owned by Despard."

"He was always too frightened to really give anything away."

"Indeed. But Mr Schmidt is very far from Mr Clean and enjoys several decades of peculation, embezzlement, skimming."

Tar raised his flask. "Good capitalist words."

"Which could be the motto of Mr Schmidt who operates as a banker without the nuisance of owning a bank. Cash on the barrel head, a high rate of interest and no awkward questions as to what the money's needed for. Similar business if a sum of money needs to be laundered. No names. No pack-drill. Frankly this all seems a touch vague to me James."

Tar shook his head. "Only if you're an outsider. Shady borrowers aren't necessarily bad risks. And Schmidt would sometimes take payment in kind."

"How so?"

"Information. You might say that Schmidt liked to invest in it. Saving something for a rainy day."

"Which supposedly has come. Mind if we take that one around the park old boy?"

Tar paused. For a moment his face was statue still. Then he

said, very slowly. "Madame Despard . . . " He stopped, rose, walked forward to look out over the town. Rossminster could no longer see his expression. "Blackmail. For years Schmidt's blackmailed Madame Despard. So she hates him. She hated what Schmidt had done to the Foundation but Despard didn't want to know and being blackmailed she was afraid to tell him. I forgot to mention that Despard had been crippled. He needed nursing. So Madame Despard gets him to make his will then scoops him up and keeps him in a Schmidt-proof house in Ireland. Good for tax is Ireland. And Despard has a stroke so there's no chance of a new will. Now he's in a coma. Dying. They give him a week."

"You know a lot Jimmy. What's your secret?"

Tar turned to Rossminster. "I've had time. A long time. Just like Schmidt has. He's not the only one who can prepare. Aye, he's not the only one with friends to help him." For the first time Tar grinned. "The friends of Jimmy Tar."

Rossminster repressed a shiver. "And who would they be? Dial a terrorist?"

Tar shook his head. "Your lads have nothing to fear. My folk are . . . " He paused for a long time. It seemed to Rossminster that he was genuinely searching for a word, the right word. "Random."

"This will," said Rossminster. "So it means, does it, that Schmidt loses control of the Foundation and then there's all hell to pay because he gets nabbed as Europe's longest serving embezzler?"

Tar raised his flask and wagged it from side to side as if it were an admonishing finger. "You can't have everything at once Henry. You have to invest. Mrs Thatcher's Spain. Let's just say that if what I hear is right then Schmidt *may* lose control of the Foundation. That's certainly one thing Schmidt's frightened of."

"Any others on offer?"

"Me," said Tar. "I think you'll find Mr Schmidt's gone into a wee bit of hiding in case I come to call. He remembers Despard becoming crippled." Tar's second grin. As mean as the first.

"How's that?"

"I shot him."

"Well," said Rossminster, "that would certainly do it. Any

special reason?"

"The lads who stayed in Spanish prisons. The lads who didn't get the free blanket or the passage to Mexico."

Rossminster was cold. He rubbed his hands together. "Very commendable. Nice to see the rich kept in line and all that and I must say I've enjoyed the chin wag but I don't see the percentage. What's in it for me and mine?"

With his non-whisky drinking hand Tar unpocketed a small oilskin pouch and held it out to Rossminster. "What I found on the hippies. What I got *from* the hippies. An advance. Eventually you get Schmidt's clients, every nasty little group of sub-criminals he ever dealt with."

"Um," said Rossminster. "Well . . . "

"And this. Like it or not the Despards lived off Schmidt's dealings. *And* Madame Despard was blackmailed by Schmidt. And who do you think is Madame Despard's stepson? And maybe Madame Despard's heir?"

"Search me."

"Esmond Claremaurice MP. Conservative MP. And don't tell me your boys at the Ministry wouldn't want a sniff at a potential scandal. Not when there's a man like Schmidt in the game. For I tell you Henry, Schmidt takes people up and he makes them over and then he owns them. He's a monster you know."

Rossminster took a risk. "You torture people Jimmy. And bury them alive. And *he's* the monster?"

Tar nodded politely as if this were a simple debating point. He lifted the oilskin package. All he said was, "Yes."

Reluctantly, nervously, Rossminster accepted the package. Tar raised his hand, palm outwards, as if quietening a crowd.

"It's in there," he said. "If it makes you feel any better to see what they deserved. What Schmidt deserved. Evidence Henry. What Schmidt's hippies had on them. What they told me. All about Schmidt." Tar leant urgently forward. "I'll give him to you Henry. I'll give you his lists. I'll give you his accounts. I'll give you every dirty little group he ever dealt with."

"Got a bit of a chip on your shoulder eh Jimmy? All sounds very general to yours truly."

Tar took a pace towards him and swayed slightly. It occurred to Rossminster that he might be drunk. That all of this might be the drunken fantasy of a deranged and murderous man . . . No he thought – this is too elaborate – there is a *plan* here.

Tar took the oilskin package from Rossminster. He opened it. He took out a photograph and gave it to Rossminster.

It was shameful.

A naked woman was on her knees. There was a man behind her and a man in front. The woman was old. The camera flash had caught the woman in an expression of discovered horror. Rossminster looked up from the photograph at Tar whose face seemed to have drawn tighter, to be held under some extra savage control.

He said, "Madame Despard. She was always a whore. That's how Schmidt blackmailed her. With them. With the hippies."

Then he said it again as if he could not quite believe it; as if it meant something special to him. "She was always a whore."

"Ah," said Rossminster. "All right Jimmy." He picked up the pouch. "I'll take it forward. But first I want to know what is in it for you. What might you want for your own particular piggy bank?"

Tar took two paces forward. He looked up at Rossminster. His eyes had grown fierce. The whisky was heavy on his breath.

"Justice."

"Steady on." Rossminster wanted to take a step backwards but his feet wouldn't move. "Tall order. Might as well ask for eternal life."

"I want what's been stolen from me."

"Ah. Ah. What's that?"

"My daughter," said Jimmy Tar.

# 12

Bert whistled through his teeth. "Well," he said. "Well well well. It's a funny old world."

Robinson poured two whiskies. They were in Robinson's spartan office in the Ministry outpost building at the dark end of Half Moon Street.

"So Tar claims he's only just found out that he's got a daughter but he won't say how he found out?"

"Yes."

"Bloody odd. Mind you so's the rest."

Robinson's swollen lip made it hard for him to drink. He scowled.

"I mean," said Bert, "why doesn't he just go up and ring Cat's doorbell – hello love I'm your Dad. Eh?"

"He doesn't say. There's a lot he isn't saying. That's his whole line. He's dangling. Stringing us along. Feeding Rossminster with enough information to get him interested – enough so he can't just be written off as some mad old no hoper. Then he says of course nobody's going to trust Jimmy Tar all at once. So you boys just sit tight. In due course things will start happening. I'll be in touch and you'll all be grateful. And no he doesn't say what things."

"Huh," said Bert. "I won't have him burying people alive on my manor. Even if they do have pigtails. If he comes to England looking for Cat we could nab him under the Prevention of Terrorism Act. Rough him up a bit. Get the whole story."

Bert glowed warmly at the thought.

"No," said Robinson. "Rossminster isn't even sure that Tar himself knows the whole story. Besides, if Tar's locked up then nothing may happen at all. According to Rossminster Tar's the one who's going to make things happen. Or so he says. No Tar, no action."

"Speaking as a copper sir I like a quiet life. Some actions are best not happening. Like murder."

"I know that," said Robinson.

"I mean," Bert swirled his whisky expansively, "we don't

want him coming over here from foreign parts knocking off anyone he thinks has kept him from his daughter. Who probably isn't his kiddie anyway. And if he's a half mad old drunk he'll probably miss and hit the Queen Mum. Cheers."

"All right," said Robinson. "But look at it like this. Look at the connections first and then the value. Schmidt's in control of the Despard Foundation but likely to lose control and Schmidt owns Catriona's club. Madame Despard is being blackmailed by Schmidt – by Catriona's boss. Madame Despard is Esmond Claremaurice's stepmother. Esmond Claremaurice has been having an affaire with Catriona. Don't tell me that's all one great big coincidence."

"No," said Bert. "I cannot tell a lie."

"Now to *value*. In intelligence terms. In terms of national security. First, Claremaurice is a Member of Parliament. He could be involved in bribery or blackmail or both. That's dangerous. I can't leave that alone. Then there's the Despard Foundation itself. For a start if it's generally lending to the dubious I'd like its list of clients. I'd like Mr Schmidt's memoirs. In fact I'd like Mr Schmidt. Our people in Morocco are still following up what Tar got from the hippies but we do know a certain amount already. Schmidt would lend money to any nasty little group of troublemakers who would pay him interest. And what exactly are the troublemakers going to do if the loans stop? I rather think they'll start showing their hands."

Robinson had walked away from his desk and now stood looking out of the window. It gave on to a blank concrete wall. So, Bert thought, there's something else bothering you. There's something *personal* here. What is it? That he fancies Cat? That he hates that upper class git Claremaurice? That he's taking a risk and working hunches? Well I'm buggered if I know but it's *something* all right. But Bert kept the doubts to himself and resumed his unctuous political manner.

"So saving your explaining too much to someone like myself sir where does that leave us?"

Robinson turned. "Us?"

He looked at Bert expressionlessly for a long time. Christ Bert thought, I'll have to be careful with this one. He could turn nasty.

"Us," said Robinson eventually. "Yes. I think I see what

you mean." He smiled helpfully as if he were cleaning up a minor problem in the golf club minutes. "I think we have to wait and see what Tar comes up with. I want you to go to work on Esmond Claremaurice and the Despard Foundation. Anything you can find. I'll take the investigation of Tar. And of Catriona Lomax."

Oh surprise me do, thought Bert. Oh you do surprise me. All right we don't know what *she* knows. All right she could be up to something with Schmidt or Tar or God knows who but I bet you start looking around from her hemline up. And look at the man now, he's gone broody.

And indeed Robinson had a far away look in his eye. But then he surprised Bert.

"Have you ever been in a war Bert?"

"No sir. Just missed National Service. Too young. Unlike yourself I expect sir."

"I was in Malaya but it's not the same thing."

"As what?"

"Spain," said Robinson. "I wonder if that's somehow what Tar's still about. It must have been wonderful."

Bert tried. "The missus and I went to Torremolinos one year. Very nice."

"I meant the war Bert. The Spanish Civil War."

"There's no accounting for tastes," said Bert.

# 13

Louis Vulliamy's flat was directly beneath Catriona's. He came to the door looking much as usual: plump and sardonic and slightly rumpled. He also held aloft a cocktail shaker. This was no surprise either. Louis was given to small dramatic gestures. They alleviated his chronic problem which was boredom. He didn't look bored now. He looked interested. He was smiling a good Louis smile; the bad ones usually preceded some large and dangerous dramatic gestures. Laughter had cracked little lines all the way around his small sharp hidden eyes. He laughed more than any other unhappy man she knew.

"Catriona," he said. "So few non-American women of your age can wear jeans with impunity."

Immediately she felt better. He had that gift but he rarely chose to exercise it. She felt grateful. For she respected Louis' sharp capacious mind and was flattered that he had, without the least suspicion of anything to gain, turned it helpfully in her direction, when she had so often seen him employ it to savage the pretensions of people who seemed a thousand times more knowledgeable than she could ever be.

She had first met Louis six years ago at a party. He had been drunk – a less usual condition in those days – standing in a far corner, his bow tie askew, the waistband of his expensive suit bulging, his sleek black rather oily hair falling over his forehead in a question mark ("unless I'm careful love I look like Louise fucking *Brooks*"), his face maintaining an unsteady yet none the less vicious scowl.

"Who's that?" Catriona asked her host.

"That? That's Louis Vulliamy. He's wondering who to insult."

"Why?"

"That what he does. I'd keep out of his way."

Downright provocation. She walked up to him. Close up the skin on his plump cheeks was soft like a girl's. He stared through her. Catriona was used to attention. When it wasn't forthcoming she demanded it.

"You might at least insult me."

His eyes suddenly focused. "Actually," he spoke with drinker's precision, "I was thinking about the end of the world. Why don't you go and insult someone for me?" He paused and added, "My dear."

And that was the beginning. But it took some time before she realised that he had meant the bit about the end of the world. He was writing a book about it.

Louis described himself as a professional failure. He did this out of aggressive self-defence. He would sneer at himself before anyone else decided to do it.

According to Penelope, who had known Louis for a long time, arrogance was the main problem. He had been a brilliant undergraduate who had never quite delivered. A succession of academic jobs had ended in disaster. He quarrelled viciously with colleagues and students. He told fools of their foolishness in terms they would never forget. He wrote intemperate reviews of others' work and bawled out the editors who tried to restrain him. Too proud to trim his opinions, or to ask for favours, he slid gradually downhill. Now he made a living from shreds and patches; translations (he was a gifted linguist), publishers' reading, and the writing of popular historical works for schoolchildren.

In the meantime he drank, travelled when he felt like it, and continued on his great cultural study of Armageddon – a task so massive that it might have been selected for its very impossibility.

Louis was more than a friend. Louis was her education.

Although Catriona had left school at sixteen her real mental severance had come much earlier. School had appeared an irrelevance to someone so unearnedly self-important. What was the point in sitting at a desk when the world was out there waiting for wonderful her? Part idler, part truant, part conceited little bundle of ego it had taken her fourteen long years before – post Monty, post Schmidt's saving intervention – she had turned with the hunger of the late learner to Louis who, though he could be a real bastard over a sloppy thought or a misplaced metaphor, lent books, listened, argued, and somehow managed to control his condescension.

Through him she learned to think not merely honestly (which after all was a part of her character) but straight. She began to understand the difference between knowledge and mere information. He added the power of selection to her propensity for fast and omnivorous reading. Conversation by conversation, distinction by distinction, she acquired the slow weight of history, the long and necessary record of human behaviour without which the present is no more than an existential jumble sale. She was grateful to him.

But now, suddenly, her usual warm-Louis feeling was swept away and she was grasping the edge of his paper-strewn ink-stained work table, sick and giddy with the memory of why she was here.

In just two movements – like many plump men Louis was light on his feet and physically deft – he had lowered her into a chair and poured a second glass from the cocktail shaker. He said, "You can drink that in a moment. I'll hold it till your hand's steady."

He stood over her narrowing his eyes in thought. Inconsequentially she found herself saying, "Esmond left me today."

"That," said Louis, "should be a subject for congratulation." Then, as he wrapped his overcoat around her knees, "I'm sorry. I really had no idea that you'd take it – or rather him – seriously. I thought he was probably some tramp that you'd been kind to once who'd come round looking for you and just decided to try it on."

"Tramp," she said. "Oh *God.*"

"Here," said Louis. "You can hold it steady if you really try."

He managed to get half the cocktail between her lips and she managed to keep hold of the glass without spilling the remainder. He stood back and looked at her, one eye up, hands folded over his paunch. "You my friend are in a mysteriously bad way."

"It's all right Louis. I want to hear. Go on please."

"He rang my doorbell. At about four o'clock today. Said he was looking for you. He'd tried your door and you were out. He looked old and very run down. Small. Very small. And drunk. Very drunk. He had a blue suit and a Scots accent. A very bright blue nylon suit too big for him. Dreadful looking thing."

"God." Catriona could see the drunk man sneering out at

her from Robinson's photograph. "Go on."

"He said to tell you that he'd see you again. He'd be in touch. And to say that your father called."

She clutched at a straw. "You're sure? There's no doubt?"

Louis frowned. "As a matter of fact he repeated it. Look Catriona I don't want to seem unduly inquisitive but I wish you'd tell me what the bloody hell is going on."

She was about to speak. Then the doorbell rang. It kept on ringing. Someone was leaning on the bell.

Catriona got up. "If you don't mind Louis I'll get that. I think it might be for me."

She had to do it. Louis saw that and moved to one side. Dear Louis she thought, yet placing her affection for him into a corner so that she could clear a path towards the clamouring bell. With a surprising steadiness she reached the door, opened it, and then leaped backwards.

"Christ!" said Louis.

A man fell into the room, sliding off the bell and landing on his hands and knees. He reeked of drink, his trousers had opened and collapsed around his ankles. He was barefoot.

But it was no father of hers. It was only Barrington Smythe.

# 14

Lying on the floor Barrington Smythe looked even taller than his six and half feet. His ectomorph's body filled the entrance hall. Looking down Catriona noticed that his completely bald head sharpened to a point. He rolled over on his back and started to snore.

Catriona found that she had started to giggle. The giggle didn't sound quite right. She spluttered a little. "He's drunk."

Louis looked at her. He looked worried. "What else would he be?" he said caustically, stepping over Barrington Smythe to secure the door. Usually he was far more tolerant of Barrington Smythe than anyone else. Years ago when challenged as to motive Louis had declared a sportsman's interest in human oddities, announcing that but for a shaky grasp on reality Barrington Smythe might have been a licensed jester. Penelope, who hated the man on the grounds of sheer spookiness, said that Louis probably meant a licensed victualler.

Barrington Smythe had not so much a past as a series of collisions. An investigation of each disaster revealed multiple smaller incidents, as if a bad driver turned out also to be secretly a bad cyclist, pedestrian, parachutist and canoeist. Yet somehow from each accident Barrington Smythe contrived to be thrown clear – shaken but sufficiently intact to tout his story around another clutch of bars – provided always that someone else was paying. Penelope said that the only money that Barrington Smythe ever had was someone else's, although (amazingly) he possessed paid employment. Despite a near disastrous university education somewhere in the provinces (his degree obtained some said by forgery, some by plain straightforward cheating), Barrington Smythe had managed to acquire work teaching a thing called American Studies in a College of Higher Education. This fact stupefied Catriona; surely anyone could see that the man was ignorant and drunk. Louis explained that this was no disadvantage in a subject like American Studies.

Suddenly Catriona realised that her giggling had reached laughter and the laughter was unnatural and high and that

Louis was asking her if he should ring Penelope and saying that he didn't want to slap her because she might never forgive him but dammit he might *have* to, and please don't make me.

Gentleness did what, with her at any rate, violence never could, and she suddenly felt quite calm and was saying yes please she wanted to talk and Louis was already on the phone to Penelope.

"She's not in. I left a message with her nanny."

"What about him? He looks dreadful."

"He *is* dreadful. That's his role in life. Leave him where he is. Move him and he'll piss or vomit. He's out cold. Can't hear a thing. Don't worry about that. Now . . . " and he sat down next to her, "tell me about it."

She had finished her story. Barrington Smythe had settled into a lurching grunting snore, bent over in the sort of attitude that gives the foetal position a bad name.

"Well," she said, "what do you think?"

Louis pushed aside the lock of thick black hair that fell across his plump forehead. "Very well," he said. "The Ministry produces a photograph of a man who is supposedly claiming to be your father. Then lo and behold up immediately pops someone who certainly seems to answer to the same description. So, what so far – and only so far mind you – are the possibilities? One, the possibility urgently pressed by Catriona Lomax; the Ministry has decided, because it wants you to perform as club manager some particularly dirty favour, to blackmail you. Not very good is it?"

"I don't know . . . "

"Yes you do. You know very well. Come along Catriona; *face it.*"

"Oh damn you. All right. They'd have to know about the Visitor. I suppose that's possible. Over the years I blabbed to anyone I was close to. But even if they did know . . . about the Visitor that is . . . why bother to use *that*? They could do something much simpler like find a way to close down the club. Then I'd be ruined. I'd never get another job in charge of something decent. And besides, they haven't even tried to blackmail me. Actually they haven't done anything except to ask me for information about . . . "

"About James Tar. All right let's fly more kites. Possibility number two; the authorities mean what they say. For some unrevealed reason – and all we currently have is a dim connection with some long ago politics – they want to find out more about Tar. They genuinely want to know whether you know anything. Especially about his putative parenthood. Well, they've certainly got your reaction to that proposition. Which brings us to possibility number three – the simplest and the one most feared by Catriona. That despite your perfectly respectable birth certificate your actual father is both alive and a dirty old drunken criminal come back to claim his daughter's hand in God knows what filial bondage. All based I may add on the very limited maunderings of your mother."

"It's easy for you."

"Yes. It is. It's easy for me and it's hard for you but that's the truth and nothing's going to change it."

"Damn you Louis Vulliamy."

"Anything to oblige. But Catriona – forgive me but I have to ask – why does it matter so much? So very much?"

And Catriona really wanted to tell him. To spit it out. To say yes I admit it; I've come a long way and I'd be embarrassed to have a lower class guttersnipe of a father. Yes, and I know that's terrible and I should be ashamed and I *am* ashamed but it doesn't change a thing; it's another of those truths you're so keen on Louis. To say that there's worse still – there's the worst of all – there's an end to all my mystery. For the Visitor can come only once and here he approaches in polluted rags and acrid dentures to take away my dreams.

But in the circumstances she only said, "I don't know Louis. I just don't have the energy. I feel so emotionally overdrawn."

The last two words roused Barrington Smythe, who sat abruptly bolt upright. He was not a pretty sight. "That reminds me," he said. "Can anyone lend me a fiver?"

Catriona and Louis began to laugh.

Barrington Smythe's finances were a mystical thing, a continual indication that the supernatural has a part to play in modern life. No watered stock ever floated so precariously, no trade in futures was subject to such longevities, no tontine found itself so systematically over-sold as the credit of Barrington Smythe.

The plain fact was that financially speaking Barrington Smythe should not be able to live. At one time or another each of the major banks had confronted the gothic folly of the man's signature. While others *in extremis* were refused overdrafts, Barrington Smythe had long been disbarred from even the possession of an account. It was impossible to meet an acquaintance from whom he had not borrowed money; it was equally impossible to find one that he had paid back. There was about such thoroughness in one so otherwise chaotic something, Catriona had to admit, of the grand manner. If unsecured borrowing had constituted an art form then Barrington Smythe would have been its Renaissance man.

A while back – some six years ago – a brief period of reform had ensued. Barrington Smythe had contracted marriage to a small silent Indian girl, a former student of his who should therefore have known enough to avoid the man, but who solved the ticklish problem of motivation for so doomed a union by being well advanced in pregnancy.

At this point Barrington Smythe had spoken of stability and new starts. Through lust or carelessness he collected two children in annual succession. The terms *husband* and *family man* were frequently upon his lips.

For a while the whole thing looked almost feasible. The silent spouse initiated reforms. She could feed four people on curried nettles. She allowed her husband only a minute proportion of his salary. She opened a bank account by which Barrington Smythe could cash cheques only if she co-signed them. Though no debtor expected repayment, there was a certain amount of awe in the air.

This was no longer so. From God knew where Barrington Smythe had obtained the means to repair the shortfall that had developed in his habits. Once again he smoked eighty cigarettes a day, was firmly drunk by lunchtime and forever buttonholing the briefest acquaintances with bibulous schemes for turning a fast buck on a small advance.

All this Louis had told Catriona with relish. Barrington Smythe's present condition, though especially dramatic, was therefore not wholly unexpected.

"No," said Louis. "No one is lending you a fiver. Why don't you have a belt, or anything on your feet?"

"Ah." Barrington Smythe regarded his feet and spoke with

a weird formality. "The authorities," he said, "have proved difficult. It may surprise you to hear that I have just been in court. After, that is, spending a night in jail."

Louis and Catriona exchanged a glance. Barrington Smythe was a habitual liar but his lies always contained some truth. Besides, his worst forays into dishonesty concerned not tall stories but rather ludicrous attempts at self-exculpation; the man was quite incapable of accepting responsibility for any one of his invariably nefarious actions.

"What charge?"

Barrington Smythe frowned and said, "Harumph." He had an incongruous way of clearing his throat. It sounded official and portentous like a merchant banker at a board meeting. Now he lifted his finger gingerly, as if fearing that it might explode, and scratched his bald head.

"Well," he said, "I think it started as attempted murder but then it seemed to work itself down to aggravated assault. There was something about drugs too but I think they forgot about that."

"Indeed?" (Louis was enjoying himself.) "But what about the belt? And the shoes and socks?"

Barrington Smythe's thickly bespectacled eyes roved about seeking a median point between alcohol and memory.

"Rather a lot on my mind just at present. Confusing. Reason for coming here. Not altogether clear. Small temporary embarrassment."

"You could have fooled me," said Catriona. "I would have put you down at least as a large permanent embarrassment."

"Bitch," said Louis cheerfully.

Suddenly Barrington Smythe's eyes flashed with a wild recognition.

"The bitch," he roared. "The bitch!" He tried to struggle to his feet. His trousers failed him and he fell. The glasses shifted on his nose.

"I've remembered. *She* attacked *me*."

"Who did?"

"Sagi."

"Socky?" asked Catriona.

"Sagi, his wife."

"With," Barrington Smythe spoke with doom-laden solemnity, "a knife."

"Good heavens Barrington," said Louis. "Not . . . a knife!"

Nodding the while Barrington Smythe used one hand to gather his trousers into a knot and the other to lever himself to unsteady feet. His swizzle stick's body now looked like an extension of his head, like something from a bad science fiction comic. He might be funny, Catriona thought, but he is also sinister. Louis claimed that Barrington Smythe's violence was all directed against himself. The man was on self-destruct. Catriona remained unconvinced. She agreed with Penelope that he looked cruel and withdrawn like a potential rapist. She now noticed that the hand officiating as trouser support was bandaged and bloodstained and, presumably through re-activation, had begun to bleed afresh.

"Your hand?"

"Bloody RIGHT," shouted Barrington Smythe in the manner of a football hooligan called abruptly to the colours. He thrust the hand out for inspection.

"Your *trousers.*"

"Ah!" He managed some late rescue work with the other hand. Catriona averted her eyes from his terrible underpants. Barrington Smythe returned to waving his bloody limb.

"Quite like *Titus Andronicus*," said Louis.

"Who?" Barrington Smythe gave a start.

"Shakespeare."

"Shake that," Barrington Smythe extended the offending member, "and I'd fucking well faint. That's how deep the cut is. She came at me *with a knife*. Have I mentioned that?"

"Yes," said Louis, "but it bears repetition. Why did she do that?"

Barrington Smythe shook a dismissive head. "Mickey Mouse stuff. So naturally I went outside because I was bleeding."

"Naturally."

"I mean she was waving this great big knife and screaming so I didn't think she'd be much help with the bandaging process. So I went to the pub . . . "

"Where?" Catriona thought she had misheard. Louis knew better.

"For the *bandaging*," Barrington Smythe said patiently, "and by the time I got back Sagi had the cops there."

"What do you mean by the time you got back?" (Louis was

already shaking his head at Catriona's naïvety.)

Bleeding, beltless and barefoot, Barrington Smythe still managed an air of injured *hauteur.* "I had a couple of drinks to steady my nerves and, and . . . "

"And as an anaesthetic," offered Louis helpfully.

"As an anaesthetic. Thank you. Harumph. Well, when they carried me out . . . "

"When *who* carried you out."

"Shut up Catriona, let him get on with it."

"When the *police* carried me out . . . "

"But why did they *carry* you out . . . "

"For God's sake Catriona."

"Shut up yourself Louis. Why?"

"They *carried* me out because I had no belt or shoes and socks."

"Why not?"

"They'd bloody well taken them away hadn't they."

"Actually," said Louis, "I wouldn't mind knowing why they'd done that myself."

Barrington Smythe gave the palpitating sigh of a suffering schoolmaster bound by duty to obtuse and recalcitrant pupils. "They thought I was violent."

"They thought you'd attack them with your socks?"

"It's a point of view," said Louis.

"I will admit," said Barrington Smythe grandly, "that it all passed in something of a rush. Whether they thought I would attack them with my shoes and belt or whether they thought I couldn't run away without my shoes and belt, or whether I might hang myself with my belt . . . "

"But not your shoes."

"But not my shoes was unclear. So they beat the shit out of me anyway. With Sagi screaming blue murder."

"She wanted them to stop?"

"Stop my arse she was egging them on. Then they were carrying me out and she started yelling I know where he keeps his drugs. So they dropped me on the steps."

"Did you escape?"

"He didn't have his shoes and belt. Remember?"

"Two of them sat on me. Damned embarrassing."

"Did they find your drugs?"

Barrington Smythe looked hurt and offended. "Certainly

not. I'd sold them."

"Gosh," said Catriona. "I didn't know that you sold drugs."

"I don't," said Barrington Smythe with an air of complete finality. "Christ are those cocktails? It's a damned long walk from Marble Arch barefoot and holding up your trousers. What with a night in the cells and another beating up thrown in for good measure. To say nothing of appearing in court like this."

"Golly." Not for the first time Catriona felt that you really had to hand it to Barrington Smythe. Though, as Louis said, if you didn't hand it to him he'd take it anyway. Louis gave him a cocktail which he downed in one.

"Happy breakfast folks."

"But what happened to you in court? Did you get bail?"

Catriona knew that Louis was thinking the same thing. Who would be crazy enough to stand bail for this man?

"Certainly not," said Barrington Smythe. "Case dismissed. No charge to answer. Sagi had pissed off somewhere. Taken the children. Which means that she thinks I won't have any money. HUH!"

"Huh?" enquired Louis.

"I said HUH! and I meant huh." Despite his drunkenness Barrington Smythe had slyly crept up on the cocktail shaker. He seized it and raised it as in a toast.

"Here's to money."

Catriona watched mesmerised as he took a huge swig straight from the shaker. Part of her job was assessing how much people could drink. Barrington Smythe looked well on the way to alcoholic poisoning. "Here's to authorship." He took another swig then turned to Catriona with exaggerated courtesy. "Ah, and here's to your father."

Then he passed out.

# 15

"All the same darling," said Penelope to Catriona, "thrills and spills. What a story. Unsurpassed for the thrillishness and spillishness of it all. Dramatic old you."

Catriona made a rude face.

"I know," said Penelope. "Agony but not boredom. You look whiter than a Ku Klux something or other. Toast and tea. That's the treatment for you."

This, thought Catriona, is what friends are for. And at this minute especially girlfriends. It was like Louis to stay away. On the other hand he and Penelope always sparred. Still, perhaps that was another example of his tact. He knew that Catriona would want toast, consolation, and not a single male intrusive firework.

Penelope had come from Knightsbridge at high speed. Despite their many apparent differences they were best friends. Perhaps they were fortunate in being attractive women of strikingly different types, so that the likelihood of rivalry diminished.

Penelope was a tall dark hawk of a thing who sometimes looked febrile and drawn to the point of fragility ("frail as a tank" said Louis), with legs that seemed to last her whole body long. She had a habit of telling potential lovers on first acquaintance that she was functionally breastless. ("Catriona, it's only fair. Like the Trades Description Act. If they know one's a bungalow they won't come expecting a first floor with a bay window.")

Catriona though was smaller, with a tendency to curve, and towards commonplace prettiness. She was saved from the latter by the peculiar grey blondeness of her hair and her oddly slanting almost orientally set hazel eyes. Their colour was a surprise. Everyone expected blue.

Neither girl was beautiful in a strictly observable sense, yet both knew where the action was. Each needed men yet bewailed her dependency. Catriona was childless. Penelope was not. Penelope was promiscuous. Catriona was not. Penelope was upper class and Catriona was not, though in this area especially Penelope had directly helped her. Penelope had done for Catriona's social behaviour what Louis had done for her reading.

There had been a time when Catriona had tried to tamper with her accent, had come close to concealing her roots. It had taken someone as self-assured as Penelope to point out the fatality of such conduct. "Be what you are darling; then choose what you want to become. You don't have to conceal something not to be common." This had been music to Catriona's ears, for she was by nature very honest. Being common – saying pardon, being overdressed, using a whole series of euphemisms – might be not a class issue but an aesthetic one. Although of course Catriona had to admit to herself that not being common was still a necessary passport to admittance to the world of men like Esmond. But then Penelope the realist knew that as well. And it had been the best thing for Catriona when, that evening, Penelope had made a typical entrance.

"Darling I came as soon as that power-mad nanny would let me. I might as well be married to the woman. Where's Louis and where's Pointy Head – you know – Whatsisface Smythe the mass murderer look alike?"

Whey-faced Catriona had sat and told Penelope the story.

She finished with the last pathetic piece of quasi-evidence. Barrington Smythe resuscitated by coffee had repeated, though partially coherent, the same story. He had happened to get drunk two days before with a man called James Tar who claimed slobbering parenthood of Catriona. Barrington Smythe told of a small old Scotsman in a blue suit. Quite a coincidence didn't Catriona think?

"Crumbs," said Penelope.

"So the end of it all," said Catriona, "is that Louis lent Barrington Smythe the twenty quid he'd come to touch Louis for in the first place and poured him into a taxi. Louis says that there isn't any point in trying to talk to Barrington again until he sobers up. He said he'd try tomorrow."

"*If* he sobers up," said Penelope with grim relish. "Here," she pushed the plate towards Catriona. "Have some buttery stabilising toast. It's cheaper than psychoanalysis and it gives you an excuse for sucking your thumb."

But for Catriona toast had exhausted its comfort potential.

"Louis says. Well Louis says lots of things . . . "

"Huh," said Penelope. She and Louis had their difficulties.

"He says I should get hold of Bert to get hold of the Man from the Ministry and find out what he really has to say. But that perhaps I should take a solicitor along. But I don't want to antagonise them any more, to have them get in touch with Mr Schmidt. Assuming they haven't already. Oh God."

Catriona had started to pace up and down. Penelope sat, her long legs arranged gymnastically round the back of her armchair. She grinned. "Wouldn't worry about antagonising them any more. I don't see how you can improve on a flying start."

"Don't. I keep thinking that they want me to do something for them at the club. But why go to such lengths? To go inventing someone . . . "

She heard herself. She was going back over the same desperate ground she had failed to hold with Louis. She wasn't convincing herself. She probably wasn't convincing Penelope, for all her toast eating sympathetic attentiveness. Father or not, the man in the blue suit could not be disinvented, hung in the air. Now she found herself just talking – to keep herself somehow going.

"And if I hadn't socked the Man from the Ministry I might have learnt a bit more. And God *knows* I wouldn't have done that – hit him – if I hadn't been half drunk and done over by Esmond."

"Ah!" said Penelope. "Maul more men. What *about* Esmond? Do tell."

Affection flooded over Catriona. Dear Penelope. She knew how impossible it would have been to tell a man – even one as oddly approachable as Louis – about Esmond.

"*Do* tell!"

She told.

"I should have suspected the moment he asked me to lunch at the Ritz."

"Why?"

"Because the tables are so large. Puts space between you. No footsie or kneesie and you know that he's a terrible toucher. Besides, it made it harder for me to get close enough to hit him."

"I must say I wouldn't have thought of that but then I don't have your speed with an ashtray."

"Besides, he's usually so stingy. Oh he ladles out the stuff when he's trying to make you but as soon as he's had his wicked way it's gosh darling there's this funny little corner rathole I just heard about from the rodent inspector. Do you *know* where he took me last time?"

"Woolworth's cafeteria?"

"A Greek restaurant."

"The inhuman beast."

"Come off it Pempy – everyone knows Greek food's the world's smelliest slop."

"Especially Greeks."

"Of course Greeks. When they come to England they make those horrible kebabs full of dog shit, but all they eat is fish and chips. And as for Greek wine . . . "

"You mean Esmond actually ordered *Greek wine.*"

"He most certainly did."

"There's meanness and meanness. Talk about getting someone on the cheap . . . I'm sorry Catriona."

Catriona's eyes had brightened with tears but she shook her head and said, "The truth's the truth. Where was I?"

"At the Ritz."

"You know what *really* made me angry? About the Ritz? He told me *before we could order*. So he got rid of me in congenial circumstances *and* saved the price of lunch."

"I expect the best you could have expected would have been the table d'hôte."

"And then dammit I kept thinking how he'd tell his next bit of stuff about his glamorous generous farewell at the Ritz . . . "

"You think there is one. A sort of bit-of-stuff-in-waiting? Hence the heave ho?"

"You know the funny thing is I don't. Otherwise he would have been – I don't know – more at ease. Better prepared."

"Well that is a new fucking one and no mistake. Esmond's approximately the most unimaginatively complacently self-assured man in London."

"And if it'd been another girl. Well he would have been prepared. God knows he's had enough practice. He's been screwing girls on the side since that broomstick of a wife first squawked I do. He must have more stories than Agatha Christie."

"So what *did* he say? I must confess I'm all agog."

"Well you can just degog because there isn't anything to gog about. Just one hurried platitude after another. Danger of people talking, political career, danger of wife finding out, thing had run its natural course. You know what really hurt. He is charming . . . "

Penelope made a face.

"Well if he's the type you like. Oh and I know he isn't kind, not a bit, but he can seem it. If he wants to. He didn't even bother. Didn't even try."

"Chum," said Penelope, "he isn't worth it. But then you knew that already."

Catriona gritted her teeth. "It doesn't help to know how stupid you've been."

"Darling no. So what did you do?"

"I told him to fuck off. Then I went to cry in the loo. The Ritz has the best one in London for crying in. When I came out he'd gone."

She didn't say how long she had stood there between the marble pillars looking to right and left – just in case he had decided to return with a bunch of cut price flowers.

"Well," said Penelope. "The sweet cheat gone. Mind you, you did tell him to fuck off. What's the matter?"

Catriona's head was in her hands. Before Penelope could reach her, embrace her, Catriona's head came up. She was dry-eyed. Her expression was fixed, determined as if a decision had been made and must now be acted on. She said, "About the Visitor."

Penelope said, "Look, there's fantasy and fantasy. Heaven knows I dream of the most extraordinary situations but aren't you going . . . "

She stopped at Catriona's expression. "I know. I know you think it's gone too far. That's why you need to see this. Nobody's seen it. Not even Louis."

"Yum yum." Penelope was uneasy; she hoped that habitual jollity still worked as a cover up. The last thing she wanted was for Catriona to fly into an offended temper.

"Come on," said Catriona.

She picked up a chair. Penelope followed her into the corridor. Catriona climbed expertly on to the chair's back and began to pull a section of grille work from the upper wall.

Penelope wondered randomly whether or not Catriona's thighs were too fleshy. Catriona pulled something out, replaced the grille and climbed down. Penelope followed her back into the main room. Catriona laid a flat oval biscuit tin on the table. Its lid commemorated the Coronation of 1953. The Queen looked as cheerful as could be expected. The lid was wrapped round by fraying elastic bands. Someone (Catriona?), thought Penelope, had spent a lot of time opening and closing this thing.

Catriona said, "Open it."

Inside Penelope encountered sprigs of white heather dried to fragments.

"It's supposed to bring luck," said Catriona. "To be rare. In Scotland. Actually it grows all over the place. It's my mother's box. I found it after she died. When she went senile she hid it in an old meat safe."

"A meat safe," said Penelope trying to fight off the gloom in Catriona's voice. "*Goodness* how you've lived."

Catriona didn't smile. Penelope found that she had carefully heaped the heather dust into a superstitious little pile. Underneath lay a bundle of material held compulsively together by a thick criss-crossed mesh of rubber bands. As she unwound them curiosity developed into amazement. Pieces of paper, symmetrically, exactly cut by scissors began to fill the box. There were two kinds.

The first consisted of thick white creamy card; smooth at the touch, heavy in the hand. Expensive stuff.

The second was bank notes. Dismembered. Sliced up money. Penelope looked at Catriona for guidance.

She said, "You can piece the cards together quite easily. To Katie on this birthday or that birthday. Ten years worth. The money must have been enclosed. As presents. Needless to say I never saw any of this."

"Gosh," said Penelope and realised immediately what a stupid thing it was to say in the face of such hoarding, such fanaticism. "But why would she cut it all up and *then* keep it?"

Catriona smiled wryly. "Perhaps she couldn't bear to part with them. Tokens of her contact with the rich world and perhaps . . . "

She paused.

"Perhaps they were there to remind her that the Visitor

existed."

That night Penelope sat up to keep watch as a good friend should while Catriona slept. This suited Penelope. She didn't need much sleep and her children were safely cared for by a tender disapproving nanny.

Penelope liked the reversal of roles – scatty Penelope cares for competent Catriona.

So Penelope sat, drank cocoa and thought about Catriona. Penelope admired Catriona for possessing not only courage (a quality which Penelope took for granted in her friends) but also guts. Catriona didn't give up. She had fought her way out of the country's most repressive class into a more expansive existence. She had been through some tough and even dangerous times but she had never given up, and she had done it all herself. Catriona might attempt to use men but only so that as soon as it could be arranged they became dispensable; and when you came down to it the men seemed to do most of the using. Still Catriona, unlike Penelope, had not passed from one man's indentured service to another's.

Most people thought of Penelope as a sort of ageing *bacchante* – an upper class eccentric, a card, a wild free spirit. Yet she herself knew this to be untrue. All her wildness (even her casual and continual entanglements with sex) was easy, comfortable, permitted.

For all her shrewd and quick-tongued disapproval of entrenched stupidities Penelope had no intention of abandoning the security blankets of position and class. Although she had run through three husbands (Louis said they could be recognised by the puncture marks above the collar), they remained chums, always reachable on the telephone, who had cheerfully settled their departures in terms of large cash settlements. She had two houses, one in town, one in the country, for she needed the right places and the right kind of money to cling to. She never had done, never would do, a job of work. Even at Oxford she had known that this would be the case. For though her mind was sharp, her education considerable, her industriousness undisputed, she could not consider departing from the pattern which others had created for her and girls like her. She had been brought up in the sweetest yet most ruthless way to live off men. Money came from husbands, fathers, lovers. It was the result of legal concubinage, the wages of the married courtesan.

But Catriona was different. She had dared. She had *moved.*

And Penelope respected her for it. But she still wondered . . .

Penelope had taught Catriona the technique of belonging *in* the upper class world without pretending to be *of* it. Penelope had simply done this to please; because Catriona wanted it. Catriona wanted to *be* something. What was that awful phrase? To make something of herself. But, Penelope wanted to know, what exactly was that *something*? Despite Catriona's denials Penelope was inclined to believe that the solution was a someone. If not a husband, at any rate a man. But Catriona had such rotten luck in that direction. A shit like Esmond was about the last straw. Although one had to admit that he was presentable.

Penelope lay back in her chair. What would have happened if the man in the photograph, the man who had called today, had not been small and disgusting and lower class? Suppose he had been in dress and appearance and accent an older version of Esmond? Wouldn't Catriona have been overjoyed? Wouldn't she even now be out there on the streets looking for him?

Perhaps therefore Catriona, for all that she was a wonder to Penelope, simply wanted that tiresomely impossible commodity desired by woman after woman – a fantasy man.

So what then? What next? What would Catriona do? What *could* she do? As far as Penelope could see Catriona could do nothing much but wait for developments – till Tar, or the sober Barrington Smythe, or the reappearance of the Man from the Ministry actually came up with something – and that wouldn't suit Catriona at all. Catriona liked activity.

That was why she loved running her club. Perhaps too it was why she liked essentially passive men – Esmond – and even in his own way Louis. They gave Catriona all the more to do. So if not enough was happening then Catriona was altogether capable of moving and shaking all on her determined own. Penelope thought of the hand that had swung the ashtray. Oh honeybunch she thought, drawing the rug around her, there's trouble ahead.

# 16

"He will only," said Yassin, "speak through the witch. It is a matter of dialects. He purports to speak little Arabic. Each question therefore one must ask the witch."

"Fine," said the Consul. "Great. Jim-Dandy. What could be easier? So ask the witch. The smell is terrible."

The room was in the Tanners Quarter, a part of the tangle of alleys that run from the Ban-ed-Debbagh, the gate of the Tanners in the Marrakesh city wall. The street below was still in full industrial use – the walls smeared with blood and fat and dyes – the curing vats and the stretching animal skins fouled the air. The Consul thought that he had never smelt anything worse. Even though it did mean more money he wished that Rossminster were here and not back in England.

The man that the Blue People had left behind sat perfectly still, cross-legged, in the middle of the bare wooden floor. The dye from his indigo garments had turned his skin the deepest darkest blue. Only the palms of his hands and the soles of his feet showed a dirt-tinted glimpse of human pink. His eyes, expressionless, still enough to be a dead man's eyes, seemed unnaturally brown, staring out as they did from beneath blue lids.

The witch sat in a rocking chair smoking a pipe. Its foulness gave even the tanner's products a measure of competition. The witch looked immeasurably old which meant that she was somewhere over forty and had false teeth which, though ill fitting, argued a good rate of return on prophecy and incantation. As a gesture of goodwill towards the authorities she had first offered Yassin a cut price curse, and then provided a tray of mint tea and small cakes sticky with granulated sugar. Hospitality compelled the Consul to try one. It tasted to him of cow carcass.

So Yassin repeated the Consul's question. Rocking and puffing the witch translated. The Blue Man nodded slowly to indicate that he understood, then spoke at length. Rocking and puffing some more the witch did another batch of translating. By the time it was Yassin's turn again impatience and the smell had driven the Consul to chain smoke three Gauloise Caporals.

"It is now," Yassin said, "permitted for him to speak by the friend of his people, Tar."

"The man who put the jest in Beau," said the Consul.

"You will refrain from interruption. You are not the proximate Milor' Rossminster. To continue *ce Monsieur Tar* had come often to them in the past. He stayed with them. He was their desert brother."

The Consul said something about Lawrence of the Gorbals but he said it to himself.

"This is in the south of Morocco in the oasis of M'hamid where the waters of the Dra river cease and there is beyond only true desert; absolute desert."

The Consul tried mentally to reassemble the map of Morocco. M'hamid was beyond Zagora and at Zagora there is no road as such going south – only the roughest of shifting tracks over the hills. The place was, even by the standards of the Moroccan hinterland, remote.

"For this Tar, you understand I summarise now, there is great respect, many compliments. On this last occasion he has come to observe, to watch the few foreigners who pass that way. It is of one particular group he is now permitted to speak. They are rich offal who come dressed as decadents."

"Like how?"

"They were of course the hippies of Señor Rossminster's attention," said Yassin coldly. "They talked much and boasted of their travels. They are full of themselves. They have no respect. They have no fear. They abuse the hospitality of the local women."

"Hold it," said the Consul. "How can that be? I thought the Tuareg women are allowed to be promiscuous. I thought that was what Tuareg hospitality was all about?"

"Not when you give the women LSD. Two killed themselves. One miscarried. One was stoned to death as possessed of djinns."

"No kidding," said the Consul. "Bad stuff. Hence the gruesome revenge."

"Hence too the witch. There were others beyond the Blue People's reach. A curse is now in order."

"What others?"

But the round of translated questioning produced the flattest answer. "It is not permitted. He will say no more. Only that he wishes money to be given to this crone. Otherwise malediction will not ensue. Pay the witch."

The Consul paid the witch. "Merci ma mère."

The witch removed the pipe from her mouth and grinned. "Hot dog," she said. "Be sure and come again. Pour le curse bébé."

"Pour le curse," said the Consul.

# 17

Next morning Penelope drove Catriona to work. Catriona had dressed to kill in Gina Fratini black slit to the thigh (and to hell with the rest of the world). Penelope remembered that it was Catriona's first post-Esmond day. Child, she thought, we're all the same. Our father may pretend to come back from the dead, but it's our ex-lover we dress to shock.

Catriona regarded Penelope's ancient Mini with distaste.

"Where's the Mercedes?"

"The bloody nanny's got it. I do hate her. I had to rush out and clear all the french letters from under the front seat."

"Don't you mean the back seat?"

"Catriona I know what I mean. Are you getting in or not?"

Penelope was a dangerously gifted driver who saw traffic as an assault course. In eight minutes they had reached the alley at the side of Green Park where Catriona's club maintained its discreet presence. Penelope parked on the pavement as usual.

"Can I come in for a bit Catriona? I do love your club."

"Only if you behave yourself. I've work to do."

"Honestly, I'll be like a little mouse with well concealed rat-like tendencies."

They passed under the green awning through the double doors down the thickly carpeted staircase. At the foot of the stairs a long curved reception desk gave on to an oblong room, galleried like a midget version of a liner's ballroom. There was no bar as such. All drinks were brought from the kitchen and served at tables. These were now piled against the walls. From the room came the clanking of slop buckets and the smells of this morning fighting the smells of last night – polish versus tobacco.

This was Catriona's empire. She never entered it without a thrill. The rich and successful who came here to waste their time and money might be reprehensible but as work objects they beat the poor every time.

Gomez came out of the kitchen.

"Good morning Miss Lomax. Good morning Lady Penelope. I'm afraid Miss Lomax that . . . "

Bert came out of the kitchen with a cup of coffee.

"And good morning to you Cat." His watchful, bogus, smiling eyes swivelled round on Penelope. He gave a little bow. "And whom do I also have the honour of addressing?"

"Lor," said Penelope, "where did you get him?"

"Where did he get himself?" said Catriona.

"Bit of a liberty eh Cat? Barged in. A treat to see all this spit and polish. Keeps a lovely club does Cat." His eyes came back firmly on to Penelope. "Eh madam, or is it Miss?"

"Lady Penelope Meadowes," said Catriona.

Bert bowed with maximum humility. "Plain Bert," he said.

Penelope clapped her hands. "Honestly. How too like a butler."

"Ha ha. Got Mr Robinson here. In your office. Having such a nice chat I forgot to mention it."

Robinson. In *her* office. Uninvited. A threat of sorts. An indication of strength. But what could she do about it? She couldn't afford a repeat of yesterday.

When, followed by Penelope and Bert, she entered the office Robinson had not sat down. He stood there looking awkward. His lip was twice its normal size and turning purple.

"Poor Mr Robinson," cooed Catriona. "How dreadful your lip looks."

"Bert said I should wait here. I hope it's all right."

Bert smiled and nodded as if this suggestion had been genuinely helpful and wholly unrelated to trouble making.

"Good God," said Robinson suddenly. He sounded disgusted. "What are *you* doing here?"

He was looking beyond Catriona. Short-sighted Penelope leaned forward, peered and then beamed in recognition.

"Humpo!" said Penelope.

"What?" said Catriona.

"Christ," said Robinson.

"Bless my soul," said Bert.

Penelope grinned broadly, made her way over to Robinson and pointedly proffered her cheek. He kissed it and scowled.

"Humpo's my cousin," said Penelope to Catriona, "and I simply never see him nowadays."

"Humpo?" mused Catriona. Bert beamed like a lighthouse. Robinson blushed. He looked even ruddier and, despite the rough maturity of his features, just a touch like a little boy. It was, Catriona thought to herself, a long time since she had seen a man blush. Penelope was now doing her gosh-how-super act; lethal in its insincerity. She hung on ecstatically to Robinson's forearms, rendering his well-clutched briefcase even more ridiculous in appearance. For a second Catriona wondered about Penelope's problems with men; a combination of cling and ridicule hardly seemed a recipe for success.

"Honestly Catriona," Penelope gurgled with all the spontaneity of a mountain brook in an old cigarette commercial. "Why didn't you tell me it was Humpo?"

Robinson detached his forearms and propelled Penelope backwards until she found herself tipped gracelessly into a chair. Catriona was amused. He now cut into Penelope's latest batch of artless chatter.

"Stop it Penelope. If you talked less you'd be more noticeable."

"Ooh beast," said Penelope. "Low blow."

And that's the thing, Catriona thought. It *is* a low blow and it hurts and for the moment you don't have anything to come back with.

Robinson turned to Catriona. "My name is Humphrey. But nobody calls me by it. Except spoilt cousins."

For the first time today – really for the first time at all – Catriona took a proper look at Robinson. He was a little under six feet and heavily, rather coarsely made. Not fat at all but raw boned. Physically strong, she suspected, in a compact solid way. But for a man with so unaesthetic a body there were odd graceful features to him. He had small feet; unlike most men of his build and colouring he didn't possess an oversized head or huge red prairies of cheeks; his head was exactly in proportion and his skin was smooth and pale and veinless. He generally looked fresh and healthy if one chose to ignore the large blue shadowy pouches that for whatever reason (overwork, worry, weariness), lay siege to his eyes. Best not to ignore them, Catriona thought, they are certainly not unsweet. She hoped they came from weariness. A genuinely weary man would make a change. She made a point of not looking at his hands.

She suddenly realised that Bert was looking on with goodwill that must suggest the presence of a venom satisfied. But what was he looking at? He was looking at Robinson looking at her. And Robinson was looking with evident appreciation. Then he seemed to come to himself and started to scowl again. Catriona felt positively gleeful. She was tempted to stand up and finish him off with the slit skirt but then decided that it might be more fun to protract matters. Besides, it was high time that she appeared in control. So now, meeting his eye (he had raised it from her neckline), and making her voice as prim as possible, she said, "I don't see that your Christian name is significant Mr Robinson."

"It is if it's Humpo." Penelope had come punching back.

"I would like to talk to Miss Lomax," said Robinson pointedly, "without the interference of silly girls."

"Ooh," Penelope let her eyebrows do the walking. "Girls he says and at our age."

"Bert, if you would show Lady Penelope out and wait outside . . . " Penelope looked at Catriona, who nodded. Penelope rose cheerfully to her feet.

"Heigh-ho. The gooseberry says farewell to the bush. A mother's heart beats once again beneath a carapace of sophistication. Even now in the village of Brompton children sob and nannies fret. Come on plain Bert – you can show me your truncheon on the way out."

"Well. Well. You're quite a wag Lady Penelope."

"Honestly Bert darling I can wag the shit out of almost anything."

The door closed behind them. Robinson shook his head. "How did you meet her?"

"Her last husband was a member here. One evening she came in to get him."

"She would," said Robinson grimly.

Catriona decided to cheer him up. She crossed her legs. He did his best to look away. She wondered what had brought on this bout of haphazard licentiousness. Yesterday he had been wholly lust-free. Gosh men were odd. Still, it was a pleasant change from Esmond. She hadn't thought about Esmond for a while until just now. And of course Robinson was Penelope's cousin. Her alarm bells rang. They rang *gentleman*.

He turned back towards her. He spoke abruptly. "James Tar," he said.

"I don't know him. Until you came along I'd never heard of him."

"Then why," said Robinson in a reasonable tone, "should he go around saying he's your father?"

That was the question she couldn't answer herself. The question that again sent a tremor of dread through her, a tremor of panic. She turned it into anger.

"How should I know? I don't know anything about him. I don't even know why you're asking me these damned questions."

Robinson made a wry face. "I seem to recall that the last time we talked you weren't in an enquiring mood."

"Don't you patronise me."

"Why not?" said Robinson.

Her jaw dropped.

Then Robinson grinned. "Sorry. I just wanted to see your expression. I see you have all your own teeth. Good ones too. Tar then. Let's just say that he recently . . . made contact . . . with the Ministry. We're interested in some information he may have. He on the other hand seems interested in an apparently long lost daughter. That's you. Ah. Sorry. Says it's you."

Nausea and anger competed inside Catriona with the conviction that this clumsy looking creature was getting the better of her. To make matters worse he seemed to have gone off the sexual boil; the deference that lust should pay to its object had vanished. Could he have made the lust up? Was it just another part of goading her? She shut her mouth tight and tried her best to stare haughtily at him.

"About Schmidt," said Robinson.

Oh God, Catriona thought. Does the blackmail start here?

"*Mr* Schmidt. What about him?"

"Well," said Robinson equably, "I rather thought you owned this club."

"Why did you think such a thing?"

"It's called Lomax's."

"That's right. Not Tar's."

"And you seem so much in control of things. So – proprietorial."

"Thank you." She tried to sound grim but she was pleased.

Robinson had opened his briefcase. "But Mr Schmidt bought it," he extracted a sheet of typewritten foolscap, "seven years ago." He read on, "With you as Manager . . .

Manageress?"
"I'm indifferent."
"Just wanted to avoid offence."
"Fancy."
"And you designed the place. Yes?"
"You've done your homework."
"Bert. Very efficient Bert. So you designed it?"
"Yes."
"An excellent job. You have excellent taste."
"Thank you sir," she said. It didn't sound half acid enough.
"And that," he was looking again at the typewritten sheet, "is why Mr Schmidt employed you?"
"What?"
Robinson looked up. "He must have had a reason. But according to Bert you seem to have done a number of – well – rather odd jobs."
She stared at the sheet of paper in Robinson's hand. My life, she thought. He has my life there. He has Monty and the Cairo job and the evidence of me in shoulder length grubby gloves, the worst member of the worst chorus line in the world. You bastard, she thought. You absolute calculating bastard. Underneath that hearty English exterior you're cunning. But then you would be. With your job. Job. She reached for the telephone.
"I think you'd better talk to Mr Schmidt. Perhaps he can explain. I'm sure he'd want to know that you're here anyway."
"Oh absolutely," said Robinson genially. "Quite right. When you've finished put him on. I'll ask if *he* knows anything about Tar."
She looked at the telephone but she didn't pick it up. Then she looked at Robinson. He wore a polite smile.
"No need to make it unnecessarily difficult for either of us."
You're right damn it, she thought. I've lost my temper once with you. It won't help to do it again.
"All right," she said. "Tell me what you want." (Apart from another inch of thigh.)
"I want to know why you're so incurious about Tar. Here a man pops up out of nowhere claiming to be your father and you don't want to know anything about him. That seems strange."

Does he know about the Visitor thought Catriona, or doesn't he? I can't tell. But I'm damned if I'll help him out.

"Of course," said Robinson, "he doesn't seem much of a catch. Socially speaking."

Christ thought Catriona, first he looks at me like a tart. Now he says that I'm a terrible snob. But if Robinson was dangling a bait she wouldn't rise to it. Instead she said sweetly, "I somehow thought you were *bound* to tell me all about him."

"Well," Robinson rubbed his ruddy chin with his big red knuckles. He looked slightly abashed. It suddenly occurred to Catriona that the randomness of Robinson's behaviour – the on/off sex interest – might actually come from not knowing much about women. It was an interesting thought.

"Well." Robinson had finished rubbing. "As I might have told you yesterday if you'd let me finish" (he touched his lip) "he was brought up in a Scottish orphanage. He served in Spain very young . . . "

"*Served* in Spain." (A waiter? A butler?)

"I'm sorry," Robinson spoke quietly but she could sense the disapproval at the back of his voice. "I thought you would have known about the war in Spain."

He sounded disappointed. As if he had thought better of her but in displaying the average rate of ignorance she had let him down. His tone stung her.

"Of course I know about the Spanish Civil War."

"Oh *good*." Robinson relieved. Robinson pleased. "Well he seems to have been something of a hero then. Perhaps he couldn't adjust after that. Of course that happened to a lot of them."

"Yes," said Catriona. She hadn't the faintest idea what he meant.

"He seems to have become a . . . " Robinson had trouble finding the right word. "A mercenary."

"You mean a soldier who sells himself for money?"

"That sort of thing."

"Someone who kills for money."

"That sort of thing."

"Oh goody."

Mercenary, she thought. Misfit. Psychopath. Then she thought of the photograph that Robinson had shown her yesterday. Is a psychopath still dangerous when he's old and drunk? For the first time in all this odd business she felt fear mingling with disgust. Yet again Robinson correctly read her expression.

"No," he said. "I don't think he's a danger to you . . . "

"To whom then?" (When angry she was always extra careful about grammar.)

"I didn't mean that either. I meant that though he's old he hasn't become Mary Poppins. He's not a man to take risks with. When he makes contact I want you to telephone Bert."

"When? Don't you mean if?"

Robinson looked straight at her. "No," he said. "I don't. I mean when. Unless of course he's put in an appearance already."

"No." She said it immediately looking bold faced straight back at him. She had spoken instinctively. But why lie? After all it would be easier to turn it all over. Get rid of it. Except that stubbornness and pride had united to say Tar was *hers* to sort out. One terrible way or another. Hers.

"All the same," said Robinson, "don't go charging around trying to do things on your own."

Catriona felt a fresh wave of anger coming over her. She said, "You silly little girl. Is that it?"

Robinson had risen. He said, "If it makes you feel better."

There it was again. That damned patronising air. He turned to go. Then, as if remembering something, he turned back. "Despard," he said.

"What?"

"I don't suppose you ever had a member here by that name? Despard?" He spelt it.

"No. Who is he?"

"Never heard the name mentioned?"

"No. I asked you a question. Who is he?"

Robinson gave a vague shrug. "Was, actually. A businessman who might have known Tar a long time ago. Dead now." He gave a reassuring little chuckle. "Of natural causes."

"And I suppose," said Catriona, "that's all I get to know about him. National security. Careless talk costs lives."

Robinson smiled his big red condescending smile. "Something like that. I'll be in touch."

Catriona couldn't bear to let him get away so easily, so

smugly. She called on the collected forces of malice and childishness.

"Presumably when you want to spend more time staring up my skirt. Humpo!"

For the second time he blushed. God, thought Catriona, what an odd man.

"You know," he said, his hand now on the doorknob, "you shouldn't try to be too like Penelope. It doesn't suit you." He paused. "Cat."

She felt as if she had been slapped.

# 18

From the depths of a leather armchair Robinson watched Esmond Claremaurice approach. He recognised two of the waiters and paused to say a few words. The waiters flushed with pleasure. For each Esmond had a smile and a little joke. Perhaps, thought Robinson grimly, that's how he got elected. A spoonful of charm, a measure of intimacy administered at just the right moment.

You had to admit that Esmond Claremaurice was a strikingly handsome man. Though in his mid-forties, his hair remained dark and full. He was tall, well over six feet, and narrowly built with that particular type of upper body on which a double breasted jacket floats but never clings. His eyes were large, rimmed with small dark smudges that had been there ever since Robinson had first known him as his senior at school; a handsome boy growing with cheerfully vacuous self-confidence into a handsome man.

Except, thought Robinson, shifting his awkward frame in his chair, there was always something slightly, just *very* slightly, wrong with Esmond Claremaurice.

His Englishness, for example, had always seemed a touch studied and therefore, to the acute observer, fragile. As if he had to take special care to avoid looking like a continental lounge lizard precisely because such lizardom was in danger of breaking through. Robinson noticed now, as the approaching Esmond greeted him with a smile, that the man's outfit – the chalk striped suit, the plain black shoes, the absolutely-not-close-fitting-or-monogrammed silk shirt – still betrayed tiny touches of café-gypsy. The watch on the wrist (hand held out now in greeting) bore a figureless Cartier dial thrust down for show; the nails, more than cut, were positively polished; the hair Trumper-trimmed was just a little too long over the collar. It seemed to Robinson that none of these small things, even accumulated into a package, *should* have mattered at all. They merely seemed strange in a man who offered himself to his constituency and the world as a not very bright, decent hearted, born into privilege, one nation Conservative. Perhaps it was because Claremaurice came from an old Anglo-Irish family. Yet that didn't ring true either. Products of that particular kennel might be only semi house trained in basic Englishness – eccentric, wild or terminally stupid – but they avoided flashiness like the plague, fearful that it might seem redolent of peasant Irishry.

Still (thought Robinson as he rose to grasp Esmond's hand), he could be wrong. His own kind of training tended to over-observation. And it would not be difficult to be jealous of a man who could pick up and discard women like Catriona Lomax.

"Rob."

"Esmond."

They sat. One of the waiters Esmond had recognised took their order.

"Rob. Don't think you know old Johnson here. Apparently he's new. Used to be at the Beefsteak."

Old Johnson here departed beaming.

"Well," said Esmond. "Short notice. So business I imagine."

Robinson had forgotten Esmond's characteristic combination of drawl and staccato half-sentences – as if because it was rather a bore to speak at all, weariness demanded that one used the least syntax.

"Business."

Esmond smiled again. "You know me. Anything to oblige."

Robinson said, "Catriona Lomax."

Esmond kept his smile but put his head enquiringly to one side. "How so?" he said.

"You're having an affaire with her."

Esmond's smile became a grin. He delivered a long wink. "Mmm," he said, and "mmm," again as if he were thinking of good vintage port or an Annabel's *mille-feuille*. Robinson suppressed a desire to punch him.

"Actually Rob . . . ah drinks. Did I tell you that Johnson here used to be at the Beefsteak?"

After more badinage Johnson went off over there. Esmond frowned for a moment. "Ah yes," he said, visibly remembering, "Catriona. Affaire. Past tense actually. What's the matter? Been a naughty girl?"

He raised his eyebrows to indicate relish at naughtiness in

prospect.

"Her club," said Robinson, "tends to attract the occasional odd fish. So my people are checking up. I can't tell you more than that."

Esmond leaned forward in shocked reassurance. "Well of course not. Of *course* not. I mean I am a *Conservative* member. I mean you chaps . . . "

He waved his hands to express appreciation of the protection offered by the secret world. Robinson said, "Why did you break off with her?"

"Frankly," said Esmond. "I always put a time limit on these things. Usually a year. This one had run double that time. But then she *is* a very fetching girl. Mmm?"

Robinson had a sudden vision of Catriona as a favourite automobile whose excessive mileage had been tolerated until its owner had regretfully but sensibly decided to unload it on the market.

"You see," continued Esmond, "after a bit they start to make demands. Telephone you at home. Leave an earring in your car. Next thing you have trouble with the wife. Not, to be fair, that our Catriona had started that, but they all do in the end. So – best to make a break. Better for everyone."

Esmond sat back and sipped his whisky with the air of a man who deserved congratulation. Robinson knew enough of Esmond's reputation to expect him to brag about women. He had not anticipated such a high incidence of myopic complacency. It occurred to him that either through innocence or calculation Esmond had so far given practically nothing away. He said, "I'd rather relied on you."

"Relied on me?"

"For a picture. As a man of the world. As her lover. To give me a picture."

"A picture of what?"

"Of her. Of Catriona Lomax. What's she like."

Esmond looked puzzled, as if such a question concerning a woman would never have occurred to him. He frowned. "In what way?"

"That's up to you."

"In any way at all?"

"That," Robinson kept his tone of voice even, "would be a start."

"Well. Rather a tricky one." He frowned some more. "Good company. Fun. Not too expensive as girls go these days." He brightened as an original idea dawned. "Hell of a temper though. Yes indeed. Have to mind your P's and Q's with our Catriona."

Robinson ran his finger along his lip. "What makes her angry?"

"Oh the usual sort of thing. Showing interest in another woman. Mentioning the wife. Forgetting her birthday. Not," Esmond spoke emphatically with especial moral self congratulation, "that I ever forget a birthday."

Robinson struggled on. "How did she behave when she was angry?"

Esmond regarded Robinson as if he were a man from Mars. "Why, angrily of course."

"Specifically?"

Esmond sighed. His expression seemed to say – I have known so many women, how can I be expected to distinguish between them? Still, as a public servant, he would make the effort. "Specifically? Well, she has a terrible tongue on her. Sometimes threw things. Sometimes hit one. Actually," he brightened at another original thought, "she tended to do it when I was asleep. I thought that was rather clever of her. I mean you'd wake up with a pain and there she'd be bashing you. Really rather original. Mmm?"

Robinson regarded this flower of the Tory party with despair – but pushed on anyway.

"Tell me. Did she ever mention her parents?"

"Her father and her mother?"

"That sort of thing."

"Not much. They were dead or something. I think she was ashamed of them for being common. Of course Catriona's common but she doesn't do a bad job of covering up. I rather like that bit of Scots accent don't you?"

"Yes."

"Oh, so you *have* met her?"

It took Robinson a moment to realise that Esmond had extracted a piece of information from him that he had intended to save till later. Well, after all, Claremaurice *was* a politician – even the stupidest of that breed possessed a certain native cunning in debate.

"So," said Robinson, "she never really talked about her father?"

Esmond shook his head. "Nor her mother."

Robinson paused. The next question was necessary but he disliked it. "Would you say she was promiscuous?"

"Her mother?"

"Catriona. Miss Lomax."

"Come again. I've rather lost the thread."

"Would you say that Catriona Lomax was promiscuous?"

"Definitely."

"*Definitely*?"

"She's a woman isn't she?"

Perhaps, thought Robinson, Catriona had bashed the sleeping rather than the waking Esmond because the man's behaviour did not admit to a distinction between the two states. Esmond tried to help out.

"You see," he said, "it's their nature."

"Do you mean," said Robinson, "that Catriona was sleeping with other men during your affaire?"

"Shouldn't think so. Expect she was satisfied with me. They usually are. You asked me what she *was*. Not what she *did*."

Once again in the midst of this astonishing egotistic smugness there came a clever little point. Robinson made a note of its occurrence. Esmond leaned back in his chair – the older man giving the younger the benefits of his urbane dissolute experience.

"You take someone, Rob, like our Catriona. Been around the world a bit. Odd jobs. Chorus girl here. Bar girl there. Then finishes running an undercover upmarket knocking shop in St James's. Must have lost track of the number of men who've been up her pearly path. Naturally enough then she doesn't want to talk about it. Naturally enough I didn't ask. After all I *am* a gentleman. Only man she ever mentioned was that swine Louis Vulliamy. Lives in that same block of flats as Catriona. But I shouldn't think there's anything there. Probably queer. Wears a bow tie and suede shoes."

Robinson, who knew Louis Vulliamy, did not intend to rise to another bait. Besides, he had something else to say.

"And what about your wife?"

"How's that?"

"Is she promiscuous?"

For the first time in the conversation urbanity deserted Esmond Claremaurice.

"WHAT?"

"She's a woman, isn't she?"

"Ah. Oh." Esmond, choosing to take it as a joke, gave vent to a nervous chuckle. "Ah. You're a bachelor. Hence the basic mistake. Never think of your wife as a woman and she'll never behave like one. Mmm?"

Again, thought Robinson. Again. It's a quick reply. It's a clever reply from a supposedly stupid man. Or was he, Robinson, exaggerating? Perhaps womanisers like Claremaurice just had an extra sense when it came to females and when that was translated into male dialogue it could easily be mistaken for intelligence or wit . . .

After Robinson had thanked Esmond for the meeting, Esmond said, "Mind if I ask you something?"

"Please?"

"Dogsbodying a bit aren't you? This sort of stuff. Hanging around that club asking questions. Isn't that Special Branch work usually?"

"Yes," said Robinson. "Usually."

"Oh," said Esmond. "Oh. Did you know you had a swollen lip?"

Robinson walked him as far as the hall. On the way out Esmond found the waiter Johnson and asked to be reminded to Mrs Johnson. Robinson walked back towards the lavatories. He intended to rinse out his mouth; what he really needed was to rinse out his mind. To rinse out the image of the furious energy possessed by Catriona Lomax converted into sex as she lay with her knees up, her throaty Scots voice urging Esmond Claremaurice on and on.

# 19

The club closed at midnight. It was another hour before the doors were finally locked and Gomez, with irritating protectiveness, walked Catriona into St James's and waved down a taxi.

She leaned back against the seat. All day she had been nervous and febrile – restless, unable to concentrate, full of dread. At any moment it could have happened. She would look up at Gomez as he cleared his throat to murmur that a strange little psychopath in an ill-fitting blue suit stood at the entrance proclaiming kinship.

What then would she have done? Called Bert as Robinson had said? She didn't know.

She had decided as a good employee she had to contact Schmidt. She *owed* Schmidt. Even if it didn't directly affect him Schmidt should know what was going on. But the Geneva answering service through which he received his calls blandly took her messages and repeated that he was out of town. Today was Friday, the end of the club's working week. If she heard nothing by Monday she would send a telegram.

There had been no word either from Barrington Smythe. Louis had repeatedly telephoned. Either he was still drunk or sleeping it off. According to Louis a twenty-four-hour detoxifying hibernation was quite usual. Perhaps, though, she should simply be grateful for one more Tar-free day.

All of which left her doing what?

Waiting.

She gave the taxi driver Esmond's address.

She knew from experience that went all the way from adolescence till now, that the-street-where-you-live syndrome, the mooning-along-under-the-beloved's-window was a bad sign, especially when the beloved in question had voted with his well-shod feet.

But she didn't feel moony. She felt bitter and puzzled.

Esmond lived in Eaton Terrace – his wife's money. "Couldn't do anything without the wife's money. Not a thing." Esmond said this immediately to any woman he wanted. That way she knew how little to expect. Esmond called it a nice little house. Perhaps he spoke comparatively. He also possessed Claremaurice House in Ireland – which he called the pile, which had too many bedrooms accurately to count and which, for some unexplained family reason, he never seemed to visit.

Although she could not remember the number Catriona found the house straight away. The door stood open. Two chauffeur driven cars waited at the kerb. Catriona told the taxi driver to stop opposite and keep the engine running.

Through the open door Catriona could see shadows cast into the hall from the passage. People crowded into the hall. None of them was Esmond. She could hear the sound of hearty English leave-taking.

Catriona looked at the house with hatred. It was so quiet, so restrained, so lovely, so rich and so not hers. Brickwork below, stucco above. Brickwork pointed scraped and glowing – yellow by streetlight. The stucco freshly white. The top floor in darkness. The nursery floor. His scrawny wife had produced three whole children. Daughters.

A knot of envy hardened in her throat. But for what exactly? Not the children. Not even the wife.

No. What she envied was a world from which she was excluded. A world she couldn't have. A world that perhaps she wanted only because she couldn't have it.

Another flurry of activity in the doorway. Four guests, two men, two women, hawed and jollied their way down the steps to the street. Esmond's wife stood framed in the doorway, cruelly lit by the overhead link. She looked dried out, spavined by entertainment. For some reason Catriona couldn't remember her name. Esmond came out now and joined her. He was smoking a cigar. Catriona could see his face clearly. It was flushed but complacent. He kept one hand inserted, fingers downwards, in the pocket of his dinner jacket. That was a habit he had. He had gripped the cigar between his teeth. It lifted the muscles in his cheeks, as if he were trying to smile like a Chinaman. He raised his spare hand and brought it down comfortingly (?) authoritatively (?) on the wife's (*his* wife's) shoulder. She gave him a little darting smile and shifted on her angular legs. Esmond puffed out smoke. He looked as if the world had been specially arranged for him. It probably had.

The wife leaned forward a little, peering out from under the glare of the link. She spoke to Esmond and nodded in the direction of the street. He bent down and followed her gaze. Oh God. They were staring at the taxi. For one brief moment bravado fought with embarrassment. Catriona's hand stretched out for the door handle and she imagined the short walk to the door, the panic on Esmond's face and the sharp bang as she blew their smug world to pieces.

But it was only a moment. "Drive on." When she looked through the cab's rear window the door had already closed. As she watched the lights in the house were extinguished one by one.

She thought.

Of course it was perfectly understandable that the wife (Catriona still couldn't find the name) should have noticed the cab. Catriona could imagine her, the good hostess, wondering if the cab rank had perhaps sent one extra for an already departed guest. So it was nothing but Catriona's fantasy which said that the woman knew that she had been there. Just fantasy.

Watching probably drove you crazy. Or did you have to be crazy to watch in the first place? It carried a weird thrill of its own though. She wondered if this was what terrorists experienced; the sweet satisfaction of observing your thoughtless victims even as you handled the grenade. Except, of course, that she had driven away. Except, of course, that she doubted that the revelation of her affaire with Esmond would amount to anything greater than a dud firework. The wife knew about his womanising or chose not to know. Such women do not quit. All that Catriona would achieve would be a scene in which the nastiness would redound on herself. After all, Esmond had given her up hadn't he? So what was she motivated by? Malice? Destructiveness? Oh the wife would be hurt all right. Badly hurt. But she was innocent. How could she be blamed for existing? For being legally married? Esmond hadn't even bothered to pretend that he was unhappy with her, or that she had in any way failed him. All Catriona's cross-questioning and probing in this direction had come to nothing. Armoured in stupidity and selfishness Esmond had grinned and changed the subject. So why punish the innocent wife when Esmond would get away? For get away he certainly would. Accomplished deceivers always did. She could imagine a dozen ways in which he could charm himself back into favour. Most likely she, Catriona, would be painted red – the scarlet woman, temptress, whore. An isolated incident. Felt frightfully bad about it. Hadn't he proved that by getting rid of the slut? And with her three children and angular body to consider the wife would take him back and shelter him with her love and her money and feel oddly proud at what, after all, was a kind of victory.

The world seemed an unfairly good place for men like Esmond.

All of which brought Catriona distressingly back to herself. Why *why* had she sat there waiting? Why had she done such a stupid demeaning thing? A thing she would be ashamed to tell anyone, even Penelope, whom it certainly wouldn't bother.

Perhaps it was all defensive. A running away. Better to think about Esmond than about the man who might be her father. But she doubted it. If all the other events of the last day or so had not happened she would still be in a ferment over Esmond.

But why? She kept returning to that damned question.

It was the truth; she hadn't really loved Esmond. So what was the matter with her? Was she only suffering from wounded pride? She tried to rake over the coals of her relationship with Esmond. It wasn't hard. They were still hot to the touch.

She found him attractive. She had enjoyed sex with him, as far as she did with anyone, though whether she *liked* it was another matter. She certainly didn't like him a bit, though she enjoyed being with him. She didn't think this amounted to some inbuilt perversion of her own. It was not the case that she desired only men she disliked. In which case there must be something special about Esmond. She searched again. He was highly sexed. Well, that had its merits. He definitely desired her. That had its merits too. He was generous, lavish even, in his praise of her charms. Good enough . . . Yet still it didn't all add up . . . She tried another ruthless look at the flaws in her own character. She was vain, capricious and wilful. Esmond also possessed these qualities. Perhaps she resented being dismissed by someone altogether too like herself, altogether too like the bad side of herself. True once again, but that was not the key that she was looking for . . . She tried harder. She hated this. She *had* to understand. She tried the things that people said. That women said. The damned fool things that you heard over and over again in magazines and cloakrooms and department stores and which always seemed to contain one humiliating grain of truth. No woman can stand to be without a man. No woman wants to lose a man unless she has another ready and waiting. Women become desperate when they're getting on, getting on, getting on . . .

God she was angry. Angry above all else that she had allowed Esmond Claremaurice to *make* her angry. And suddenly she had her answer. Esmond thought that she was nothing more than a piece – easily acquired, easily discarded.

"Chelsea Mansions lady."

She paid the driver and looked at her watch. It was two thirty. On the corner two Arabs were arguing with an underage whore in a postage stamp of a leather skirt. Further down the street a punk wearing a kilt and a razor blade as nostril decoration sat in the gutter drinking lager.

What with one thing and another it seemed a fitting end to the day. Except of course that Catriona still had unfinished business. When she had telephoned Louis earlier to find out about Barrington Smythe Catriona had made a request of the kind that Louis loved to grant.

Hanging from the doorknob of her flat's door was a carrier bag. It contained three books on the Spanish Civil War.

Louis was a great marker of passages. For Catriona he had also turned down chunks of pages. He was not one for the silly little girl syndrome. She had asked for information in a hurry and he had provided it. Though as for that she wanted not so much facts as flavour feelings – the what-it-must-have-been-like for men like James Tar.

Catriona read. She read of a different war. Of men who simply laid down their tools and left their factory benches – of men who left behind the deadening unemployment of their mean streets – of women who left hospital patients or shop counters or the cold garrets where they endured as servants – to go and do what they could for a Republic under siege. To join the International Brigades. To fight in a distant place of which they were almost wholly ignorant for a cause which they defined perhaps too simply but which was still magnificent. The war against totalitarianism. The war for the future. Which they *could* not lose. Which in the end was lost.

Catriona was apolitical. She couldn't care much for the factionalising – for the doctrinal splits that divided the Republicans – Communist against Anarchist against Left Republican.

What she cared about was the people.

And James Tar had been one of them.

It was four o'clock when she turned out her bedside lamp.

In the street outside Madame Despard looked up from the hired Mercedes and saw Catriona's light go out. She turned to Busboy who sat behind the wheel.

"I should have gone in."

Busboy shook his head. "Mr Tar. He say wait."

"I hate him," said Madame Despard.

"Oh sure."

"Oh Busboy," she said, "all the things I've done."

"Lady," he said, "you done wrong. Now you do right."

She looked up again at the darkened window as Busboy turned the car towards the Dorchester and Madame Despard's rich and sleepless suite.

Robinson also read late into the night. He had missed the last train long ago. This happened often. He had little to go home for. There was a service bed he could use – down the passage from the raw looking office in Half Moon Street – where he sat over instant coffee, a chaste two fingers of whisky, and a very limited quantity of information. The contents of Tar's oilskin pouch and such skimpy files as short notice could produce.

Of course he – no more than Rossminster – hadn't the slightest doubt even on the hippie front that Tar had held a great deal back. Yet the known material was not insignificant. They had performed a task for Schmidt and before Robinson was the evidence of a job well done. The woman was more or less naked and old and apparently (so the back of the photograph read) Madame Despard. The hippies were also naked – one before and one behind her. Whatever the nature of the act, the taking of the photograph was a much more corrupt thing. As corrupt as the trail they had cut across Morocco and for which they had cruelly paid the price.

What did they mean – the other photographs. Surely Tar must know but (except in one case) he hadn't told. One was of a wall with a low plain door in it, taken in bright sunshine. The second was of part of what seemed to be a Georgian – or perhaps neo-Georgian – building. It had tall steps. A dumpy girl stood at their top. If the house had a number the girl obscured it. She was ringing the bell and looking fearfully down the street. The last photograph seemed to be of the back of a tenement building, probably concrete, possibly high rise. On the ground there were scattered beer cans intermixed with discarded syringes.

Yet the last photograph *did* count. There was snow, and a low bridge, and a collection of buildings and a field with animals, although the setting was otherwise urban. In the background the skyline of Copenhagen stood up out of the snow. Walking towards it was a pasty faced fat man in a camel hair coat. The back of the photograph carried a message – Tar's message. It read *Schmidt* and where to find him.

Maybe, thought Robinson. Just maybe we know where to find Schmidt. It's about all we do know. He looked down at the single sheet of paper in the file. Name . . . date of birth . . . a solid educational ascent from kindergarten to accountant's office . . . the directorship of the Despard Foundation. So, thought Robinson, we find him and what then? We ask him questions? And to get him to answer them we have to offer something? We have to offer him what he wants. Robinson gave a little smile. He had thought of something that Schmidt might want. Something or someone.

And what about the rest? Despard and Madame Despard came down to no more than a few glossies from thirty-year-old magazines. Despard in a wheelchair. Madame Despard tall, elegant, face shaded by a hat. Despard's origins seemed simply and plainly rich. He was on nobody's list of wicked deeds, nor was she. If either or both had indeed been in Spain there was no record of it. And if there had been such a record then so what?

Much the same importance attached to the Despard Foundation itself. It was not a charity so it could legally do what it damned well pleased. Its home was in Switzerland which was as if to say its records were in an armour plated vault. There was absolutely no indication that the *famille Despard* had done anything other than engage in a spot of sporadical chic and pull out just as soon as their money was endangered.

Robinson turned his attention to Esmond Claremaurice. Like all Members of Parliament – actual or prospective – he had been vetted. Robinson always thought vetting pretty useless. Anyone who had a good enough lie would have thought, well in advance, of a way of covering it up. All the same Esmond Claremaurice seemed to have been honest enough. School, parents, regiment, a couple of non-executive directorships and a genial declaration of the fact that he lived on his wife's income. Wife being, Robinson further noted, the daughter of bristlingly respectable Knight of the Shires. Indeed there was stepmother listed too with an address in New York. Nor was much to be gleaned from Esmond's womanising – not one of his women seemed to have been the member of anything more political than the *Sunday Times* Wine Club.

Which left what? It left too damned much. Who were the people that Schmidt was involved with? The people who were likely to turn nasty? And who were the friends of Jimmy Tar? Where did his information come from? Come to that what, if anything, was the real significance of Spain?

But for Robinson all of this was overridden by one indisputable and awkward fact. There was only one thing that bound together Tar and Schmidt and Esmond Claremaurice.

Catriona Lomax . . .

# 20

Catriona woke to the insolent clamour of the doorbell. The flat was in darkness; the curtains still drawn. She looked at her watch. Ten o'clock. She was half asleep when she reached the door. Not until it was open did she remember who it might be. Horror and panic swept over her. But it was too late now. She pulled the door wide open.

"Good morning," said Esmond's wife. "May I come in please?"

"Of course," said Catriona automatically, as if this were the most natural request in the world, and stepped back to let her pass inside. The woman stopped in the centre of the room.

Suddenly Catriona remembered that this was the morning after a long night. She was a slob in a dressing gown; unwashed hair, hung-over eyes, suddenly and cruelly exposed by a long-standing rival. Then she took in the awkward flat-chested woman who stood before her shifting from foot to foot. If Esmond's wife had tried entrapment she had made a grave mistake. Catriona was capable of looking terrible but never plain. Whereas this woman could never look anything else.

Her hands had been folded like an aid to thought. Now they flopped clumsily to her sides. "Oh dear," she said. Catriona thought she meant the room's mess. She narrowed her eyes. Esmond's wife saw and understood. "Oh no," she said. "Oh *no*. I didn't mean that. I couldn't." She sounded humble. "*That* would be none of my business."

What, thought Catriona, am I supposed to do? Ask what *is* your business?

But Esmond's wife anticipated her. "You know who I am."

Catriona nodded.

"And of course I know who you are or I wouldn't be here." She laughed nervously and looked around the room. "Goodness how bohemian." She sounded as if she were trying to put someone at ease, but who? Herself? Catriona? Both?

"I don't know your name." Catriona realised that these were her first words and that they sounded ridiculous. "I mean. That is I mean I don't know your Christian name."

God, that was even more ridiculous. What did her Christian name matter? She was here as Mrs Claremaurice. She didn't need a Christian name. Not for this visit.

"My name's Theodora." She gave a high nervous laugh. "I always hated it. I don't know why. Well I do know why of course but it really wouldn't interest you." She gave another nervous laugh. Catriona didn't speak. She still felt stunned. "But it's my name. How do you do?"

She actually held out her hand. In default of other ideas Catriona shook it. It was moist.

"Catriona. That's a beautiful name. But then you are beautiful." Theodora Claremaurice was biting her lip.

"No," said Catriona.

"Oh yes," said Esmond's wife and turned away. She looked at the table where the books on the Spanish Civil War lent by Louis lay scattered. "You read a lot," she said with tremulous politeness.

"No," said Catriona. "That is. Yes."

"Bohemian," said Esmond's wife and nodded as if this were an especially happy confirmation. Catriona realised that the woman had been trying to find a place for her – a groove, a rank – and bohemian was apparently it.

Catriona Lomax. Party girl. Someone who lived on her looks and her wits. A messy girl with a messy room who could sleep in as sluttishly late as she wanted. Was Catriona wrong or did she detect in Theodora's nervous, eager, curious glance a glimmer of envy? No wife of Esmond Claremaurice's could really want these surroundings, this life. At the same time she wouldn't like the fact that her physical appearance disbarred her from the role of sexy-single-girldom. Theodora Claremaurice could never have hacked it as anyone's mistress.

Yet this gave Catriona no satisfaction. In fact she felt dreadful.

"Look," she pushed a hand through her hair. "I need some coffee."

"Oh. Of course. I don't want to disturb you."

Is that right lady? Then why the hell are you here? Catriona stopped herself just in time. Something about this woman made her want to act up as the hard-boiled shop-soiled hand-on-hip houri who ate husbands raw.

"Do you want some? Some coffee?"

The question seemed to agitate Esmond's wife, as if she were being offered some dangerous extra-curricular temptation.

"Well," she hesitated. "You see I had breakfast with the children."

"I expect you did," said Catriona nastily. "I asked you if you wanted some coffee now."

"Oh you know I *would*." She made it sound naughty. "It's very kind of you."

Catriona felt a fresh fit of hard-boiledness coming on. You bet. Oh yeah. Tell it to the marines. I'm from Missouri too. Any one of the cinematic clichés that fitted the hooker to whom the script writer has yet to issue a heart of gold . . . Except that this woman sounded as if she meant what she said – that it really was kind of Catriona, who had slept with her husband and spied on her home, to provide coffee. There was altogether too much disarming innocence about for Catriona's taste.

They went into the kitchen. Catriona started to fiddle with the percolator. She was glad to have something to do with her hands. A little gasp made her look up. Theodora Claremaurice was staring with widened eyes. Catriona stared mutinously back.

The kitchen was curtainless. The sunlight was very bright and, for Mrs Claremaurice, harsh. For the first time Catriona was able to see her, literally, in the worst light.

She was tall – five foot eight or nine – and thin. Probably no thinner than Penelope but with none of the latter's smoothness and elegance. Penelope's dark skin was lustrous, her hair thick, her hips delicately but distinctly fleshed. Mrs Claremaurice's possessed none of these advantages. She was thin to scrawniness, with little knots of stringy muscle. Her legs from knee to ankle were tubularly straight. Her hair, which was dark, going grey, was impoverished. She allowed it to hang as it grew, lankly straight, with a simple right hand parting. The hairdresser's despair, Catriona thought, given up on long ago. Mrs Claremaurice's face was long with a flat forehead and a broad muscular jaw. Her mouth, though wide, showed sparse timid lips. No lipstick. In fact no make-up at all. Nothing to mitigate the sallowness of her complexion. This was particularly odd when you realised, as Catriona now did, that her eyes were far and away her best feature. Set very wide and fringed with thick coarse lashes they were of a deep anxious hazel. Kind, sensitive, troubled eyes. Eyes that had got that way partly through the anguish that came from having been dealt these looks. Your adolescence, Catriona thought, must have been hard, very hard. She felt a sudden and considerable pity for Mrs Claremaurice. Then she remembered, just as suddenly, that she *was* Mrs Claremaurice. That despite being physically ill-favoured, despite doubtless pains and rejections she had managed to acquire a husband and three children. All Catriona had acquired was the managership of a club and a tiny drunk posing as a father. Then Catriona's unkindness again gave way to sympathy when she remembered what bound Esmond to his wife. Money.

But why – at this particular moment – should she have started to stare so intently at Catriona? The expression changed. She bit her lip. She looked rueful – in a miserable sort of way almost amused.

"I wondered what had happened to that dressing gown. He said that he lost it on a trip. I suppose you were with him."

The dressing gown had been Esmond's. He had given it to her in New York. On examination Catriona had noticed that it was fraying. Obviously Esmond had finished with it. She remembered spending an afternoon on a bench in Central Park wondering how she could stay involved with so transparent a cheapskate.

Theodora gripped the door frame. She looked white about the mouth. She said, with a noise that tried to be a laugh, "I don't know why that should hurt so much. Particularly. But it does."

"Oh no." Catriona felt dreadful. All her emotions turned over at once. It was like being sea-sick in your feelings.

"Oh *no*." She put down the coffee accoutrements and crossed the small kitchen. She took Theodora by the elbow, steered her towards the one kitchen chair and thrust her down into it. As an action it seemed perfectly natural. Not until she was moving back towards the sink did Catriona realise that she had touched, taken charge of, semi-comforted Esmond's wife, and had run one hell of a risk in the process. If Catriona had been the wronged wife on whom the mistress had laid hands she would have done her best to tear her into little pieces. Catriona wondered if she was dealing with a saint or someone almost insanely submissive. Either way it didn't make much difference. Catriona was beginning to like this woman. And that might be an awful problem.

"Coffee," Catriona said. "I'll hurry it up." As if coffee would solve anything.

"Thank you. It's so silly of me."

"No," said Catriona, hurling the coffee together.

Theodora sat with her legs slightly apart and her large workmanlike hands on her knees. Once upon a distant time someone had told her to sit still and not be a bother. It had stuck. She looked up with a shy little self-knowing smile.

"Oh yes," she said. "Very silly. I ought to be used to it. Better able to cope. It's just too important to me."

"Look," said Catriona. "I don't know what's on your mind but I think you ought to know that Esmond has . . . that Esmond and I have broken up."

Theodora replied instantly. Her expression once again anxious. "Oh I know that. That's what's worrying me."

"I think," said Catriona, "that I need a cigarette."

"Of course," said Theodora.

Catriona wondered how many times she said it in an average day. When she returned from the drawing room Theodora sat in exactly the same position, staring at the wall. Catriona had a sudden vision of all the evenings she must have sat in waiting for Esmond. The coffee had boiled. Catriona turned it off. Poured it. Lit her cigarette.

"I'm sorry," she said. "Do you want one?"

Theodora put her head on one side and stared at the packet as if a matter for serious consideration. "Do you know," she said, "I always rather thought I'd like to smoke but Esmond said that he didn't like to see women smoking. He said it was unfeminine." She looked at the cigarette in Catriona's hand and started to giggle. "Oh my," she said, "Oh my oh my oh *my*."

"Yes," said Catriona. "He tried that one on me."

"What did you say?"

"I told him to fuck off."

"*Did* you. Did you really?"

"You bet I did."

The giggles ceased. Theodora shook her head. "I suppose

that's the difference between us." And then, quickly, in case she had been impolite about Catriona's charms, "That is, *one* of the differences."

"Here," Catriona handed her a cigarette. She accepted it gingerly, held it between thumb and forefinger as if it were a pill. "What do I do?"

"What do you do?" Catriona wondered impatiently if this helplessness was an act for a male audience. If you're short on female equipment then play the little girl lost for all it's worth. No sooner did this thought occur to Catriona than she reproached herself for ungenerosity. Still, she was damned if she would let guilt change her temperament. A silly question gets a silly answer. "*Do* with it! You put it in your mouth and light it."

This Theodora did without mishap. "Mmm," she said blowing out. "I'm sorry to be so stupid."

She looked down at her cigarette and took a deep breath.

"You see, I don't make a habit of this. This is the first time I've talked to . . . to one of Esmond's . . . to someone of Esmond's."

"Yes," said Catriona. "That's what I thought."

"Is it that obvious? I'm sorry."

"Look," said Catriona. "Do you mind doing something for both of us? Stop apologising!"

"I'm . . . " She stopped herself just in time. "Yes," she said as if confirming something. "You must have been a change from the others. They always tended to be rather silly or nasty. When you've been married to a man for a long time you get to know him very well. I suppose it must be the same if you've lived with a man."

"Wouldn't know. Never done it."

"*Haven't* you? I thought that's what everybody did nowadays." She sounded wistful.

"I like being on my own. Look," Catriona hesitated, finally got her tongue around the name, "Theodora. Why *are* you here?"

"Oh yes," Theodora seemed grateful for the reminder, "well, you see I usually know when he's finishing an affaire. He's extra nice to me and he spends more time with the children and he doesn't make so many silly excuses. And he's doing all that. He *is*. But there's one difference."

"I can't wait," said Catriona. She meant it.

"He isn't *relieved*. Usually, you see, he's relieved."

"Oh?"

"But he isn't relieved. He isn't relieved at all."

"He isn't?"

"No."

"Oh."

Impasse, thought Catriona. It was too early in the morning for conversations like this. She tried her very hardest to concentrate.

"But Theodora what in the world has this got to do with me?"

Theodora had blushed. "I'm afraid," she said. "Afraid that this time . . . it . . . you . . . that it was more important to him. Afraid that he might leave us."

"Us?"

"The children."

"Oh." Children again.

Theodora stumbled on. "Because you see it wouldn't suit him. He *needs* my money. And he needs someone who makes life – convenient."

"Christ Almighty," said Catriona. "No one could say that you're not a realist."

The flush deepened. It did nothing for the woman's looks. "I suppose you think that I'm humiliating myself." She paused. Then she went on. Although she spoke hesitantly, her jaw had set in a firm defiant line. "Perhaps I am. Perhaps it's because I have no choice. I couldn't expect a man like Esmond to desire me or be faithful. Not when he could sleep with someone like you. I *would* be a fool if I believed that. Wouldn't I?"

In all her tally of adultery Catriona had never encountered a wife like this. She wondered how Esmond managed to lie to her. Theodora must possess some way of making it easy for him. Catriona would be a complete brute if she did not provide what honest ease she could.

"Look," said Catriona. "Look. Listen. Look. Esmond is not leaving you for me. He never was. He never would. I wouldn't want him to. Didn't. Don't."

"Oh." She looked both relieved and puzzled.

"I do not love your husband."

"Oh." Theodora's face was suffused with pity. "But how terrible for you?"

"What? Why?"

The blush had returned to reach maximum intensity. "Sexually."

Catriona was surprised that the word even came out. Did this woman think that sex and love were inseparable? Perhaps just for women. Otherwise Esmond's conduct looked pretty odd. Perhaps she envisaged girls as living martyrs sacrificed on the altar of Esmond's lust; perhaps that explained how she could pity them.

"Relatively terrible," said Catriona.

Theodora managed to smile – a shy one of course. "You're making fun of me."

"Only relatively."

"You know," said Theodora, "you're jolly good fun."

Fine, thought Catriona. If Schmidt sacks me I'll know where to go for a reference.

Theodora had risen to her feet. She looked additionally anxious; she had something more to say. It took its time coming.

"I don't suppose," she said, "that you've met Esmond's mother?"

"Not that I recall."

Theodora gave the thinnest available smile. "She's not a woman that you forget."

"I didn't even know he had a mother."

"Stepmother actually. His real mother died when he was just a mite."

Catriona felt that her pool of sentiment was drying up. "Haven't met her either."

"So Esmond didn't mention her? Stepmama I mean. He didn't talk about her?"

"We never talked much."

It simply slipped out. Catriona could have bitten her tongue. Something in Theodora kept tapping into veins of subcutaneous unpleasantness. But Theodora didn't seem to have noticed. Hello thought Catriona; what's so important about this stepmother business? Theodora was moving into full agitation.

"I know you'll think I'm fearfully silly – well you probably think that already – but, well, I wondered if she . . . Esmond's stepmother that is . . . well, played a part?"

"A part in what?"

Theodora took a deep breath; the next statement needed an extra effort. "In you and Esmond. That is in making Esmond . . . stop."

Suddenly Catriona had a distinct vision of that lunch at the Ritz, of Esmond's shifty implausible behaviour. Then she had another vision – weak-kneed Esmond nodding to stepmummy as she told him to leave that common little hostess alone.

"Oh," said Catriona, "and just how would such a thing come about?"

Her tone was cold. Theodora looked even more wretched.

"You have to understand. She's rich you see and the money ought to go to Esmond."

"Fine," said Catriona. "I feel better already."

"No really *please*. You see it's not that. It's the *house*. Esmond's house. Claremaurice in Ireland. You see Esmond's father died fearfully poor and the house would have been sold. Except that stepmama married this seriously rich foreigner who took a lease on it in stepmama's name. Now *he's* just died and so the house ought to come back to Esmond."

Catriona felt colder. Here was another material thing to show her true worth to Esmond. Catriona the disposable. Catriona the throw-away woman.

"Ought to? But if it's his . . . ?"

"I don't know but there's some trouble about the lease. And even then we're not rich enough to keep it up. Now that the second husband's dead I expect she'll be rich as rich. He has to do what she says."

"*Has* to?"

"You didn't know did you?"

"Know what?"

Theodora's smile was that of the brave little girl accustomed, yet again, to combat tears. "You see the house is what he *really* loves. It was his father's. What was taken from him. So you see we both come at the heel of the hunt. That's how it is."

Sisterhood had its limits. "Except," Catriona said, "that you're riding and I've been disbarred and I want to know *why*."

Theodora came to her and took her hands. For a moment Catriona tried to pull away but when Theodora held on with a fierce and surprising strength, she relaxed and let herself be held.

"Catriona. His stepmother. You have to understand. She's hateful. She's one of those horrible rich jet set women. All clothes and power. Esmond hates her. She's a sort of American."

"Oh well," said Catriona, "that would do it."

"You are quick. It must be nice to be so terribly quick. I'm slow you see."

"But not so slow that you can't see I'm quick."

But Theodora was paying attention to something inside herself. She frowned hard like a dim schoolgirl trying to understand a theorem.

"You're sure? Esmond's never talked about any of this? Not his childhood or his stepmother? Not even . . . you know . . . pillow talk?"

"No. Not even, you know – that."

"Because," Theodora was still concentrating fiercely, "it must have been awful for him. His own mother died when he was quite young. And for a while it was just him and his father and his father was always rather a drunk and then he married stepmama and then his father died you see. Esmond always hated her and it must have been frightful. She was, well, an awful tart. A sort of orgy person. I mean she *paid* men. Actually paid them."

Catriona was tempted to say good for her. But a picture of young Esmond got in the way. Esmond with an unhappy childhood was something new. In fact Catriona had never thought of Esmond having a childhood at all. He seemed to have sprung whole from some platonic conception of a tailor. Nor had he ever seemed the least damaged by childhood. He wasn't neurotic. Just plain selfish. Theodora was still talking.

"She has a sort of black manservant who goes around arranging things like that. She's a – I don't know – she's a *freak*. She keeps places for that sort of thing. Love nests. Well lust nests."

Theodora was now pressing Catriona's hands as if to persuade her of something. Catriona rose and as gently as possible disentangled herself.

"Theodora. Why are you telling me all this?"

Theodora hung her head. "I've got it wrong. I always get things wrong. I haven't explained properly. I only thought that she might be playing some game. She likes to hurt people. So if she thought that Esmond really wanted you and not me then she might make him break with you. Just out of spite."

"Except that according to you he wants the house and the money to run it. Remember?"

Catriona reached for another cigarette. Her hand stopped in the air at what Theodora said next.

"But suppose he just did what she said – broke up with you – in the meantime. And then he *got* the house and the money. What would he do then?"

"Oh," said Catriona. "Oh."

Theodora pushed a strand of thin hair away from the lank little girl parting. She looked passively suffering at Catriona – an animal used to punishment, defenceless with no escape, wondering if the worst beating of all was on its way.

"No," Catriona said. "No."

"But you do see don't you? He wouldn't need me then. He might want *you* then."

"No. My dear no. He wouldn't. And I wouldn't. I would not do that."

Theodora stared achingly into Catriona's face. "Not now. But I thought . . . I thought you might have planned it together. That he told you . . . "

Sitting rigid in her chair Theodora was crying, her hands clenched on her knees, no attempt made to wipe away the tears.

"He never told me any of this. Not a word."

Catriona searched frantically for the truth. If Esmond had actually proposed would she have accepted – accepted the broken marriage and the guilt? Perhaps. More likely that she would have rejected him for the purely selfish reason that he was an indifferent human being whom she could neither trust nor properly love. She didn't think that would cheer up his wife. But there was one certain truth that might help.

She said, "I would never have played such a filthy trick."

Then Theodora was sobbing in her arms. A few moments passed of back patting and squeezing and physical separation and nose blowing. During it all Theodora said, "You have to forgive me. I was afraid."

Before such honesty Catriona had nothing to offer but a box of Kleenex.

When Theodora finished wiping her face red-raw she rose to go. But she was embarrassed and awkward and angular and so felt clumsily that she had to leave on a social note.

"I wish I'd worked like you. Your club. It must be fun to be surrounded by a lot of chaps."

Surely is, thought Catriona, if you want to screw other women's husbands, but instead she said, "Look, you may not like this but you need to hear it. You're worth ten of Esmond. He's vain and greedy and stupid."

Theodora considered this, then spoke slowly and thoughtfully.

"I wonder about the stupid. I sometimes think that's the mistake his stepmother makes. He's really rather good at getting what he wants with no risk to himself. Other people do things for him. Like us. You know," and Theodora extended her hand, "we could have been such chums."

And Catriona had thought that there were no surprises left.

# 21

And then it was quiet. Completely quiet. And Catriona was more confused than ever in her life. Well she said you have no man, quite likely no job. You feel an adulterous swine. You have an Intelligence Service bearing down on you over a part of your fantasy life concerning a dirty little Father Pretender who doesn't even – and she put down the telephone after the tenth call to Barrington Smythe – finally appear . . . Louis and Penelope had said was it all right because honestly they'd stay but Penelope had to go to the country with those bloody children and Louis had to have lunch with a weekendaholic publisher but he'd be there in the afternoon to go sniffing out Barrington Smythe if she wanted?

Yes. That was all right. Really.

When Catriona felt an especial need for luxury, she always decided to go out, head for Bond Street and buy herself something expensive to wear. She damned well wouldn't sit still. She remained herself. She would behave like herself.

So she set her small chin at a determined angle, took longer than usual with her make-up, put on an Ungaro skirt and blouse and examined the results in her bedroom's full length mirror.

Well she thought, you haven't done too badly with the looks you've been dealt. You may not be a beauty but you are an attractive well turned out woman with exceptional colouring who looks a lot younger than her thirty-eight largely misspent years. You may not be everybody's taste but you are definitely *a* taste.

She felt better already. Primping might constitute a primitive form of reassurance but it worked.

It worked for ten minutes and three hundred yards of pavement.

She walked up the Earls Court Road looking behind her for a taxi when she collided with someone. The someone seized her by the arms. She looked up into the face of Barrington Smythe. His breath was like a public health warning.

"Ah," he said, "Lucky this."

"Let go of me."
"What?" Barrington Smythe bent down from his useless height, grimaced at the traffic noise and thrust his left ear closer. Its interior, clearly visible in close up, reminded Catriona of the bottom of an ashtray.
"I said let go of me."
"Oh. Ah!"
"Listen," she said. "I've been trying to get in touch with you."
He released her. "Understandable. Popular man. The other evening eh? Complicated business. I imagine we were all a bit under the weather."
He smiled forgivingly. She wanted to kill him; perhaps he knew that for there was an I-know-what-you-don't-know glint in his eye as he said, "To speak frankly, I fancy a pint."
Catriona didn't hesitate. The most likely way of getting anything out of Barrington Smythe was by establishing a chain of free drinks.
"All right," she said. "Where?"
"Here." He was right too. They were six inches from a pub's door.
"Come on," said Catriona and went in ahead of him.
"Afternoon Cyril," said Barrington Smythe to the barman.
"Morning Barrington," said Cyril.
Barrington Smythe lived two miles away in Bayswater. Catriona wondered how many barmen along this and similar routes were on Christian names with Barrington Smythe. She didn't ask. He might have told her.
"What will you have?"
To her amazement Barrington Smythe extracted a roll of notes from his top pocket. She dismissed the notion that they were forged; he was too generally incompetent. Besides his hands shook.
"An orange juice," she said. Barrington Smythe turned to the barman.
"Double vodka and orange and a pint harumph."
Normally this would have driven Catriona to militant abuse. She hated anyone (but particularly men since only men ever did it) deciding that they knew best. Now, however, a number of factors restrained her. Barrington Smythe's acquaintance with non-alcoholic drinks must surely be

minimal. For all Catriona knew he might genuinely think that this was what she meant; that orange juice implied the attendant presence of vodka. Then again there was the miracle of watching him not only pay for a drink but pay for a more expensive one than was necessary. Besides, the combined effect of the last two days probably made alcohol a medical necessity. In this whole weird hide and seek Barrington Smythe seemed to be the only person who had any proper contact with the man in the blue suit. All the same she wished that Louis were here. He if anyone knew how to handle the man. All she could think of for now was to plunge straight in.

"Barrington. About the other evening. You said you'd seen . . ."

"She'll be back."

Barrington Smythe had a habit of forgetting not only whom he addressed but whether they had any previous information about the subject in hand.

"Who?"

"Sagi."

"Who? Oh. Your wife. Good."

"I had to get heavy." He closed one eye and nodded knowingly.

It was an alarming sight. Catriona didn't have the faintest idea what she was supposed to know about. More than that, this sudden presumption of intimacy gave her the creeps. What occurrence in the shadowland of Barrington Smythe's imagination had brought on this spurious closeness? She suddenly felt glad that it was daylight. She began to think that Penelope might be right. Barrington Smythe was more than just a drunken clown. He was, in part at least, sinister. He was still nodding with one eye closed. Catriona wished that he would stop.

"Heav-ee."

"Oh," said Catriona. "How nice."

"Ha!" He gave a wild defiant snort of laughter.

Some people at the bar turned around. Barrington Smythe immediately adopted an attitude of theatrical secretiveness. Catriona saw the barman shake his head.

"Mmm," said Barrington Smythe, "better keep my voice down. Never know who's about." He raised and wagged a nicotine inlaid finger. "Oh yes. I can be heavy."

"Ah," said Catriona, not wishing to risk a repeat of how nice. She had been right about needing the vodka.

"I," said Barrington Smythe, "will show them. Oh yes. I can see them off. I can handle them."

"Handle who?" asked Catriona. "That is whom?"

"Who or whom. Makes no difference. Mickey Mouse people. Forget them. Let's concentrate on *you*."

Barrington Smythe was nodding again and had picked up a sinister smile along the way. It came to Catriona that not only was his behaviour increasingly self-important but that it was intended to impress her.

"Barrington, what are you talking about?"

"Point one I was coming to see you just now when point two I was able to stop you from falling over."

"When you *what*?" Her tone was so outraged that for a moment Barrington Smythe noticed something other than himself.

"Well I suppose that's not the point." He offered this as a manful concession and continued. "Point three."

"Point two!"

"What?"

"If the original point two wasn't point two then this one must be point two."

Barrington Smythe sneered. "You sound like Louis Vulliamy."

"And what's wrong with that?"

"Not a bad fellow Vulliamy but arrogant. Thinks he's too clever."

Catriona was genuinely amazed at this combination of ingratitude, effrontery and something pretty close to treachery. But his attitude was so bizarre that it made him almost worth listening to. Barrington Smythe clearly interpreted curiosity as respect.

"But not, I concede, Mickey Mouse. Now harumph point four . . . "

"Point three surely. If it isn't point two."

"Point *four*. I have a message for you."

At first Catriona, almost despairing of relevance, thought she had misheard. "A message?"

"Must watch that. Tendency to inattention. Expensive business in your line of work. Be taken advantage of. Free drinks that kind of thing. Message. Your father."

He leaned forward and gave an even bigger one eyed conspiratorial nod.

"You old Dad, right?" He grinned with what seemed to be thinner lips, yellower teeth. "Not quite *one of us*." He did an exaggerated imitation of Penelope's delivery. "Somewhat a member of the lower classes harumph. We've risen in the world a bit haven't we?"

Catriona gripped the sides of her chair. Looking down she could see her knuckles whiten. "You said a message. That's what you said."

"I think I'll have the other half thank you. Large Scotch."

Catriona stayed where she was. "Message first."

Barrington Smythe leaned back as one at ease, stretching his legs. He said with insulting breeziness, "He's in a spot of bother. Needs a helping hand. Tell you himself."

"Where is he?"

"Oh he's at my place. Couldn't turn him away could I?"

"Where did you meet him? How long has he been with you?"

"Getting to sound a bit like Vulliamy. Have to watch that. Too many questions. However," he now cast a pointed look at the emptiness of his glass, "the facts are somewhat in dispute. The old memory," he tapped the side of his torpedo-shaped skull, "a touch fuddled. Bumped into him in the pub. Introduced himself. A number of jars. Then it all gets a touch vague."

"But when did he move in with you?"

"Touch vague."

"Come on then. Let's go."

Barrington Smythe didn't budge. "I fancy the other half."

"If," said Catriona, "*if* he's at your, at your . . . "

"Place. At my place."

"Yes. You get one whole bottle of Scotch."

"Fair enough. But you buy the bottle now. There's an off licence next door."

"All right."

Barrington Smythe rose to his feet and then paused to take a courtly farewell of the barman. "Bye Cyril."

"Bye Barrington."

"I'd like to stay for the other half but I have to go."

"That's all right mate."
"Spot of business."
"That's the way."
"Are you," said Catriona thinly, "or are you not coming?"
"Musn't keep the lady friend waiting eh?" He leered from the barman to Catriona and all the way back again.
Catriona wondered about his wife. What could make a woman with the good sense to leave this man, return?
"Come on," said Barrington Smythe, "get a move on. I want that Scotch."

"Why don't you have a car?"
"What?" Catriona had been looking out of the window trying to forget that she was in a taxi with Barrington Smythe and his breath.
"Why don't you have a car?"
"Why should I?"
"Hmm." Barrington Smythe fell to consider this.
"Could you move opposite?"
"Why?"
"Your breath smells."
Barrington Smythe accepted this with surprising equanimity. He lowered one of the small seats opposite and perched on it. He adjusted his spectacles. Catriona noticed that the bridge had been secured with masking tape.
"Why don't you have a car? I thought you'd have a car?"
Catriona ignored him and returned to looking out of the window. They had reached South Kensington Underground Station. That meant at least five more minutes of Barrington Smythe.
"You're earning enough aren't you?" A reproach, not a question, with more than a flavour of sneer. "How much do you make? You must be doing all right."
Catriona wished that she were back in her club so that Gomez could throw this man out into the street. Except, of course, that he would never have been admitted in the first place.
"Do you ever think about anything but money and drink?"
This energised Barrington Smythe. "Ah," he began to rummage in his pockets. "Good point."
"I hope it's the only one."

"What?" He pulled out and discarded used tissues and empty cigarette packets.

"Since you can't count above one."

He didn't understand. She left it.

"Here are the kiddies."

He unfolded a large coloured photograph. Two children smiled cheerfully at the camera. Studio job. They wore matching sweaters of a particular Fair Isle ghastliness. Still, considering Barrington Smythe was their father they looked miraculously normal, revealing no conspicuous signs of outward contusion or internal damage.

"Aren't they handsome?"

"What? Oh yes."

"They're very handsome. They'll be back. When the book comes through."

He nodded wisely several times. Catriona thought that he was probably trying to look like a sage; the actual effect was of a fallen turf accountant contemplating comeback.

"What book?"

Barrington Smythe adjusted his glasses with an air of formality. He seemed to be struggling with the difficulty of summarising a mass of complex material, and finally said, "Cross cultural study."

"Of what?"

Barrington Smythe looked at Catriona as if her stupidity was amazing beyond calculation. "Culture of course. What colour do you think they are? The kiddies?"

Catriona now remembered that Barrington Smythe's wife was Indian. In terms of the children's looks was this supposed to be a good or a bad thing? She went back to the photograph. They both looked mildly foreign.

"French," she said, playing safe, but Barrington Smythe had already moved on to a more pressing matter – himself. He leaned forward, smacking his concave chest.

"I am," he said with a terrible violence, "a very devoted family man."

Catriona decided that desperate measures were called for. She pulled the bottle from her bag. Barrington Smythe's eyes glowed with a mystic light. "Look," she said, "if I give you a drink *will* you shut up?"

"You're being heavy."

"Yes."
"I had to be heavy. I may have mentioned that."
"Yes."
Barrington Smythe's lips closed around the neck of the bottle.

Barrington Smythe lived in a peculiar place.
"Are you sure mate?" said the taxi driver.
Barrington Smythe harumphed directions. They finally turned through several narrow streets into a mews so constricted that it amounted almost to a slit. It was dark, claustrophobic and depressing, filled entirely with warehouses except for one extremely small unit of flats (one could hardly call it a block) that looked as if someone had left it there by mistake. Here the taxi stopped. Clutching the bottle Barrington Smythe eventually found his keys and, as Catriona paid the driver, pressed him to come inside for a snifter. The driver declined. Barrington Smythe set off across the two feet of dirty untended grass that fronted the building.
"Excuse me asking Miss," said the driver, "but are you all right with him?" He jerked his head in the direction of Barrington Smythe who, kicking a few empty beer cans out of the way, had managed to open the door.
"Yes thank you," said Catriona.
"Oh well," said the driver. "It takes all sorts." He didn't sound convinced.
The hall of the building was tiny and dark. It contained a dismembered bicycle and smelt of tom cat and old creosote. He lived on the ground floor. Catriona was glad she didn't have to go upstairs. She might have caught something from the banister.
"Never been here before eh?"
"Never," said Catriona. She could hear the gratitude in her voice.
He pushed the door open and waved the whisky bottle in encouragement. "Enter," he said, only just managing it. The top of his bald pointed head almost touched the ceiling. The walls brushed his shoulders. Although it was daytime the hall was completely dark.
"Stay where you are." He tiptoed forward holding the bottle carefully aloft until he found a light switch.

Louis had told her something of the grimness of Barrington Smythe's living conditions but he had not prepared her for what she saw. The walls of the hall had been painted amateurishly in high industrial yellow; the paint discarded from one of the neighbouring warehouses. It was now streaked and stippled with sticky finger marks. The bare boards of the floor had been incompetently varnished. Bubbles of dirt pushed up under the varnish and rough splinters had broken through. To the right a doorway led to what must be the children's bedroom. It was only just large enough to hold a set of bunk beds covered in rumpled makeshift blanketing. Broken toys lay scattered across the floor and the doorway. To the left there was another room, no more than half again as large, where Barrington Smythe's family carried on what passed for living. Parts of what might have been sofas or what might have been beds, covered in long unwashed curtain material, lined the room; these with age and wear had attained a shade of mid-vomit. It was empty.

"Where is he?" said Catriona.

"Harumph," said Barrington Smythe. "Through here perhaps."

She followed down the tiny remainder of corridor and into another bedroom only marginally bigger than the first, painted another job lot colour, filled by a bed and a mountain of dirty clothes. Just like a shoe box, Catriona thought – like a shoe box divided into hideous humanoid compartments and made worse when filled with human detritus. Barrington Smythe called out, "Lomax." Catriona almost asked what he was doing with her name. Had the man been using it or had Barrington Smythe for once in his life made a normal deduction? There was no reply.

They went past the empty lavatory (Catriona quickly averted her eyes), into a hell hole of a kitchen. Here all thought of colour vanished. The place seemed wall to wall biryani. Months (years?) of variegated foodstuffs had spattered everywhere and dried at their points of arrival. An ancient stove stood mournfully beneath a thick impermeable crust. But these were the only signs of humanity. Catriona turned enraged upon Barrington Smythe and shoved him with all her weight. Taken by surprise he staggered backwards, almost fell and steadied himself by seizing the cooker. The crust turned out to be permeable after all; his fingers sank into it. Catriona seized the bottle from his other hand.

"Where *is* he you stupid slob?" She threatened to spill the bottle.

The terror of losing several free drinks suddenly fixed Barrington Smythe's powers of concentration. Revelation dawned on his unhealthy features. "Wait," he cried out. "I've remembered. Out the back. Just be careful with that will you?"

He made his way across the slippery floor to a back door that Catriona hadn't noticed. "A bit paranoid your old man if I may say so. Kept thinking someone might come to get him. Children's play area."

The children's play area was a six foot strip of concrete hemmed in either side by the high walls of surrounding factories. Beyond it lay a brick outhouse – the remains perhaps of a laundry or a scullery or a set of privies abandoned when the flats had been built. From inside it, distinct and repeated, came the sound of a human cough.

Catriona hesitated. This couldn't be happening. It was ridiculous and wrong. What lay out here must have nothing to do with her. Not in this pathetic appendage to this filthy flat. The cough came again. She wanted to go away but she also wanted to go forward. She needed to know however bad the knowledge. She was already sure that it would be very bad. How could it be otherwise?

"Here," she passed the bottle to Barrington Smythe.

"Ah," he said. "Strong words back there. However," he said portentously, "one understands."

Catriona had no time to insult him now. He walked back into the kitchen nursing the bottle and licking the crust from his fingers. Catriona turned and walked towards the outhouse and whatever it contained.

The smell came first. A mixture of decay and body odour and stale beer. It had one more property. The indefinable but unmistakable aroma of age. It was dark inside the shelter. Catriona could make out a board raised from the floor on two packing cases. A figure slumped on it – a small man with his knees drawn up to the chin. He coughed again then put a hand to his mouth. "Beg pardon," he said.

Catriona felt her gorge rise. Nothing thus far – not the place nor the smell nor the offering of this travesty of a father – nothing at all struck at her like these two words. For a moment she couldn't speak at all. The man coughed some more. She could see him more clearly now.

He was very small, not much above five feet, with a thin stringy body. It was difficult to tell precisely for the body was lost inside a capacious suit with extra wide shoulders and flared trouser legs. This suit was composed of a coarse synthetic material. Violent blue in colour. All in all it was a garment that had been rarely seen in England and certainly not for a quarter of a century. With a pang of resignation Catriona remembered Robinson's photograph at the night club. When the man had finished coughing he reached into one of the misshapen side pockets of the suit and extracted a can of lager. He pulled off the strip top and raised the can in a hesitant toast. When he tried to drink from it he coughed again; a narrow plane of spray shot outwards and struck the wall.

Catriona started an internal litany, her eyes closed. Imagine the worst and it does not matter. If he is your father it does not matter. Your parents are not you, they need not matter. You have nothing to be ashamed of, it does not matter.

But when she opened her eyes and looked at him it mattered like hell. In Scotland there is a particular word for the weasel-like whey faced pinched physical attenuation that comes from undernourishment. The word is *schilpit*. The man who might be Catriona's father was schilpit.

She couldn't stand upright. She found an orange box to sit on. Her skirt would be filthy. It was very hot in the shelter. She felt moisture start between her thighs. Like sperm. Why had she thought of that? Because she, with her smooth fair body and her expensive clothes, might have been made from the sperm of the wretch opposite? And all the while she couldn't speak. Yet the man seemed, after all the fuss of bringing her here, in no particular hurry. Eventually she managed to break the silence.

"Why . . . "

But then she stopped. Again she felt like choking. She put her head down to get her breath. Silence, except for the gurgle of his drinking. She looked up. He wiped his mouth nervously with the back of a trembling hand. His face strained to a point. His skin was seamed and folded, stained. It had not been clean for a long time. His eyes were small and dark.

And very frightened.

Not shy, not embarrassed. The man was terrified.

And this was one thing she hadn't anticipated. Sweat began to trickle down the back of her neck. He reached out a trembling hand, saw her expression, withdrew it. He screwed up his face, took a deep breath and said, "Katie."

"Catriona. I'm Catriona now."

He frowned as if he had been interrupted, grimaced as if the next words had to be got out at all costs and only concentration would do it. The result was like a badly learned recitation.

"Katie. Katie. James Tar has watched over his little girl."

He began to cough. The cough stopped and he drank some beer. His hand trembled; the can chattered against his teeth. Some of the beer spilled. His eyes looked desperate. He tried to smile but the cough started again. Catriona gripped the sides of the orange box; she pulled her hands away, sticky with cobwebs. Sweat trickled down her face. The man tried to be helpful.

"It's that hot. Would ye like a wee beer?"

He reached obligingly towards one of his huge bulging pockets. Her expression stopped him. He said with pathetic courtesy, "It's all I've got."

Pity and disgust acting together finally pushed the words out of her. They came in a rush.

"I don't believe you. You're not my father. Who are you? You're not my father. I don't believe you."

Yet even as she spoke, even as she told herself that the man before her could never have been what Robinson had described; heroic or even strong, she felt ashamed. Ashamed of her snobbery. Ashamed of a selfishness that bordered on cruelty. She knew then that if this man was her father she could not, whatever the consequences, turn him away.

"I have my orders," and then self-importantly, "I've a meeting."

"What orders? Whose orders? Who are you meeting?"

"Oh aye," despite the fear and the sickness his eyes had gone sly. "You're invited. At a price. Five hundred pounds. Then you'll know everything."

Her heart sank. It was even worse than she had thought. He had come for money. He had come for extortion.

She looked at him for a while. He hung his head.

"I'm sorry," he said, "but I'm bad in the chest." She remembered she was a businesswoman used to negotiation.

"It's Saturday. The banks are closed."

He began to rock from side to side and moan.

"I'm feared. I have to go."

"I'll get the money," said Catriona. "Do you want me to come back here?"

"Christ no."

"Where then?"

"The platform of Earls Court Station. Number two. Three o'clock or I'm away on my own. Away home and no mistake."

She rose into a half crouch to leave. He turned away to pull another can of lager from his pocket. She said, "Tell me one thing now."

He looked up, dribbling a little.

She wanted to say long ago were you ever someone different. Were you ever my Visitor? But the nearest she could get was, "Were you *ever* rich?"

He replied with a strange grace that she would not forget.

"Fortune and I," he said, "have always been strangers."

As she walked across the midget's play area she heard his cough start up again. Inside the flat Barrington Smythe lay asleep on the sofa. She looked at the whisky bottle. He had not left the other half for Mr Manners.

She let herself out.

# 22

"You're a miracle worker," said Catriona. "You really are a genius," as Louis handed over the five hundred pounds. "Where did you get it so quickly?"

"I borrowed it from the head waiter. I told him that lunch had inspired me and I had to rush out and buy all the foie-gras at Fortnum's."

"I ruined your lunch."

"We'd got to the coffee but not the contract. I'm not sure I like this Catriona. Is he dangerous?"

"No poor thing. There's no danger. You'd better come if you're coming."

"Oh I'm coming all right," said Louis. "I've an investment to protect. Two if we include you."

She knew that he was trying to keep her going. "You say the sweetest things."

"Well sod it," said Louis. "Somebody has to."

The Earls Court Underground Station is exceptionally long. It possesses two exits, both populous; one gives on to the Earls Court Road, the other on to the even seamier and busier Warwick Road. These face each other. Each exit has its own ticket booth, turnstile, guards. Catriona did not know which way the man would come so she stood in the middle of the platform. From there she could see the steps which descended from both exits. Louis placed himself against a kiosk and settled down to watch.

It had begun to rain heavily outside; this gave the station an eldritch beauty of its own. The platform where Louis and Catriona now stood was not, properly speaking, underground. It was merely sunk beneath street level and then surmounted by a fine Victorian canopy, its lamps lit early this dark afternoon. The colours of the massed passengers' clothes, the unfolding flap and flutter of umbrellas, the reflections cast up from greasy puddles and the hiss of spray across the headlights of the halting trains created a spectacle that Catriona had come to love but now failed even to notice. Bad tempered passengers, steam rising from their clothes, jostled their way past Catriona.

She wondered if he had a coat. The rain, she thought, will be bad for his chest. She thought of the things she ought to say – come with me now and I'll get you a bath and hot coffee and a medical check-up. If you are my father. If you aren't my father. You need someone to help you, not just a bundle of banknotes. But inside her was another voice. And it said you never know, maybe he'll disappear. Maybe even in this crowd you'll miss him. Miss him. You'd prefer that, wouldn't you?

Louis saw him first. Catriona saw him point towards the Warwick Road exit. She turned in that direction.

There he was, the man who had claimed to be her father, coming through the ticket barrier, swamped in his cheap blue suit, carrying a plastic bag, coming towards her.

Something was wrong. He glanced once, then twice behind him. On the Warwick Road bridge he tried to run but the crowd was too thick. He started to push with his elbows. She could see people gesture indignantly.

He reached the steps and, small as he was, disappeared into the descending crowd. Catriona moved forward but there were people in her way as well.

He emerged at the bottom of the steps, saw her, moved towards her.

But now something else was wrong. He began to stagger. Your cough, she thought inconsequentially, this must be bad for your cough.

Crowds have instincts all their own. People parted on either side of him as if suddenly aware of something abnormal come amongst them.

His staggering had become a zig-zag. His knees buckled and then straightened. He dropped his bag. Cans of lager careened across the platform. Someone in a disgusted voice said, "Drunk."

He had almost reached her, his hand out, opening and closing his small ferret's eyes, protuberant with fear and pain.

He clutched at her and they fell together to the platform. He was in her arms and she was keeping his head from striking the ground.

He was not drunk. He was dead.

A crowd had gathered. She could hear Louis yelling to be

let through.

She looked up at the surrounding faces. All she could think to say was, "He isn't my father."

An elderly man with a toothbrush moustache bent over her, over them. He looked carefully into the seamed and dirty face she cradled.

"No. I don't think he is," said Señor Rossminster.

# Part II

# 23

We want you to understand, Catriona.

They kept saying that. Robinson and then Bert. But she didn't understand at all. Everything was broken up. Mess. Confusion. They were patient. They said she was in shock. In the end they gave her pills and let Louis take her away.

Nothing was clear, but some things were distinct.

She could see the station platform; the crowds roped off, the small body covered with a coat, policemen chalking round the place where he had fallen; the place where she had knelt.

Distinct too, after much repetition, was what the man called Señor Something really meant. The dead man on the platform was not her father, because the dead man on the platform wasn't James Tar at all.

In fact it seemed that James Tar had done something really rather clever.

He had sent someone else to die in his place.

The Consul crossed the city's last bridge, found the canal path and followed it. For all its smug cleanliness the Consul had a softish spot for Copenhagen. Red lights were permitted as long as they shone on clean streets. A decade ago he had done a brief trade here in hard core pornography and live sex shows. Tourists paid well to see a blonde perform – particularly with the right sort of animal.

But now he approached a different part of the city. Europe had long lost patience with communes; each time another was levelled its inhabitants headed north to seek out the protection of the tolerantly civic-minded Danes – to dig the heels of their Doc Martens into what must be one of the few remaining barricaded student ghettos.

There was the boundary – a wall of sorts reinforced with packing cases and builders' rubble. A gap seemed the only entrance. The Consul stepped forward firmly. He wore a donkey jacket, a blue peaked refusenik's cap and heavily laced second-hand industrial boots. Instead of a sweater he wore three ill-sized shirts. He bore an armoury of badges proclaiming solidarity or dissatisfaction or superstitious disquiet. He had omitted to shave. He thought that his nails, extra long and black, gave a nice finishing touch.

There was a brazier at the entrance and people round it dressed in the same nuisance-uniform as the Consul. It was cold. The first snow that turns Copenhagen crystalline was in the air. Behind the fire he could make out part of the buildings. Half the old warehouse area remained. Someone had thought up some grass and a goat, a cow, a few unlovely chickens. He tried not to laugh.

The faces around the fire stared hostilely. He stepped forward and spoke slowly in English.

"I am John Consul from Morocco," he held out the oilskin packet that Robinson had sent him. "Give him this and he will see me."

Somebody said, "Give who?"

"Mr Schmidt of course," said the Consul.

Penelope always apologised elaborately for Kesteven. It was so beastly dull in Warwickshire. Nowadays one had to do the cooking oneself. Besides it wasn't a proper country house – just a farm knocked through into a pair of adjoining cottages. It didn't *even* have any land or stables – just two acres of paddock and a couple of loose boxes.

To Catriona it was haven, never more than now, as Louis turned his ancient Ford out of Shipston-on-Stour. Catriona loved the shabby elegance that simply seemed to happen around people like Penelope. Kesteven was a chintzed and inglenooked womb – full of the smell of woodsmoke, the gurgle of bathwater, the chiming of innumerable clocks and the never failing generosity of mad Penelope . . .

Beyond exhaustion, somewhere beyond shock, Catriona felt pulped. She had talked herself – and been talked – to a standstill. The body on the station platform unlocked her tongue. They listened, Bert and Robinson and the old man in the toothbrush moustache whose name was prefixed not by Mr but by Señor, and then went back and forward over the same points.

The drunk man in the blue suit who had come calling at her flat; the taxi ride with Barrington Smythe; the meeting in the squalid hovel at the back of his squalid flat. Then there was the Visitor. She told of him too – with her head held high precisely because she felt such a fool.

But when it was their turn she felt worse, although Señor Rossminster spoke very gently.

"Not Tar. I can assure you. Know him. Seen him recently. Not the slightest doubt."

Bert was less delicate. Bert was angry; as if someone had made a fool of him. Perhaps someone had. "Maxwell," he said. "Stanley Maxwell from the Rowton House Hostel for useless old gits in Leith Scotland. Pulls up roots and comes down to London to play being James Tar. Ponces around in the blue suit Tar wore in Morocco . . . "

"You remember the photograph," said Rossminster.

"Oh yes," said Catriona. "I remember the photograph."

"Which suit," said Bert, "you could recognise anywhere. So Maxwell goes around advertising himself as Tar until bless my boots he gets himself bloody killed as Tar."

"Killed? What do you mean killed? He was ill. Didn't he just die?"

Bert looked at her as if she were the thickest infant in a kindergarten for the backward. "No he didn't *just die*! Unless he decided to jam a bloody great needle into the back of his thigh."

"Needle? Thigh?" It was as if they were speaking a foreign language.

"Botched job too. Someone who didn't know what they were doing . . . "

"As I say," Señor Rossminster interrupted, "that couldn't be Jimmy."

"Dirty great hole. Government warning. Heroin can severely spoil the cut of your horrible old whistle and flute."

Robinson said, "We have to wait for the autopsy. We don't know that it's heroin."

"Heroin is *cheap*. Not that it matters much. An old wreck like that – an injection of Bovril'd do the trick."

"What are you talking about? I don't know what you're talking about."

"I'm talking about this." Bert had planted himself four square in front of her – big and flushed. A cartoon policeman steps down into the audience. "I'm talking about the joker who swans about saying he's your dad for reasons best known to his bleeding self and by means best known to his bleeding self setting up one down and out derelict Scots git Maxwell to get killed in his place."

"Steady old boy," said Rossminster to Bert, who had gone pink around the collar stud. Robinson said nothing and watched.

Catriona took it slowly. "You – mean – that . . . You mean that Tar knew that someone else was going to try to kill him and he got Maxwell to imitate him so that Maxwell was murdered? In Tar's place?"

"Spot on," said Bert.

"But that's HORRIBLE."

"All the same I'd like to know how he got Maxwell to do it." Bert had switched to grudging admiration.

Rossminster cleared his throat politely but firmly. "To be fair that's not what Jimmy said . . . "

"*Said*?!" What was this; yet another thing to be kept from her?

Rossminster responded with what she was beginning to recognise as a slightly foxed version of old world courtesy. "Oh dear me yes."

"You mean all this time you've been talking away to him while I . . . "

Robinson intervened. "Catriona. Listen now." (Robinson sounded anxious; perhaps by now she was looking especially wild eyed.) "It was Señor Rossminster with whom Tar first made contact. They knew each other in the past. So Señor Rossminster was to be Tar's contact. Henry?"

Rossminster tugged at his moustache in embarrassment at Catriona's expression. "The fact is young Miss that Jimmy telephoned me. That's how we were at the station. He said to meet him there."

"To meet him or Maxwell?" ("Exactly," muttered Bert.)

"Perhaps both."

Another snort from Bert. Robinson shook his head. Bert subsided. As he nodded for the old man to continue Catriona noticed how attentively, how respectfully, Robinson listened to Rossminster.

"Of course," Rossminster still sounded apologetic, "there's a great deal, a *very* great deal we don't know – that Jimmy's keeping from us naturally, his nest egg so to speak, his investment – but I think a certain amount is pretty clear. He set up Maxwell to *show* us, to show you too young Miss, that someone would be out to get a person whom *they* thought was James Tar. So Maxwell arranged the meeting as Jimmy told him in a very public place. Where, in fact, any attempt on Maxwell would be obvious. Except something went wrong. Maxwell didn't keep to the plan. The injection that killed him was administered *outside* the station."

"None of which alters the fact that even if things had gone right Maxwell might still have got his. That Tar was quite prepared to see Maxwell used as a sacrificial victim. A Judas goat?"

"Oh yes er . . . Bert." Rossminster's tone was even and reasonable. "Quite prepared. I think Miss Lomax needs assistance."

For a while Robinson held her head between her knees. When she brought it up again she felt as if she had bitten permanently into something green and bitter; the bile would never leave her.

She looked around the room at this collection of men who had charged in and broken up her life. She wanted to get angry, to fight back, to say something hurtful. But all that came out was feeble sarcasm. "I don't suppose he had time to leave a message."

Rossminster took her seriously. His face glowed with a polite and conventional brightness.

"Silly of me. Almost forgot. Sent you his love."

"I hate love," said Catriona aloud.

"Best thing to do with it," said Louis as he drove off the last tangled country lane and across the gravel sweep in front of Kesteven. The windows blazed with light. Penelope ran out; she had been listening for the car's engine. She wrenched open the passenger door and flung her arms around Catriona.

"Heavens, the drama! Strict orders from Humpo. Mainstream pampering. He says you're being a brick considering – and that you're probably for a sedative and bed though one naturally longs for you to babble like a fountain. I can't believe you're letting them start again tomorrow. Louis you are just this once an angel; I know you hate driving and loathe the country."

Penelope's chatter filled the space from car to house but in the light of the doorway she saw Catriona's face – stopped – then said, "Darling!"

Catriona stood, her face full of the platform in the rain, with the small stinking bundle of humanity dying in her lap, and of the colossal ride that someone out there was taking her for.

She set her chin. "Pempy," she said, "I won't stand for it. And now for God's sake get me to bed."

It was as the Consul expected. In the late sixties most cities still had quarters like this; by the eighties City Halls had started to bulldoze them. The place in Copenhagen was a late surviving equivalent of a Victorian rookery – adjoining buildings pecked away at from the inside to leave a series of interconnecting lofts and corridors – through which no outsider could find the way – with a number of escape routes into the streets and sewers of the outside world. The Consul was searched and blindfolded; then marched up and down enough staircases and corridors to scramble his sense of direction. Schmidt was taking very good care of Schmidt. As long as he stayed here he would not be an easy man to get at.

The blindfold came off. The Consul had expected a filthy corridor, its rooms containing the usual mishmash of mattresses, trunks and posters that put the solid into solidarity. In fact he found himself thrust into a room where the walls were recently painted white, the bare floors scrubbed and smelling of disinfectant. There was a very large trestle table – also scrubbed. It was stacked high with boxes of different board games. Before the table sat a pudgy pasty man in his fifties. He had a wide square face and tiny eyes and incongruously yellow hair, neatly parted and just one shade off the expensive camel coat into which he huddled, although there were two calor gas heaters and the room was warm. He had a glass of buttermilk and a piece of dry toast. He lifted the glass in the Consul's direction as if inviting the appreciation of a connoisseur.

"You see the cows out front? My idea. I got a nervous stomach. Fresh milk – that is one necessity for health. These young people," he gestured with the toast as if to acknowledge a genial proprietorship over the rookery's inhabitants, "these are nice alternative boys and girls – you unnerstan' my meaning. But diet! Biscuits! Potato chips! So I say to these nice people that I try to help you have to have a cow for when Schmidt comes a cow is necessary." He tapped the top of the glass so that the little chunk of yellow dissolved further. "But for the butter they have to send out. You take a seat John Consul from Morocco."

There was a single chair positioned exactly opposite Schmidt but a good ten feet away from him. The Consul sat like a single candidate at an interview. Schmidt looked up and down his trestle table.

"You like board games?"

"An evening without one is like a day without sunshine."

"Sure," said Schmidt. He put down the buttermilk. From behind the Monopoly set he extracted the contents of the oilskin pouch which the Consul had handed over earlier – the first photographs that Tar had extracted from the hippies. Schmidt laid them before him one by one in a line as if they were patience cards.

"Prints, huh?"

"Yes," said the Consul.

"But you got the originals?"

"Yes."

"Sure you do." He dipped his toast in the buttermilk. "Where you get these things?"

The Consul gave his glad-to-be-of-assistance smile. "I believe they were originally in the possession of the fun-loving fornicators in front of you." The Consul pointed to the photograph that caught Madame Despard in mid orgy. "Hippies," he continued. "In Morocco. Claimed they worked for you."

Schmidt stared impassively at the Consul.

"So maybe these people got my name from somewhere. But speaking personally I search my memory and frankly I never see them before. Where these people now?"

"Dead."

"That's a pity."

"Buried."

"That's nice."

"Alive."

"That's not."

Schmidt started to chew the softened toast.

The Consul was a good pimp – he had spent years assessing

the weaknesses and vanities of the human race. But Schmidt was close to opaque. He was fat, unhealthy, a coarse looking man with a rich coat and an odd diet. But these points apart the Consul could be sure of only one thing – Schmidt was sure not only of himself but also of the situation. He should have been under pressure but he looked as if he had just patented the ring of confidence.

Now he turned his attention back to the photographs.

"So," he tapped each with a pudgy finger. "You got me a snapshot of Schmidt. Nice view. Shows where to find him. You got some old whore who gets a little action fore and aft . . . "

"Madame Despard."

"You're a well-informed person. Eager beaver. What you reckon to the rest Mr Beaver?"

"We thought you might tell us."

The Consul had begun to notice something about the way Schmidt looked at the photographs. Each time the fat man glanced down his eyes flicked quickly over four of the snapshots but paused at the fifth – that which captured the low wall, and the plain door, the sunshine. Either you are acting very beautifully, thought the Consul, or that's the only photograph you don't recognise.

"Never mind that for now," said Schmidt. "Maybe later you earn that information." (Almost exactly, thought the Consul, what Tar told Rossminster.) Delicately, charily Schmidt swallowed his last morsel of pap. "So these hippies are dead. So where you get this stuff?"

"James Tar."

"Uh-uh." Schmidt's piggy eyes moved from the Consul to the photographs and back again. "And where would Jimmy be? Maybe in some jail somewhere?"

"We think not."

"So what is this we? We who? We what?"

"An interest. A British interest."

"What kind of interest?"

"Government."

"What kind of government?"

"The quiet kind."

Schmidt showed no sign of any strain other than dyspepsia. He gave a little belch and brought a large white silk handkerchief to his mouth. "You can prove that? Maybe the Queen gives me a telephone call?"

"I can arrange . . . "

Mr Schmidt waved a silencing handkerchief.

"Forget it. Sure we get to that. A meeting or something. Some bigwig with a big badge maybe. Never mind. I believe you. Schmidt is a very believing guy. Anyway you're the pimp who turned tricks in Morocco for the old fart. Whasisname? Rossminster?"

"My," said the Consul. "We do cover the waterfront."

Schmidt looked benign – like a man who has fed well and never heard of buttermilk. "Sure. I ask. I listen. I store." He raised a finger, turned it in towards his chest as if his person was an exhibit. "That's me. Mr Information."

"Completely," said the Consul. "Absolutely. Counting on it."

"You Quiet Boys got the right idea. You want information – you come to Schmidt. I got all kinds of information."

This was sparring. Schmidt was advertising his general goods store in preparation for any particular request. The Consul could spar too. He smiled encouragingly and waited for Schmidt to make a real move.

For a moment Schmidt regarded the Consul impassively. Then he said, "So what then? Jimmy goes to you? So he's got to go to someone. I mean he is no spring chicken. Alone – don't make me laugh."

The Consul smiled his polite smile – the one with all the yellow teeth.

Schmidt rearranged his coat against a non-existent draught. He sucked in a long O of buttermilk, his piggy eyes watching the Consul over the glass. Yes, thought the Consul, for the first time you're on the defensive.

"So Jimmy's crazy mad. So he's dangerous. So he's also one old drunk. So what he asks you for – back up, pick up, whatever? He tells you lots of crazy things. So what does he want? So what do you want?"

"Actually old chum," said the Consul, "what we really want is to make a deal."

"You got a silver tongue," said Mr Schmidt.

"A bit of old England, eh sir?" said Bert. They had crossed the little orchard at the back of Kesteven and walked towards the house. Bert's spate of temper had passed; he had recovered his usual mixture of ingratiation and insolence. Robinson was preoccupied. He wondered how far the Consul had got in Copenhagen. He wondered about Tar. From time to time he glanced up at the first floor where Catriona Lomax slept the day away.

Now they had reached the walled kitchen garden. Robinson pushed open the little iron gate.

"Does your heart good, a place like this," Bert inhaled with unnecessary force. "I do like a nice row of cottages."

"For some odd reason," said Robinson, "they make me think of suburbs."

"I like a nice suburb."

"I don't. I have to live in one of the damned things."

Aha, thought Bert, no money of your own eh? All socks and no suspenders. Want a place like this and don't like your cousin having it.

"She's a real lady."

"Who?" said Robinson irritably.

"Why Lady Penelope of *course*."

"She's a mad tart but she has her uses."

"You don't say sir?" Bert made it sound as if he had received a state secret that he would forever treasure.

Robinson said nothing. He was staring up again at the first floor bedrooms.

"Getting her beauty sleep all right, eh? Our Cat."

"I'm pretty certain that she didn't know anything about Maxwell or Tar. All of that came as a real shock. And she was completely blank when I mentioned the name Despard. If she'd known anything about a connection to Schmidt or to Esmond Claremaurice I think there would have been some reaction. Some."

"She used to be an actress sir."

"A bad actress by all accounts."

"On the stage sir. Life's different."

"So they say," said Robinson. "Which leaves us waiting. For what Tar does next. For Schmidt if we've got to him."

"Most likely sir we're really waiting for someone to contact her. For her to get moving."

They had reached half way to the kitchen. Robinson

turned. Another figure had come through the iron gate at the far end of the garden.

"So there's still no sign of this Barrington Smythe character?"

Bert shook his head. "Could be on a jag. Nothing unusual about that. Disappears on the razzle for a week at a time. Probably why the wife left him. We've got a man watching the place."

"I want you to go over it. With someone who knows Barrington Smythe."

Bert followed Robinson's gaze. Plump Louis Vulliamy picked his way with evident distaste at the messiness of rural life towards them across the cabbages.

"Could we," said Louis, "get away from those verminous green things?"

They walked round the back of the house until they reached the paddock. Bert had been dispatched, sulking, into the house.

"All right," said Louis. "I'll give Bert a hand with Barrington Smythe's flat. As long as you look after Catriona."

"The only way to do that is to lock her up and guard her door."

"She wouldn't have that."

"No. We'll do our best. So far no one seems to want to harm *her*."

Louis stopped and pushed the question mark of black hair out of his right eye. "That would be in the big picture. Not just in the little picture that we simpletons know about."

"Such as it is. Yes."

"All right. Don't tell me – you can't tell me."

"I can't tell you."

They walked on. "Believe me my lad," said Louis, "you will have trouble with Catriona."

Robinson gave a big red grin. "What do you mean *will*?"

"Me I'm broad church," said Mr Schmidt. "Me I'm liberal. Live and let live. Everybody gets a bit – everybody's happy. Me I'm a very helpful person. I help people. Doesn't matter who. My young friends here," he waved a rookery-embracing hand, "or the highest in the land."

"Which land?" asked the Consul.

"*Any* land. Lot of lands. Lot of people. That's how come Schmidt knows so much. How Schmidt's got so much to share with people like you."

"At a price?"

Schmidt chortled synthetically as if sympathising with a bad joke. "You ever hear of something free you keep it to yourself or someone else is going to come along and put a price on it. Anyway you ask a question with your permission I answer it."

"Actually I asked you several questions."

"Patience. Like I got also. One thing at a time. So I work my way up. So I rescue their Foundation which as you unnerstan' is entropy, chaos, mess – whatever bad word you can think of. This Despard believe me is someone who requires to be sincerely rich. I mean to be the big philanthropist you got to have the money in the first place."

The Consul said that this seemed a sound proposition to him.

"Undoubtedly. So I do well. I cut back. I invest here. I invest there. I keep Despard rich and I keep that whore wife of his in all the suspender belts she can buy. Year after year. So now what do I get in return? I get hatred."

The heat of the room and the smell of buttermilk got on the Consul's nerves. Increasingly Schmidt spooked him. The man was nervous enough to hide out in this hair shirt flower child give-the-revolution-a-kiss fortress, yet he was still indefinably confident.

"Forgive the village gossip," said the Consul, "but that wouldn't have anything to do with your fingers in the till? Lot of fingers; big till? Or with blackmailing Madame Despard?"

Schmidt put his head on one side and smiled. It suddenly came to the Consul that he looked like Toad of Toad Hall. Mr Toad without the lovableness and with thirty times the watchfulness.

"Schmidt's a very legal guy. Legality, that is one impressive thing. I got organisation. I got method. Catching Schmidt is not believe me easy."

In other words, thought the Consul, your peculation is scattered across different banks in different countries. And back home in good old Switzerland you have a nice numbered account that dares not speak its name. Except . . . Except why are you hiding? Except why are you interested in a deal – in any kind of deal?

"Seems to me I heard something about a will. Your losing control of the Foundation."

Schmidt's next smile was fifty percent amused tolerance, fifty per cent complacency. "*That* is not the problem."

"So what is?"

"Jimmy," he said. "Jimmy's the problem."

Catriona woke to distant church bells. Vespers. Sunday *evening*. She had slept away the remainder of the night and most of the day. The sedative had certainly worked; she could still taste it. She swilled out her mouth with the bedside bottle of Malvern water and ran her bath. She bathed and dried herself and turned to the clothes that Penelope had provided. Since they were of radically different shapes, all girlie borrowing was out and Catriona had to make do with the vestiges of a departed husband. The checked shirt looked becomingly outsize; the trousers – pillar box red numbers from Beale and Inman – had to be rolled up below the knee. She tied them at the waist with a silk scarf.

Penelope came into the room.

"Cor," she said. "Ain't she sweet. At least Humpo won't be able to stare at your legs in that outfit."

"I feel like something out of the Market Snodsbury Light Amateur Dramatic Society Production of Li'l Abner."

"Don't change the subject. What about Humpo?"

"For Christ's *sake* Penelope!"

"Sorree." She was clearly unrepentant. "Anyway he's waiting downstairs. With the others."

"Let him wait. Let them all wait. God knows I'm having to. I don't know what's going on. Perhaps they do but I doubt it. I think they just know bits and pieces and they just tell me whatever bit or piece that suits them. And all the time *he's* out there. What does he want? What *can* he want? They don't know how it feels. They can't. But they don't want to."

"Oh well darling, *men*. They're always scheming at something. They're basically very silly. It's just as well they have cocks and things."

"Things?"

"You know."

And you can't understand it either Penelope – how foolish and horrible it is to find yourself *parented* against your will; to find that a foolishness becomes a nastiness and a nastiness becomes a horror.

"Catriona? Are you frightened? I should be you know."

But Catriona seemed to be thinking of something else.

"You know what I really can't stand? What I can't endure? It's just waiting. Being dependent. Just stuck."

"But let's face it darling what *can* you do?"

"I can bloody well move," said Catriona.

They're in charge Catriona thought as she entered Penelope's drawing room. Whatever you say they're in charge of me – Robinson, Bert and even old apologetic Señor Rossminster. They know what's going on and I don't. They can always sit back smugly and mumble something about security and need-to-know and tell or withhold just as much as it suits them. They can say the murder's nothing to do with me and I'm safe as houses or they can say I should stay inside and lock all the doors and buy a can of mace and subscribe to the Phone-a-Rottweiler service and I wouldn't know which to believe.

Louis, in his usual faded corduroy jacket and blue spotted bow tie, was dispensing drinks. (It was one of the few areas in which Penelope bowed to Louis' technological prowess.) Bert, in a High Street jacket of grotesque hirsuteness and cheap cavalry twills, beamed goodwill at the fireplace, the portraits, the bookshelves, as if trying to worm his way into their unsuspecting confidence. Señor Rossminster had made uncomfortably the wrong effort. He wore a starched collar, pin-striped suit, heavily watch-chained at the middle and shoes of a startling continental patent leather. All this set off his olive skin and made him look more than ever like an actor miscast as an Englishman in a foreign movie. He was on the receiving end of Penelope in full swoop.

"This divine Señor Rossminster thought I had a butler's pantry. Too humiliating."

Catriona felt a little better. Rossminster didn't.

"Quite," he said uneasily. "Times change."

"If *only*. Break heart for the modern world."

"That's enough Penelope," Robinson turned from the fire.

Catriona's hackles rose. You rude man, she thought, you *coarse* man. You ought to know better. Penelope put her tongue out. He ignored her. The heat from the fire had built up an extra flush on his already ruddy countenance. He seemed more alert, more vigorous than he had in London. In fact he looked like a gentleman farmer at ease with his acres and his sense of superiority over the female sex. But just for a moment his gaze went to Catriona's trousered legs. Penelope noticed and winked at Catriona. Robinson caught a corner of the wink. He looked determinedly at a space above Catriona's head. He sounded gruffer than yesterday, as if his supply of sympathy had now been used up.

"Good rest?"

"Good," said Catriona.

"Good," said Robinson.

"Goody all round," said Penelope. Robinson glowered at her. She looked around the room brightly, as if a point of general interest had just occurred to her. "Suppressed desire is very bad for the temper."

Robinson did his best to pay no attention. He turned away to face Catriona.

"Catriona I know none of this can be easy but I want you to listen to Señor Rossminster for a while. He's the only one who knows Tar. Then I have a proposal to put to you."

Catriona folded her arms, ignoring the drink that Louis had prepared for her. "All right. What's the next thing that nobody's told me?"

She realised that mild Señor Rossminster was looking at her with definite disapproval.

"With permission" – he made it sound reproachful, as if Catriona had impeded him – "what he believed in. What he was. In my opinion what he is." He cleared his throat. "The man inside. No – don't believe anyone's told you about him."

"OK," said Schmidt. "I admit it. Schmidt is a frank person. I didn't reckon on Jimmy. The Foundation and Jimmy, that was long gone. Settled. So for all I knew Jimmy was dead somewhere. I mean killing people is one high risk profession you unnerstan'. What with that and drink . . . Anyway, not so. That sperm sack Madame Despard gets hold of him – which thing I firmly believed she would not do – she pumps him full of this and that. The next thing he's going to kill me."

"You're sure of that?"

"So what else? Jimmy's a seriously violent person. Give him the right weapons and he kills maybe half the human race. Believe me Jimmy's the worst kind of loose cannon. The kind they only just brought back on deck after too long in the dark. It shoots anywhere. Not just me. You too. Anyone."

The Consul remembered with a shiver the scene in Marrakesh; down on his knees as Tar held a razor to his cheek. "Very likely but what's Madame Despard got to do with it?"

Schmidt stretched out his plump hands and from the little pile on his table opened the box containing the Monopoly set. He laid out the individual tokens – the dog, the car, the flat iron, the top hat, the locomotive.

"Me, I like board games. Up here no one plays. They got no sense of humour. Monopoly, that means the evils of capitalism – you know the situation. So I get to play with myself. I sit. I figure the odds and the stakes all on my own. And now," he lifted his head and looked straight at the Consul. "I figure that you don't know too much. I like you John Company . . . "

"Consul."

"Whatever. Something imperial. And Schmidt needs his Empire protected before he tells you all the things you don't know. Like," Schmidt tapped his little line of photographs. "These. Interests of Schmidt. You play ball you get much more than these."

So, slowly but surely the deal was being cut.

"All right. What's your price?"

Schmidt's piggy eyes glinted.

"I want Jimmy off the scene."

"How's that exactly?"

"Exactly is your business. You put him in jail for the next two thousand years, you put him on a desert island, you put him painfully to sleep. I don't want to know. I don't know. All I know is no more Jimmy."

The Consul felt his palms go moist. The fat man meant what he was saying. "Mr Schmidt. You're a rich man with connections. There are people you could pay to do this. People like Tar himself."

Schmidt tapped the top hat up and down on the board like

a song writer looking for a tune. "But Tar is not in touch with them. I mean they would have to go and find him. Besides, as I say, I'm a very legal guy and I got to consider the future. The immediate future. The Foundation. Despard's will. There could be questions. No one can benefit legally from a crime. And," he smiled, "what you guys do is not a crime. You use a cut out, accident, whatever."

Years ago the Consul had learned a certain number of firm trade rules. One such said that in a tight corner you promised anything.

"So Jimmy's a nuisance to us. A criminal yes. Suppose it's in our interest. Suppose it's hunkey dorey, satisfaction guaranteed. What then?"

"Very fine," said Schmidt. "So now I give you something. Good faith. A bond. You don't come across that's all you get."

"Understood."

"So I let you in on a deal. Me, I like to buy futures. This has been my policy always. Long term investment. Growth potential. I give you a part of my best resource, best stock. I give you why with Jimmy gone I can't lose."

"Which is?"

In a surprisingly decisive gesture Mr Schmidt tossed the little tin hat into the air and caught it.

"Miss Catriona Lomax. Strictly limited issue."

"We want you to understand."

There it was again; this time the phrase used by Robinson to launch Señor Rossminster.

"Moors," said Rossminster. "That's who I commanded. Moorish *regulares*. Mercenaries. Tremendous looking chaps. Red caps and blue djellabas. They were *good* troops." Rossminster looked around the room as if he were pressing their claims for employment. "Skirmish, deploy, the best shots on either side. Even managed to cope with the cold. Treated badly too. Bad casualties. Bad pay. Sometimes even paid in bogus currency. Despite all that with good officers they were disciplined. But once let off the hook . . . Well as far as massacre goes no fairer to blame the Moors than anyone else. No worse than anyone else. Neither side had a patent on atrocities. Still, that's not how the Republicans saw it. Terrified of being taken by the Moors. Cut to pieces, crucified, eaten alive, God knows what. Brave men you see; they could face straight death but not the Moors. Sorry to go on. Context you see. Enter Jimmy."

He paused. This time he directed his visual apology at Catriona. Here was a topic that, for most of the modern world, had outgrown its relevance. He didn't want to seem rude.

"About Spain. The war and so on. How much do you know?"

Catriona didn't know what to answer. Louis spoke up.

"Enough."

Rossminster nodded, continued.

"I met him twice in the war. Both times he was a prisoner. This was the first time. A place called Mantelete. It had been taken, then re-taken. Hand to hand fighting. Bad business. In the end we had some prisoners. Mixed bag – some Spanish, some International Brigaders from the British Battalion. Jimmy was one of them. Looked like a small scarecrow. There were quite a few who looked like that. Undernourished boys who'd walked their way to the war and gone through conditions that would have killed men twice their size in perfect health. They believed, you see . . . "

He *likes* him Catriona thought. It isn't just respect. He actually likes him. And not in the past tense either. Now.

"I remember," said Rossminster, "that parts of his skin that had been out of the sun had gone so pale as to be almost green. He was very fair. Like you young Miss."

Catriona's stomach twisted.

"They had to be marched away from the lines to the Base Camp. My Moors as escort. Prisoners strung out three deep; the Moorish cavalry pushing them on none too gently with the flat of their sabres. Not in a tolerant mood you might say. The trouble started with the prisoners singing. I didn't care what they sang if it kept them moving and I don't think the Moors understood a word. At first there were just a few protest songs – *Ay Carmela* – that sort of thing. But then some of the Brigaders started up the *Internationale*. Then all hell broke loose. The Anarchists and the Left Republicans started screaming at the Communists and they started yelling back."

"Another fine war you got me into," said Louis.

"Just so. Well you can imagine young Miss" (the third time he had used that phrase – trying to avoid slipping back into

Señorita). "The Anarchists yelling that the *Internationale*'s a foreign anthem, the Communists yelling that the Anarchists are a bunch of undisciplined part-time soldiers and my Moors having to break things up which they don't like and no mistake. I mean if the other side wants to go killing itself why not join in and save a march. At which point up pops Tar. Little bantam cock. Makes a speech. Up and down. Punching the air with his fist. Do they want to give the Moors an excuse to start murdering? Don't they know that every dead prisoner means more rations for the Moors? Do they think the Moors are that well fed? So make up your minds – *hijos.* Are you soldiers of the Republic or amateur martyrs and class traitors? It worked but it was an awful risk. He could have been killed by either side – the prisoners *or* the Moors. And that was the first time I met James Tar."

Catriona didn't know what to say. She felt that everyone was watching her. When she remained expressionless for long enough Rossminster continued.

"As a matter of interest," Penelope interrupted, "how did Tar *make* the speech? Surely the proletarian warriors didn't speak any English. Had Tar learnt that much Spanish inside a year – "

Rossminster shook his head.

"So who translated?"

"Well," Rossminster looked sheepish, "*I* did actually. Didn't want any more slaughter, don't you know."

"Not only a dish," said Penelope, "but a humane dish."

Rossminster, uneasy at whimsical compliments, hurried on. "The second time I met him was six months later. By then everything had changed. I'd been wounded so I was back at the Base interrogating prisoners. A few of the last British Brigaders. I don't think there were many illusions left. Life slowly squeezed out of the Republic. The end just a matter of time and the International Brigades being withdrawn altogether."

"Just a moment," said Robinson. He was starting to fill a noxious looking pipe. "I think you'd better explain that for Catriona."

Gee thanks, thought Catriona. More lessons for a little girl. She nearly said it out loud but then she saw first the smile on Louis' face, then Rossminster's expression. Worried, pained, concentrated. He's so *serious* about this. It must be important. I must listen to him.

"As I said everything had changed. The end was coming, a bigger war on its way to make Spain a sideshow. Hitler had just been given the Sudetenland by Chamberlain and Daladier. Stalin was getting scared. Wanted to appease Hitler so he would withdraw the thing that rightly or wrongly gave the Republic its widest publicity. He persuaded the Republic to send home the Brigades. By then anyway they'd changed out of recognition. So many of the originals were dead or repatriated. Half the members had become Spaniards and some pretty reluctant ones at that. Jailbirds. Conscripts . . . "

He had gone dreamy for a moment. Robinson coughed. Rossminster twitched back into narrative.

"About repatriation . . . You see all along, for the whole course of the war, a lot of International Brigaders who were taken prisoner were repatriated. Good publicity. Decent treatment of POWs et cetera. On the understanding . . . " (and Rossminster wagged a finger to illustrate the one-sidedness of the understanding) "that if they came back and were recaptured they were shot on sight. Summary execution. Even the Communist Party HQ in London told people not to go back."

"All right," said Catriona. "Don't tell me. Tar did."

"There I was," Rossminster smiled, "standing in front of my table. We looked at each other and we knew. Both of us. All I had to do was tell the guard. They wouldn't even have bothered with a check. Just act on my word. An arm under each elbow, outside, a bullet in the back of the head. No ceremony. No pack drill."

"What did you do?" Despite herself Catriona was gripped.

"Well actually," Rossminster sounded self-deprecating, "I suppose I saved his life."

And so again she listened, though with increasing detachment. This was nothing to do with her. Once again Robinson was playing with her. Just wearing her down by setting this kind old man, whom it would be rude to interrupt, on to her. The fire was warm. She could smell the brandy in her now-cold coffee. She just didn't know what was going on but she would not show weakness. They wanted something from her and to get it they must first make her weak. It was not – well of course it wasn't – that the kind old man's story wasn't moving, merely that it described a person who, no matter his name or his claims, had long ceased to exist. He was simply a good thousand light years away from herself. In this spirit she listened.

There had been an officer at the Base who had been on the staff of Franco's military attaché in London. He had seen photographs of each repatriated Brigader, for just the eventuality that had now occurred. There was no doubt that he would have recognised Tar, and that Tar would have been shot. So (and Rossminster offered no motive) Rossminster had taken Tar and moved him from place to place, job to job – now in the recesses of the kitchen, now in the latrines, now in the foul pit behind the hospital to burn the wound dressings and the amputated limbs. And so Tar survived to be sent home a second time, marched away between half starved cripples towards the railway station of a concentration camp over the French border. (Tar had not thanked Rossminster nor had he asked him for an explanation. He had simply said he would not forget.) And at the border he had watched the expatriated Communist troops as they gave three cheers for the Ribbentrop pact and for the new ally of the Left, Adolf Hitler.

And all the while Catriona was nodding politely, as if it all had nothing to do with her. It was in the same polite tone that she said, "So why did you do it? Not do it? Save his life?"

Señor Rossminster looked up at the ceiling. "Oh," he said vaguely, "one more death. Why kill any more, and then" (and now he levelled his gaze at Catriona as if seeing if she could possibly understand, if she had any inkling of what he meant) "you see it was such a remarkable thing. All over Europe these little people – no not little – these *poor* people just stopping what they were doing, laying down their tools, going to fight in Spain. There was never anything like it. Ordinary people. Yet he, you see, was not at all an ordinary man."

Catriona wished this was going to happen to someone other than Rossminster – to Robinson perhaps, whose now-lit pipe had lived up to its promise of foulness. On the other hand it was Rossminster's story, Rossminster's Tar, and Rossminster who was now squarely in her sights.

"Well good," she said. "Fine. You said you wanted me to understand. Understand *what.* That a man I've never seen, who's probably a lunatic and certainly a murderer, who goes around for absolutely no reason saying he's my father, was once upon a time a gallant young revolutionary? For Christ's sake!"

It was Rossminster who spoke now – with a combination of purpose and dignity. "I wanted you to know a little of the quality of the man who says he loves you. I wanted you to realise that the love of such a man would not be a negligible thing."

The door opened. Penelope's nanny stood there looking at the assembled adults as if they weren't much of an advertisement for ex-childhood.

"The telephone," she intoned, "for Miss Lomax." She gave the prep school outfit a dirty look.

Catriona went to the telephone in the hall. She picked up the receiver to hear Gomez's cultured Goan tones.

"Miss Lomax. I didn't know where you were. I've been trying to reach you."

"Yes Gomez?" (Catriona the steady responsible employer.)

"And so has Mr Schmidt."

Robinson, Rossminster and Bert walked back across Kesteven's paddock towards their cars. Half an hour had passed since Louis' old Ford had pulled away from the house taking Catriona back to London. Just afterwards the Consul had made contact from Copenhagen. Robinson had just finished giving Bert and Rossminster the substance of the Consul's meeting with Schmidt. Bert cleared his throat.

"You wouldn't be going to tell all this to our Cat would you sir."

"I would certainly not," said Robinson. "Any more than I told her what Tar told Henry here about the Despard Foundation or about Madame Despard being Esmond Claremaurice's stepmother. I want it all to come to her *fresh*. I want to see how she reacts. I want to see how she *runs*. Especially if she really is as important to the future of the Foundation as Schmidt claims. Schmidt could be lying. She could be lying. Tar could be lying."

"So we wait and see sir?"

"Wait, *watch* and see Bert. So little is certain. Tar would hardly have bothered to kill Maxwell. But Schmidt asks the Consul to get Tar killed, which means that he, Schmidt, didn't kill Maxwell-posing-as-Tar. So who killed Maxwell? Who thinks they've killed Tar?"

"But we do pretend to Schmidt that Tar's dead and we did it for him? I mean the timing's a bit off."

"Can't be helped," said Robinson. "It's all we've got. Do you agree Henry?"

Rossminster stood by the open car door looking sentimentally over green and English Warwickshire. "Tar stays dead. That means that Schmidt or whoever else feels freer to move. Oh yes, Jimmy stays dead and everything will happen. The trouble is that rather a lot of it may happen to Miss Lomax and then . . . well!"

"Well what?" Bert was becoming tired of Rossminster the Sage from the European Community.

"Well I know it's a question of what he really cares about or what he most cares about but if she *is* his daughter – well I wonder how long he'll want to stay dead."

"Which may depend," Bert said, "on how much she gets up to."

"Yes," said Rossminster. "It has become a case of I'll do it myself said the little red rooster."

"Hen. Little red hen."

"No." Señor Rossminster gave his old sad smile. "I was thinking of something altogether more forceful."

# 24

Catriona heard the woman first – the creak and crackle of expensive leather as she dropped into the seat across the aisle and the train began to move out. For the moment Catriona's attention was otherwise engaged. Preoccupied, she stared out of the window as the first stages of the journey to Scotland began to slip away.

Back in her flat she had sat and waited for two whole hours. When the telephone rang she had seized it like a lifeline. There was something secure, something un-Tar-tainted about Schmidt's Americo-Swiss voice. Boss and employee – surely that would be solid and normal.

"Mr Schmidt you'll have to speak up. It's a bad line."

"Sure. Sure." Schmidt's voice seemed to come from a great distance along a cable repaired by hammering goblins. Suddenly the line cleared and Schmidt's voice came clearly through. "Ireland. You got that?"

"Ireland. Yes. What?"

"Dublin, right? Milburne Hotel. I got one day to fix things here. Then I meet you there. You wait for me day after tomorrow. You wait. You got that?"

"But . . . "

He talked over her – the employer pulls rank. "We got some business. A new venture. This is one exciting prospect you unnerstan'."

"But Mr Schmidt you don't understand. It's about the club."

"One club. Two clubs. Why not? Believe me, this Irish deal. There's a lot of possibility."

"No. Mr Schmidt about *this* club. About Lomaxes. I've had some trouble with . . . "

Trouble with what? When it came right down to it all the trouble was not with the club but with herself. And irrespective of what Robinson had told her about keeping Tar dead, any tale involving the events of the last few days would only underscore her unsuitability. Surely no one would choose to employ a girl in such a god-awful mess. She found herself saying, "I've had some people asking . . . well asking questions." She had never sounded lamer.

"Oh sure. Me too."

"You too!"

"Undoubtedly. Some Ministry personage."

Her mouth went dry. Then she heard Schmidt chuckle. He was pleased with himself as if he had done something clever.

She said, "But who . . . I mean . . . ?"

"This is no problem. Schmidt is behind you one hundred per cent. We talk in Dublin. Sort it all out. Milburne Hotel. You got that? You really got that?"

"Yes. Yes."

The line had gone dead. That was one of Schmidt's peculiarities. He never said good-bye.

So here, she thought, is another thing Robinson kept from me; the Ministry has talked to Schmidt already. But about what? Surely not the full extent of the Tar/Maxwell business? Schmidt could not then have sounded so sanguine. Perhaps – though this was one more matter that she didn't want to think about – they were taking Schmidt for a ride. Still, he hadn't been nobbled. He wasn't going to fire her. Quite the reverse. In all this mad mess Schmidt alone seemed solid. Schmidt was certain. Schmidt existed. Schmidt was *there*.

And Catriona, with a day to spare before the meeting in Dublin, put Gomez in charge of the club, dressed in a fire-engine red cashmere dress (defiance? a call to battle?) and took a morning train to Edinburgh. Sick with conditionals she sought an absolute. She wanted what mattered to *her*. She wanted the truth of her birth. She wanted confirmation of an actual father. Or did she? Even as the conviction formed in her mind Tar stepped out of his photograph and over the body of poor degenerate dying Maxwell to embrace her body, stiff already in recoil.

No, she had to know. Had to do her best to find out. It was no use being protected and namby-pambied. She didn't want the male game that made her a spectator sitting still and doing what she was told under an umbrella of masculine patronage. Catriona gritted her teeth and looked out at the rails as Stevenage shot by. So here she was, on her own, heading back to the only place that might provide the beginnings of an answer; towards the only possibly remaining family figure (unless she was dead too) from what Louis had called her relativeless childhood. Perhaps the idea was stupid – doomed to failure – but at least she would be doing something.

Just then Catriona picked up the reflection of the woman opposite, looking in Catriona's direction. As Catriona turned the woman herself turned away; to look out of her own window. I really am slowing down, thought Catriona. All this ridiculous razzmatazz is blunting me. In no time at all I'll be useless at my job. I won't be noticing *anything*. For the woman opposite smelt of money. Scent and skin (animal and human) had combined to say firmly I am simply as rich as hell – to be frank I represent a wholly different kind of money.

She was tall and diet thin. Her long narrow legs pushed straight out under the empty seats in front. She wore a cape and boots of matching brown leather, a calf skin skirt in a softer similar shade and a cream silk blouse, open at her long thin throat. Catriona's apprenticeship in upward mobility, her watch-and-ward of class and style, had not been wasted. She knew immediately that the cost of these garments extended beyond anything that even prosperous Penelope would have contemplated. Only the blouse had seen the inside of a shop. The rest was, and in the *real* sense, designer made. Each garment had been prepared for this woman and this woman alone. And there was something about the way she now sat carelessly – her face averted looking out at the passing landscape, the chattering track – that said she wore just one of a hundred perhaps a thousand such outfits, created anywhere from Milan to Tokyo, wherever she happened to be at the time, wherever it was amusing to have something made. Catriona drew in her breath at the effortlessness of the spectacle. Every day, she thought. Just like that. I'm sure of it. For, she thought, this woman doesn't so much wear clothes, she *assumes* them, just as she has assumed control of the empty seats before and beside her, scattering magazines, handbag, scarf, taking up all four of them with breathtaking effrontery.

What's she doing on a train Catriona wondered? Most probably afraid of flying.

A guard came down the aisle checking tickets. He was an unhappy fat man with pop eyes, the kind thought Catriona who gives blood pressure a bad name, for whom officialdom is a way of marketing a private grudge. He paused a little to misunderstand a question from a Japanese tourist, then moved on to Catriona's ticket and gave it a surly punch. He turned now to Lady Leather who continued to stare out of the window as if he wasn't there.

"Ticket. *If* you please."

Lady Leather turned and looked blankly at him. Not rudely, just blankly. It occurred to Catriona that the woman didn't know what he was there for, and therefore that she was wholly unaccustomed to train travel. So much for the fear of flying theory. But the guard had become aware of something better than a showdown over the production of a single ticket. His eyes gleamed as he cast them over the three vacant seats on which Lady Leather had spread her belongings. Each bore a reserved card clipped into the seat's headrest. The guard began to breathe heavily as over a pornographic picture.

"These . . . seats" (each word was a slow savoury mouthful) "are . . . taken."

For several moments, a count perhaps of five, the woman stared, playing back to the guard his own slow paced impertinence until the returned insult was unmistakable and his complexion had gone brick coloured. Then, very slowly, summoning a servant across a crowded room, she raised her arm.

She had moved a little and Catriona now had a better fuller view. Her face was long and strong with a firm clear jaw line and a high forehead. Her nose was long too and perfectly straight; her eyes were narrow, wide-set, which together with her hair lent a slight but distinct touch of the equine, though (and Catriona could see now *how* un-English was this woman's style) nothing of the horsey. Still her hair had the thick long silkiness of a mane – toned with a dozen different greys swept straight back from the high hair line, groomed to a follicle and tied (deliberately? defiantly?) with a red ribbon far too young for her age.

Her age. It was a surprise. Catriona had made a rough calculation in favour of middle age, but this was a face that had left that far behind. Her skin, tight with face lifts, had taken in the sun on too many fashionable beaches – it was worn and tense and lined. She was well into her sixties yet, after the surprise of that clothed body, there was little attempt at concealment. She wore a very minimum of make-up.

"Taken," she said. "Yes they are. By me."

Catriona thrilled to the expression which the woman turned upon the guard. Perhaps it was a part of being Scots but to Catriona it was sublimely un-English. It took even Penelope a little time to warm up to a confrontation with authority; after all darling one had to be absolutely *sure* that the peasants really meant to be beastly. But here there was nothing of the apologetic deprecating politeness which the English controlling classes guiltily use on those notionally less fortunate than themselves. The woman looked at the guard as if he were a fly foolish enough to have landed on the edge of her jar of cold cream. She said, "Look if you like."

Her raised hand had produced a definite result. Standing beside her was a black man in a bottle green chauffeur's uniform. He must have come from the rear of the carriage silently and at speed. Although over six feet he looked shorter for his body was deep and wide with an evenly spread solidity of muscle, thick all the way through with a neck like a chest and wrists like Harrods hams. Bouncer, thought Catriona. Ex-heavyweight. He smiled a gold-toothed smile and extended a sheaf-ful of tickets. The guard took them and backed away, looked at them, returned them gingerly at arm's length.

"Obliged," said the black man.

The guard made one more desperate play. "May I ask why Madam has reserved four seats?"

"No," she said. "You may not."

The black man raised himself on the balls of his feet. He no longer smiled. "You go."

The guard went. As he passed through the pneumatic doors separating the carriages Catriona heard him mutter something about money and selfishness. The black man went back to his seat.

What a woman, thought Catriona. What a woman!

And then she smiled at Catriona – a small smile of acknowledgement; of complicity in mischief. Catriona felt warm, flattered. Just as abruptly the woman turned back to the view. Catriona felt a slight twinge of disappointment; still she understood disliking as she did instant intimacies, journey bores who cannot be shaken off. Besides, anyone who bought four seats must naturally want to be left alone.

By now Catriona was growing drowsy. She had simply

forgotten how tired she was, how much the last few days had taken out of her. Marvellous woman she thought, drifting. So independent. So in command. Like a racehorse only momentarily stabled. No. Too old for that. You didn't think of racehorses as old. Not in that way . . . Still there was so much *in* that woman that Catriona would wish for herself . . . Why didn't they show girl children different models? Older women instead of all those simpering little boy-tickling-men-pleasing-pop-star-popsies. A woman's images in youth should be of age . . . Except that in that face wasn't there . . . perhaps . . . what was it? Something also to do with money. Disappointment? . . . or worse and less than disappointment – discontent? . . . Just before Catriona fell asleep an odd fact which she had recorded earlier and shelved now returned. They had something in common. They were alike. For like Catriona the woman had no luggage. Something in common then. Something odd yet also oddly comforting. She murmured to the rhythm of the rails "Lady Leather has no luggage," and fell asleep to the beat.

The first class dining car was almost empty. Catriona had a table to herself. She was glad. This was the second lunch sitting and if you didn't mind the staff clearing up around you, you could stay at your table all the way to Edinburgh drinking, smoking, adjusting to the craggy newness of the Scottish scenery in solitude. Catriona needed the solitude – needed the time to adjust the approaching beauty of Edinburgh to the killing bungalowed boredom of her own childhood. There is a problem in pulling up your roots and then denying as far as you could the place where they had been planted; it is a process that leaves you uncertain and guilty and defensive. Oh and envious too; let's not forget envy. She felt a sour taste in her mouth. The sardine salad was actually quite good but she pushed it away. The wine was not so good and over-refrigerated but it was wine. She took a gulp and lit a cigarette. Outside Northumberland was speeding by. Suddenly Lindisfarne, girdled with mist, stood up out of the grey hard sea. Getting closer all the time she thought – nearer to not-home.

For years she had not gone back; long stupid years when she tried to pretend that she wasn't Scots at all, tried to lose her accent until Penelope taught her how to modify it and told her not to be an idiot. When the very thought of going back gave her the dry heaves. It had been worse after Kirstie's death. Catriona did not make the journey for the funeral. She told herself that since she had failed Kirstie in life she had better stay away from her in death, but really was too honest to believe her own telling. Catriona simply did not want to be reminded of her earlier self, did not want to go to the place where it had lived, had waited like an unclaimed pledge in a pawn shop, a piece of left luggage perpetually uncollected.

"You don't mind."

Catriona looked up. Although the dining car was almost empty Lady Leather was easing herself into the seat opposite Catriona. Half a dozen tables further back the black heavyweight sat at an empty table. What *is* he, thought Catriona? Chauffeur? Servant? Bodyguard?

"No," said Catriona. "Not at all. Please."

The woman no longer wore her cape. The sleeves of her blouse were rolled up to show long finely fingered hands; it was a shock to see that they were dotted with liver spots. Catriona smiled and the woman gave back the same conspiratorial smile that she had used earlier. Catriona noticed the little folds along her neck. It isn't fair thought Catriona. She doesn't want to be old. Why should she be old?

The steward had arrived at their table. "I'm sorry madam. I'm afraid we've stopped serving."

The woman raised her arm. The black man walked down the car and stood at the woman's shoulder. The steward paled. "Busboy. Twenty."

The black man took out a twenty pound note and gave it to the woman who placed it flat on the table. Catriona noticed that her hand trembled.

"That's all Busboy," and as the black man returned to his seat, "Coffee. Twenty. No change."

The steward took the money as gracefully as greed would permit. "I'll see what I can do madam."

"No," said the woman. "Just get the coffee."

But as the steward retreated and Catriona was about to say something admiring about the shortest way with officialdom she saw the woman's eyes close as if in pain and her hands develop an added tremble.

"Aren't you feeling well? Here have some of my wine while you're waiting for the coffee."

Catriona pushed her glass across the table. Instead of saying a normal thank you, opening her eyes the woman stared intensely at Catriona as if trying to discover something in her face, and said, "You'll do."

She took a gulp from Catriona's glass. Her shaking hand set the rings on her fingers banging against the glass.

"I'm Alice. I have occasional trouble with my nerves. It comes with being rich." She was still staring intently at Catriona. "You must think me a very impertinent . . . " (it took an effort to produce the next word) "old woman."

"Actually," said Catriona, "I think you have the most tremendous style."

As if in recognition of a truth rather than in the acknowledgement of a compliment Alice lifted one hand to her forehead and shakily smoothed her already smooth hair. She said, "And you are the only other woman on this train who knows how to dress."

Catriona felt a warm glow, a flush of pleasure. "I'm flattered."

"Don't be. It's the truth." Approval, thought Catriona. That's why she's been staring at me.

The steward arrived with the coffee. He looked worried as to what extra the payment of twenty pounds might entail. Alice acted. "Just put it there. Don't stand about."

The steward left with an uneasy look cast in Busboy's direction. The hand that held the glass now held the coffee cup. It still shook. Alice drank and made a face. "The British still can't make coffee."

This gave Catriona an opening. "But you're English aren't you?" Before the woman had begun to speak Catriona had half thought she might be some species of intensely up-market American. Yet her accent was undeniably upper class English though of an earlier derivation than the drawling extravagance of Esmond or the buoyant affectation of Penelope. Yet the rhythms, like the diction, weren't typical.

"I was born in British India," said Alice. "I've lived a long time away from here. America mostly. But you're Scots?"

"Yes. I'm Scots."

"What's your name?"

"Catriona Lomax."

"That's a nice name. Catriona that is."

"Thank you."

"It suits you."

Catriona felt slightly embarrassed. The conversation was straying towards formality and she wanted her contact with this special woman to remain special. Yet what came out next was travelling companion cliché.

"So why are you going to Edinburgh?"

The woman looked at her with a polite sharpness as if this were a real and testing question.

Catriona floundered. "I mean do you have family . . . "

The woman didn't speak but as she shook her head slowly she continued to stare as if she looked for something in Catriona's face.

" . . . or business?"

The spell broke. She smiled down into her coffee. It was a sad smile.

"Business. Yes. That's what I have. I have business."

It was Alice's turn to ask about Catriona. Instead she kept staring at her coffee as if speech itself had suddenly failed.

Catriona wanted to help. She said, "Look. My favourite part of the journey."

The train was on the Scottish border passing through Berwick. Red roofs, grey stone houses clustered across the river, spilled out towards the frozen beach and the wild sea. The rain, picked up by the wind (there was always wind here), hissed round the train, twisting the fishing boats on the estuary.

"Get off the train."

"I'm sorry?"

Catriona turned politely away from the view. But she hadn't misheard.

"You have to get off the train."

The woman/Lady Leather/Alice wept. Tears made ladders down her thin lined cheeks and fell on her blouse, darkening it in streaks like the streaks in her hair. Her trembling hands reached out and seized Catriona's.

"What do you mean? I don't know what you mean. What do you mean get off the train?"

Catriona tried to pull away and couldn't. Her hands were

held in a trembling vice.

"The train doesn't *stop* anywhere . . . please . . . " Did it stop? Didn't it?

At the back of the dining car Busboy had risen.

"What do you *mean* get out?" Catriona pulled away. Alice fell forward on the table. Catriona scrambled out of her seat. "I'm going to Edinburgh."

"Don't. Turn around. Take the train back. Anything. I know."

"Know?" Catriona retreated down the car. "Know what?"

Alice had risen. Alice was coming after her, arms outstretched.

"Lady," said Busboy.

"I know . . . "

Busboy was beside her. With gentle dignity he took her arm. She started to nod; to say without saying that Busboy was right.

"My dear," she said, "my dear, you have to forgive me."

It was as if a rift had opened in the woman's personality, now some sudden alchemy closed it. The wave of hysteria had passed. She stood up straight. Her body seemed to rearrange itself inside her clothes.

"You see . . . you have to understand – there are some things in life you can't control."

"Oh yes," said Catriona. "Yes."

"Lady. You come."

Catriona watched Busboy lead her away, then sat down heavily. How awful, she thought. How mad, how sad, and how just like my current luck. The woman she had so admired departs with her keeper. So much for the value of her admiration, so much for that as the beginning of something. Well, thought Catriona, the only thing you can say in favour of the journey is that for a while it took your mind off your own problems.

Until the Waverley Station. Catriona disliked the pointless rush to disembark; she hated being jostled just as she hated being promiscuously touched by strangers, by casual acquaintances. So she waited until the other passengers had gathered up their luggage and left. Only then did she descend from the train.

The platform was empty except for Busboy. He stood there, wearing a chauffeur's cap now, squarely in her path. When he saw her he saluted and waited stolidly for her to approach. When Catriona was standing in front of him he held out his hand. It contained a small slip of paper folded over many times. She took it.

Busboy said, "You be mindful of the Lady. She's had pain. You don't add to it none. She want you, you come."

Catriona took the paper and began the slow unfolding process. It was a page from a Van Cleef and Arpels diary. The writing was hurried, jagged, the ink splodged. It took time to read. She turned the thin rich paper in her hand, held it up to the light and read aloud.

"I am not insane only distressed. Please come to me this evening at the bar in the George Hotel. I think you will want to." It was signed Alice Despard.

"I'll be there."

"Oh I'm aware of that," said Busboy politely.

# 25

Catriona was tense all the way. It took twenty minutes before she came face to face with the sources of the past which she had so fiercely attempted to deny.

The taxi left the station and swung out on to Telford's magnificent bridge. The beauty of the city's great contrast – the medieval town hunched around the castle, poised upon the hill behind, the great Augustan new town spread below across the plain – went begging. Catriona shivered. She was up against it. She had no comfort. The city seemed hostile. The Auld Toon looked as if it might launch itself upon the New and devour it for smugness. Before it had been cleaned up, just before her own birth, before the great tourist clean up, the gutters of the Auld Toon's slums had run with Saturday night blood. Now the violence had been exported; the barbarians were held off in the housing estates that ringed the city – banished to drug-infested high rise vertical caves stationed beyond the city's invisible gates. Yet for Catriona there was still menace; past and present had combined to put violence in the air.

The taxi ran the length of Princes Street, took a short cut through Charlotte Square, headed out along the Queensferry Road. By Orchard Brae the great Georgian capital, the watch fobbed uncle of Bath and Cheltenham, had been left behind. At Blackhall she passed her childhood bungalow. She looked away. Now they were in ugly monotonous granite territory though in less than a mile the big boring villas of Kirstie's Barnton would proclaim their prosperous superiority. But Catriona wasn't going anywhere like that.

The taxi turned right off the wide Queensferry Road, wound past a series of little fantasies – past Cosie Nook and Bide-a-Wee, essays in suburban granite schlock-and-squat – until she told the driver to stop at the end of a potholed cul-de-sac with a narrow footpath at its left hand corner. She let the taxi go and headed for the footpath. She had not been here since her adolescence. She could have got it wrong. She walked on from memory. Memory was right.

The footpath ran along the railway track. Disused now. The branch line into Edinburgh had closed long ago; the level crossing gates were long removed. In the distance, across a mile of tufted grass and empty Tennants lager cans the hideous council estate of Pilton shambled skywards. Here genteel Edinburgh had deposited its social conscience and walked away as quickly as possible.

Out of a long terrace of railwayman's cottages only four had survived demolition. (Catriona supposed that the tenants had found some legal way of hanging on.) Three were boarded up; windows filled with breeze blocks, roof tiles removed, crumbling pebble dash façades smeared with desultory graffiti. Her father (or the first man to claim parenthood) had been born in one of these, a railway labourer's son. Once upon a time the virtuous working classes had struggled for such a place – the decency of a whole house as against the miscellaneous horror of the Scottish slums where huge families squeezed into segments of tenement floor in vertical cold water villages. Escape was everything. First from the tenement, then from the cottage and finally from the shame of a lower class past. So with her parents: the flight to the dead bungalow had been a moral positive, an *ab initio* good. With that knowledge Catriona stood now surrounded by the vestiges of those roots which her gentility-seeking mother had so vehemently repressed; which had decayed into this stretch of deserted nothing at the end of a disused railway track.

The fourth cottage remained occupied. The only definite relative that Catriona knew of lived here – Aunt Jessie, her father's older sister, railwayman's widow and, to Catriona's mother, an embarrassment, a discardable social nuisance.

Catriona pushed open the little wooden gate. The path of paving stones was split apart by weeds; the roses ran to seed.

Age, she thought.

A younger Jessie, aflame with proletarian pride, would not have tolerated neglect any more than she had tolerated the embourgoisement of her weak gardening brother and his family. In her entire youth Catriona could remember only a handful of meetings with Jessie, each defined by Mr Lomax's shuffle-footed guilt at his inability to handle two women – Jessie and Catriona's mother – at war. They had hated and despised each other. To each the other was the class enemy.

Perhaps that was why Catriona had not questioned Jessie before. She wasn't sure. Being sneered at was certainly a deterrent. To approach socialist Jessie with dreams of a rich Visitor was merely to invite scathing rejection. Besides it was simply inconceivable that Catriona's mother would not have successfully hidden her adultery from a woman she loathed. Equally had Jessie known of that adultery it was inconceivable that she would not have brazened it forth.

But that was then, and now was now. The case was altered. And the difference consisted in James Tar whose world seemed to have so much in political common with Jessie's. Besides – quite simply – the game had changed and in that changed game Jessie was all that Catriona had. For even the chance of information Jessie was all she had to go to.

The bell worked but it took a long time for Jessie to answer. Age had bent her into a question mark. She looked closer to ninety than eighty. Her hair had grown thin and wispy – turned to the texture of a baby's fuzz. Through a stroke, or perhaps arthritis, one hand had turned in on itself. The fingers almost touched the palm. Time seemed to be twisting her into the foetal position in preparation for a second darker womb. From chest height she peered up at Catriona with rheumy eyes. Catriona felt a flush of embarrassment pass across her face.

"Jessie," she said, "its been . . . You won't remember . . . "

For a moment Jessie stared out uncomprehendingly, her eyes dull behind a film of grease. Then her lids flicked like a lizard's on a rock and her eyes shone black and bright.

"Oh aye," she said. "It's you that never comes."

"I've come now," said Catriona. "Can I talk to you?"

"What else would ye do? Come ben the hoose."

Catriona remembered that one of her mother's most persistent disapprovals had been of Jessie's determination to use what was, depending on how you looked at it, authentic Scots dialect or illiterate urban slang – the yobspeak of a more romanticised and earlier proletariat. So ben the hoose it was but ben wasn't far. A tiny hall led into a tiny sitting room. Stiflingly hot, it smelt of embrocation and animals and old age. The lumpy ancient furniture was covered in coloured crocheted blankets. The thirties gas fire popped and hissed. Catriona could feel Jessie's gaze on her as she took it all in.

For there was, after all, one truly remarkable feature. Despite all the badges of age and class, despite the smell of Friars Balsam and the budgerigar in its cage, despite the copies of *People's Friend* and *Home Notes*, the room was nothing less than a shrine to socialism. The walls were covered from floor to ceiling with the insignia of the Labour Movement. Here – framed in *passe-partout*, captured on postcard or box Brownie or newsprint, tinted the colour of a lung under mustard gas – were Lenin and Shinwell and Keir Hardie and John Burns. Here, spilling on to the mantelpiece, was the female section. Catriona could recognise Beatrice Webb and Krupskaya and La Passionaria and even Daisy, Countess of Warwick. Further along there was a framed cigarette card set of the first Labour Cabinet minus Ramsay MacDonald.

Louis, Catriona thought, what would you make of this?

Catriona turned around; she knew that Jessie had been watching her. Patronise me, said the old woman's look, at your peril.

Now Jessie lowered her half-hoop body into a chair next to the budgerigar's cage. The effort hurt. The eyes closed. She dribbled a little, lifted her hooked hand awkwardly to wipe it. She dribbled some more. Left it alone. Fell silent. It struck Catriona that Jessie had simply forgotten her presence. Catriona's guilt at her own callousness and selfishness gave way to panic. What if Jessie were senile? What if she didn't understand, wasn't able to . . .

But eyes flicked open. The lizard look was back and it moved up and down Catriona's body taking in hair, make-up, shoes, clothes. Catriona suddenly remembered the cut and colour of her Bond Street dress.

"Fine feathers," she had managed her mouth into a purse of disapproval. "Ye look a trout."

Normally Catriona would have snapped back. Particularly since, like many unhappy children, she did not necessarily revere age. In her experience a nasty old person was simply a nasty young person with a few extra miles on the clock. Old age was a condition, not an excuse. Yet now she felt – all other sins of omission apart – guilty of a most absolute breach of good manners. In this chapel to Labour, where the union memorabilia had become Holy Relics, she felt like a loutish brazen infidel whose dress and presence constituted an offence, who should have known enough and had the common decency to stay away. Still, she was here and here for a purpose. She *had* to stay. She started to apologise. Jessie ignored her and started to talk again, this time with a definite sneer.

"Catri-OH-na Lomax. You that was Katie. Aye no doubt *Mrs* Lomax . . . (she leant heavily on the words with a bad imitation of the anglophile Morningside drawl) "*Miss-is Lohmex* would be proud of you if she'd been spared. Mind" (a little cackle, more spittle) "she'd have been jealous forbye. You've grown beyond what she wanted. She wanted respectability, not red dresses. Aye altogether too good a specimen of the boorjoyzee?"

Catriona felt that she was being looked at like a larger budgerigar; something brightly plumed, good only to do tricks on a perch.

"You make it sound like a Russian chimp."

"What's that?"

"Bourgeoisie."

"Oh I do beg your pardon. Oh I do. That would be an English joke. Aye ye were ever a pert girl. I mind well your bitter wee face. But I preferred the look of you then."

The room was hot. Catriona had come a long way. She hated condescension. The words came out before she could stop them.

"You haven't exactly changed for the better."

The thing was said. And Jessie didn't seem to mind it.

"Ah well," she said reasonably, "I'm dying. What's your excuse?"

Catriona shook her head. "I've never been much good at excuses. I can't make myself believe them."

Jessie nodded in slow approval. "Aye. A pert child but a truthful one. Truth's best."

Guilt began to sweep over Catriona. "Are you really . . . are you very ill?"

Jessie tut-tutted death away. "I've a bad case of Anno Domini. It's just to be expected. There's no pain in wearing down. No nor shame either. So what is it that you've come here for, Catriona-that-was-Katie?"

Catriona had nothing planned. She had no idea where to begin. Perhaps the deep end was best. She said, "It's about my mother. It's about someone . . . about someone called James Tar. He says . . . He says he's my father."

Jessie began to pull herself up from the chair. Her face twisted in pain. Catriona took a step forward – then stopped herself. In this territory pride had declared a hands off policy. Something creaked. Catriona hoped it was only the chair. Jessie now stood as upright as she could.

"I'll boil a kettle. Ye'll have biscuits. Though they're nothing but shop made."

Insults and biscuits. Demotic Scotland, Catriona thought. You would probably be insulted. You would certainly be given tea.

"Wee Jimmie Tar?" Jessie chuckled. "Oh I knew him well enough. He was a larrikin right enough. But all for the Struggle, all for the Movement, that was Jimmie. Oh he was a brave lad. But in the end he couldnae settle. That was maybe when he got a taste for the drink. Aye there were a lot like that. Just never quite the same again." She sighed. "Call it Spain."

Jessie had left her biscuit to soak in the tea cup. It had disintegrated. Her eyes had drifted again – had gone to visit some cloudy past far away from the hissing gas fire and the budgerigar and the anxiety of Catriona's questioning.

Catriona felt at bursting point. She wanted to make demands, to shout questions, but she was terrified of tilting Jessie over into full senility. She was afraid that somewhere in the randomness of Jessie's recollections the matter of her birth would be overlooked. She leaned forward.

"Jessie. Please Jessie. I need you to go on. It's just you see that I have no one else to ask."

"Ask what?"

God, Catriona thought, but then click! The eyes refocused. Is she putting it on? *Could* she be? Could she be playing with me, testing me? And how, in any case, could I tell? There was a little smile on Jessie's withered lips.

"Your legs are young. Up on that stool with you. In the corner press. Top shelf. And mind ye're careful how ye bring it down."

The box was marked SPAIN. Catriona looked inside. Then she gawped down at the bent old woman beneath her. "I

never knew you were in Spain."
"Ye never asked," said Jessie.

Photographs. Clippings. Brochures. Tickets. Menus. Maps. But mostly photographs. Jessie narrated, shuffling in and out to the kitchen for more hot water, losing the strand and then recovering while Catriona clung on trying to remember everything.

. . . So she hadn't met Jimmy till Spain for Jimmy was from Glasgow and she from Edinburgh . . . though she'd heard of him through the Party and what with him no more than a wee lad and still on every rostrum he could find. Well, how he'd got to Spain at his age past the fascist authorities and then joined up, it was a pure miracle . . . of course she was older, Jessie, by a lot, and seven years a qualified nurse at the Edinburgh Infirmary when the chance came. A special Ambulance Unit was being founded and formed in Edinburgh . . . not mind that it was the only one but it was a grand act of giving and how the people responded to the Cause . . .

(The Cause. There was a lot about the magnificence of the cause but Jessie became too excited, incoherent. She sat for a moment quietly, eyes glazed, a handkerchief held up to stem the dribble till she was strong enough to start again.)

. . . And Jimmy was out there already and they met when he and some of the other Scots lads were wounded when the International Brigades had stood and saved Madrid . . . and the courage . . .

(Jessie was crying now; slow old tears that she brushed fiercely aside with her hooped hand.)

The Edinburgh Ambulance had been to and fro, treating the dying in the streets, taking the wounded to hospital . . . Aye it was terrible and wonderful at once . . . Madrid. It was the first time for bombing a city like that. The first of all the blitzes . . . but the Madrileños digging away and singing back at the shells . . . The University City away to the West was plain devastated . . . oh, here it is. Here we are . . . After Madrid. On the way down to Valencia.

Catriona took the photograph.

Somewhere near the sea. No city. No evidence of fighting. An ambulance stops by the sand. For the sun, for the view, for a little peace-in-wartime, for the photograph.

Jessie explains. Jessie isn't in the photograph. Jessie held the camera. Jessie points. There's Jimmy. Aye that's Jimmy right enough. A little sinewy man with almost white-fair hair (Catriona's hand goes upwards, touches her own hair). His shirt is off. He enjoys the sun. There are taller men either side of him. The taller men have their arms around his shoulders. Aye says Jessie there's the Irish lad Patrick. She squints up at Catriona. Catriona says oh. And wasn't he, says Jessie, the great lad for spouting the workers' struggle though him with the big house and a member of the upper class. Patrick and Jimmy stepped in to drive when the original drivers were killed. Jessie scratches her nose. The other lad with the dark curly hair – she can't now mind his name. Nor the woman in the corner drying her hair who'd just been for a swim, or a wash in the sea more like for water was like gold. No. She's old and she can't remember their names.

Jessie looked at Catriona as if the photograph should produce some direct effect; as if Catriona was supposed to ask something. Catriona didn't know what to say. Jessie then spoke slowly and deliberately as if enunciating a lesson which Catriona had failed to understand.

"Ye've no idea of the nobility. For it's all forgotten now."

Catriona was moved. She felt guilty but she was getting nowhere. "No, Jessie. Perhaps I . . . "

Jessie cut in abruptly. "Has Jimmy been to see you?"

What could she say? Yes? No? In a sense? Maybe? "He sent me a message."

"Do ye have a paper?"

"What? What paper?"

"A writing? Something written?"

"You mean from Jimmy?"

"A paper?"

"No."

What the hell did she mean? But Jessie had lost all interest. Her eyes had gone far away. She crooned wordlessly to the budgerigar.

Catriona felt desperate. "Please Jessie. I don't understand how he could say I'm his daughter. I don't see how it's possible. Can't you help me at all?"

Jessie's eyes were alive again. What *was* this? Senility as flirtation?

"Don't you see what I'm saying?"

The little smile returned. "Oh aye," said Jessie. "It's a wise dog that knows its own father."

"That's a cliché. Jessie please . . . "

"It's a good Scots saying. How am I to know what happened in another woman's bed?"

"Well if you don't know all you . . . "

"I know this. If Jimmy Tar says he's your father then there's a reason."

"For God's sake Jessie I don't want reasons – I want the truth. The truth's best. Didn't you just say that?"

Jessie raised her crab shaped hand. "There's no God, Catriona-that-was-Katie." She turned her bad hand in a circle to take in the room's four walls. "There's only this. And as for truth," she made the same curling motion for the second time, "there's only this as well."

Catriona felt like screaming. The room's heat, the smell of linctus, didn't help one bit. She couldn't respond to the courage it must take to wait here for death with only this flinty philosophy for comfort. All she could feel was a claustrophobia of opinion, a deliberate narrowness that left no space for her own plight. Though as for that what did Catriona expect; she had made no attempt to see the world Jessie's way – let alone enter it and elbow out some living space for its crushed inhabitants.

Catriona dug her nails into her palms. Calm. Be calm. She remembered one of Schmidt's rare morsels of business psychology. "Someone says you can't have something. Most people go away you unnerstan'? You don't. You stand there. You just go on asking. Ask ask ask. Maybe there's a way. Surely you can fix it. Think again . . . Nine times out of ten they get tired. They give you it. Believe me."

"Jessie. You knew my parents. You knew things I couldn't have known. You must have. You must be able to tell me something."

Jessie had started once more to dribble. She sucked at her lower lip but when she looked up she had again the lizard look.

"You mean," she said deliberately, "could your mother have done it with Jimmy?"

"Yes."

"If they met I never knew of it. Not that I saw Jimmy more than a dozen times after the war. When were you born?"

"1951."

"I've no memory of him here then. Not that it signifies. They'd hardly have asked my permission."

She scooped up some melted biscuit with her spoon using the twisted hand as if insisting on the egalitarian rights of each limb. Yet all the time her eyes watched Catriona carefully.

"But in any case Jessie surely it couldn't be possible? Not him and her? Not ever?"

Jessie licked her spoon but her eyes went on watching. "Ye may be right. Tar the larrikin and her as tight as a button boot. To say nothing of politics. Still, I was a trained nurse in time of war and I've seen stranger things. A prim wee girl – wee Missie Mouse – and then up with the skirt. Not that I'm against revolutionary promiscuity if it serves an end."

"What end?"

Jessie looked at her blankly. "The Revolution of course." As if there were only one.

"And that's all you can tell me?"

"That's all I have."

Bowed and twisted as she was Jessie insisted in taking Catriona the few painful steps to the door. Watching her move brought back Catriona's guilt. Here I am, she thought with disgust, nagging away at this poor old gallant woman, thinking only of myself.

"Jessie. There must be something I could do to help you . . . to make life a little easier."

"Ah wheesht. East West hame's best. I'm no sae housebound. There's wee student laddies that come to run my messages."

Catriona translated. "To do your shopping. I suppose it's voluntary."

Jessie gave a cackle. "Oh aye voluntary work for an old volunteer."

"I'm sorry to have been such a nuisance . . . "

"Wheesht. Away."

" . . . but it was very interesting even if you didn't know anything about . . . about me."

"Of course," said Jessie, "I never knew where Mrs Lomax got all that money."

# 26

Money, thought Catriona as she walked past Randolph Crescent. I should have thought about the money. How could I have been so stupid? Everything in the end comes down to money. Money is the system of exchange by which human beings have to live. Money is the spoor by which we hunt the human animal.

Mr Lomax had been a railway clerk. Steady job – low salary – no tips. Catriona's mother had never worked. There had been no inheritances. No one on either side had possessed anything to leave. So where *had* it all come from – the money for the things she had despised as well as those things that had sent her on her way; the bungalow, the little car, the private schools, the insurance policies?

Because Catriona's schoolfriends had always been so much richer than herself, she had simply never thought of her parents as unreasonably affluent. Until Jessie told her, she had no idea that the money trail stretched back to her birth. There was the layette, and the hundred pound perambulator but most of all ("aye and all on your father's wee clerk's pay") the expensive private clinic to which she now hurried. Without any clear sense of direction Catriona Lomax seeks a rendezvous with her birthplace, and seeks perhaps the evidence of the Visitor's existence.

It was early evening. The autumnal dusk had set in fast. In Scotland summer nights come reluctantly in a thin pale light no darker than a cloud. But when winter approaches the nights draw in black and early. Between the tall curlicued street lamps there were pools of darkness. As Catriona reached the street's end and turned the lights of the Georgian New Town set up their reflected sparkle on the Water of Leith.

Here the tall houses had been subdivided into offices. Catriona stopped before a small brass plate that read Ambo Clinic. As the yellow pages had said the place was still in some sort of medical use.

She pressed the heavy brass doorbell. What was she going

to say? Good afternoon . . . oh, evening . . . silly me . . . Well anyway I was born here so I just thought I'd pop in here on the off chance that you might have some thirty-eight-year-old files so I could see who paid my mother's bills. You do? Well isn't that the *nicest* surprise!

There was no reply. She thought it an odd way to run a clinic; presumably the sick had to be admitted before they could be treated. The wind was cold. She set about belabouring the doorbell. Eventually and slowly the door began to open.

Catriona had been expecting a white starched medical receptionist but what she actually got was a scrawny woman devoid of teeth aged God knows what dressed in a Woolworth's grey nylon overall, holding a bottle of industrial disinfectant. She stared at Catriona, shook her spavined head from side to side and gave a sigh of deep vexation.

"You another one?" she said.

"Yes," Catriona said.

"So ye didnae get the message?"

"Message?" said Catriona. "No."

"So ye've an appointment?"

"Yes," said Catriona. Heaven knew it was odd to find herself again appreciating Schmidt's training. (You want to get in enough you say anything. Later on you say some misunderstanding sure sorry. If they throw you out they would have thrown you out anyway. Life is too short. You want to get in, get in. You take what's on offer.)

The woman jerked her toothless head from side to side as if Catriona was one more recalcitrant stain in the path of her mop but she made way all the same, though she clearly wanted acknowledgement of the world's marketplace selfishness.

"It's no right," she said, "them all going. And me for the door with my own work to do."

"No," said Catriona, and tried to look as dumb and health worried and unobservant as possible, for what she saw all around her in the large marble floored hall were signs of an enterprise under dismantlement. A succession of laundry baskets were piled high against the walls. Before them stood ranks of filing cabinets, their drawers pulled out and piled separately on the floors. In one corner a heap of mattresses reached half way to the ceiling.

"Ye'd best wait here. Doubtless he'll be to send you away in his own time. For," and a vicious Scots happiness dawned on her countenance. "Ye'll get no satisfaction here."

The woman muttered her way off stage through a green baize door that gave a glimpse of kitchen.

Double doors dominated the hall. Catriona opened them. She found herself in a consulting room heavily carpeted to the point of utter hush. It had been stripped bare. The carpet showed heavy marks where the furniture had been removed. In the middle of the room a tall bald swarthy middle-aged man in a fat cat silk suit stood stuffing a white lab coat into a crocodile skin briefcase. He was in a hurry. He was worried. He was not pleased to see Catriona.

"How did *you* get in?"

Catriona thought this was a good time to be girlie. She opened her eyes wide, fluttered a hand in the direction of the kitchen and the unhelpful help. "I'm sorry . . . I . . . "

"You shouldn't be here." He sounded indeterminately foreign. Catriona bit her lip and made her eyes wider.

"What do you think this is," he let his raised eyebrows include the room. "Business as usual?"

Catriona shook her head from side to side. Dumb bunny meets an empty room.

The woman who had admitted Catriona came in. She wore a coat and carried a basket. "Ah'm off, Doctor."

"Yes. Yes." The Doctor was nervous. He had trouble with the clasp on his briefcase. The woman gave Catriona a look which combined loathing with disapproval and went out. Catriona heard her footsteps in the hall and then the bang of the big front door. The Doctor turned to Catriona.

"Didn't you listen to the answering service?"

The man opened a cupboard, pulled out what looked like an overnight bag, but his eyes were on Catriona – still looking dumb.

"For heaven's sake" (worry made him exasperated, aggressive) "you were supposed to *telephone*. Then you would have got the *answering service* to say we were stopping. Don't you see? I can't help you."

"You can't?" At drama school Catriona had possessed a single gift. She could make herself cry. Now she filled her curious green eyes with tears.

"I thought you could."

The Doctor was impressed – no doubt about it – but he was also, she now saw, frightened.

"I tell you I can't. You have to go now. Me too. I have to get out of here."

Catriona let a tear do the rolling.

"You can't be that far gone anyway." His eyes were on Catriona's abdomen. "Who sent you? No. Don't tell me. I don't want to know. Go back. That's all you can do. Ask for them to find someone else. That's all. You have to go. Here. For the fare."

She looked down. He had pressed a hundred pounds into her hand. She nodded, retreated from the room tearful, inarticulate, grateful.

Catriona made as much noise as possible going down the hall. She reached the front door, opened it, banged it noisily and slipped back across the hall. Holding her breath, praying the hinges were oiled, she pushed open the door of the Ladies lavatory. No noise. She crossed the carpeted floor and crouched behind the large armchair that faced the vanity unit. Don't breathe, she thought. Don't cast a shadow. There's no reason for him to come in here. She didn't really believe herself – then she heard footsteps in the hall. A light switch snapped down. The big front door banged shut.

And the house and Catriona were completely in the dark.

Catriona was afraid. Afraid *of* the dark. Afraid *in* the dark. Not more than most people but enough in a superstitious way (dark as woman's enemy, in from the garden at dark said Mother in case the bogeyman comes calling) – enough in a practical way (dark as woman's enemy, dark the rapist's mantle). It was no use trying to lose her imagination on this landing of this house in this particular darkness.

The place where babies had been born – her own birthplace – had switched roles to become an abortion clinic. Sick joke time. Turned turtle to snatch rabbits; she snapped down on the silly, frightened, bad taste giggle that almost escaped. She despised hysteria. But then who was there to hear her? The place was empty. Wasn't it?

She started up the beautiful dipping staircase grasping the mahogany balustrade, waiting for her eyes to grow accustomed to the dark. She touched the wall and recoiled at its perfectly ordinary coldness. Ghosts. Penelope believed in ghosts. Louis too? No, Louis favoured some theory about the energy released at death leaving a deposit, a charge. Catriona shrank back. Perhaps these walls were porous with human misery – sunk in, retained like damp. There are no joyful abortions she thought, not even, however defined, the necessary ones. She thought of the misery of all those women . . . And then the foetuses? Did none of their pain and abandonment stay behind here, in a final parody of their rejection, to impregnate this place?

Somehow she made herself move.

At the main landing she could see a little better. She stood and strained her eyes. Straight ahead was the open door of a sluice room. She could see kidney dishes, bottles of disinfectant. She moved on. Swing doors stood wedged open. Through them were two small interconnecting wards. Bed frames were stacked against the walls. She went back on to the landing and up the stairs. On each floor the room arrangement was the same until the very top. Next to the sluice room was a door marked *office*. Beneath that door there showed a small sliver of light.

Catriona stood and looked at it. I am frightened, she thought, but I have come this far. I can't go back so I must go on.

The room was empty but someone had been here before her. The wall cupboards stood open. In the corner a safe door swung on its hinges. The safe was empty; the floor covered in files. A breeze lifted their covers. Catriona looked across the room. The floor length window was open. An iron fire escape stretched down to the back of the house.

"Well," said the high-pitched little-girl sing-song voice behind her. "Aren't you the pretty one."

Catriona jumped backwards and half fell against the window frame.

A massive woman in denim overalls filled the doorway. Her features were sunk in folds of flesh. Somewhere at the back of the flab she had eyes but they were hard to find. Her hair was combat cut, nail-scissors ragged. She was tall, six feet at least. Her rolled up sleeves revealed leg of lamb forearms. She put her big head on one side, simpered and said, "I'm Baby Mary.

What's your name?"

Her voice was terrifying, incongruously sinister, little girl bitsy poo. Dear God thought Catriona. Dear God Almighty what's this?

"Catriona Lomax. I . . . I was looking for the Ladies and . . . "

"No." Baby Mary swung a finger like a chop and waggled it in front of Catriona's nose. "Tell the truth and shame the devil."

Catriona stared at the finger. Her mouth dried up. The woman gave out a whinnying noise – part giggle, part snigger.

"Catriona. Cat got your tongue?"

Catriona dived for the window and its fire escape. She hadn't a chance. With astounding lightness of foot Mary caught her and lifted her clean off her feet. Somewhere far away Catriona's brain told her that this mobile pork barrel was *trained* – a professional of sorts who shook her as easily as Gomez shook a cocktail. She smelt of a bad diet – of grease left to rot at the chip pan's bottom. The great slopes of her face settled into a sneer but the voice was Marilyn Monroe cutesie-breathless.

"Wanted to pee pee did we?"

The meat axe of a hand came up to tap at Catriona's cheekbone. Testing a barometer for accuracy. No, thought Catriona. She's going to kill me. She's going to disfigure me. She's going to break my *face*.

"Tell Mary. Who do you work for? Spit it out."

Catriona spat – straight into Mary's open mouth. Mary let go and punched Catriona expertly just below the ribs. The shock was immense. On her knees, she didn't have the strength to fall any further. Her breath came up in rasps.

"What do you mean work for?"

Mary took a step forward, smiled and cuffed Catriona playfully on the head. Being driven into a brick wall couldn't be worse than this.

"Answer the question dearie."

What did she want to know for? What difference could it make? Mary raised her hand.

"Mr Schmidt. I work for someone called . . . "

She was yanked fiercely upwards, then scooped up under the woman's arm as if she were a parcel and carried out of the office, through the sluice room to the room beyond. It bore the last vestiges of an abortion ward; a trolley, a steel hospital bed surmounted by a pulley mechanism from which sliding stirrups dangled. Catriona twisted, tried to bite into an arm.

"Uh-uh. Mary does her *own* biting."

Catriona landed on the bed and landed hard, the breath she had recovered driven from her. Her eyes had stopped focusing. She heard the pulley clank. Big fat hands clasped her legs and swung them upwards. She felt a stirrup clamp around each foot.

"Now," again the whinny, the thin mincing voice and the thick chip pan smell, "that'll keep you out of mischief. Now we can find out why you're here. We can have an ex-am-in-ation."

Catriona hated the smell. She hated this travesty of abortion. For a moment anger overcame terror. She yelled like a bullied child in a playground.

"Why don't you WASH. Because YOU'RE TOO FAT FOR THE BATH. Because you're too fat EVEN FOR THE SHOWER."

Smack! A red light occupied Catriona's head. "Sticks and stones," trilled Baby Mary.

She managed to open her eyes. Through a haze she saw Mary holding a gin bottle. She took two deep swigs, then brought the bottle to Catriona's lips. She trilled.

"Sticks and stones. Sticks and carrots."

A great gush of gin poured into Catriona's mouth. She had always hated the stuff. The filmy fuel oil texture made her sick and far too quickly drunk. Now she gagged and spat. The stuff kept coming. Dead drunk. Literally. I will choke to death, drunk.

"MARY. STOP IT."

Mary stopped it. Through a blur of pain and gin Catriona saw Madame Despard, with Busboy behind her. She reached out and took Catriona's hand.

"Katie," said Madame Despard. "Katie."

Catriona smiled. She said, "I know who you are."

Madame Despard's hand tightened. "And who am I?"

"I always expected a man you see." Catriona shook her humming head but it wouldn't clear. "But you're the Visitor."

# 27

Busboy can do everything; Catriona thought that – drifting in and out of the gin stupor, being carried down the iron steps blanket wrapped like a casualty, Mary's voice whining an excuse that contained Schmidt's name, the car, the back of Busboy's wide neck as he drove. She slept. She could vaguely remember being carried, up steps this time – Busboy again. He had a sweet scent like camphor wood. When she woke he was there with what saloon keeper Catriona recognised as a prairie oyster – tomato juice, Worcestershire sauce and a raw egg. Catriona slowly lowered her legs from the bed. Her head hurt. She felt terrible.

"The Lady. She say drink."

Catriona drank, shuddered, felt better.

"You know it makes sense," said Busboy. He picked up a large white towelling gown. "We got no shower. You want a full bath maybe?"

Catriona looked around. The room was square, anonymous with dull expensive matching furniture. "Where are we?"

"This one of her places. A Lady place. She got several. This one Mary takes care of. To get away from Despard. She got several all over."

"All over what?"

"The world," said Busboy. "Neighbourhood here is name of Leith."

"Leith!" Catriona thought of the run down docks, the disused tenements and Madame Despard's rich and raddled glamour. "Why Leith?"

"Miss Lomax, you got a whole lot to learn."

"All right," said Catriona. "What was Mary doing there? Why is she Baby Mary?"

Busboy grinned. "Professional name. Mary wrestles. She a little touched. One time she lose a baby. Maybe that was it. She owes the Lady. She loyal to the Lady."

"Tremendous," said Catriona acidly.

"She wanted the files."

"What for?"

"You ask the Lady." Busboy laid down the towelling gown and left on the balls of his boxer's feet.

Catriona rose gingerly. She was glad to be out of her clothes. They smelt of train and fear. The bathroom was large and clinical. She was stiff. The soak helped.

When she came back Busboy was waiting.

"You want clean clothes." It was a statement. He pointed to the large purpose built cupboard that covered one wall. Catriona went to it.

"No," said Busboy. "That side the Lady keeps locked. You try the other side."

Wondering vaguely why anyone should lock a wardrobe, Catriona did what he said.

It was full of clothes; dresses, coats, three shelves of underclothes, even hats and shoes.

She didn't realise until she held the sixth expensive dress. She turned gaping.

"Yes," said Busboy. "She got your size. She always had your size."

Catriona's hands trembled as they moved from hanger to hanger. She started to pull garments from the rack because this had to be wrong. She had been hit on the head. She had gone mad.

There was an outfit in her size for each period of her adult life. None worn. None used. All virgin.

"That's right." Catriona spun around. Busboy had gone. In his place stood Madame Despard. She wore a black silk kimono. Above it her face was white – swathed in cold cream – her dark eyes staring from a mask of white. A figure from a cargo cult. The white goddess dressed in black.

"Once a year from when you were fifteen. Before that children's clothes. In the end I threw them out. A pity. Some of them were damned nice."

Catriona didn't know what to say. She stood there with her arms full of clothes. Finally she said, "Why?"

"Why? Why what?"

"Why everything?"

"There's a lot of that," said Madame Despard. "There's a lot of everything."

"I am not likeable," said Madame Despard. "You have to

understand that."

She applied cold cream to her face. She did it methodically – dab dab dab – her hand went up and down. A ritual. A soothing ritual. A way of keeping calm. Now and again she would clear a little space only to dab more cream, to begin again.

*Understand.* Catriona thought of Robinson. But this was different. This was really to do with her. Out of the nightmare a dream was pushing through. Magic was worthwhile again.

"Also I've made a mess of this. That's what I do you know. Make messes. I shouldn't have come for you. I should have waited."

You should have come for me earlier. You should have come for me long ago. But that too would have to wait.

"I knew you see. When you said Katie. Not Catriona. Katie. But I really think I would have known anyway. By the way you touched me."

Madame Despard's hand stopped its creamy journey. It shook.

So far, despite her greed for knowledge, Catriona had been the one who talked. She couldn't prevent herself. The words had spilled out. So she had taken Madame Despard back to the hysterical whisperings of the bungalow, to the sad evidence of the Coronation biscuit tin with its torn up cards and shredded money. She was about to get to Jessie when Madame Despard had said that she wasn't likeable. She said it twice.

"No. I am not likeable. In some ways I am . . . " (she paused, she thought) "cold."

Now she used one hand to grip the other. The shaking stopped. Catriona wondered how often she had to do that. "You're pretty. Very pretty. It's a lousy world for a woman who isn't. And very often for a woman who is."

Her hand had taken up the cold cream routine again.

"Jimmy," she said. "Have you seen Jimmy? Have you talked to Jimmy?"

Cold, Catriona thought. It is I who feels cold. This exotic woman may be my Visitor but out there Tar is still waiting.

"I . . . no."

"But" (hand up, pat) "he sent you a message?" (down, pat). "He told you?"

"Yes."
"What did he tell you?"
Catriona found she was whispering. "He says he's my father . . . *Is* he?"
"Yes," said Madame Despard. "That he is."
"Oh." Catriona felt the bruise on her head come back to life. She felt dizzy.
"You don't like that?"
"I . . . No . . . No!"
Madame Despard's tone was flat yet tense, as if it tried to steer a course between extremes. Her expression lay back there hidden under white. Perhaps, Catriona thought, this mask is deliberate. She needs to hide.
"Jimmy was something you know. He *did* things. Fought in wars. Shot people. Something . . . Vital . . . What would you prefer? Mr Lomax?"
She thought of fierce, independent Jessie whose blood she no longer shared. "I would prefer the truth." The words were anodyne but Catriona delivered them with force – Jessie's force.
Madame Despard reached out to an octagonal ebony box. Her fingers stuttered through the pile until they clasped a cigarette. Her hand left a smear of cream across the others.
"Your mother," Madame Despard lit her cigarette; it took some time. "Your mother certainly considered an abortion. After all the circumstances of your conception were hardly – convenient. In those days the clinic was mine. One of my interests. It did straightforward gynaecological work but it did abortions too. Legal ones."
Madame Despard exhaled smoke from the totem mask of her face.
"You have no idea, someone of your age, no idea what an unwanted pregnancy was like in those days. Knitting needles, septicaemia, death. Oh there was a legal way all right but only if you had the money. Pay two psychiatrists to say you'd go nuts if you had the child, pay the surgeon and there you were. Pay pay pay. At the clinic we tried to help. My subsidy. We helped a lot of women for nothing. We had some cheap performing psychiatrists. I called them our male clowns."
Helped? Aborted. Helped? "But not my mother?"
"But not your mother." The cold cream caused Madame

Despard's cigarette to smoulder; its smoke flickered for a second with a faint blue light. "In that way. She was getting on. You were her last chance. Otherwise she might never have had a child."

Catriona shook her head. "It's so hard to imagine" (she thought of her mother; buttoned up, bourgeois-tight) "my mother even knowing someone like that."

Madame Despard shrugged. "Sex."

"And my fa . . . Mr Lomax? Did *he* know?"

"Perhaps. I never met the man." There was a dismissive edge of snobbery to Madame Despard's tone. Now it softened. "Your mother meant the best for you. Always." She leaned forward, spilled some ash, stubbed out the cigarette. "That's why Jimmy never knew. He was hardly the ideal father. Anyway Lomax's name is on your birth certificate."

"So he really never knew? Tar?"

"No."

"But he knows now?"

"Yes."

"Who told him?"

"I did."

"*You* did? You told him and not me?"

Madame Despard's hands had begun to shake. "I thought it would come better from him. From your father."

Catriona got up, yanking the towelling gown around her. "Christ. This sounds so normal but it's INSANE."

"Whoever mentioned normality? Don't come to me for that."

Catriona could feel a tide of anger rising in her. In another moment she would fly into a temper. She looked long and hard at the black silked white masked figure who sat across from her . . . There was something between them, some emotional current by which Catriona knew that Madame Despard was holding on to calm by will alone. She had issued her body orders of self control but they had broken down on the way to her right hand. It twitched upwards; she put it to work removing the cold cream from her cheek.

Catriona said, "What is it?"

"Jimmy hasn't talked to you?"

"I told you. No."

"And you don't know?"

"Don't know *what*?"

"I'm Esmond Claremaurice's stepmother."

Catriona's mouth opened and closed in stupefaction. Then ideas raced through her mind. She remembered Theodora's description of Esmond's stepmother. Of course it fitted Madame Despard exactly.

Catriona said, "You knew this. About Esmond and me?"

"Hell no," said Madame Despard. "Didn't have a clue till Jimmy told me. Correction, let me know. I imagine Schmidt arranged it."

"Schmidt!?"

"What else? Bought the club. Stuck you in there. Esmond's a member. You're divine looking. The rest is history. Steered you Esmond's way. Schmidt's not a fool."

But I am, thought Catriona. I really am because I can't follow this. And although a slow red anger was dawning in her – the anger that comes from manipulation – she still kept mentally steady.

Somehow. Somehow did it.

"But what's the point?" She heard herself say it. Actually it sounded quite reasonable. But all she could think of was that her already shameful affaire with Esmond (she thought of Theodora and tried to shut out Esmond's hands) had been additionally, shamefully arranged. She wanted to be angry, to rage, but all that came out was, "Me? Esmond? Schmidt? What? Why?"

"Jimmy will tell you."

And now the anger had a focus, a nodal point, a trigger.

"Jimmy. Always bloody *Jimmy*!"

But although she had to repeat herself Madame Despard talked over Catriona as a parent disregarding a child's tantrums.

"*Esmond*!" She sneered him away. "Schmidt!" She spat him away in a cloud of gelatinated lip salve. "Listen to me. And let Jimmy tell you the rest."

And because Catriona wanted the information she fell silent although anger was in her, waiting for a red and violent dawn.

"Esmond," said Madame Despard, "is a mental and moral irrelevance."

Join the club, thought Catriona. I think so too. But you might at least give me the let out of saying that he's gorgeous.

"Esmond is just a sideshow. It's Schmidt that matters."

Schmidt again. Everyone shits on Schmidt. But for the moment Catriona controlled her red anger.

"But," Madame Despard continued, "you need to know the story.

"Esmond's father, Patrick Claremaurice, was my first husband. He was a drunk. When he died I married a rich man Honoré Despard, a Swiss. He set up a – a sort of charity – called the Despard Foundation. And I had parts of it to play with" (the *play* rolled bitterly off her tongue) "like a good little wifey. The clinic was one of those parts. Then the whole Foundation went to hell in a handcart. What that clinic did was alternate butchery and robbery. Now things have changed. I'm going to get the Foundation back and the clinic with it. You can see how they've packed up and panicked. I sent in Mary first in case there was trouble. I wanted all the files I could get for evidence."

"And?" said Catriona.

"Silly of me," said Madame Despard. "I guess that Schmidt airbrushed them years ago. I never was much of a one for business. Never was much of a one for anything. One last try, that's all I've got."

But Catriona did not wish to discuss Madame Despard's problems. She had her own shame to pursue.

"Esmond?" she said.

"He's a shit," said Madame Despard. "Always was. A shit as a child too. And of course he's male. That helps."

"I know he's a shit. What I want to know is if you told him to stop seeing me?"

For the first time Madame Despard seemed amused. "I didn't."

"You *didn't*?"

Madame Despard snorted. "Good God no. He's a twerp but a girl's entitled to a little fun with the dumb. Still, you're far too good for him."

Catriona felt a flush of pride. Then the nagging questions returned.

"Wait a minute. Why now? Why did you tell Tar now? Why is he coming for me now?"

Madame Despard stood up. "Because now I need you. We need you. With Schmidt."

"WITH SCHMIDT?"

Catriona couldn't believe her ears.

"What has Mr Schmidt got to do with it?"

"Schmidt's evil. Jimmy'll tell you."

"I know him. I work for him."

"Ha. Jimmy'll tell you."

Everything shifted. Everything was tilting. "No," said Catriona. "That can't be right."

"No? Who do you think ran the Foundation like a cash register and the clinic like an abattoir? Who do you think put Esmond Claremaurice in your bed?"

"Stop. I don't believe you. My mother's been dead for eighteen years. Eighteen years when you could have come and told me who I was . . . "

"I couldn't. Because of Schmidt. Jimmy'll tell you."

"And why send me things? It doesn't make a damned bit of sense. You aren't telling me the TRUTH."

Madame Despard's cold cream mask had liquefied in streaks of tears. Catriona could see patches of lined skin – cracked earth under melting snow – but she had no pity. She was very very angry.

"Schmidt . . . " tried Madame Despard.

"Schmidt was the only person who ever helped. Helped me while you were playing your games . . . "

"Jimmy . . . "

A wave of new anger, black anger swept over Catriona. She was being twisted, cheated, deceived – neglected, abandoned, derided. And suddenly she wanted to smash things up, to hurt, to give pain, to repay the harm done to her. And all that was available for hurting was the woman now before her. And instinct told Catriona how to do it. Instinct put the lie into her mouth.

"It's no use saying Jimmy because Jimmy won't tell you anything. Jimmy's dead. Jimmy was murdered on Earls Court Station last Saturday."

Madame Despard was completely still. Still as a stone. Pale as a ghost. She had stopped crying. She shook her head a little and Catriona suddenly had the image of a weary horse refusing a fence.

"I really always do make a mess of things," said Madame Despard.

* * *

Twenty minutes later Catriona changed back into her own clothes and came out of the bathroom just as Busboy burst into the room.

"Where the Lady?"

"I haven't the faintest."

"Jesus. What you done to her?"

The locked half of the closet stood open. The scattered contents could have been a stripper's mail order catalogue. Stockings, garter belts, corsets, huge bouffant wigs . . .

"Come on," said Busboy. "We got no time to spare."

Leith. A tangle of alleys. High derelict warehouses. Presumably there were pubs; the drunks they passed had to come from somewhere. One lay on the ground lapped in his own urine. They were near the river. Catriona could smell dirty water. Busboy jogged on, turning left, right, left again without hesitation. Catriona found it hard to keep up. Twice he stopped briefly to let her rest, then dragged her on again.

"How do you know?" she gasped.

"She always takes the same route."

Busboy, who had become suddenly grammatical, stopped and sniffed the air. Then Catriona caught it too – heavy clinging scent, expensive female scent too heavily applied.

"Come on."

It was dark and difficult to see. An open derelict space of some kind. Piled up rubbish – packing cases, cardboard boxes, tin cans and a wall. Madame Despard and a man were against the wall. The moon came out.

It was a miserable sight. Madame Despard wore a beehive wig of synthetic hair. Her cheap red dress was hitched up at the front and torn away from her shoulders. The black stockings on her thin legs were wrinkled; they looked artificial as if they had been painted on with a large defective brush.

As the man pawed at her Madame Despard's head was back, her eyes closed, her mouth open as if she were reminding herself to breathe. Her face was blank – no passion, no eagerness, no disgust. She might as well have been dead. This was an act of premature necrophilia.

The man was having trouble. He was probably too drunk. The hand that pressed Madame Despard to the wall still held a beer can. With the other he pulled swearing at his uncooperative flies. Sweat ran down his tee shirt's back.

The man started to spew obscenities like an actor in a bad pornographic movie. Madame Despard simply stood there. In the silly stockings her legs looked pinched and old and erotically pointless. Something – her passivity, his impotence? – drove this man beyond the drunken anger with which he routinely confronted the world. He drew back the beer can to strike.

"No," but Busboy didn't mean the man. He referred to James Tar, who had come from the darkness on the other side so quickly that he seemed to have materialised, as if he possessed the power to reconstitute himself from shadows.

He drove his elbow into the man's kidneys, then used the side of a hand on his neck. The man fell and lay on his back. His big red genitals flopped spongily, dribbling slightly like a badly fastened tap. Tar looked down on him.

"Mr Tar," Busboy again. "Be careful or you kill him."

Tar looked up. His hair was white in the moonlight. He was small and old yet hard. Old and hard with a goblin's age, a goblin's power.

"Yes," he spoke reasonably and sensibly. His accent was slight, his tone restrained. "Only a poor working man. No fault of his."

Madame Despard stepped away from the wall. Her face had come alive.

"Jimmy. I thought you were dead."

Tar looked at her. "You were always a whore," he said.

And against all the odds that the whole wide world could offer Madame Despard became, for a moment once again, magnificent. She made no attempt to rearrange her clothes. She showed no shame. She expressed no embarrassment. She stared back at him.

Then she said, " . . . I didn't want to live. You know that."

Tar said nothing. Madame Despard gave a little smile. Tar turned abruptly away and walked across the waste ground to where Catriona and Busboy stood. He stopped.

"I'm your father." He put out his hand.

In the circumstances Catriona could think of nothing better to do. She took it.

She drew in her breath. She was looking into her own eyes;

the green hazel colour, the slight oriental setting that men – that Esmond – made much of. The eyes that saved her face from commonplace prettiness were staring back at her – wrinkled and pouched and weather veined and mean but the same eyes, the same genetic signature. He had seen it too. He cleared his throat but nothing came out. Catriona tried to help.

"Jessie said . . . Jessie said . . ."

"Jessie?!" His voice went up, urgently. "You've seen Jessie? Where? When?"

He had dropped her hand. "This afternoon. At home. I mean her house. In Edinburgh."

"Oh Jesus," said Tar.

# 28

Bert had a way with locks. He stepped aside to let Louis move ahead down the dark narrow hall of Barrington Smythe's flat. Louis inhaled the mixture of dust and booze, of dead cigarettes and ageing curry that passed for air.

"Blimey," said Bert. "Pongs a bit."

They went into the small front room. Like many physically indolent men Louis was tidy; he looked with a shudder at the stained cushions, the filthy glasses, the hillocks of unemptied ashtrays.

"So," said Louis, "what are you saying? That you can't find him? That the earth's swallowed him up?"

"Don't reckon the earth could keep him down. Not if he smells like this lot. What I'm saying is that we try to find where he might be. You start in here and I'll go out the back."

Bert departed. Louis started on Barrington Smythe's paperwork. There was a lot of it. The two bookcases, the corner cupboard with the missing door, substantial sections of the filthy floor were infested with loose paper. The sum total constituted an epic mess. Louis sighed and went to work.

Really the job was like taking apart a mountainous multi-layered sandwich. Unopened bills were jammed next to unmarked student essays – some two years old. The bailiff had not been a stranger. Threatening letters from the college dean objected to Barrington Smythe's work habits in increasingly litigious language. Across these Barrington Smythe had inscribed WANKER in large letters. But there was nothing to do with the business in hand; nothing to do with Maxwell or Tar, or Barrington Smythe's apparent disappearance.

Then Louis found the photographs.

The first four seemed pretty unremarkable. A wall with a low door shot in bright sunshine; a girl at the top of the steep steps leading up to a Georgian building. The girl was looking anxiously over her shoulder. Then – Louis turned the photographs over carefully, as a neat man who disliked leaving smudges – a snap of a fat man in a camel coat, walking in the snow. Next what seemed to be some waste ground at the back of a tenement building – garbage, beer cans, used syringes scattered all about.

But the fifth and final photograph was a different matter altogether. Two men, youngish, long haired. One woman, old and on her knees. All naked.

It took Louis a moment or two before he grasped what it was that made the photograph familiar. He looked away from the naked bodies; at the edge of the picture was the corner of a bookcase, part of a chair . . . The photograph had been taken here, in Barrington Smythe's flat, in this very room.

Louis took the photographs and went out through the filthy kitchen. Bert stood looking at the concrete shelter with a satisfied grin.

"Well, well," said Bert. "Come and see what I've found."

Bert unscrewed the disused drainpipe at the side of the outhouse. He showed Louis how the top of the pipe was blocked off and how easily the centre unscrewed to leave a neat dry hiding place.

Inside, the shelter stank of beer and piss. Maxwell was dead but the odours of his living body still lingered. "Watch," said Bert. He knelt and pressed heavily with both hands. Three of the floorboards came neatly loose. "Hiding place number two."

Louis bent and looked into the gap. It was empty.

"You reckon your drunk chum did this?"

"No," said Louis. "He's far too clumsy. What about these?"

He handed Bert the photographs. Bert whistled. "Unless I'm very much mistaken these are the same photographs that Tar gave Robinson. Prints of the same that is. So how did Dipso Dan get them?"

"I will thank you harumph," said Barrington Smythe, leaning on to the kitchen door for support, "to adopt a more respectful form of dress."

"Dress?"

"He means address, Bert," said Louis.

"I said address. Address is what I said and address harumph is what I meant."

"Christ," said Bert.

Although Barrington Smythe sounded like a merchant banker he looked more than ever like a tramp. His clothes were stained and torn. His shoes were lightly dusted with vomit.

"Moreover," he said, continuing with the same crazed formality, "I am in a position to make a full settlement."

He pulled a handful of crumpled notes from his jacket's torn pocket. Bert turned to Louis.

"What's he talking about?" Like most people Bert looked at Barrington Smythe as if he were a combination of freak show and cabaret turn.

"He thinks you're a bailiff. For God's sake Barrington where have you been?"

Barrington Smythe dropped a bundle of fivers. Louis picked them up.

"I have been looking, unsuccessfully as it happens, for my wife and kiddies."

"Tried all their usual pubs did you?" said Bert.

A slow drunken suspicion dawned over Barrington Smythe's yellowed features. "You know Vulliamy, this bailiff reminds me of a policeman."

Then he slid quietly to the ground.

They let him sleep for a couple of hours. Bert used the time to turn the place inside out and then replace the mess in its original disorder. There were no more revelations, no more hiding places, nothing of significance.

But when they woke Barrington Smythe up the story was different.

He had a bad case of the shakes; his defences were down. As usual his conversational style was in a meandering ramble but slowly and persistently Bert made sense of it.

The chappies in the photograph – the long-haired chappies; he leered shakily – had needed a place for this kind of thing. They paid well too. So when they were in London they'd give him a ring, he'd make sure that the wife and kiddies were out and bob's your uncle. It paid well. But after a bit it got on the wife's nerves. Well you know how women are.

Bert and Louis said they did.

The arrangement was always the same. They'd ring. He'd give them a couple of hours when the wife was at work and the kiddies at school. They had their own key. Only one rule. No one around. Not that he minded. No questions asked eh?

But what about the photographs? How had these come to

be here? He had no idea. Never seen them before. He supposed they must have just stuffed them in with his papers. No, he didn't know the places in the photographs.

They took him outside. Bert repeated his act with drainpipe and floorboard. Barrington Smythe announced that he was gob-smacked frankly, and didn't they think it might be time to pop out for a snifter?

# 29

Tar neither apologised nor explained. He concentrated on driving fast. Catriona, alone with him in the car, supposed that she should have been frightened but she wasn't. She was excited. She was fascinated. She was no longer excluded. Whatever was happening she was *necessary*. He stopped once only, on the way out of Leith at a telephone box. She kept looking at his fierce little face.

"Did no one ever tell you not to stare?"

"Yes," said Catriona. "The man I thought was my father at the time. You know how it is."

"No. I was in an orphanage."

"Oh I suppose that excuses everything."

"Suppose what you like. I don't make excuses."

This conversation wasn't going Catriona's way. She was supposed to be the aggrieved one, the recriminator. Tar short-circuited that. He didn't seem interested in her. He seemed interested in something else but she didn't know what it was.

He swung the car down the Mound, past the National Gallery, grey and formidable by moonlight, over the Princes Street traffic lights.

"So what's it like – killing people?"

"Don't be silly." He hunched forward watching the road. He was a very good driver.

She tried another tack. "So where should Jessie be? Instead of in Edinburgh?"

"Ireland," said Tar.

"You know, I don't believe you. I don't think I should believe a single thing you say."

"Quite right. Most people wouldn't. That's the point."

"What's the point?"

"Making you see. You can't deny what you see."

"See WHAT?!"

"I don't have time for this now."

He pushed the accelerator all the way down to the floor.

They swept up the cul-de-sac and stopped behind another car

parked at right angles to the path leading to Jessie's house.

Tar was out and running. Catriona followed. She slipped on some gravel from the disused railway track. By the time she steadied herself Tar had reached the tangled garden. He stopped. She caught up with him as Jessie's door opened. Señor Rossminster stood in the doorway.

"Old boy," he said. "I wouldn't let Miss Lomax go in there. Best not."

They paid no attention. Tar pushed past him. She followed. She heard, she felt, his intake of breath. He said nothing; Catriona was fool enough to call out, "Jessie."

But Jessie was as dead as dead could be. They didn't come any deader than Jessie.

Her neck had snapped so that it lay sideways to her shoulders like a game bird in a butcher's shop. Her eyes were open; her expression terrified. Somehow Catriona especially didn't want that. Somehow Tar understood. Kneeling beside Jessie he looked up at Catriona.

"Even the bravest of us are afraid."

Yet, in that moment of brief and flinty comfort, she made herself a promise. I won't forget this. I won't forgive or forget this. Ever.

"There are worse things than fear," said Tar.

Then the smell hit her. Jessie's sphincter had broken.

"The indignity." She felt vomit rising in her. Tar pointed a fierce finger.

"You can't throw up here. I'll not have it. You'll have to wait."

Her body obeyed; just as if she were a real child and he, once upon a time, a real father. Señor Rossminster patted her shoulder.

"Evidence d'you see. Don't want some local bobby analysing it."

"No. No, of course not." Gagging, Catriona wanted these to be nice men. To agree with them. To win their approval. To have them take her away to a nice place with cocoa and blankets and what survivors of normal disasters are supposed to get.

"Henry?" Tar again.

"Look for yourself," said Señor Rossminster. The tiny room had been ransacked. Drawers stood open. Labour politicians and feminist commanders had been torn from the walls and ripped from their frames. The box marked Spain was torn open, its contents scattered.

"She let them in," said Rossminster. "Door not forced. Given that it's dark and she lived alone she probably knew them."

"The students," said Catriona. "She said that some students came to do her messages."

Rossminster looked blank.

"Errands," translated Tar. He was running his eye around the room, first clockwise, then anti-clockwise.

"Ah! Scots phrase," said Rossminster politely. "Marks outside. Motor cycles I'd say. Easy to get away over the railway tracks and on to the derelict land."

Tar nodded. There was a chirping noise. For a moment Catriona imagined that Crazy Mary had wedged herself into the tiny room. Then she saw the budgerigar on Jessie's sewing table. Next to the cage was the magnifying glass that Jessie needed for reading. The photograph she had shown Catriona lay beside it. Catriona was glad that Jessie had had these things near to her. Memories at the end. Memories in the face of the barbarians. Then she was angry again.

"Why? Why should they murder her?"

"They didn't," said Tar. "It went wrong. They threatened her all right. She was afraid. She fell. She hit her head *there*," he pointed to a mark on the sewing table's edge. "A neck doesn't break like that from a blow unless it takes half the head away. Sorry Catriona. It's the truth."

It was the first time he had used her name. Not Katie. But then he had only met her as Catriona.

"Glad you haven't lost your touch," said Rossminster.

"So the aim wasn't to kill her and then cover up by making it look like a burglary. The aim was to find something. And she wouldn't tell them where it was. She died and they didn't find it."

"How do you know that?" said Catriona.

Rossminster and Tar exchanged a glance; who should take on the chore of explanation?

"Well," said Rossminster, "when most people *search*, d'you see, when they reach the point where they find whatever they seek, they stop, take it, go. In other words *something* remains undisturbed, still in place. But they've turned over everything. Upstairs is just the same."

"She slept down here," said Catriona. "Close to the fire. She felt the cold."

"They didn't find it." The moment's tenderness when Tar had knelt by Jessie's body had been replaced by the absolute concentration he had shown in the car. He frowned at the room for keeping its secret. Señor Rossminster looked professionally worried as if a meeting of commercial travellers was going badly. He cleared his throat and sounded embarrassed.

"Fact is Jimmy we need to know what *it* is."

Tar stood considering whether to tell him. Whether to tell her.

Catriona spoke. "She asked me if I'd got a paper."

Rossminster cocked an eyebrow. "That be it old boy?"

"I think so," said Tar. He said cautiously, "That sort of thing. Not big."

Rossminster looked round the room and gave a helpless sigh.

"The bird." Catriona went to the sewing table.

"What about the burd?" Tension had broadened Tar's vowels.

"Usually at night she would have put a cloth over its cage so it could sleep. That's what you do with budgerigars. But look."

The cloth lay next to the cage. Tar picked it up. "So she couldn't sleep. Needed company."

Yes, thought Catriona, she relied on the company of birds.

"But would she have cleaned out the cage at night? I don't think so. Besides Jessie was neat. She was too infirm to do the garden but the house was clean and tidy. She'd never have left that mess."

The two men followed the line of Catriona's finger. On the surface of the sewing table at the base of the cage lay a dusting of sand speckled with tiny droppings.

"Hush," said Catriona to the fluttering bird. Slowly she drew out the detachable tray that made up the bottom of the cage and extracted a flat manila envelope.

"You know," said James Tar, "you're *good.*"

And that was the first praise which Catriona received from

her father.

She stood on the gravel track waiting. Tar had returned to the house to close Jessie's eyes. "It's the least I could do." Now he came out of the little house followed by Rossminster carrying the budgerigar in its cage. Tar hurried her to the car. He turned to Rossminster.

"Take care of that bloody bourgeois bird."

Rossminster smiled brightly as if he were keeping a pet for a vacationing friend. "Fair exchange," said Rossminster. He reached into his own car and extracted a small bag which he passed to Tar. "All present and correct," said Rossminster. "As per instructions."

Tar took the bag. Rossminster lifted the caged budgerigar in salute. "Old boy," he said. "Teach it to whistle the Internationale."

"*Ay Carmela*," said Tar, then to Catriona, "Come on."

They got into the car and drove off. They crossed the empty night-time Queensferry Road towards Corstorphine. Tar made several turnings, checking for following headlights. Then he pulled away from streets and houses to stop out of sight of the road, between a golf course and a wood. He leant across and opened Catriona's door. He had to stretch. How small he was. How small and old and tough and mysterious. How not in a blue suit. How not like Maxwell.

"All right," he said, "now you can be sick."

She thought of Maxwell and Jessie; she had no trouble vomiting.

Tar paid no attention. "Don't worry. Nobody'll have you in for questioning. The Ministry'll see to that. What the local police get there it'll be another case of mindless vandalism." Tar the businesslike.

"Don't you have any feelings?"

"Yes."

He passed her a handkerchief. She wiped her mouth. She paused. "So you work for the Ministry?"

"It would be more accurate," he looked straight ahead picking his words, "to say that we're in association. Via Rossminster."

He started up the engine. Catriona said, "Do you mind telling me where we're going?"

"Glasgow. You can get the first flight for Dublin. That's where Schmidt told you to go."

"How do you know that?"

"Because he had to."

"NOBODY TELLS ME ANYTHING."

He had to pull the car up sharply. She banged her fists on the windscreen, on the dashboard, then she went for him. He seized her hands and held them. He was strong. After a while she subsided. He put his hands back on the wheel.

"You're right," he said. "I'd feel the same."

"You can't know what I feel."

"No. Nor you what I feel."

It was evidently true but she just hadn't thought of it.

"All right," he passed Jessie's envelope to her. "Look inside."

"What happened to your wrists?" She had noticed when he held her; now the car's interior light showed a fading blue stain around the backs of his wrists.

"I had an accident. Look inside. Then I'll tell you a story."

For these contents Jessie had died. Catriona extracted them slowly.

First there was a letter from a Dublin solicitor. He acted for the Despard Foundation. In accordance with the wishes of the late M. Honoré Despard he wrote in the belief that Jessamine Lomax had a legal interest in the future disposition of the Foundation. This interest could be exercised only at the official solicitor's meeting of sharers. The date of the meeting was two days away. The place was Claremaurice House.

"That's Esmond's house!"

"Despard leased it. He died there. Go on."

A document of sorts. Yellow. Old. On very cheap coarse paper. Typed, using an archaic continental typeface. It was in Spanish – stamped and officially re-stamped and finished off with elaborate seals. Catriona looked at the date. Here was the one memento of the Spanish struggle that Jessie had hidden.

"I can't read Spanish. What is it?"

"It's a *permisión*, an *Autorización*. For the Ambulance. Because at the time we were going away from the front. Away from Madrid to Valencia. Of course that looked wrong. Running away. We could have been shot as deserters without that.

We had trouble enough as it was."

"We?"

"The names are on there."

They were. Hispanicised but there all right. Patricio Claremaurice. Alicia Cook. Jessamina Lomax. Jaime Tar.

Catriona looked up. "Jessie was testing me. She mentioned the others but not . . . "

"Not Alice Cook. Not Alice Claremaurice. Not Alice Despard."

Cook, thought Catriona. How could she have started life with a name so mundane? She felt herself whirled around in the same old spiral of frustration.

"But so *what*? I mean it's all very nice and historical but for now, for this minute, what *is* it?"

"It's evidence. Evidence of who was in the Ambulance. The Ambulance that took Despard and about three-quarters of a million pounds worth of Spanish gold out of Spain so that neither Stalin nor Franco could get it."

"But what has that to do with the rest? With this Despard Foundation thing?"

"Because Despard was a guilty man and wanted to make amends. The future of the Despard Foundation will be decided by what's left of the Ambulance Brigade plus one, minus one."

"What?"

"Minus yours truly," Tar smiled. "I ceased to be Despard's cup of tea. Plus Schmidt. Who's run it for years. Who wants to go on running it. Whom Madame Despard hates. Who hates Madame Despard."

Every moment seemed to suck Catriona further into the spiral. She fought to keep her aching head clear.

"You mean that's why Jessie was murdered? No. You said she wasn't murdered."

"She wasn't," said Tar flatly. "Someone wanted those. Don't ask me why because I don't know and I don't like it. It wasn't Schmidt."

I will burst, thought Catriona. I will simply burst with all of this. "Of course it wasn't Schmidt. What do you *mean* Schmidt? Mr Schmidt's a businessman. Mr Schmidt doesn't kill people. *You* kill people. You killed Maxwell. You killed that poor pathetic old man. He died in my arms. If you talk about seeing I saw that all right and he died in my arms. And you killed him."

But he wasn't moved. He drove on steadily, looking straight ahead.

"First, as I keep telling you, Jessie's death was an accident. Second, I didn't kill Maxwell. If he'd done what he was told he'd be alive but he was too drunk and too greedy. But yes I used Maxwell to prove that someone would try to kill me."

"Oh don't tell me! Mr Schmidt."

Tar shook his head. "It's possible but I don't think so. Not his style. That's what worries me."

"So Maxwell was expendable."

"Maxwell was a traitor. He was a bosses' nark in the union movement for the best part of twenty years. No wonder he took to drink. Pure guilt. Well I was the one who found him out and I let him live on condition that he did what I told him. Odd jobs and little bits of information. If it makes you feel any better he was dying anyway."

"It doesn't. Why didn't you do it yourself. Stake yourself out."

"Because, you damned fool, I might have died. And if I died Schmidt would keep control of the Foundation."

Perhaps it was his tone. Catriona forever after was never sure, perhaps it was some pure intuition of the blood, but out of nowhere Catriona said, "That isn't the reason though. That's not why you're doing all this."

Tar turned to look at her. His green eyes lit up in the passing headlights.

"I was right. You're good."

Good! Perhaps soon I'll get to plan my first murder. We can take family snaps and compare them. "Why then?"

He tried to tell it in a matter of fact way, concentrating on his driving, on the road ahead. But it wasn't a matter of fact story and in any case his voice had a strange edge of dreamy bitterness. This was the rest of the story that Jessie hadn't told.

Catriona knew about the gold? No? Well at the start of the Spanish war Stalin had given shelter to Spain's gold reserves. But in Uncle Joe's case shelter meant expropriation. Of course no one of the Republican side wanted to admit that – for one thing the Russians were the only real ally in sight. Only the

Russians were providing arms and equipment. And whatever anybody said about the purges – the Communists' covert policy of executing Left Republicans or Anarchists – the truth was that only those same Communists had the discipline to run the war. Here Tar paused and shook his head as if he couldn't quite believe what he'd seen. The Anarchists didn't believe in officers. They wanted a conference before each offensive. Some of them wanted to fight the war during the day and return to their villages at night. Some of them wanted to fight part-time so they could tend their crops. Then there was the *paseo*. Members of the middle class were all guilty of crimes against the people, and on sight should be taken for a walk to a quiet place and a bullet in the head. So Communist discipline was vital. So Stalin was vital. So no one wanted to believe that he'd stolen the very gold that could have armed the Republic.

Well almost no one. Or maybe it was just inefficiency but about three-quarters of a million pounds worth of gold never went to Moscow. The idea was to get it secretly out of Spain. Patrick Claremaurice had been blockade running in his boat. Despard would take charge of the gold and buy arms to be run back in by boats. But first the gold had to reach the coast and Patrick's boat.

So Tar had thought of the Ambulance. It was less likely than most vehicles to be attacked from the air. They had painted a big red cross on its top. But the real fear was being stopped by the Anarchists or the Left Republicans. And to make matters worse Despard was terror-stricken. A week in wartime Spain and the man was a wreck. Just another (Tar wrenched the gear lever viciously) bloody intellectual tourist.

And so they had used the suit.

It went like this. If you wore a suit (no he was *not* making this up) the Anarchists would shoot you unless you had worker's hands – hands that said manual labour. If you had these they assumed you'd stolen the suit. Now Tar had worker's hands and no mistake. So he – Tar – had worn the hideous office worker's blue suit that Despard had acquired in a rare moment of solidarity in Madrid.

But, asked Catriona, why bother at all? Why didn't you all dress as peasants? Because, said Tar, when they were stopped (it happened a dozen times) the suit gave the stoppers something to think about. Gave them something to do. Kept them from poking around and finding the Ambulance's false floor. A distraction, like Alice.

Like Alice?

She was then, said Tar, exceptionally beautiful. They were too busy gawping at her to look at anything else.

Yes. Exceptionally beautiful and brave as a lion. She had come for the ride and she loved it. It worked. At least getting the gold and Despard out worked. But it was too late for the Spanish Republic. The war was all but lost; the gold redundant.

So – Catriona jumped ahead – Despard stole the gold. Was that it?

No, said Tar. Despard was rich anyway. Still rich in those days and though a coward he possessed a conscience of sorts. The Despard Foundation helped Spanish veterans and Despard (or so he said) was sitting on the gold till it could be used for something big. Something, Tar paused to find the right words, something for the real Spain.

Bribery, Tar said. A huge bribe to be paid in gold. A bribe for prisoners. Three hundred former Republican soldiers who had spent more than a decade in Franco's stinking jails. It had taken five years for him to arrange it, slipping in and out of Spain with one identity or another. The prisoners were brought by boat which stood off the North African coast opposite the border with Spanish Morocco and Morocco itself. The gold was to come in from the Moroccan side to be handed over in Melilla; the boat would then sail on and dock in Tangier, then a free port where the right kind of palm greasing smoothed the way.

At the last minute the gold had not come. It seemed that Despard was far poorer than he had thought. Without the gold as collateral his new adviser Mr Schmidt would be unable to reconstruct or recycle or renegotiate or whatever the correct term was for staying rich. So Tar had stood wearing his wartime blue suit for identification and watched through binoculars as the ship was scuttled. Its cargo was too incriminating to send back. The men had all died. They were long gone. Nothing could help them now. Perhaps it was instinct. Perhaps it was accident but for one cause or another she reached into the bag that Rossminster had given Tar. She drew out the blue suit in which Maxwell had died, in which this father of hers had stood long ago upon a distant shore.

"Why?" she said. "What do you want with this? What?"

He smiled at her with a cold cold smile. "There'll come a time for me to wear it. You'll see. When it's time to pay. When the Foundation does its right job."

Catriona wanted to get it right. "So that's it? You've come for the Foundation?"

Tar shifted in his seat. "That and what it stands for."

Along the motorway the outskirts of Glasgow put in an appearance.

"Don't cry," said Tar. "Not if you can help it."

For the first time in a long time there was something Jessie-human in his voice.

"I know it's silly. I just thought that perhaps . . . I thought you'd come for *me*."

His voice had gone husky, his accent increasingly Scots. "I did. But I can't be what I'm not. I can't pretend . . . "

"Love," said Catriona. "You can't pretend love. So what then? Why involve me?"

"I didn't know. I wasn't sure . . . what I heard about you . . . then over Maxwell I knew it would be all right."

"So Maxwell was a test for me. Apart from everything else."

"If you like."

"You still haven't answered my question. Why involve me?"

"Because you're involved already. And because I need you." That, she thought, was what Madame Despard had said.

She closed her eyes. She had never ever been so tired.

"So what do you want me to do now?"

"I want you to sleep."

She should have stayed wide awake, haunted by his ruthlessness.

But she was exhausted. So she did what she was told. She slept.

Four thirty on a cold grey autumn morning. The airport was empty except for a team of miserable Indian cleaners and a single lorry driver sulkily throwing freight on to the causeway. They talked in the car. Catriona had woken feeling terrible:

battered, aching, with a sheep dip mouth. Night flying was banned so all the cafés were closed. Tar went to the edge of the concourse; through the windscreen she saw him giving money to the cleaners. He came back with a thermos of Indian prepared coffee.

"How did you do that?"

"I've been around the world. I know how to get things done."

"But this is theirs?"

"There's a price for everything. That's capitalism for you. Sometimes you have to collaborate for the higher good."

"Which is?"

"In this case – you. In one piece and able to go on."

"What makes you think I'll go on."

"It's in your blood," said Tar. "You'll want to know."

She drank some coffee. Then, abruptly, Tar said, "You mustn't be too hard on her."

"I wasn't. I'm not." There had been an uncomfortable edge to his voice. "You find her disgusting don't you?"

For the first time internal conflict showed in his face. "And you don't?"

"It's *her* body . . . But I find her . . . strange, I think."

He stared at her – surprised – as if she had said something original or remarkable. He looked almost pleased. But that didn't add up. She probably couldn't read his signals.

"She said you'd tell me about Mr Schmidt."

"No," said Tar. "You'll have to see for yourself. You wouldn't believe me. You don't believe me now . . . "

But I want to thought Catriona. The trouble is that I want to believe Schmidt too. It doesn't seem fair. I want both. Do I want everyone to be a father?

"I don't think you can have got it right. He made everything possible. He gave me independence."

"I'll tell you what he did – like he did to a lot of other people – he gave you dependence on a long string and now he's going to pull it in."

"So how am I to see?"

"You go to the lawyer who sent Jessie that letter. Despard's lawyer. Do it first thing, before you see Schmidt. Then you can judge what Schmidt has to say. Will you do that? For me? For Jessie? He'll need someone to tell him about Jessie. He knows you'll be coming from me. But you don't mention my name. Officially I stay dead."

My name. Your name. "You know," Catriona said, "I don't know what to call you."

"Call me McIshmael. What's so funny?"

"I hadn't thought of you reading." In fact I haven't thought of what you did with the rest of your life – with all the spare time in between killing people. But she didn't say that. It would have been rude.

"And what will the lawyer do?"

"He'll tell you how you're involved. Then you'll know why we needed you. Then you can listen to Schmidt. You see; you choose."

"Aren't you taking a risk McIshmael?"

"Lassie," he said, "only if you turn out wrong. Only if you hate us too much." (Us?)

It was time for growing up – for giving him a proper name. But it was too early for Father. "Jimmy, I don't hate you. Suppose you're right about anything important – suppose you're right about *everything*. What should I do with Schmidt?"

"It's a political world. Agree with him until you have the chance to do what you want."

He was full of advice. The way some fathers are. Catriona looked at her watch. "It's time for the flight."

"Yes."

"We're embarrassed," said Catriona. "We don't know how to say good-bye."

"Amongst other things."

She opened the door on her side. Then a final thought occurred – a hanging thumbnail, a split end of a thought. It was about Madame Despard.

"Jimmy? Did you know that she bought outfits for me every year and that she sent me money and cards?"

"I didn't."

"Why, do you think?"

He looked away from her. "You'd better ask your mother."

"But she's dead. Surely you knew that?"

He stared at her with that blank look that he had worn before. He went pale under his tan.

"God," he said. "Oh God. I should have known. She didn't tell you did she?"

His expression was frightening. He looked like a man repeatedly deceived, who had believed one final futile time too many.

"Tell me what? Jimmy? Tell me what?"

Tar reached out his hand, then drew it back as if Catriona might, within the next few moments, reject it.

And then it came. The thing she should have thought of. The thing she should have noticed – no, not all along – but surely since the dabbing with the cold cream, the closet with the clothes.

He said, "Madame Despard is your mother."

# 30

Catriona crossed O'Connell Bridge and made her way past the Post Office until the end of O'Connell Street. Instead of carrying straight on towards the handsome greenery of Parnell Square she turned right, past the Gate Theatre. A narrow passage gave suddenly on to an untidy lop-sided squarish place – one of the remaining courts in Central Dublin which neither developer nor gentrifier mucked about or removed. Three sides of the court consisted of store houses – the wood of the window frames discoloured and twisted by the rain; the fourth side from ground to roof levels had been painted red. Probably, thought Catriona, an old warehouse with a separate exit at the back. Over the low wooden door letters were painted with what looked like deliberate crudeness. They said *Donovan Myers – So What?* There was no bell, no knocker. Catriona could hear voices inside. She pushed the door. It creaked back. She entered.

The interior was strange beyond non-Irish understanding. The rough stone floor was covered with newspapers of considerable antiquity. At Catriona's feet a yellowed De Valera stared without embarrassment up her skirt. The furniture came from scavenged pieces of discarded wood. The tables had been fashioned from abandoned doors mounted on decorator's trestles and covered with more newspapers on which lay tin mugs, Smethwick's bottles, lumps of soda bread. On broken chairs, milk crates, orange boxes there sat a number of old men and one old woman. The old woman was knitting. Further over against the walls other figures lay on mattresses. They all seemed very old or very wrecked.

The place smelt of ageing bodies and illness and not much washing but it didn't seem to Catriona nearly as bad as the bomb shelter at the back of Barrington Smythe's flat. Then she realised why. It was fear-free. Yet the place was cold – from the raw Dublin damp.

A voice roared out from the shadows at the back of the barn.

"Read the notice. On the wall by the door." Catriona

turned. The notice was painted in large letters.

Attention
No prayers to be offered here.
If you want to pray go somewhere else.

Catriona looked up. A large man of about fifty with a long straggling beard dressed in a shapeless Arran sweater and a French beret came from the back. He pointed at the notice, at Catriona, then back to the notice again.

"I won't," he shouted as if for the benefit of the deaf, "have anyone in here believing in God."

"All right," said Catriona, but he didn't seem to notice.

"I won't have it will I?" he roared at the derelicts behind him.

"Ah ye will not," said the woman with the knitting.

"That's the trouble with this damned country – religion. Isn't that so?"

The derelicts muttered that Glory be to God It Was. A couple crossed themselves. Catriona shifted uneasily from foot to foot.

"Yes," she said. "Fine. But I'm looking for . . . "

The man strode forward beaming. He swept off his beret dramatically and held out his large hand. Catriona took it.

"Donovan Myers," he said. His was a precise Irish accent that clipped words as if guarded about the easiness of sway and rhythm; the enunciation of the debating chamber and the law court. "You're a wonderful sight for the eyes, Miss Lomax."

There was nothing lecherous here; he sounded as if Catriona really amounted to a visual treat. After the last few days this cheered her up considerably. He pumped her hand up and down as if she were the long awaited friend of a friend, as if they were going to have a terrific time together.

Catriona said (and immediately thought how foolish it sounded), "So you *were* expecting me."

Donovan Myers grinned even wider. "Who else and none better. We'll be off straight away."

He turned round and addressed the derelicts. "I'm away now till tomorrow. Fair's fair. No praying while I'm away. Biddie, you're in charge."

The woman at the table made a shooing gesture with her knitting needles.

"I'll lead the way."

Donovan Myers strode ahead of Catriona. He walked fast, talking as she worked hard to keep up with him. He had arthritis and limped. On the other hand he limped at speed. The climate he said gave you the limp; then you had to limp as fast as you could to get indoors away from the climate.

"The only atheist refuge for down-and-outs in the whole of Dublin. No! The whole of Ireland. Every other place where some wretch wants shelter and something in his belly he has to go crawling on his knees to God, who put him in the mess in the first place. Huh! None of that for me. Dignity! And do they appreciate it? Devil a bit. The moment my back's turned you know what they're up to. Not just praying. Worse than that. Praying for *me*. It isn't even polite."

As they walked through Dublin, now alongside the Liffey, Donovan Myers did not modulate the volume of his voice. Half of O'Connell Street either smiled at another Dublin character or, like a parcel of passing nuns, greeted the poor touched unbeliever with Christian warmth, to which Myers politely raised his beret.

"Diseases of the liver," he continued in mid-bellow as they reached the Guinness Brewery. "That's what I specialise in."

Catriona thought of the prominence of empties at the Myers Refuge for Atheists.

"You mean you get these people treatment?"

"Not in the slightest," said Myers. "I get them drink. Kills them off quicker. Pretty painless on the whole and a damned fine anaesthetic. Annoys the priests too. Though you'd think by now they'd be used to hearing drunk confessions. And here we are."

A Georgian house now divided into offices. The largest plate proclaimed Donovan Myers' qualifications as a solicitor. His office was on the ground floor.

"Sit ye down. I'll not be a minute. I have to get into my pox doctor's outfit."

She sat in an old leather chair by a coal fire. She took a deep breath. They were alone now and she could delay no longer.

"Mr Myers, I have a message. That is I was asked to tell you . . . Jessie's dead. It happened yesterday."

Donovan Myers cocked his head on one side and pursed his lips in a noiseless whistle. "Natural causes? No. Don't tell me. I'm a lawyer and it's best I shouldn't know. Ah well I never knew her personally and you can't mourn what you never knew. Pox doctor's outfit. It's a certain aid to concentration."

A spotty young clerk brought her a pot of tea. She stared into the fire and thought.

She had no doubt about it. At the airport Tar's collapsed face had told an undeniable truth. Besides, it all fitted in: the clothes, the cards, the torn up money, the fears of . . . of Mrs Lomax that a rich visitor would call.

So Madame Despard was her mother. A mother who had never tried to see her, never lifted a finger for her, who even now had been unable to tell her the truth . . . Acknowledgement . . . The word stepped straight out of the pages of a Victorian novel full of fallen women and deceitful squires, but it was a word that counted. It had been eighteen years since Mrs Lomax had died. In all that time, even up to the present, Alice Despard had never acknowledged her daughter's existence. The reason wasn't hard to find. She had been married to a rich man. She had hated him but she had not wanted to lose the money. Her child had been less important than the money. It was as simple as that. A few days ago Catriona's innate romantic snobbery would have leapt at a Mother/Visitor so elegant, so arrogant; would even have admired the sheer independence of her wild uncontrollable sexual kink. Now she felt disgust and anger. The woman's long ritual of guilt just seemed sickening. An indulgence. A third-of-a-century-long excuse for taking no action. The old lag's, the recidivist's sentimental excuse.

Catriona also felt ashamed of herself. Snobbery had made her cringe at the idea of Tar. Now, for all her fear and confusion, she knew that he was someone important. She might live to regret it but he had moved her and he had won her respect. Yet snobbery and selfishness would not quite go away. Catriona wanted to help it but couldn't – her actual mother could have given forty times over the sort of life that the young Catriona had dreamed of. She felt envious, deprived. She felt dispossessed, she felt cheated. And in doing so she felt ignoble.

All of which left Schmidt. Yet at the moment he had to be

the villain of their piece, not hers. For whatever they said the plain fact remained that Schmidt had not been the one who abandoned her to seek her out only when she became suddenly and mysteriously useful. Schmidt deserved his chance. She would see Schmidt soon. The thought made her feel stronger, firmer of purpose.

Donovan Myers came back into the office. His pox doctor's outfit consisted of an old fashioned black jacket and striped trousers; its formality was diminished by the beret which he continued to wear. He saw Catriona stare and pointed upwards.

"Never let your head be cold. The first rule of health. A terrible thing arthritis of the head."

He grinned broadly so she supposed this was a joke. He opened a cupboard and pulled out a bottle of John Jameson's. It was ten o'clock in the morning – Catriona didn't point this out as she refused a drink. She was forming the impression that Donovan Myers was a strong minded man who disliked interference with the way he lived his life.

"I'm a nuisance," said Myers. "That's the type of solicitor I am. I take difficult cases. Always have. There are plenty of difficult cases here. I have a reputation for independence."

"I can believe that," said Catriona.

He was tapping his fingers against the teapot as if he needed a rhythm, a tune to listen to.

"Perhaps that's why Despard used me. That and the fact that I knew what you'd call the context. My father was Old IRA. He was in Spain with Jimmy. Wounded at Brunete when Major Nathan was killed. He didn't live long enough to see the Provos. He wouldn't have liked them but he would have believed in their legal rights. Though maybe that helped too in Despard's mind. I was less likely to be put off or bullied. Anyway Despard used me to draw up his will. It's a very . . . " he leaned back and paused, looking upwards until he could pluck the right adjective from the air, "unusual will. And he didn't want any slips."

"Unusual?"

Myers leaned forward. "Catriona. I'm a solicitor. I represent the estate of the recently deceased M. Despard. Not the Despard Foundation. Not Madame Despard. I'm the executor. I'm the one who puts the will through probate. And I can't do anything that will endanger that legal authority. The only thing that could hold up the settlement of the will would be if I were disbarred. Otherwise the provisions of the will *have* to stand. And what happens to the Despard Foundation is one of the provisions of the will. Let me take you back to the first of it. At the time I didn't know a thing. Only that I'd been summoned. I suppose you think Ireland's a small place but it's big enough in all conscience to be ignorant about. That was the way with me. My world stopped at Waterford. I'd been to the Arran Islands for a jaunt but that was about the size of it. But I did what homework I could. It was no surprise to find Claremaurice House in non-Claremaurice hands. Three-quarters of the gentry houses still standing are American or German. Who else could keep the great fossils that they are up? Not that Claremaurice House was exactly kept up. More turned into a barricade and a sick room downstairs and the rest shut up tight. Despard was a frightened man and a bitter man. And he was no better for not knowing who to believe. His wife – " he paused.

"Go on."

"Well, she was enjoying it. She had power over him all right, you could see that. But so had he over her. Ah they were a wretched miserable rich pair. And what each had on the other was the will. It took me time to get to grips with the whole thing – two full days to make the will and have it typed and witnessed, there and then, and watertight – but essentially the matter of the thing was this. He was terrified of what he'd done in the past and of death and of being abandoned or worse. The will was his insurance policy. And so it was insurance for her too. Let me explain. It wasn't a question of Despard's fortune alone, though to me that seemed a great sum of money. It was a question of the Foundation that bore his name and which, by all accounts, belonged to him. According to the wife it had been run in a terrible corrupt way."

"By Mr Schmidt?"

"I'm not naming names but you get my drift. And I think she'd persuaded him half way. But half way wasn't good enough. For though he distrusted a certain gentleman I'll not name he distrusted the wife too. Oh he hated her and yet he was obsessed with her. Then too he was full of terrible guilt.

And she played on that. He had a debt. He owed. If he were a man he'd do the right thing, and he a poor broken hate-filled fellow in a wheelchair. *But*," and Donovan Myers lifted an emphatic hand, "*he was sane*! Well, in the end between themselves they agreed. It was a correct will, properly made with her not even on the premises and witness brought in who'd never heard of the man. So it's a good will and there's no doubt of its validity. What it came down to was precisely this. He wanted a balance. He wanted a shared decision in which neither Madame Despard nor Mr Schmidt had complete sway. So if you like there'd be a test of the evidence as to the truth of what had been happening to the Despard Foundation and where it's to go. Right?"

"Right," said Catriona.

"So he wants his shared decision," continued Donovan Myers, "and the best way of doing that is to leave voting shares to certain individuals who will vote in such a way as to produce his balance, his compromise."

"Individuals? What individuals?"

"Patience now," said Donovan Myers. "For there was more on the man's mind. More on his conscience. A powerful sense of guilt had Despard. About Spain. About the way he treated his comrades. Didn't he babble on about them. The white knights. The original keepers of the flame. So he wanted his nice voting balance but at one and the same time he wanted to assuage his conscience."

Catriona thought of Jessie and the Ambulance and James Tar standing years before on that distant dock looking out to sea as the boat was scuttled.

"A little late," she said grimly.

"Precisely," said Donovan Myers. "He wanted to repay *and* he wanted to use for his own ends the members of the Ambulance. With of course one exception."

Catriona thought of James Tar. Of the bullet fired into Despard's spine.

"My fa . . . Jimmy?"

Donovan Myers nodded solemnly. "Jimmy was out. But Despard was obsessed with the Ambulance. The closer he got to death the guiltier he became. Ah it was all mixed up with the Ambulance as the only decent thing he'd done and then he'd gone and betrayed his principles. Now that was all fine and dandy but once you cut Jimmy out who is left of the original crowd? Well Patrick Claremaurice is dead. So all that's left is Jessie and Madame Despard herself. Not much chance of your balance or your compromise there. One old Communist who'd vote for the devil before she'd uphold Schmidt and the Madame who hated Schmidt."

Donovan Myers leaned forward and waved an arthritic finger at Catriona as if it was a pointer and she the blackboard.

"Now Miss Lomax I wish the closest attention. In addition to members of the Ambulance, Schmidt was to have a vote. He knew too much to be left out. It was he who knew all about the Foundation's finances. He was too important to exclude. He had to be part of the eventual compromise. Except . . . "

But Catriona was there before him. "Except that so far there couldn't be a compromise. It would be two votes to one. Jessie and Madame Despard against Schmidt. And they'd probably go straight to crucifying him."

"Not probably. Certainly. Very messy. No. Despard wants a tie so that when he dies there's as little scandal as possible. They all have to work out the thing together. Schmidt gets to keep what he's got already but goes legal. Madame Despard doesn't get to take revenge on Schmidt. All of which has to be filtered through the Trustee, yours truly, Donovan Myers, Solicitor-at-Law."

"I'm sorry," Catriona said. "I still don't see where this tie would ever come from."

"Well here it comes," said Donovan Myers. "It amounts to Esmond Claremaurice." Donovan Myers gave her a sly look. "The same. The descendants of Ambulance members got a vote. And once again I require your closest attention, for this is not straightforward. To be sure Despard sees that Esmond Claremaurice will produce the famous balance. The man is a Member of Parliament; won't want a scandal; all for compromise. And besides he hates his stepmother Madame Despard. He'd probably vote against her, no matter what."

"You mean that I have a vote?" (You mean that I'm important. You mean that I have to be counted? You mean that I *count*?)

"Yes and then again no."

"*What?*"

"Forgive me. No Irishisms need apply. But there's truth in what I said. There's the question of proof. Legally you're Catriona Lomax. Not Madame Despard's child. Not the heir of the Ambulance. And unless you can provide the right proof – with no vote at all."

Catriona sat back. The fire had ceased to warm her. She was no one again. Nobody. She was nowhere. And then she remembered that whoever she wasn't she was still the someone she had made for herself. And she steadied herself. She thought.

She said, "But if I don't have a legal claim, if I don't have a vote then none of it makes much sense. What's been done to me."

"No my dear," said Donovan Myers gently.

No, thought Catriona, no one has come for love of me. They have come for convenience. But suffering would have to wait. It was more than ever necessary for her to think.

She thought.

"Jessie's dead. That's going to make a difference. My . . . Madame Despard loses a vote. If I *had* a vote she would need it just to force a tie, whereas Jessie's death would convince Schmidt that he had a natural majority – that he didn't need me. Except . . . ?"

"Except?" asked Donovan Myers politely.

Catriona remembered Tar on Jessie's death: Schmidt was not responsible.

"Except Schmidt may not know that Jessie's dead."

"Ye have an interesting time ahead," said Donovan Myers.

# 31

Catriona paid the taxi driver and looked in puzzlement at the Phoenix Park racecourse. She knew nothing about horses and less about the places where people bet on them. Schmidt's message at the hotel had simply said the racecourse. She thought she would have trouble finding him. She didn't. There he was detaching himself from a laughing jollying group of tweeded punters drinking their morning champagne outside a big white marquee. He saw her, waved, put down his glass of milk and waddled towards her. He had made no concessions to out-of-doors Dublin. He wore his yellow camel coat and highly polished hand-made shoes. Somehow he had kept the mud off them. He was smiling; he looked pleased to see her. He looked as if he had backed a winner. Perhaps he had. Perhaps he did this kind of thing a lot. The people he had been standing with plainly knew him. She had never known that Schmidt was a racing man or any kind of gambler. But then what really had she ever known about Schmidt. *Really* about Schmidt himself. And that started her heart hammering again.

She had thought it out. *Christ* hadn't she. Schmidt had stepped off the streets of Cairo into her life to save her the very year that Despard had made his will. Perhaps it was a coincidence. Possibly Schmidt was not the villain she had been warned against.

Certainly he had offered her nothing but employment and independence. He who owed her nothing had, by any standards, behaved better than her parents. Yet the awful doubt continued its logical gnawing process. He knew about that will and so he picked me up and took me and used me and he was so damned clever about being nice to me that when the crunch came, *if* the crunch came, it was to the neutrally nice non-manipulative Mr Schmidt I would be grateful. But then the other voice started up. The other voice said grow up, don't be so dumb. Even if Schmidt's the crook they say he is he can't be using you. Because legally my dear you aren't worth a damn.

"Catriona. Sure." Schmidt beamed. "This is very good. You comfortable at the hotel?"

"Yes, I . . . "

"Fine. This is a very fine thing. Look who's here. I got an old friend for you." He started to wave the genial wave of one who beckons over the shy, the politely unwilling, the embarrassed.

"Mr Schmidt I must talk to you. I *must*."

"Sure. Shooore." Schmidt laid a reassuring hand on her arm. "You been through some things, right? I got a number of people against me. Some very unscrupulous people you unnerstan'. We talk. Naturally. But first, here – I got one old friend."

Standing in front of her, smiling sheepishly, was her first employer Monty Mont.

He looked older and thinner and more worn but he was otherwise the same Monty. He had a loud hand-painted tie and a suit of checks that would have startled Liberace.

"Doll."

"Monty."

They embraced. "This is very nice," said Schmidt. "So Monty. It's my impression some people have been giving maybe a bad press release to Catriona. Schmidt the thoroughly bad person. So what's your view?"

Monty beamed all over his kind Jewish face. "Mr Schmidt! The man is an angel. He bailed me out of London. Set me up here. I'm a bookie now doll and a damned good bookie too."

"Damned good," said Schmidt. "That's a fact."

"He did it all doll. A FRIEND IN NEED. I pay him back a little bit a month. I have the wife here and the kiddies . . . And you. Look at you. I bless the day I told Mr Schmidt about you."

"That's wonderful Monty." (Wonderful and on cue.)

Schmidt nodded like Moses confirming the validity of a commandment.

"Schmidt does not forget a friend. This is one very sentimental occasion, but business first Monty boy."

"You're right there Mr Schmidt. You want to take this little lady away?"

"Sure Monty. You say your goodbyes."

She went to hug lovely ordinary just-normally-corrupt Monty but he seized her hands and held them tight – lifted them up in a deliberate squeeze. "Doll. Remember your old Monty."

She supposed he was about fifty-three but she said yes anyway.

As she hurried away Schmidt said, "OK. Now we talk some turkey. Schmidt is nobody's fool and it's an inevitable matter that some prominent people come and tell you things. Let me say you've got people coming round bad-mouthing Schmidt to his best manageress. A lot of stuff about the past. Correct me if I'm wrong."

"No Mr Schmidt. You're not wrong."

"So you wonder. This is bound to happen. You wonder about Schmidt. Maybe he lies to me. Maybe he cheats me. Maybe he's from a long way back a bad man. You don't be afraid to tell me. Am I right?"

"Yes Mr Schmidt."

"Well I make you a promise. Together we make some beautiful music. But this has got to be for you a free thing. You say no? OK. You go. But first you need a full and frank disclosure which Schmidt is going to give you. Schmidt is different from the others. He has proof. He has documents. Naturally. Sure. No problem. Certainly. So you go back to the hotel. You rest. Have a little lunch. You stay in. I pick you up – what – three, four o'clock. Right now I got business. I got documents to collect."

"But Mr Schmidt I thought now . . . "

Schmidt lifted his hand. "So far you're still my employee. We keep it that way soon who knows you're my partner. Besides," and he allowed himself a good solid burgher's chuckle, "you seriously think a bad man turns you loose, gives you time to hang around, listen to who you like? Enjoy yourself. I see you later."

Seriously . . . Seriously he was either speaking the truth or utterly secure that he would succeed. Normally though she would have stood her ground, demanded explanations right then and there. Something more serious had held her back.

At parting, as Monty had held her, she had felt him press his crossed fingers into her palm. It was his old office signal. It meant be careful; somebody is lying.

The hotel lift was either monopolised or stuck. Catriona took the stairs. Her mind buzzed. What *about* Jessie's death? Who could have wanted the things that Jessie had hidden? All those who whirled around moving her about couldn't possibly need such things; Tar, Madame Despard, Schmidt – they all knew the membership of the Ambulance Group, knew that Despard's will had been based on that membership. So whoever it was either hadn't known or possibly thought they were looking for something else. How did they relate to the killing of Maxwell? Were they the same people, the ones who had thought they were killing Tar? And surely people who would go to such lengths ought to *figure* more prominently. Was it all something that the Ministry and Tar had cooked up together – Tar's *association*? . . . No, she didn't believe that the Ministry had been involved in Maxwell's death. She had been there. She had been questioned. She had watched their reactions. As for Jessie's death, even if Jessie had been killed by accident she could accept neither that Rossminster was involved nor that he would have put on an act like that.

So here she was – for all her brave thoughts of action, of finding out herself – waiting again. Waiting to discover what Schmidt had to say to her; what Tar was going to do. She paused by the door to her room. A wave of self-pity came over her – for Catriona the rejected, Catriona the manipulated, Catriona the about-to-be somehow used, Catriona the passive. Then she lost her temper with her own self-indulgence.

"Damn," she turned the key in the door. "Damn," she pushed the door open. "Damn all of it." She kicked the door shut with her heel.

"Hi," said a voice behind her. She spun round terrified. Busboy stood flat against the wall next to the door. He had a revolver which he was now politely putting away. He wore a polo neck sweater, jeans, sneakers and a grubby raincoat. He looked different out of his chauffeur's uniform. The deference had gone. He had left inferiority behind with his braided cap. He had always looked powerful. Now he also looked very tough.

"Sorry to frighten you. It might not have been you."

He smiled reassuringly. He sounded different. His voice remained Southern but without the black molasses. His English had ceased to be non-standard. Catriona remembered the brief moment in Leith when under pressure he had become suddenly grammatical.

"Busboy. What are you doing here? How did you get in?"

"Miss Lomax, a new born child could open that door with its pacifier."

She looked at the door. The lock looked solid to her. She looked back at Busboy. He shrugged modestly and grinned in a cheerful sorry-if-I-seem-to-be-menacing-you fashion.

Catriona walked across the room, found her cigarettes and lit one with unsteady hands. "Who are you Busboy. *What* are you?"

"A friend. A friend who owes the Lady a lot. So a friend that's helping out. Helping the Lady. Helping Mr Tar."

"Why the Jim Crow act?"

"It was necessary. For the general good."

"Don't tell me. You've got a college degree and you work for the CIA."

"Oh my," Busboy chuckled, "two degrees. And I'm only what you might call a freelance. A freelance helping friends, and maybe paying some old debts. Now when you saw Mr Schmidt at the race track what arrangement did he make for meeting you again?"

"He said three, four o'clock. You were having me watched. You and who else?"

"You are the cynosure of all eyes Miss Lomax. I can spell cynosure too. Due to those college degrees."

"You didn't answer me."

"No," said Busboy. "So are you coming or not? I mean you can sit here on your fanny or you can come with me. Jimmy said you'd want to come."

"To do what."

"To *see*," said Busboy.

It rained. Soft Irish rain, midway between mist and spray. Catriona wore a raincoat with a hood. Busboy had brought it with him. She thought back to Edinburgh. Busboy could do everything. Or perhaps he had been well prepared; told exactly what to do. He paid the taxi off. She pulled the hood over her hair and tightened it. Busboy was bareheaded.

"You'll get wet."

"Can't be helped. I want to be noticed."

"Why?"

"Because there's only one reason a black man goes where we're going."

"Which is?"

"You're here to see. Remember?"

They weren't far out. Not more, she supposed, than half a mile from the Liberties but Dublin the Beautiful seemed as distant as the moon. They walked through lines of poor ugly pebble-dashed bungalows built close enough to drip on to each other. Religious statuary abounded. One window had three plaster figurines of the Pope; perhaps someone had misunderstood the Doctrine of the Trinity. The house two windows along had an electric Virgin palming a bleeding heart that flicked on and off like a roadside burger sign. Catriona shivered. "Ugh."

"You'd better prepare yourself for worse than this."

He was right. They turned off the bungalow-strewn road. Ahead three tower blocks loomed out of the mist; a dingy modern version of the siege perilous – lard coloured concrete, smashed windows, the ground in between trampled down and refuse covered.

"Stick close to me," said Busboy. Catriona needed no encouragement.

The buildings looked abandoned but they weren't. Some windows were boarded up. Two or three had become holes blackened by fire but at some there were faces staring blankly out like prisoners in cells.

They walked on, then turned into a narrow space between the two buildings into the remnants of a badly planned playground. The concrete blocks on either side would have kept it in perpetual shadow. Not that this mattered now. Only the skeletons of recreation remained – the cast iron frames of swings, of roundabouts, of a slide and a see-saw. The wood and the chains had been stolen, Catriona supposed, for warmth or weaponry. The ground was scattered with discarded syringes. Straight ahead there was a small fire and around it a cluster of dirty ragged children.

"Oh no," said Catriona.

"Welcome to the twentieth century," said Busboy. "The twenty-first is going to be a real lulu."

The tallest of the children got up and approached them. He was very dirty. He smelt of ageing piss. His wrinkled mean face had a running sore on each cheek. His eyes seemed unnaturally small as if they had used themselves up by seeing too much, by looking at a bad eclipse. His pupils had shrunk to nothing. He wore a man's jacket far too big for him. He was probably about nine years of age. He gave Busboy a nod of professional recognition. Busboy returned it. The boy gave Catriona a sidelong glance and reached into one of his pockets, pulled out a small cone of paper and extended it to Catriona. For a moment she thought she was being offered a mouldy sweet or a half used chip. Then she saw it was full of white powder. What should she say? Not today thank you? As if this nine year old pusher was the milkman?

Busboy intervened. "Put that away. You mind your manners. Here."

He pulled out a fifty pound note. He tore it into two halves – put one into his pocket, gave the other to the child. The child took a pinch from his snow cone, sniffed it, resealed the cone, pocketed it along with the half banknote and ran off towards one of the tower blocks on sole-separating plimsolled feet.

Busboy again took Catriona's arm and moved her slowly in the same direction.

"I've seen whole cities in the States go like this and now it's coming here. The stuff is cheaper than Guinness and it works quicker. In Catholic Ireland where condoms are illegal you have one mighty AIDS epidemic coming down the road." He jerked his head at the little figures huddled by the fire. "Maybe they've got it already. Maybe their parents have died of it. There's fifty per cent youth unemployment."

The hopelessness. The complete ruin of these lives before they had even properly started. That was the worst of it. The robbery of childhood. By comparison any complaint she had ever made about her own life was blind and selfish.

There was a discoloured sign over the tenement's side door. It read, pathetically, Youth Project. In the doorway the representative of youth beckoned. No speaking, thought Catriona. Perhaps drugs had rotted his tongue. They followed him through two battered rooms. They came to a door marked Office. The child had a key. He opened the door and summoned like a bad fairy in a bedtime book. They followed him inside.

Busboy handed over the other half of the banknote. "This,"

said Busboy, "is Mr O'Rourke. He used to run the Youth Project."

Mr O'Rourke was in a hell of a mess. He had been comprehensively beaten up. His face was a mass of bruises. He lay against the wall at an angle which said that his body was bruised the same way. He wore designer jeans and Reeboks and a sharp leather jacket. His long expensively styled hair was matted with blood. He looked up at Busboy and with an effort got his lips moving.

"The money?"

"You stay." Busboy meant the urchin who was making for the door. He kept going. Busboy produced the revolver. The urchin promptly and unemotionally sat down against another wall. Just like that. No fear, no feeling. Just the way it was. Cause and effect.

With his other hand Busboy produced an envelope. O'Rourke said, "Let me see."

Busboy let him see, then took the envelope back and let it drop on the floor between them.

"Tell her. And keep it simple."

He kept it simple. He was probably glad. It was hard for him to speak. Besides, like so many of the worst things in life, it *was* simple. All you had to do was raise the money. You wrote a letter asking for a grant. Then it was explained – by telephone because the respondent never wrote to you – that there were no more grants. But perhaps a loan could be arranged. You got a loan – in cash. Then you invested – O'Rourke rolled his eyes in the direction of the living investment in the corner taking another whiff from his personal snow cone – and you repaid in cash at three times the normal interest. That was that. Once off and once only. That was how the Despard Foundation worked.

They left the envelope on the floor and went outside.

"It's got a lot of merits," said Busboy. "It's clever partly because it's cautious. Schmidt operates through what looks like a respectable front organisation. Here this Youth Project shit. Nothing's written down. Well that's O'Rourke's problem. Nothing says that Schmidt has to write things down either as he notionally pays his taxes. And Schmidt's not greedy. Better to make one quick profit and move on. He keeps out of the way of the law and he keeps out of the way of the big boys who start moving in on something like this. That's his method. A little at a time but over the years it all adds up. Schmidt scams a little, puts a little back into the Foundation. Both ways invests what's been made in legal business, and in judicious gambling."

Catriona thought of Monty and his bookmaker's business. She thought too that Busboy sounded like Louis when he was summarising a well known, well researched topic.

"And legally speaking it's hard as hell to catch him. He throws up his arms. How could I have known? Anyway the bastard operates from Switzerland where bank accounts are numbers and he keeps his nose very clean. And don't believe what you've heard about the Swiss disclosing account ownership. That's head of government arm twisting stuff. No, the criminal law won't get Schmidt."

Catriona looked back through the mist at the rubble and the filth-filled little figures huddled about the fire. She thought of her slum born father. He had fought poverty and won at the least a sort of personal victory. But that poverty had not enlisted drugs on its side. She turned wearily to Busboy. She supposed he knew about the will; he seemed to know everything else. And now it was crystal clear to her.

"Except of course if he lost control of the Despard Foundation."

She looked back again into the tunnel of shadow and mist between the tenements.

Catriona let herself into the hotel bedroom. This time there was no Busboy. She put down the new clothes she had just bought in Grafton Street.

She looked at her watch. It was still only a little after noon. It suddenly occurred to her that what she needed more than anything at the moment was to feel good about herself – and that the principal obstacles to this were feeling scruffy, hungry, and very badly in need of a drink.

Yet as she changed clothes thoughts continued to race through her head. So Busboy had shown her a Schmidt horror. That was to say a Schmidt-induced, Schmidt-permitted horror. Could it have been staged? Surely not, and what anyway would have been the point? . . . And then Busboy? What *about* Busboy? Who did he *really* work for? Where was

Robinson and the Ministry in all of this? What did Tar mean by their working in association? Where did she, Catriona, fit in? Was she part of some trap into which Schmidt should walk? But how could she possibly bait it? After all what use could she be to those for or against Schmidt – to the whole future of the Foundation. If there was no proof of her birth she had no vote. She was irrelevant. She was Miss Nobody from Nowhere . . . Yet that didn't fit. It simply made no sense at all. Everyone behaved as if she was relevant. So she couldn't be Miss Nobody from . . .

She put down her lipstick with a bang. Surely that had to be it. Somewhere there *was* that proof.

When she hurried down the hotel staircase Catriona wore a silk blouse, a tweed skirt and had gathered her hair in a black silk scarf. She looked at her reflection in the stairs mirror. Still blonde – keep going and you'll turn white. Well if you've got it flaunt it while it's there. She swung the coat that Busboy had brought her. She would leave this flat modern nothing of a hotel, walk a block to the Shelburne and sit there drinking champagne and looking good. Then salmon. She remembered how Penelope always talked about the Shelburne's salmon.

Still when she reached the Shelburne Catriona chose a quiet corner of the dark bar and sat with her back to the door. Wanting to feel attractive was one thing; encouraging passing men to do double takes and ogle quite another. She sat for a while with newspaper, cigarette and champagne cocktail.

She looked up. The barman placed a second – unordered – champagne cocktail in front of her and withdrew with a discreet but filthy smile.

"All alone," said a male voice behind her; an exquisitely tailored sleeve in Glen Urquhart check came over her shoulder. At the sleeve's end was a beautifully tapering hand grasping a whisky glass. She would have known Esmond's hands anywhere.

But he didn't know her.

"Ah, Catriona." He got it out quickly because where women were concerned he was almost never at a loss, but she knew instantly that he had walked into the bar, seen the rearview of an attractive woman and came to pick her up. Besides, he would only have bought an expensive drink for a new girl.

"Don't smile so hard Esmond. I can practically read your dentist's bill."

Esmond went on smiling. "Sharp. You always were sharp."

She thought of her childhood. Think you know it all don't you Catriona. So sharp you'll cut yourself. Well she felt pretty blunt now. I despise you Esmond. You are pointless. You are useless. You lie just by standing here with your only-girl-in-the-world smile. But oh dear God Almighty you are attractive. And that isn't fair or right or reasonable. But then, said a small voice inside Catriona, what is?

He reached out and touched her cheek just underneath the bruise. "Mmm," he drawled. "Got a rough boyfriend. Didn't take you long I must say." Uninvited, he sat.

"I bumped into something." (You fool. Don't explain to him. Don't send him any signals.)

"So what brings you to Dublin?" Very gently he took her hand and began to massage her thumb.

Now, she thought. Stop it now. Take away your hand *now*. She didn't.

"Business. And you?"

"Family business."

Of course you are. And I know what business. And you don't know I know. And of course I should get out of this place, this bar, this situation, this hand wrapped round my hand right this minute. But if you stay, said a little self-serving dishonest voice, you might learn more.

He moved from her thumb to her forearm. He knew how she loved to have her forearm stroked. She tried to hate him. She certainly hated his presumption. She hated how she was beginning to feel. But she did not move her arm. This man was dishonourable. He is my inferior. So why in the wide world do I want him so badly to make love to me?

Suddenly, as clearly as if she had been in the room, came the image of Theodora. Good plain decent Theodora who was worth a dozen of her husband, whose betrayal came closer by the moment. So, said the voice, would one more betrayal make any difference?

"Your wife?" Catriona meant it to sound moral. It sounded strategic. Esmond had reached her thigh now, stroking beautifully.

"Gone ahead to my house. We're getting the dump back.

She loves the bloody place."

Wait a minute, thought Catriona. Dump? Bloody place?

"You threw me over Esmond. Just last week." She expected a bogus excuse or a glib joke.

Instead he frowned. "That might have been a mistake."

For a brief moment Catriona felt sympathy with men gripped by a sexual obsession. Men who came again and again to her club just because the shape of a worthless breast, the turn of a meretricious neck drove them erotically crazy. After a while they had to pretend that their little lust bundles really cared for them after all. Perhaps she was doing the same but Esmond now seemed to be looking at her *personally*.

He took his hand away. He would never have done that usually.

"Fact is I'm worried."

"Can't you speak in sentences?" (She who could hardly speak at all!) He not only looked beautiful. He sounded like a human being.

"The fact is that I need you, Catriona."

And she was sunk.

There was no shame like the shame that comes from pleasure. It's worse for women, thought Catriona, as Esmond rolled away. We always give that bit extra and they always take it. However you cut the pleasure cake men get the bigger slice. Not that she hadn't enjoyed herself. She had. Oh she had. It was just that Esmond could now sit on the end of the hotel bed while she felt like a villainess, a scarlet woman, a traitress.

But – and it was a large but – this wasn't the usual Esmond. As a lover he put ego first. He liked to spend a long time and be told he was wonderful. His lust was vain and epicurean. This time he had been hungrier, as if trying to find or get rid of something. Usually he would be polite afterwards; he would always have a plausible excuse to get away quickly. Besides he was ageing and conceited; he didn't want his body looked at too long in the wrong light.

Yet here he still was – sitting there like a man who had run out of small talk.

"It's Theodora," he said. "She's up to something."

"What?"

Be careful, thought Catriona. There are things you aren't

supposed to know. Remember Catriona. You've betrayed Theodora again; that's enough.

"Damned if I know really," said Esmond. "I keep getting the feeling that she's . . . " he searched for the right word, "deceiving me."

Catriona sat up. "You mean with someone else? Another man?"

"Dunno. No. I don't think so. No. But it's *like* that. Something she doesn't want me to know."

(Like that she visited me.) "I didn't realise that you paid so much attention to her?"

"I don't. That's what bothers me. See here – don't you work for that Schmidt fellow?"

(Careful Catriona.) "He owns the club."

"So that's why you're here? Club business?"

"Yes."

"Some sort of secretarial thing for him I suppose?"

There was no point in taking offence. A manageress and a secretary would always be equally female-menial to Esmond.

"That sort of thing, Esmond."

"Mmm. Well then I expect you realise that he's a fairly dubious proposition. Sails pretty close to the wind. Not that most businessmen don't do the same. Besides he's a shifty looking bastard and a Swiss. Fat one too."

"What's that got to do with it?"

Esmond ignored this question as rhetorical. "Of course he *may* be all right but one has to be cautious. And Theodora's usually cautious."

"Please Esmond."

"It's a family thing. To do with my bitch of a stepmother's husband's will. It seems there's some sort of trust and one has to choose the bitch or Schmidt to run it. Well I hate the bitch but I'd like to hear a bit more before I give this Schmidt fellow the go-ahead."

"Esmond? How do you know he's dubious? Mr Schmidt?"

"Asked a fellow I was at school with. Robinson. He gets around. Picks things up."

(Robinson. She pulled the heavy linen sheet around her.)

The talking seemed to help him. He reached for his clothes.

"Theodora, Esmond. What about Theodora?"

"She's pushing for Schmidt."

Surely she thinks . . . Catriona stopped herself just in time and did some quick rethinking. "Don't you stand to gain? One way or another? Now you've got your house back won't you want more money – to run it?"

Esmond gave a nasty laugh. "The bitch wouldn't give me a penny. When she dies she'll make some home for left-wing cats very happy. I suppose Schmidt might come across with a retainer. But it mightn't be too clever to get mixed up with him. You'd think Theodora would understand that. I am a Member of bloody Parliament after all."

"The house, though?"

Then he really surprised her. "Hate it. Pointless great barracks of a place. Gloomy great white elephant. Besides my father drank himself to death there. Gives me the abjabs. The land's unfarmable too. If I can't sell it to some fool it'll have to be pulled down." He straightened his tie and reached for his jacket.

"Esmond. Why *did* you chuck me?"

He took no offence. He had needed Catriona. Now he didn't. Things were no longer personal.

"Told you at the time. More or less. Theodora was sniffing around altogether too much."

"Was that all?"

"That's what she always does. Her pattern if you like. You don't want to underestimate Theodora. She's tough."

"Then why are you here?"

Esmond grinned his complacent rooster's grin. "She's being tough somewhere else." He had reached the door. "We'll have a drink in London, mmm?"

"Esmond, why do you hate your stepmother so much?"

He stood grasping the handle, the door half open. Then he said, "She's the world's biggest whore."

Catriona knew how she felt.

Catriona had lost track of time. She was late. She hurried across the hotel lobby. But there was no Schmidt, no message from Schmidt. She didn't understand it. She was making for the lift to return to her room, to wash Esmond off her when Theodora Claremaurice rose out of a chair, stood in her way and said, "Deceit."

Catriona froze. She had always made a bad adulteress. Yes,

it was a free world and if a man wanted to be with her and not his wife that was his choice and there was no point in inflicting pain so that was why the wife was kept in the dark. These things she had told herself, but they had never really worked. And that was at the best of times. These were the worst of times.

Theodora stood before her pulling with raw hands at the string of pearls that hung limply on her twin set. Her face twisted in anguish. She had been crying. She had trouble speaking. She said, "Esmond." Stopped. Sniffled. Then, "Deceit. Deception. Whatever you call it."

"Yes," said Catriona. Theodora must have seen them. She must not have gone ahead but waited in Dublin to spy on Esmond. Had she listened outside the door as well? Catriona could feel the trickle of sperm that Esmond had left on her breast. All right. Let it start now. Let it all come out. Get on with it. Punish me. I deserve it.

Theodora managed to speak.

"I feel so terrible about it. About deceiving you."

Theodora sat on the bed. She should have looked better in country clothes but she wore them with gawky ill-ease. Catriona took the arm chair; she didn't want to go near a bed for a long time.

She put down the telephone. There were no messages at reception . . . Yes, if one came they would telephone immediately.

Theodora was eager, awkward, apologetic in distress and so obviously devoid of sin that Catriona felt no relief at not being caught. In fact she felt even worse.

"You see I knew. When I came to see you at your nice flat . . . " (bohemian Theodora; say it) "that you worked for that Mr Schmidt. I checked you see. As to who owned your club. I was so worried about you and Esmond. Of course that was before I knew what you were *really* like . . . " (go on, rub it in) "so I thought you might be conspiring. You and Esmond. So perhaps you and Esmond might run away together. I mean this Mr Schmidt might have arranged it."

An alarm bell of a question as big as a migraine went off in Catriona's head. How did this incoherent fear of Theodora's possibly fit with Esmond's declaration that Theodora was pressing him to side with Schmidt? Catriona couldn't ask about it without revealing that she'd just been with Esmond.

"I expect it's because he just thinks I'm a silly woman – no one tells one anything when one's female . . . " (welcome to the sewing circle Theodora, I know just what you mean) "so Esmond won't tell me but I think he may be somehow involved with this Schmidt. Ugh."

She made a schoolgirl meets a creepy crawly face.

Concentrate, Catriona told herself. You must concentrate.

"You know Schmidt?"

"Oh I met him. Years ago. Yuk." (Same face.) "I don't suppose you have a cigarette. You remember the last time you gave me one."

"Yes Theodora, I remember." Catriona got her a cigarette. Theodora puffed out a straight tramline of smoke.

"The point is that Esmond doesn't think he'll ever get any money from stepmama. So I think he may have got himself mixed up with Schmidt. For money."

Take it slowly Catriona. One step at a time. "But he has money."

"My money." Theodora said it flatly, looking down at her cigarette. "Esmond's expensive. And the house," she looked up and gave a tremulous smile, "Claremaurice House, it is beautiful but it will cost such a lot to put right."

Catriona tried to defamiliarise her tone. "You think that Esmond wants that?"

"Oh *yes*." A moment of girlish enthusiasm; it was quickly replaced by the old anxiety. "But I haven't explained at all have I? About the family thingy. I shouldn't even be here. It's just that I don't have anyone . . . anyone to talk to." She stopped talking. She just sat there, hands folded, silent and bereft. Catriona's heart went out to her.

Catriona made a decision. She leaned forward.

"Theodora," she said. "I have something to tell you."

"Why it's like a fairy tale," said Theodora.

You don't know the half of it, thought Catriona. In fact you know about a quarter. No Visitor, no Tar, no Ministry, no Maxwell, no Sanatorium, no Leith, no Jessie, no Busboy, no trip this morning to the tenement where the Despard Foundation made a living. Catriona had told what she believed to be Theodora's due. That she had been adopted. That a hysterical Madame Despard had returned to claim maternity. That she had been told of the Foundation settlement by Donovan Myers. That without legal proof of birth she had no vote. That therefore she was useless as an ally to either Madame Despard or Schmidt. That she was in the dark.

Now she said, "Fairy tales have happy endings."

"You'll be rich," said Theodora. Again that flat tone when she talked about money.

"But I told you . . . "

"No. Madame Despard's own money. Who else would get it?"

(The cat's home, said Esmond.) "No. I don't think so."

"You wait and see. Ever so rich. You deserve it. She abandoned you. What about your father? I mean your actual father?"

"He's dead," said Catriona quickly.

"Oh. If you *did* have a vote, what would you do Catriona?"

"I don't know. I suppose I'd wait and see."

Theodora was on her third cigarette. She had learned quickly how to smoke properly.

"You can only follow your conscience." From anyone else it would have sounded pompous. From Theodora it sounded simple and true. Theodora got up from the bed and walked over to the window.

"Things will change for you. They won't for me. Esmond will go on not telling me anything. He thinks I'm nothing really. It won't change. It'll be like this for the rest of my life. Esmond's women too . . . "

Theodora turned to face Catriona. "I think he's got someone else already. Here in Dublin. I'm sorry. I didn't mean to hurt your feelings."

Guilt wrenched Catriona's features; "No. No. I was thinking of you."

Theodora smiled her sad smile. "I'd better resign myself to it."

(I thought you *had* Theodora – but perhaps you just told yourself that – perhaps I was naïve to believe it.)

"You know he doesn't have much of a conscience, Esmond. So it's up to me to see that he does what's right. As you said, wait and see. I mean about the will. The woman thing is hopeless. He's too clever for me."

Catriona wished she could sit down with Theodora and unburden herself completely. She couldn't though. Instead she needed to think. She remembered then that Esmond too had said something about deception.

"Theodora do you never think of . . . " (she struggled for an available euphemism) "of being unfaithful to Esmond?"

"Oh yes. I am a woman you know." She said it gently yet Catriona felt rebuked. "But . . . " Her rueful smile finished the sentence. It said don't you realise that for someone like me that is utterly impossible?

The telephone rang. The desk had a message for Miss Lomax from someone.

# 32

The brothel was just beyond Sandymount. The taxi wound around the bay, left the suburb, came into open country, then turned into the drive of a square suburban villa. This, Tar had said, was Catriona's last bit of personalised seeing, her last sample of Show and Tell. She still had no idea where Schmidt had got to. All she could think of was to leave the address at Reception.

Catriona had never knowingly been in a brothel. She didn't know what to expect but she was certainly unprepared for the atmosphere of solid respectability that started with the quiet uniformed maid who answered the door and continued through the wax and camphor convent smell of the broad hall. The place was silent. Presumably it opened for business later in the evening.

The maid showed her into a heavily furnished thick carpeted parlour. A lumpy matronly woman as solid as the house rose from a pile of accounts. The woman shook hands with robust cheerfulness. She neither gave her name nor asked for Catriona's. She sat Catriona down at a tea table piled high with thick-crusted ham sandwiches. "Ye look famished."

Catriona was. She hit the top sandwich like a marine going for a bridgehead.

"I'll not waste time," said the woman. "Ye're here to listen to me and meet someone. In that order."

Mouth full, Catriona nodded. In a day and a half she had hardly eaten. This was the world's most necessary sandwich.

"What you see here is clean and well run and it's thanks to Madame Despard. For I wanted something that wasn't like the places I'd worked in when I was a girl. She didn't charge; not she. It was a loan where she never cared for the interest. We'd take the girls in and clean them up and give them the best clothes. They were taught about contraception and never a one had to take a man who was dirty or brutal. We even made the men wash, can you imagine that?" She gave the cheery laugh of a county wife at a flower show. "We had a doctor who checked regularly. We saved a proportion of the girls' money too, so at the end they'd have a nest egg to leave with. Many a girl got married on that. Yes and went on to be a good wife and mother too. The best tending a girl could have. For that's what's needed. Tending. It's a rare girl who comes to this life who's not had a bad thing or two done to her; who's not in need of better care than she's been getting. And who, if she takes to this game in Holy Ireland where contraception is illegal never mind abortion, is likeliest to find herself pimp-ridden and diseased and drunk and dead with children left to squawl upon the streets. For I'll tell you this," the woman pointed a severe finger, "whether you approve or not she did good. Ah she did much good. She was a realist. There'll always be places of this particular nature. There'll always be places where men exploit women. That's what Madame Despard said. This way the men paid and the girls at least got something out of it." She smiled. "Don't think of selling your bodies – that's what she'd tell the girls – think of renting them."

Catriona nodded through her ham sandwich. It sounded like approximate sense to her.

"And then," the woman had ceased to be genial, "things changed. Madame Despard was no longer in charge and the loan had to be paid back with the interest rate doubled. I got the money together somehow and repaid quickly. I was afraid of what might have happened to the girls, what he might have put them through."

"He?" But Catriona knew the answer in advance.

"The new man was name of Mr Schmidt."

Catriona pushed the plate of sandwiches away; her appetite had gone. The woman lifted a large handbell and gave it two shakes. The maid reappeared bringing with her a square sturdy girl who, even in the cosy muted lamplight of the parlour (dusk was setting in), had farm written all over her. She came into the room shyly and with a shamefaced awkwardness. For a moment Catriona was reminded of Theodora but she drove the thought away. She couldn't afford guilt at the moment; she had no more space for it.

The girl had a weathered complexion; work had already begun to age her. Catriona guessed that she was only about eighteen, though she might pass for ten years older. She had a large head which might have seemed masculine but for the singular submissive sweetness and innocence of her face. She could have been the primitive madonna of some crude wayfaring artist.

"Now down ye sit, Dolours."

Dolours sat. She was visibly pregnant.

"Now Dolours just you tell what you told me."

She told her story. It was very terrible.

There had been a farm and nine children and she Dolours the eldest. And their mother had died with the last one. So didn't Dolours have to take care of the house as well as the hens and help with the milking. Her father was not the same since her mother died. At night he would take a drop too much. Then he would weep and be violent until finally he visited his grief and his appetite together upon Dolours.

Now she began to weep softly. He was not a bad man. They must not think that. It was only that he had his sorrows. But because he was a good man no one would believe her. Not the priest and not the nuns. She who had done nothing was now doubly wicked. So she had run off looking for a certain kind of address. She had come to Dublin. She had come here. It was at this point in the story that Dolours most impressed Catriona by her strength.

"It was a terrible sin but it had to be done. Else you see Miss there would be no life for anyone." She meant that otherwise she could never go back to take care of her brothers and sisters.

Except that it never happened. She had gone twice. First the man had asked her for money and then when all she had was just enough to make the journey and back he had said he would operate if she did . . . things . . . And she had done the things. And told to come back in a week, and then they were closing the place down.

What place? The place in Edinburgh. The clinic. Which once upon a time had run at Madame Despard's charitable behest. Schmidt had changed that.

Catriona was herself close to tears. Her own problems melted into insignificance. Cruelty of a kind she had seen. Brutality she had seen. She could even find a small corner of pity for Dolours' drunken, selfish, irresponsible father but she simply could not understand the kind of monster who could take the desperate pleading agony of a girl like this and play with it.

The woman said, "There were others who were less lucky. Two that I know of are dead. One swallowed a packet of drugs to smuggle and the thing burst inside her. Another they just killed with carelessness during the operation."

"What will happen to Dolours now?"

"Ah she'll have the baby. We'll help her yet. Off with you now Dolours and take the plate with you."

Smiling gratefully Dolours took up the plate of sandwiches like the healthy girl she was.

"But" (as Dolours left the room), "she'll never see her family again." She paused. "And of course there's a sister just a year or so behind her that she'll never have the chance to protect. Ah well I'll leave the two of you now."

The door that had just closed behind poor Dolours re-opened. Madame Despard stood in the doorway.

Catriona stood up. Madame Despard was back in leather. Perhaps she was travelling light. Perhaps she wanted to remind Catriona of how they had been together on the train. Perhaps leather was simply good for damp Dublin. In the comfortable bourgeois plush of the brothel she looked magnificently out of place; as if she had stepped down from some photogravure Olympus to do a little charity work. She stood very straight. She was in control again.

The hostess looked backwards and forwards between them. She had half recognised something that was none of her business. "I'll leave ye together."

She hurried past Madame Despard, who merely inclined her head. Catriona heard a scrap of conversation with Dolours in the hall. Then the door closed and they were alone together.

"Well," said Catriona, "I've heard the reference. You're a wonderful human being. To other people."

Not to your daughter – but she couldn't get the words out. Madame Despard knew them anyway.

"I told you I wasn't lovable."

"Yes," said Catriona. "But you didn't tell me you were my mother."

Madame Despard advanced into the room. "I was going to. Then you said that Jimmy was dead. That finished me. I thought that everything was over."

Everything?

"You knew," Madame Despard was closer now. "That was cruel of you. Perhaps you got that from Jimmy. The cruelty. Though he always had a Cause to hide it under. I just ran away. You're not like that."

Catriona saw again the wardrobe in Leith, the annual purchase of clothes that she would never wear. What had it taken to do that? To teeter on the brink and then, time after time, retreat? What had she felt, this unlovable woman? Had she been going to tell Catriona the truth for about a third of a century?

"You think," said Catriona, "that you haven't been cruel? You think that this isn't cruel?"

"You hate me," said Madame Despard. "I knew you would."

Suddenly Catriona was yelling. "I don't hate you. I don't not hate you. I don't *anything* you. You could have told me the truth. YOU COULD HAVE COME FOR ME."

"Yes," said Madame Despard. "I could. But the truth is I'm not much of a catch."

That stopped Catriona short. Madame Despard walked across the thick dull carpet to the desk. She took a cigarette from the packet of Sweet Afton that lay there. She made a face at the brand but lit the cigarette anyway. As on the train she had to use one hand to keep the other steady. Nerves? Distress under the carefully tailored control? Or just the fact that her elegance continually concealed – that she was old?

"I made a mess of everything. I married Patrick Claremaurice and that was no good. Patrick was a drunk. I went to work for Despard. Then I married him. I liked the Foundation. Ideals, excitement. But I made a mess of that too. And I conceived you. By Jimmy. I think you will have gathered that I like . . . " she paused, "that sexually I like . . . "

"You like rough trade," said Catriona.

Madame Despard looked defiantly at Catriona. "Yes. That disgusts you."

"No." Disgust of that kind was for the censorious world of judging men. A world that forgave itself for visiting brothels and vilified the women who staffed them. Besides, her own taste for Esmond was bad enough. She said, "God knows why any of us like what we like."

Madame Despard laughed. "I know all right. I got the taste

from Jimmy. Long ago in Spain even before I was married to Patrick. It was always Jimmy you see. Always Jimmy."

Catriona had no doubt. She could see Tar's face as he had talked of Madame Despard, fierce and straight ahead over the steering wheel. She had no doubt at all. These parents of hers had loved each other.

"I wonder what you'd have done. I wonder. There I was married to Despard. There was Jimmy the quasi-terrorist. Off somewhere else and I don't just mean geographically. Jimmy was always running some private revolution in his head. So what if I told him – what would he have done? He'd have said abortion. Even if he hadn't, what kind of a life would you have had? . . . Here are my parents the assassin and the whore."

"Don't say that." She was trying to hurt herself, Madame Despard.

"So I found a childless woman and I went ahead. And I never told Jimmy. I had the clinic so that was easy enough. But I told you, I make a mess of things. I kept thinking . . . maybe one day . . . I knew I'd be no good for you."

"But I don't understand how you got away with it? Anyway couldn't you have said that it – that I – was his?"

"Despard was impotent," she paused. "Jimmy shot him. A month after we got married. At the base of the spine. Quite deliberately. So he could never screw me again. He was in hospital for a long time. Including when I was pregnant."

Catriona sat down.

"I told you that Jimmy could be cruel. Don't be deceived. Just because he's nice to us. He's still Jimmy."

"My God."

Madame Despard came and stood next to her. Catriona felt as if she were drowning in competing emotions. She put up her hand but Madame Despard didn't take it. She now spoke slowly and carefully, each word squeezed out. "Don't be deceived about me either. I could have walked away from Schmidt's blackmail. I should have stopped him taking you up and making you over . . . "

"Wait a minute. Just hold on . . . "

Madame Despard actually stamped her foot as if Catriona were a child over whom she had some rights. "Dammit let me finish. It's hard enough to say. But I didn't have the guts. So when I say I need you that's selfish too but it's *right*."

Catriona grabbed Madame Despard by the shoulders. "Don't you understand. I'm not legally yours. I don't have a vote. You didn't even give me your name."

Madame Despard looked down at her blankly as if Catriona were an idiot. "But of course I did. Of course you do. You're hurting me."

Catriona screamed like a child. "What do you know about hurt? You've got it all wrong. I don't have anything."

Realisation of a kind was happening to Madame Despard's long lined face. "Jimmy didn't tell you about the birth certificate? The original?"

Catriona released her and stared. Madame Despard said, "Schmidt's got it."

Suddenly the air was filled with the clamour of an electric bell. The hostess' genial untroubled face came round the parlour door.

"No cause for worry. 'Tis nothing but a police raid. Just for formality's sake they do it once a month. They telephone first so that we can get all the clients out in time. Then the police lads have a nice drink with me. Off they go and it's all back to normal. Ah well," she checked her watch, "They're too early for clients tonight. All the same we'll not be wanting awkward questions so we'll take you through to the back and out of harm's way. Come here Dolours. You too."

She ushered Catriona, Dolours and Madame Despard across the hall, through a large kitchen, then into a pantry. She opened a door to the outside. Catriona could smell animals and the water from Dublin Bay. Night had fallen.

"The old farmyard. The boys never come out the back. It's a good understanding that we have. Here now." She reached up and pulled at a clothes line that ran outwards into the lightless darkness. "Just you find yourself down that a little way and you'll find a nice enough bench to sit on."

Madame Despard swore under her breath but she went first, her black leather melding with the dark. Dolours put one hand on the rope and with the other gripped Catriona tightly.

"Ye don't mind?"

"Of course not."

They edged along the rope sightlessly like Great War gas victims. Catriona heard the sound of a car engine. The police, she thought.

Then everything happened fast. Beyond the farmyard a single beam like that of a torch but with the force of a searchlight snapped on to them. It blinded Madame Despard, who fell against the bench shouting out and pulling Catriona with her. "Get down. Get your head down."

But Catriona was slow to realise. She pulled back and looked up to see Dolours, who had slipped a little, steady herself with a rope and then fold like a petulant fan, her forehead gone red. Only then did the shot sound. Catriona wiped Dolours' spattered blood out of her own eyes.

Madame Despard was screaming. "Busboy!"

He was running from somewhere. "Lady." The light had gone out. Another report. Perhaps Busboy's own gun. Catriona crouched over Dolours. Madame Despard tried to pull her away but Catriona had to get close enough to see.

Dolours had no more sorrows to seek. Her quiet suffering submissive face was mutton-dead. Jessie-dead.

Busboy fired again. A motor cycle started up. Roared away.

Now there was the sound of a car engine coming round the side of the house. Yes, there were the car's lights. Catriona scrambled up and, waving her arms, frantically ran towards the police.

# 33

The rear door of the long black limousine swung open. Catriona clutched at it, yelling. Then from its dark interior she was grabbed by arms – strong arms – and pulled from her feet. The car started to move again. Her knees bounced once, twice, painfully on the ground and she was hauled inside. She sprawled on the floor as the car picked up speed.

"Stop! Don't you understand? You have to stop! Someone's been shot."

She rolled over to bang on the door. She had to get back – to Madame Despard, to Busboy, to the body that had heaved blood out of two lives as it hung from the washing pole line.

But the car was going even faster. She heard the click of a central locking system. She sat up. A big man with a broad face, dressed in jeans and a tee shirt showing huge biceps, looked at her impassively.

"So what you wait for? You help Miss Lomax to a seat."

Schmidt hunched into his camel coat had huddled against the extreme corner of the back seat, as if trying to put the maximum distance between harm and himself.

"Mr Schmidt you have to stop."

"Miss Lomax. Catriona. This is a bad thing you unnerstan'."

"*You* don't understand. She was shot. Killed. A poor girl. A poor pregnant girl. Back there. I think someone was trying to shoot Madame Despard."

Schmidt shrank back further. "She's got a lot of enemies. But shot. That's a bad thing."

"She's all right. It's the girl."

"Sure. A poor pregnant girl. I hate to blaspheme but Jesus. This is a very unsafe place."

"WE HAVE TO STOP."

"Sure."

The car drove on. "You calm yourself."

He had calmed himself all right. Death was further behind them. He leaned forward.

"This is a very terrible world. But we stop? For what? They

got police. They got the big shot Madame Despard to sort things out. Schmidt can't spare the time. We got things to do. Look at you. Best manageress I ever had. Huh! What a mess. You ignore my messages, you get like this. Help Miss Lomax up."

Biceps reached out. He had professional Heavy written all over him.

"She was *dead*," said Catriona, "and if you touch me again I'll claw your eyes out."

"A lot of people are dead," said Schmidt. "You aren't. Get off the floor."

Despite everything Catriona the employee reacted to the boss's voice. She reached up, pulled down one of the jump seats (she wanted to be near neither of them, especially Biceps) and got herself on to it. She sat with her back to the chauffeur's glass panel. She smoothed down her skirt. Her tights had torn. Her knees bled.

"What instructions? You were supposed to send me a message."

"Sure I sent you a message. Come round to my hotel. Then we have a nice chat thoroughly. I put you in the picture. Then we make a nice journey in comfort."

"There was no message." Although this was true and she was in the right Catriona found herself speaking defensively, like a stubborn child repeating an implausible excuse. Perhaps it was the way Schmidt looked at her – quizzically, one yellow eyebrow up.

"There *wasn't*."

Schmidt sat back and sighed. "Hotels. OK. Schmidt believes you."

"Thanks," said Catriona. "I want to get out."

"We all want something," said Schmidt philosophically. "Me I want a camel coat that fails to scratch my back and a quiet life. What do I get? Always some itching. Rescuing my best manageress who turns against me."

"Stop the car. You don't own me."

Catriona had never seen Schmidt angry. He was angry now. An outsider would not have noticed. He didn't rage or shout as she had just done. He didn't even raise his voice. But his slack body went tense and his tiny eyes seemed to grow a millimetre closer to each other.

This is important to him, thought Catriona. *I* am important to him.

"So very well. People tell you bad things about Schmidt. So I could tell you some bad things of my own. But you want to get out. Schmidt believes in free choice. Liberty hall."

He rapped on the glass panel. The chauffeur pulled the car into the side of the road and stopped but left the engine running. A click; the rear door on Catriona's side swung open.

Outside Ireland seemed to stretch forever. No lights – she could hardly see the road. There was neither traffic nor habitation, only the smell of the earth and the light drilling of rain on the car roof. Catriona was a city girl in empty country.

"Oh sure," Schmidt was saying. "Other people get to explain but not Schmidt, who gives you a job and never puts one small piece of blaspheming pressure on you. You got a funny way with thank-yous."

The night and the countryside looked back at her with the cold impassivity of hell. There was only the smell and the darkness and the fearful prospects of a lone woman on a lonely road.

Perhaps fear returned her to reality. No staying with Schmidt, no solution, no endgame. Besides, she realised with the purest of pleasure that she had him worried.

"I go away, I only have to come back for you. You concerned? You ask the driver where we're going."

He tapped the panel. It slid back.

"All right," said Catriona. "Where are we going?"

The driver she saw was another big man, from the same stable as Biceps.

"Claremaurice House, Miss."

Catriona closed the door. Schmidt beamed. He looked at her knees.

"Schmidt says ouch. Maybe we got some items for that."

He pressed a button and opened an ugly walnut cabinet that squatted between the jump seats. It contained drink and peanuts.

"Huh!" said Schmidt. "No first aid kit. Some limo." He became solicitous. "You give Miss Lomax the brandy. I mean a glass I say a glass. You give her the bottle. Your hands clean? You surprise me. So with your clean hands then."

Catriona took the bottle and, passed by his fingertips, one of

Schmidt's beautiful silk handkerchiefs. He never touches you, she thought. She gestured at the bodyguard.

"I want him in the front."

"You're a demanding woman. This is good. You say what you want. We do business. You climb over."

Biceps hesitated. Schmidt chortled. "I got to fear my best girl that I made? Do what you're told."

He climbed over. Schmidt pressed a button. The panel closed. Catriona began to dab at the cuts on her knees. The brandy stung. My best girl, she thought; that I *made*.

Schmidt made conversation. "These are local boys," he meant the two large creatures in the front. "A little crude but effective. There's a lot of unemployment. I like to help local boys. Not too directly you unnerstan'. I do good, but for Schmidt the word is always indirection."

Catriona pictured the pile of syringes, the tenement urchins pursuing their own version of full employment. She dabbed angrily at her smarting knee but said nothing. Wait and see, she told herself. Wait and see.

Schmidt was disapproving further of the cabinet. "This car got no possibility for buttermilk. All alcohol. A very unhealthy thing."

Actually Schmidt didn't look healthy. His skin was too pale. Anxiety? Stress? Some hidden excitement? Catriona wondered not only what Schmidt was up to but what he was really like as a man. What made him live? What *ran* him?

"There's some mineral water."

Schmidt shuddered. "My bladder! Believe me."

She went back to her knee. When she looked up she realised that Schmidt had been staring at her. He wore the expression she remembered from their first encounter, long ago in Cairo. He was assessing.

"So. Schmidt does not blaspheme but maybe some blasphemy is necessary. You go sniffing round. You listen. You believe everyone but Schmidt."

Catriona made herself sound professionally prim. "Mr Schmidt. You have not talked to me. You have not told me one single thing."

"I been busy," said Schmidt vaguely. "I had to keep out of the way while business got sorted."

He might have been describing a missed appointment. He

smiled reassuringly. He was the old Schmidt – self-confident, sure of himself.

"Anyway, maybe it's all for the best. You went talking with other people first. You form an impression without Schmidt making an influence."

(Tar's point she thought, but played back against Tar. Everyone pretends that little Catriona gets to make up her own mind.)

"Furthermore how could I keep you from the old woman? She makes up her mind to see you how can I stop you?"

The old woman. First she thought he meant Jessie but no, he meant Madame Despard. Well, one way of preventing a conversation would be by killing her. Exhaustion crept over Catriona. It was such an effort to think, yet thinking had never been so important. She used the pain in her knees as an aid to concentration.

"So. You see the old woman and you see the lawyer. What do they tell you?"

Perhaps exhaustion lends insight; Catriona knew immediately that Schmidt had no idea that she had talked to Tar or Jessie or, if it came to that, Theodora. Or Esmond. (But she never wanted to think about Esmond again.) He spoke smugly with a totality of knowledge. Catriona drew a deep breath.

"My parents. My real parents. The Foundation. What happens to it. What's to happen to it. Madame Despard told me a lot of stories about you."

Schmidt was pleased. "Stories. I like that word. You bet one large fat ass she told you stories."

"You used me."

"Using." Schmidt leaned forward, the employer explaining a point of industrial etiquette. "Using is not a crime."

She fought back the recriminations. They could wait. Get to the point that mattered *now*.

"The lawyer. Mr Myers. He told me that . . . that despite who I am I don't have a vote."

Schmidt looked positively delighted. "Oh, ho, ho."

(Christ, Mr Toad as Santa Claus.) To stop herself from speaking she took a long swallow from the brandy bottle. The alcohol rushed to her brain. Sleep pulled at her.

"You are going to be pleased." Schmidt beamed. Schmidt the bearer of gifts. Schmidt the present-giver. "First I ask you one question. All the time you know me does Schmidt ever do one thing to you that wasn't good?"

There it was. Whatever all the others had told her one indisputable fact stood in the way. Schmidt had never done her anything but good.

"No Mr Schmidt."

"I got documents. I got all kind of documents. I got who you are. And I got who you can be."

She sounded like a little girl over-tired at the party's end. "Thank you Mr Schmidt."

"Sure. We got a long journey. You sleep."

The last person to say that had been her father. She remembered him. She closed her eyes but she waited. She opened one eye.

Schmidt was already further back into the seat, his great pallid face folded down into itself. Catriona had watched drunks fall asleep; in two ticks of the clock they could turn their terrible burdens into a brief passage of temporary forgetfulness. Schmidt did not drink but he slept the same quick unhappy way.

She took another pull at the brandy bottle, and slept herself.

The place was a lodge, Schmidt said. For fishing or shooting or something; she didn't really listen. He had rented it to spy on Despard in his last paraplegic years. Claremaurice House was three miles downhill; close enough with good binoculars. The lodge was perched on top of a hill, sheltered by a little break of trees. There was no garden; the scrub came up to the very windows.

The two thugs lit a fire in the small sitting room and retreated to the kitchen.

Schmidt smacked his lips. There was buttermilk and for Catriona soda bread and instant coffee. She wondered how Schmidt stayed fat. He sat next to the strong box that had been brought from the limousine's boot. He unlocked it and looked up.

"I know," said Catriona. "You've got documents."

Schmidt had stopped pretending he was a host. It was all business now. He dug into the box with greedy hands. Catriona looked out of the window. It was almost light. "It's stopped raining."

"Huh. Give it time. You build a geodesic dome over this country maybe then you get some climate to live in."

He had made as neat a pile of files and papers as their different sizes would allow.

"Now we talk. So everyone tells you Schmidt's a bad man and you believe them. Let me tell you something. From way back certain people think Schmidt's a nothing. Just some piece of defecation material. So when Schmidt starts doing things, when Schmidt saves their dumb Foundation for them, when they've got to have money and Schmidt's the only one to get it for them – what do they do? They *hate* Schmidt."

It made sense of a sort. The incompetent resents the rescuer. But for the moment the resentment was all Schmidt's.

"They look down a lot of noses. Poor boy Schmidt. Hard scrabble Schmidt who works his way up, gets some qualifications, speaks funny and he's the one who saves them."

Catriona thought of Madame Despard's nose. There was a lot of it to look down. Schmidt laid a plump hand flat on his paper pile.

"You're a quick study. In a minute you get to look all you like. I got it all here. Schmidt was present at the creation. You owe me everything. You owe me to be here at your age with food, some clothes, a job. It was Schmidt who watched over you. And now it's Schmidt who comes to give you your big chance."

She stood mesmerised at the fat hand resting on the papers. He nodded, pleased that she was getting the message.

"I got you here Catriona. I got your life here. I got documents."

She stared. He smiled.

"Sure. All the places that I greased your path. The job with Monty. The money to go abroad when Monty folded. Then I came to you in Cairo. When you were no good for nothing. I bought the club for *you* little girl."

A trapdoor started to open inside her. In a moment she would fall straight through it. The mysterious bailing out that had given her strength, respect, independence was now, in the worst way, clear.

"So I was never any good at anything. It wasn't my doing a good job for Monty. It was you picking me up. It was," she struggled for the right word; she couldn't find it, "patronage."

Schmidt shrugged. "Suit yourself. You turned out good. You run a good club."

But – there was no point in saying it out loud and besides it hurt too much – if she had been a disaster he would have kept her on just the same, for the time he needed her. For this moment. For now.

She spoke slowly, trying to make the whole business clear to herself. "When Despard made the will. You planned it from then?"

"You get that from the lawyer? Huh! Document!" He lifted the top folder and threw it in front of her. "Purchase of clinic where you get born by Despard Foundation. Authorisation: Schmidt. Document. Payments to doctors at same. Cash payments. Authorisation: Schmidt. Lump sum payment to Mrs Lomax. Provided by: Schmidt. Document. Insurance policies on life of John Lomax; standing orders from Scottish Co-operative Bank: receipts for cash payments in same amount retained by Schmidt. Document. Purchase of bungalow . . . "

"Stop. Just stop it."

Schmidt looked disappointed. "This is seriously notarised shit."

She was at the very edge of the trapdoor now. She would fall through, clean off the edge of the world. Everything solid would be left behind. Nothing would be the same again. Keep calm. You must keep calm. Tar had told her. You have to see.

"You. You did all of it. From the very beginning."

"Who else? Naturally."

"But you blackmailed her? My . . . Madame Despard."

"So. Blackmail, whitemail, what's the difference? It suited her. She needed someone to make the arrangements. She needed a person to keep it all from Despard. And we know why. You and me huh?"

"No." But she did.

"Sure. You're like I said a quick study. You've seen her. She needed someone to keep her seriously rich."

"But you *blackmailed* her." Catriona stuck to it doggedly. She had to stick to something.

"Nothing's for nothing. She gives you some philanthropic baloney. Schmidt does not. Figure it out for yourself. All she had to say was go to hell Schmidt. Go to hell Despard. I have the child. I take the child. I go. I live with the child. But then she has to say go to hell money."

For a while Catriona was stunned. Then rage swept over her. She hated everybody but only Schmidt was there, so she took it out on Schmidt.

"All that time. My whole life. *You* could have told me. You should have told me. You're like some horrible fat calculating machine."

Now it was Schmidt's turn for rage. He was on his feet scattering his files, gesticulating like an urchin.

"Grow the fuck *up*. Who do you think you are? You're the bastard of some low life creep Communist murderer and some money mad whore. You get conceived against maybe a toilet wall and you want that it's Schmidt's fault. Like what? Schmidt was the wall? Schmidt should be there with a condom so you never get born, so you never have to go through nothing? So fat Schmidt's a bad boy 'cos he didn't come on a magic carpet to give you a long white dress and a crown? 'Cos he's the one who saves you from being some dull provincial bitch, with the job he makes for you?"

He had seized another file. He waved it like a weapon.

"I protected you when no one else gave a damn. I made you what you are. And you had better not let this fat man down. I GOT A DOCUMENT."

She took the file. It contained a single sheet of official paper. It was a birth certificate. She supposed it was this she had come for. Her parents were listed as Alice Despard and James Tar. She had, however, been born a day earlier than she thought.

"This is legal," she said. "It's registered. How did you do it?"

Schmidt was modest about his practical gifts. "Easy. Double registration. Two certificates and you register them at different places. Some cock and bull story about delay. A backhander to the Registrar. In which case *that*," he pointed at the evidence of existence which Catriona held, "being the first is, you unnerstan', the legal one. One for Mrs Lomax who didn't have no chance of adoption. One for you know who. Just in case one day she changed her mind and comes back for you. When it suited her."

I want to get out of here, thought Catriona. I want to get

out of everywhere. "I need some air."

She walked across the room and wrenched open the french window. She looked at the rough scrubby hill that fell steeply away from the house. She turned back.

"Everyone used me," she said. "Except my father."

Schmidt calmed down. "Jimmy I give you, yes. Jimmy believed in shit sure but he stuck close to it. But Jimmy's dead. It's a crooked world. You want a place at the top table or not?"

"Why should I vote for you and not Madame Despard?"

"Jesus," Schmidt's objections to blasphemy were long forgotten. "You got no powers of observation. She's crazy. Anyone can see that. She's mixed up in the Foundation before. She wrecks it. Hence Schmidt. You think that rich bitch turns into a philanthropist? In a year she spends the whole lot on shoes."

He came closer.

"Listen. I know how you feel. Schmidt's a crook. Schmidt cuts corners. You come in with me. We tidy the whole matter up. Go legitimate."

"Explain the vote to me."

"You know the damned vote or we wouldn't be talking."

"Explain it. I want to be clear."

"Me I want to be warm."

"Leave the window. I want to be clear," said Catriona.

"One side me and Esmond Claremaurice. The other Madame Despard and the old woman from Edinburgh."

A new feeling swept over Catriona. It took a moment to identify. Then – excitement. He doesn't know. He really doesn't know about Jessie's death.

"So," Schmidt was saying, "I need your vote or it's a tie. With a tie things become very difficult. Possible for Schmidt but difficult certainly."

"Esmond will vote for you?"

Schmidt grinned. "It's a certainty."

No it isn't. Something else you don't know. But *why* don't you know it?

"I could say I'll vote with you and then not do it."

"No," said Schmidt. "You're too proud. I know you."

Catriona laughed. She held up the birth certificate. "But if I say I'll vote against you, you'll risk a tie and destroy this. So I won't be able to vote at all?"

"Schmidt's told you the truth little girl. What else could I do? You got to choose. Nothing's for nothing."

"No," said Catriona. "It isn't. I'll see to the window."

She turned and jumped through it.

# 34

It's easier in the movies. The escaper rolls tidily down tiered lawns. But from Schmidt's lodge window a three foot drop launched Catriona on to what seemed a trainee cliff; covered in bracken and wet stinging wild grass. She went over and over in a bruising roll till she crashed into a stand of bamboo. She struggled out of it and into a freezing, hard pebbled stream. On the opposite bank stood Theodora Claremaurice. She held a shotgun.

Dublin flashed into Catriona's mind. She's found out about Esmond and me in Dublin. I am up to my knees in an Irish stream, out of sight of any habitation, confronted by a fully armed woman whose husband makes love to me.

"It's *you*," said Theodora.

"Yes," said Catriona.

"Heavens." Theodora the Good broke open the shotgun, tucked it under her arm and reached out her spare hand to pull Catriona out of the stream.

"Come on."

"That's Schmidt up there."

"I know. Come on."

Theodora pulled Catriona powerfully from the stream. She set off down the hill hauling Catriona behind her. Here, in the countryside, Theodora was not clumsy. She took Catriona forward at speed. She stopped twice to listen.

She shook her head. Then to Catriona, "Wait for a minute. Here." They stopped in the shelter of a small grove.

She gave mud-spattered Catriona a large man's handkerchief and strode a few paces back up the hill. She wore an oilskin waistcoat, corduroy leggings and Wellington boots. This was her habitat. She fitted into it like a figure in a print.

"Theodora? Why the gun?"

"Rabbits."

"Oh."

Catriona shoved the handkerchief deep into her pocket where it lay over her crumpled birth certificate. She looked up and, so it seemed to her, down the barrels of Theodora's shotgun.

"Stay right where you are."

Catriona screamed with terror. "Theodora? THEODORA?"

"Not you Catriona. I mean the chap behind you."

She turned around. The chap behind her was Robinson. He stood at the edge of the clearing looking rueful. He held his hands away from his sides, palms upward, in a gesture of mock surrender. 'Nothing up my sleeve."

"Catriona?"

"It's all right Theodora," she supposed it was. She was too tired to think otherwise. "I know him."

Theodora lowered the gun.

"Oh yes," Robinson advanced genially. "I know Cat."

"If you call me Cat I'll get Theodora to shoot you."

Theodora's eyes went back and forth between them. She took in Robinson's outfit and his accent. He grinned with what seemed to Catriona the whole expanse of his big red face. He strode forward, hand out.

"Mrs Claremaurice I presume. I was at school with Esmond as it happens." He pulled his grin round to Catriona, back again to Theodora and winked.

You actually winked you bastard, as if Theodora was being let in on a lovers' secret.

"She always gave me a hard time did Catriona. Hit me once with an ashtray. Good God girl what's happened? Who's been hitting you?"

"Theodora. Can we get out of here?"

"Robinson. Humphrey Robinson." He had his hand out. Theodora took it.

Theodora's class clock was ticking. "Aren't you a cousin of Penelope Meadowes?"

"Yes. She introduced this young thing here to me."

"For God's sake Theodora," said Catriona. "Let's get away from here."

"I rather think we're trespassing. Yes. Trespassing." (Theodora pretending normality.)

"Absolutely. Off we go then," said Robinson. "Very touchy about their land are some people."

They were nearer the road than Catriona had imagined. Robinson had become even more obscenely roguish about Catriona's disarray. Cat been to a party had she? Cat been to an orgy? Couldn't keep a good girl down even in the wilds of Ireland. Theodora started what would undoubtedly have been an utterly implausible story but he mercifully interrupted with further roguishness.

Gentlemen didn't ask questions. Ladies had other reasons. Pity though. What a coincidence. Could dine out on it.

Theodora had a fat wide Volvo. A newer estate version of the same was parked behind it. Its interior was a mess of fishing tackle and assorted bags. A top hat and highly polished riding boots sat on the back seat. Robinson babbled on sounding more like a silly ass version of Esmond by the moment.

Fishing. Hunting. Further to the west. He mentioned two packs. Did Theodora know them? Theodora knew the packs. Did Theodora know the Masters? Theodora knew them. For some reason he lifted the tailgate of his car and raised it.

So here he had been in Dublin. Same hotel as Cat, mmm? (And the same noise God help me, thought Catriona, that Esmond made.) Nice to see her again. Old times, mmm?

"So," he slapped the tailgate, "I've got two words to say to you my little flower of the night. Ingrate and suitcase."

"Suitcase?"

"There you are," Robinson replied to Theodora. "Ingratitude taken for granted. Going to meet me for a drink and she vanishes. I ask at the desk and you've left your suitcase. Right say I. Address Claremaurice House. On my way drop it off. Please don't worry . . . "

Theodora's politeness light had just flashed on. Catriona saw her trying to think of a reason for not offering Robinson hospitality.

"Wouldn't dream of getting in the way. Pure fluke. Here Cat, give me a hand with your case." He rummaged inside. Catriona joined him. He spoke in a lipless whisper. "Are you able to vote?" Catriona gave the smallest available nod. "Good girl. Stick with it."

Robinson insisted on carrying the case to Theodora's car, putting it in, holding first Theodora's, then Catriona's door. Theodora made conversation. What house was he in at school? Old Someone's. Same as Esmond.

"Though they were squeezing me in at the bottom while they were squeezing him out at the top."

"Mr Robinson . . . ?"

"Humphrey. Humpo." He said it without a blush.

"Forgive me but why were you – well – *here*?"

Catriona had dreaded the question, though would have liked the answer herself. Robinson put his head back and roared with Humpo-ish laughter.

"A bloody great piss. Best to Esmond. Ladies."

They drove off. Some way back Robinson bobbed along behind them.

"Well I must say," said Theodora. "You get around. You seem to know men simply everywhere." Theodora drove fast and efficiently with a long-wristed action on the gear lever.

"Ugh."

"I thought he was rather dishy."

"Theodora. What the hell were you doing there?"

Theodora was watching Robinson in the rear view mirror.

"Actually I was thinking I might shoot Schmidt."

"Oh God Almighty!" (What next? What now?)

"Of course not *really*." Theodora's face twisted in pain. "If only I could. If only I were that sort of person and I could just *do* something like that and not go to jail. I wanted to talk to him. Esmond's behaving so strangely. I'm sure he's blackmailing Esmond. And I was frightened so I took a gun."

"Jesus Christ Theodora!"

"I know. I'm a fool. Esmond always says so."

They slowed down to turn right. Robinson passed them on the inside with much honking and waving.

I give up, thought Catriona. I give up wondering about anything. But she was wrong. They were going fast now along a tangled avenue of huge untended trees. Then it ended. Catriona drew in her breath. Here was a different thing to wonder at.

There was a huge bay and an immense sea. Dawn crawled along it, taking its time with the big bare cliffs; a smudge of deep rain-led purple hung over the house.

And what a house. Three stories of crumbling Georgian masonry swept out in a delicate curve towards the sea, as if reminding rough nature that it could grow but not build. It stood there in the middle of nowhere, willing the world to come to it. There at once, in one extended glance, Catriona realised what it was that she had wanted to love in men like

Esmond. Self-confidence, grandeur, indifference, style. Esmond and his kind were a vestige; off centre shadows on the walls of Plato's cave. Philistine and cheaply glamorous they still carried a hint of the beauty that had seeped into generations of landowning clodhoppers against their will.

"Oh *yes*," said Catriona.

For a moment Theodora laid her hand on Catriona's. "I thought he'd want it."

The house's beauty was the beauty of loss. The gardens had gone back to undergrowth. Many of the windows were boarded. In the carriage sweep a tired sundial had fallen over. Then Catriona noticed the rest. The security. Concrete bollards meant that no car could come within a hundred feet. At ground floor level the windows sported metal cage screens, as did the front door. Catriona almost laughed; Despard had done his best to turn Claremaurice House into a fortified bungalow.

For a moment the two women sat there together.

"And he doesn't? Want it?"

"No. I got it wrong."

Catriona heard the thud-thud of an approaching helicopter. Theodora sounded abstracted, dreamy.

"I was the girl next door . . . well you know what I mean . . . " she raised her hand from Catriona's to indicate the countryside rolling away in each direction.

"I was six and I saw Esmond ride past. That's when I fell in love with him."

The helicopter had landed. Madame Despard appeared at its door.

"I expect that's everyone," said Theodora. "Except for Schmidt."

Catriona insisted on carrying her own bag.

"Catriona." Theodora had stopped. She was biting her lip. "Follow your conscience. That's what *I* say. What else can any of us do."

It was, for Theodora, a rhetorical question.

# 35

Half an hour later Catriona came into the library; while she had washed herself in brackish water in a vast gloomy bathroom she heard car doors slam, and Schmidt's voice in the hall. The library like the rest of the house that Despard hadn't colonised was a kind of ruin. The books had been sold at some distant auction. The shelves (the long labour of a craftsman's skill) were stained with mould, twisted with damp. The room was freezing. At either end of the room a turf fire burned. The smell was beautiful, the heat minimal. Madame Despard huddled herself next to one of the fireplaces. She wore an enormous fur coat and dark glasses. She looked at Catriona's knees but said nothing. It was impossible to tell what she was thinking.

There was little furniture. A battered desk – behind which sat Donovan Myers in his pox doctor's outfit topped by the beret – an armchair with Schmidt perched on its edge, as if he might catch a disease from the unhygienic upholstery. Esmond stood by the other fireplace, a bottle of whiskey in one hand and a half-full tumbler in the other. He wore yesterday's suit and yesterday's shirt. He had not shaved. You've been up all night, thought Catriona. Theodora stood looking out of the vast french windows with their view of the desolate park and the high cliff beyond.

"Well," Esmond lifted his glass in Catriona's direction, "fancy seeing you here."

Wait a minute, thought Catriona. Esmond could be unkind, he could be brutally selfish, but he was never nasty. Perhaps he thought it was common. Perhaps he thought it suggested a lack of control. But he was nasty now and, if one looked at him, not particularly in control.

"My wife's little friend eh?"

"Esmond!" Theodora turned imploringly from the window. Catriona suddenly realised that no one else was drinking. Esmond was an abstemious man; he was too vain to risk spoiling his looks. And it was early in the morning. You've been drinking all night she thought. You're drunk, or on the way.

Now he stared belligerently at Theodora, who stood there suffering.

"Oh well fuck it," he said about nothing in particular. He turned to the fire and kicked a stray piece of smouldering turf. He would not have done that normally. His shoes were hand-made. He took care of them.

The room was cold through more than temperature, thought Catriona. The room was full of hate. Donovan Myers looked at them over his half glasses.

"Miss Jessie Lomax I am informed will not be with us. She died a few days ago."

Schmidt looked up. His mouth hung open.

"Now that we're all here," said Donovan Myers, "I'll begin." He was not going to waste any time. He had an appointment later in Dublin. He would do best without interruptions (this with a glance in Esmond's direction). He reminded those present that he was here to discuss only that part of the will which dealt with the Despard Foundation. The remainder of the estate passed to Madame Despard and was a matter for herself alone entirely. The details of Despard's intentions for the Foundation were known to all present. So to procedure. Did or did not Miss Lomax have the necessary proof of her entitlement to vote?

Miss Lomax felt them all watch her as she walked to the desk, drew the handkerchief from her pocket and then from beneath the handkerchief, weighted down with coins, the curled up ball of paper. She placed it before Donovan Myers. She smoothed it out. It was damp but dry enough for him to read the evidence of her existence. He held it up.

"I am satisfied as to the validity of this document."

"For Christ's sake speak English," said Esmond.

"She gets to vote," snapped Donovan Myers. "Does anyone wish to examine this?"

"Christ no." Esmond drained the tumbler and started to refill it.

"Esmond?" Theodora pleading again.

"Theodora." Esmond raised his glass in a mock toast.

She bowed her head. Madame Despard lit a cigarette and blew out a smoke ring. It stayed undispersed unnaturally long, resting on the room's damp air.

"Very well." Donovan Myers had said he would get on with it. The late M. Despard's provisions were exact. Anyone who challenged them would receive precisely one pound.

"Pound Irish or pound sterling?" said Esmond. The lawyer ignored him.

"Those entitled to vote are Madame Despard, Mr Schmidt, Mr Claremaurice and Miss Lomax." He nodded as he spoke each name. Only Schmidt responded with a little continental half nod. "Two candidates permissible at a time. Candidates may nominate themselves. Candidates may vote for themselves. No more than three rounds of voting allowed. In the event of a tie I will operate as sole Trustee."

"Answer all the questions right and you win a Metro."

"Esmond." Theodora was still trying.

Esmond rounded on her. "Just shut up Theodora. We all know it's nothing to do with you."

Whatever it meant it went home, as private gibes made public do. Theodora bit her lip; the corners of her mouth were pinched white.

"Oh all right," said Esmond. "For God's sake get it over with."

Donovan Myers rapped the table. "Nominations?"

Schmidt and Madame Despard both raised their hands. Esmond snorted.

"Splendid choice. A tart or a crook."

What in heaven's name has got into you Esmond? I have never seen you like this. What's happened since yesterday?

Madame Despard ostentatiously ignored the fireplace and ground out her cigarette on the fraying carpet. Theodora winced. Schmidt looked straight at Esmond. He spoke slowly in case Esmond was too obtuse or too drunk to get the point.

"Sticks and stones. Sometimes you got to cut a corner. You're a political person. You know how it is. Sometimes you got no choice."

"Schmidt." Esmond sneered the name in Donovan Myers' direction. "I vote for the completely honest Mr Schmidt."

Now they waited for Catriona. They all watched her except for Madame Despard, who showed nothing from behind her black orbs. Perhaps Schmidt is right, thought Catriona, and you will be a disaster. Perhaps too Schmidt is not all that you say – is less corrupt than I think. But none of that makes any difference.

"I vote for Madame Despard."

"You got some regrets coming." Schmidt's tiny eyes had got smaller.

"Right," said Donovan Myers. "Tie. First ballot over. Second ballot. Nominations?"

Theodora, who seemed to take comfort from the view, turned away from the window. "Why doesn't someone nominate Esmond?"

She had asked before and, Catriona could also tell, got nowhere.

"Not on your life," said Esmond. "An MP dipping into their little bran tub. Not on your life."

Theodora would have said more but Esmond held up his whiskey glass like a policeman halting traffic.

"Besides this bunch wouldn't vote for me. No. I think this is someone else's mess don't you Theodora?"

"That's right," said Jimmy Tar advancing into the room, followed by Busboy. "And I know just the person. My daughter."

"Hello Jimmy," said Donovan Myers equably. "Outsiders can't nominate. Something wrong Mr Schmidt?"

Schmidt gaped in terror. "You're supposed to be dead."

"I wouldn't say he looked that bad," said Esmond. "Is he really your father?"

"Yes," said Catriona. "He's that."

"Well tell him to find another tailor."

Tar wore the hideous blue over-large suit of the photograph; the suit Catriona had last seen on the dying Maxwell. Schmidt rose from his chair. He moved back until he hit the wall.

"Well I can," said Madame Despard. "Nominate. I nominate our daughter."

Theodora turned, stiff with offence, on Tar. "How did *you* get in here? This is my house."

"No," said Esmond. "Actually it isn't."

"Catriona," said Schmidt. "You tell them. You don't accept."

Catriona turned to Tar, who stood with his bantam stance in the centre of the room. Busboy had first looked round the room. Now he strolled over to the window.

"How did you *get* in here?" Theodora's voice was shrill; it cracked.

"Catriona," said Schmidt. "Listen. You *owe* me."

"How?"

Esmond lost his temper. He shouted. "Theodora. Just bloody well shut up."

She began to cry. Later Catriona was to think that these were tears not of distress but of rage, but now she said, "Why? Why should you want me to have it?"

Tar smiled at her. "You're all right," he said. "You may hate us but you'll do the job. I've watched you. You'll do what's right and you'll do what's best. You're the one who can see to the truth."

As Tar talked his gaze shifted from Catriona to Schmidt. She didn't mind. It was the best reference she could ever have.

"You owe me," Schmidt was whining now. "You *owe* me."

"No Mr Schmidt. I don't."

"Do I take it Miss Lomax that you vote for yourself?"

"Yes Mr Myers."

"And you Madame Despard?"

"You bet," said Madame Despard.

Schmidt pointed a finger at Donovan Myers. "This is a stitch up."

Donovan Myers looked at him stonily. The beret increased the impression of a hanging judge wearing a black cap.

"You have a quaint way with colloquialisms Mr Schmidt. Do you also have a vote?"

"Sure I got a vote. I vote against. You think you're so damned clever. So what have you got? Another tie."

Esmond had been leaning against the mantelpiece watching, turning his head in the direction of each speaker with the exaggerated precision of the drunk. Now he pushed himself unsteadily away from the wall. He was angry. He was terribly angry. He spoke with the bitterness of the aggrieved, the left out, the disregarded – perhaps also, the deceived. Catriona knew; these were emotions which, until a moment ago when Tar spoke, she could practically have patented.

"It seems to me," Esmond swayed a little, "that I am being taken for granted." He paused and took another swig of whiskey. "You know you make me sick."

Who did he mean? Schmidt? But he looked vaguely ahead.

"Oh Esmond," Theodora folded her hands together. The knuckles were white. "Esmond. Esmond."

He mimicked her. Catriona was surprised at his accuracy. "Esmond. Esmond." He caught his wife's querulous suffering reproachfulness.

"Mr Claremaurice," said Schmidt. "You don't want to disappoint me."

"Catriona," said Esmond abruptly. "I vote for Catriona. Where do we sign?"

"He's drunk," shouted Schmidt. "It don't count."

"Drunkenness is no legal impediment in Ireland. Would you sign here?"

"I ain't signing *nothing*." Schmidt was in the middle of the room gesticulating.

Esmond, Catriona and Madame Despard signed. Donovan Myers asked Schmidt politely if he was still in the same negative frame of mind. Schmidt swore.

"No matter," said Donovan Myers, gathering up his papers in his briefcase and straightening his beret.

Theodora, drying her eyes, recovered herself as a hostess, clutching for the everyday. "This way's quicker." She opened the great windows that stretched from floor to ceiling. Donovan Myers passed through them. Schmidt went to follow. Tar stepped into his path. Schmidt shrunk back. Theodora walked up to Esmond.

"I hate you Esmond," she said.

Esmond looked blank, then turned his back on her to stare into the fire. In another flood of tears Theodora ran out through the window. Catriona watched her run across the neglected park, then slow to a walk, moving away from the house, her head down, her shoulders shaken with sobs. From overhead came the thud-thud of Donovan Myers' departing Dublin-bound helicopter.

James Tar stepped forward. His face had set hard. Catriona was reminded of photographs of men going into battle. "Well now Erhardt." He meant Schmidt; Catriona had never thought of Schmidt as having a Christian name. "You remember the suit, don't you?"

He came forward, extending his arm as if inviting Schmidt to feel the nasty blue material. Schmidt shrank back against the wall; he looked wildly at the bookshelves as though he might climb them to safety.

"Oh you do Erhardt."

"No Jimmy," cried Madame Despard. "That's enough. Busboy. Stop him."

Busboy had been watching Esmond, who stood staring obliviously after Theodora. "No, Lady," said Busboy. "It's personal."

"Jimmy," Schmidt actually shook. "It wasn't me. You're completely crazy."

Catriona noticed that Busboy had started to frown. He looked again at Esmond; his frown deepened.

Tar said, "A walk outside. That's what you made them take didn't you Erhardt. A *paseo*. A short walk. The shortest walk there is. Your turn to take it. A Spanish walk on an Irish cliff."

Catriona couldn't stand Schmidt's abject terror. She remembered what Madame Despard had said about Tar's cruelty. He looked at Schmidt with the eye of a cat watching a crippled bird. Catriona would have intervened but Madame Despard was there before her, pushing between the men. Somewhere along the way she had dropped her glasses. She turned her ravaged face to Tar.

"We're old Jimmy." There was a tone in her voice that was new to Catriona. It was tender. "Leave it Jimmy. Come away with me. Just leave the whole thing."

Tar couldn't speak. His face struggled with a reply but there was too much emotion in the way. She put her hand on his arm.

"You know that's what you always wanted Jimmy. Come away with me now. It's over."

Tar looked up at her. The difference in their height should have made them look ridiculous. But it didn't. He closed his eyes. He said, "Spain's never over."

Schmidt bolted.

"GET AWAY FROM THE WINDOWS." Busboy shouted but he was too late. Esmond fell backwards. The side of his face was no longer there. The second shot caught Schmidt as he foolishly continued to run forward. It lifted him into the air where he flopped like a seal after a fish. Tar managed to pull Madame Despard and Catriona to one side before the third shot struck him. He fell awkwardly on to his knees, hands clutching his upper body.

There were no more shots. Outside a woman was screaming. Theodora? Busboy was yelling too. Catriona crawled over to Tar, now knelt cradling him. The blue suit that Maxwell had died in was reddened. Madame Despard held one of his hands. Tar's breathing came hard. He managed, "Your mother."

Catriona knew what he wanted. She reached across his body and took Madame Despard's spare and quivering hand.

Madame Despard said, "Jimmy. Not now. Not after everything. Don't die now."

He was trying to tell Catriona something. She bent closer to hear through Madame Despard's sobbing. He forced the words out.

"It couldn't have been Schmidt."

"No," said Catriona. "Of course it couldn't."

He squeezed her hand. He was pleased with her.

"Please Jimmy. Not now." Madame Despard begged him not to die.

He smiled in resignation up at Madame Despard. He was already at a sort of peace.

"Oh aye," he said. "Now. Oh aye. *Ay Carmela.*"

Then Catriona's father died and she held out her arms to comfort her mother.

# 36

Catriona knew the truth – it was just that she couldn't believe it. She had to be wrong. It was impossible. There were neat explanations. Let them stand. She didn't want to accept the trail that Tar had set her on or the legacy of evidence he had left her to inherit. It was all too much for her. She was simply an ordinary girl with a bizarre history; a real person who had longed for a fairy tale and found a horror story. She wanted to be ordinary again, to escape from the bizarre, to put it behind her.

It wasn't possible. The bizarre caught her up and overtook her and stood before her, beckoning and pointing to the road ahead. In the end Tar had been right. She was his daughter. She could no more leave the past than he could. But time passed before she took the journey to Morocco and the final rendezvous with the truth she wished she could avoid.

First there was the fuss. The fuss that was also the fix. Then the funerals.

Robinson was good. There was no doubt about it. She supposed that Tar would have thought so too. She had possessed no sense of the authority that Robinson and his kind could exercise. In retrospect Esmond's superiority had been a feeble class-led thing.

They had been moved out of Ireland with the smoothest kind of courtesy. Two groups of Irish police – the ordinary ones in green who tramped stoically about Claremaurice House measuring, searching through the undergrowth, giving hysterical broken down Theodora and catatonic Madame Despard tea laced with John Jamesons; and their equivalent to the British Special Branch – asked a run of very ordinary questions. Just as if a bunch of terrorists had acted on the commonplace impulse to assassinate a British MP and his assorted chums.

As Schmidt had said to Donovan Myers – it was a stitch up. Catriona let the fabric lie untorn. Busboy agreed. In England someone would explain. Very well. She would wait for Robinson.

Within hours the British Press reported the story; within a day the tabloids had created an unquestioning and adamantine myth. Schmidt and Tar were sidelined as uninteresting light-industrial corpses – the glamour factor was Esmond. The banner headlines churned out the usual meretricious stuff: handsome dashing politician, grieving wife, bereaved kiddies. Theodora had a brief period as a heroine. Catriona had her own memories here – Theodora running, screaming across the empty park towards Esmond's body, slumped between the open french windows, stopping silent with no screams left when she saw that half his beautiful face had been erased. Within a few days Theodora's remarkable strength reasserted itself. By Esmond's funeral the popular papers paraded her as this year's *mater dolorosa*. Yet Theodora would have none of it. She gave no interviews, issued a few brief dishonest pieties concerning Esmond the politician, and retired into dignified widowhood. Everyone said how wonderful she was and then forgot about her. For a while a few semi-serious articles continued to talk of the dangers of terrorism shifting from Northern to Southern Ireland, or of the extension/retraction of this or that part of the Anglo-Irish agreement. But these too faded away. The newspapers had been fed their favourite pap. There was no point in asking further questions.

Except for Catriona.

But first the burials of the dead. She stayed away from Esmond's; in death at least Theodora was entitled to full proprietorship.

Jessie had disposed of herself through the Co-operative Society. She had wanted a quick cremation and no religious service. Afterwards Catriona collected all Jessie's Civil War memorabilia. No one else had wanted them.

Schmidt it turned out had a number of relatives eager to accept the burial of his body as a means of making some claim on his estate. After the autopsy his remains were whisked away to Switzerland. By some irony he had died intestate and, as might be expected, legally rich.

Tar was buried in Ireland at the Old Hillyard cemetery where the Church of Ireland had long given up expecting non-Catholic deaths; where there was plenty of space for the dead. Donovan Myers shook out some veterans from Spain for a parade of sorts. Madame Despard watched from the closed windows of a chauffeured limousine.

Increasingly that seemed to Catriona to be Madame Despard's real position in life.

That was one of the odd things, she thought; how right how many people had been about so many things.

Madame Despard, for example, had been right about herself. She was not lovable. In fact she wasn't likeable. Catriona didn't like her a bit. Schmidt too had been right. She was spoilt and selfish and insanely extravagant. As Catriona wrestled through the dishonest doctored accounts of the Despard Foundation, unsuccessfully trying to establish Schmidt's network of subtle theft, her mother's spending left her aghast. Yes, Schmidt had been right; Madame Despard had nearly ruined the Foundation once and would certainly have ruined it twice. Charity was what she gave from her purse to the beggar who waited in the rain while she finished buying fifty pairs of shoes.

Yet Tar had been right about Madame Despard too. She had been magnificent once in a daring past. Now she babbled about it the way the old do. Indeed she was slipping fast into age. In the service apartment near the Dorchester (she had wanted to be "near" Catriona) she shopped compulsively by telephone, and paced the floor and mumbled. Gradually she came to remind Catriona of Mrs Lomax. Like mother like mother she thought grimly. Tar had loved Madame Despard but Tar was dead. And Catriona had something else to think about. Catriona had Tar's message.

*It couldn't have been Schmidt.*

"Yes," said Robinson. "Nobody's disputing that."

He spoke patiently to her in his office in Half Moon Street. She hated the place. It was spartan and ugly. It made him look bigger and redder and more coarsely alive. Of course most of her recent male acquaintances were corpses. He kept giving her whisky. She kept taking it. He kept being avuncular. She kept hating it.

"All right," she said stubbornly. "If not Schmidt who then? All those deaths? Maxwell, Jessie, the girl Dolours at the brothel, Schmidt, Esmond," she paused, "and my father. Who then?"

"Not who. What. Terrorists. Accept it. Things are best left

as they are."

"Whose terrorists? *Why* terrorists? For Pete's *sake* they're different crimes aren't they? Maxwell is killed because someone thinks he's my father. Jessie is killed by accident because someone's looking for the lawyer's letter and the Ambulance Brigade stuff. Dolours is shot by accident because someone misses Madame Despard and God knows why three such ill-assorted people got shot at Claremaurice House!"

Robinson nodded in a soothing way. "I think you need to look at the big picture. But in looking at it remember this. Do not assume consistency. Life is messy. People get things wrong. Murderers and assassins and terrorists are just as incompetent as everyone else."

"Great," said Catriona. "I'll get that done in pokerwork. Could we get on with the big picture?"

Robinson smiled a big ruddy co-operative smile. "Tar came to us via Señor Rossminster. Effectively he offered us Schmidt, which is to say information on Schmidt's dubious operating of the Despard Foundation. We weren't sure but we played along. Next comes the death of Maxwell. Tar persuades Maxwell to imitate Tar, and while he imitates Tar Maxwell is killed. We know that the killer was not Schmidt because Schmidt makes a separate deal with *us* to remove Tar. Of course that suits ourselves and Tar equally. The more Tar is believed to be dead the more Schmidt comes out into the open. Who then do you think killed Maxwell-cum-Tar? Well I frankly don't know but there must be a number of candidates who hated your father. For example your father assisted in Morocco in the murder of two of Schmidt's associates. They may have had friends."

"Oh come *on*." Catriona banged her glass on Robinson's desk. "May, might. Come on!"

"Come on yourself," said Robinson. "Remember this. Schmidt had dealt with some dubious people but so had Tar. Perhaps in staking out Maxwell Tar *was* intending to draw out some of Schmidt's associates – associates working independently of Schmidt – but that fact would be completely consistent with my thesis."

"Don't tell me! Terrorists."

"Let me go on. By now we were interested. Very interested. Like most people who have something to sell Tar trailed too large a coat. He spoke of friends in the plural but he did have one friend, Busboy, who protected Madame Despard. In the past there had been – I don't know – at least one attempt on her life. By whom?"

"Begins with a 't' does it?" said Catriona.

Robinson ignored her and kept on going. "By almost anyone I should have thought. Her life was *louche* enough heaven knows to get a whole phalanx of irate wives after her. Anyway, from our point of view, we keep going along humouring Tar. You go to Edinburgh. You visit Jessie. She dies. You go to Ireland. Practically everyone dies."

"Thanks," said Catriona.

"And you say to me there is a pattern and that pattern must have to do with the Foundation."

"Yes. But not Schmidt. Schmidt thought Tar was dead. He was sure of himself. He thought he'd win. He had no motive to kill anyone."

"Yes. Yes. Yes." Robinson waved the last points away as if they were too obvious to bother about. "But after all who did?"

"Did?"

"Did have a motive of course."

"How about you?" said Catriona.

Robinson rolled his eyes. "We got what we wanted. But look, you say Jessie died by accident when people were looking for those documents. But what value could they have had? And suppose she just hid them as senile people hide things. A couple of tearaways may just have decided to ransack her place for fun."

"It's too much of a coincidence."

"*Is* it? You see Catriona you want a pattern and you want it to have to do with the Foundation. Perhaps Tar wanted that too. But it just can't be. Think about it. Schmidt believes he will win anyway. Surely no one associated with Schmidt, no one afraid of the consequences of Schmidt losing would bother to try to kill Madame Despard outside a brothel or anywhere else. Maybe poor Dolours' father had a go, I don't know but I do know this – shooting Tar and Schmidt and Esmond *after* the future of the Foundation was *settled* makes no sense at all unless . . . "

"Unless it's random." Catriona was getting angry. "Is that

what you're going to say? Person or persons with assorted grudges? Varied nuts?"

Robinson produced a wicked grin. "Unless you did it."

Catriona almost fell off her chair.

"You bastard. You absolutely dishonest bastard."

Robinson was still grinning. He liked the idea.

"Well, you have an alibi for Maxwell's death and those at Claremaurice House but, on the other hand, we're not precisely talking about a single finger on a trigger. You could have taken out contracts and after all Catriona you're the only person I can think of with a complete set of motives."

"That's ridiculous."

But of course it wasn't, as Robinson robustly demonstrated on his square fingers. "You're a snob who would have hated the idea of Maxwell as a father. You wanted to find out more about your own past and the Foundation's disposition so you had Jessie roughed up. Dolours is killed by accident – you wanted it to be Madame Despard, the mother who abandoned you. Later on the Foundation comes your way which, of course, makes you the only person to gain from this whole business. Then you get the deaths of three men who abused you – ex-lover Esmond, common little murdering father Tar, manipulative cheat Schmidt. *And* you make sure that Theodora Claremaurice, whom you like and with whom you sympathise, is well out of the way."

Catriona gaped. "You're crazy. That breaks down at every point. You know that can't be true."

"Of course it can't. But it's a pattern. And it's as good as anything you've thought up."

Catriona got to her feet. She had had enough, but there was one thing left to say. "You said that you got what you wanted. What is it?"

Now Robinson did not smile. "You. In a sense. In the same sense as Tar. He wanted you to run the Foundation. We wanted that too. Now we can go through the records. Every dirty little deal. And don't say you can stop us. You can't."

"No," said Catriona. "I don't suppose I can."

Robinson politely preceded her to the door. Handle in hand he said, "I don't suppose you could have dinner with me."

Catriona stared up at him. She wanted to slap his face but all that she managed was, "No."

"Oh well," said Robinson looking away from her furiou
stare, "it's just that I like women who do things."

"I'm overwhelmed," said Catriona. She took his hand fror
the door knob and turned it herself.

"Only . . . " said Robinson. You swine, thought Catriona
now you're going to try lunch. "Only if you did have a theory
About motive, let's say. You'd need proof."

Catriona had left the Ministry building and was half wa
towards Piccadilly before it struck her.

She stood transfixed, staring blankly at the traffic haze ove
Green Park. I *know*, she thought. And he knows too. But h
can't do anything about it.

So now it's up to me.

It's *mine*.

For twenty-four hours Catriona Lomax sat alone in her fla
She neither ate nor slept. She existed on black coffee an
cigarettes. For long periods she kept perfectly still; only he
hand was at work scribbling and re-scribbling, crossing ou
drawing diagrams, trying to piece together her own big pic
ture. Sometimes she forgot things. Sometimes she despaire
that the lines would ever run straight to the right plac
Sometimes she ringed another item in the mess of Despar
Foundation accounts that spread across the table.

Then she moved.

Bert was relatively easy. He was angry. Catriona shut him u
in her office and got him comprehensively drunk.

"He's shut up shop Cat, that's what he's done M
Humperdinck Robinson or whatever his bloody name is.
murder done on my manor and I'm supposed to forget abou
it. What do you think of that?"

"I want to see them Bert. The photographs that Louis tol
me about. Show me the photographs."

She looked at each slowly, carefully, in turn.

"All right Bert. Let's stick to the area you really know
Everything to do with the Maxwell business. I want to mak
sure that I've got it quite straight, that all the bits and piece
I've got from other people fit in with your version."

"Fair enough, Cat." Bert helped himself to another drink

"So," said Catriona, "Barrington Smythe's flat was used a

a what-do-you-call-it, a drop for people going about Schmidt's business. The people in the photograph for example . . . "

"Sad about your old Mum being that way inclined."

"The people in this photograph, say, would enter the flat when it was empty, use one of the hiding places to leave whatever they had to leave – payment in cash or kind – they'd leave and Schmidt's representative would pick it up later, perhaps a few days later even. Yes?"

"Yes."

"So that way they wouldn't ever meet or see each other. Correct?"

"Correct Cat."

"But why?"

"What do you mean why?"

"Why was it so all-important for them not to be able to recognise each other? I mean these hippies are public enough aren't they? They pick Barrington Smythe. They pick the flat. They're put on to . . . "

"Your old Mum," said Bert.

"Yes. So it's the collector who doesn't want to be seen. Because that person can't *afford* to be seen. Because it is absolutely essential that this person keeps out of the way. Quite possibly because that person is – how shall I say – recognisable. Now think of something else. James Tar knew about the use of Barrington Smythe's flat. He got it from the hippies. He got the way it was used. But he didn't know the name of Schmidt's representative. If the hippies had known it they'd have told him. So Tar put Maxwell into the flat to flush that very person from cover. The person who knew the name Tar. A person with a very long involvement," and Catriona tapped the photographs. "A person with a lot to lose and a lot to gain. A clever person who may well have been considering a little blackmail on the side when the time was ripe. But above all a person *who could not have been some random terrorist.*"

Bert sat upright. "This person. Got a name has he? Give me a name."

Catriona gave him a name. Bert dropped his drink.

"Holy Mary Mother of the Metropolitan Line. No wonder Robinson's shut the lid. You'll never prove it. And even if you did . . . "

"I can prove it. The even part – well that's up to Robinson.

But I need you. Go to Robinson. Tell him I want a meeting with Rossminster and Busboy. Give him the name, not that he doesn't know it already."

"The sod," said Bert admiringly.

"Now," said Catriona. "Let's get back to the photographs. With one exception each has to do with some aspect of the Despard Foundation's corruption. The clinic in Edinburgh. The housing estate in Dublin. Schmidt's hideout in Copenhagen. My mother's . . . life. Yes?"

"Right on the nose Cat."

"And you say that there are two sets of these same photographs. One batch Tar got from the hippies and another batch kept here. So these are important photographs. Potentially they could be sold to someone as information and they are useful for blackmail. In other words the hippies are preparing to do a little business on the side. Yes?"

Bert was very still. He said, "I'm with you. Go on."

"Now," and there was a note of growing strength, of gathering conviction in Catriona's voice, "we come to the exception."

She held up the photograph of the low wall and the door and the bright burning sunshine.

"Which must not, which *cannot* be an exception. Otherwise they wouldn't have kept it. It must fit in with the others. It must be some part of the Despard Foundation's corruption. Now remember that our photographers didn't know Schmidt's representative here in London. But let's suppose they were curious. Let's suppose they were sniffing. They hadn't found the person but they'd found the place."

She tapped the photograph. She placed her finger on the door in the wall.

"I mean what would you do? You'd want to get some money out of the country just in case. You'd want a safe and secret bolt hole."

Bert bent over the photograph.

"I wonder. Bright sunshine. Morocco?"

"Perhaps. You need to check travel plans. They'll lead us to that house. It's only a matter of time. Not long now I think. We need to get moving. Our detailed financial snoop should tie it up."

Bert poured himself a newer, heftier drink. "Not bank accounts Cat. The Ministry won't wear it."

Catriona laughed. "Don't be silly. Cash is the point. Anything else would be far too risky. No. It's all about cash. And insurance. I want you to check some insurance companies."

Never before had Catriona seen Bert nervous. With quiet satisfaction she realised that she had frightened him.

"All too unfeminine for you, Bert?"

"Christ. Look Cat. Listen. What if he won't play ball? Robinson that is."

"Go and tell him that my mother is a very rich woman. I'm sure that she can afford a superior and wholly unrandom class of terrorist."

"You're a dangerous woman Cat."

"Well you know how it is," said Catriona. "I take after my father. I like to rely on my friends."

Louis Vulliamy had spent all day in the Karl Marx Library in Clerkenwell, working patiently in its International Brigade Archive. He had to continually cross refer. There was always a possibility that Catriona was wrong. In any case he was fat and liked sitting down. He found the Scottish Ambulance in five places. The references – in this memoir – in that small bit of newsprint – were perfunctory, and leaned heavily on the proletarian-heroic style which stressed the struggle of the masses at the expense of individual names.

But there were some names. Jessie was mentioned three times, Patrick Claremaurice once. Nowhere was there a full list of members.

He walked back to the desk holding the scholar's bonafide, his little list of references.

The Archivist looked up – a kindly helpful woman who was annotating *Marxism Today* for ideological impurities. What he really wanted he said was to establish the actual membership of the Ambulance. The full membership. Now if he could perhaps contact Jessie Lomax . . . On the other hand if someone else had got there before him then his monograph would be useless. Perhaps if the Archivist could check. He, Louis, rather thought that old so and so had made a similar enquiry some time back.

Oh yes, said the Archivist, she remembered old so and so quite well. So odd for someone like that to be interested. So agitated too.

Louis said thank you and went to telephone Catriona.

"Cash," said Penelope, her eyes saucer-wide. "Can you *imagine*. Cash for simply everything. I mean it's so uncharacteristic don't you think?"

Catriona didn't reply. She sat looking at her office table as if for security.

"Darling," said Penelope, "you look pale. Are you ill?"

"It's probably nothing. Probably just that I don't want to believe it. Even now. I'd prefer not to."

"Well you jolly well have to. I've worked it all out. How much everything would cost. It's *so* expensive living like that. And you were *so* right about the smoking."

But Catriona had left the room to be sick.

They walked together in the dusk across Hyde Park – Catriona, Robinson, Señor Rossminster, Busboy. Catriona did most of the talking. She waved her arms. Once or twice she punched her fingers into Robinson's chest like a cab driver demanding a fare.

For a while they stopped by a children's sandpit. Using twigs first Rossminster and then Busboy scratched diagrams in the sand. Catriona looked and nodded, although occasionally she turned to watch the children leaving with their nannies.

Finally Robinson stood up. He thrust his hands deep into the pockets of his British Warm.

"All right," he said. "We'll do it."

# 37

Although Rossminster had explained the layout to her, the place still surprised Catriona; it was so perfectly enclosed. Just a well and a gate and somewhere behind it the only remarkable sound – that of rushing water in a dry land.

The rest of Morocco was behind them. They had flown over the High Atlas and gone on by Land Rover. After Zagora the going was hard, but finally they made it all the way south, past the forts and the camel fairs, to the last oasis on the very edge of the Sahara.

She pulled the heavy lever that worked the bell. A male servant came to the gate and unlocked it. He said nothing. Either he was a mute or there were orders to admit any European. They went through two sets of doors, through two open courtyards. Then the servant bowed Catriona forward. She turned a corner and there was the white expensive house and what, in the dazzling refraction of the light, seemed to be an enormous pool. Emerging from it, levering out in one strong-armed motion, was the brown muscular flat-chested figure of Theodora Claremaurice.

She walked dripping towards Catriona. The once lank hair was sleek like an otter's fur. What had seemed in London the knobbly awkwardness of her body now revealed itself as strength. There were ridges of muscle in her shoulders. Yes, Catriona thought, this is your place. Water. Strength. Another element.

"Catriona! Did you see my dive? Don't *you* get about!"

Catriona did not walk towards her. She stood stock still and said, "Insurance."

"I'm sorry?"

"That was what finally explained it. Otherwise I couldn't understand why you did it."

Theodora had come closer. She looked politely concerned as if the sun, which had made her bloom, had affected Catriona's brain. But she also looked completely in charge. There was not a shred of her customary nerves, her habitual hesitancy.

"Did what?"

"I know Theodora. I know the whole thing. I've worked it out."

Theodora looked at her quite calmly and with a measure of appreciation. Then she said slowly, "I underestimated you. I should have known it would be you."

"And everyone else never estimated you at all."

"Just a moment." Theodora turned and called across the garden. "Darling. Would you mind?"

At the garden's far corner by a wall, a male shape in a g-string and a large straw hat, rose gracefully from a sun bed. Theodora wore a sly triumphant smile.

"Surprised?"

"No one," said Catriona, "has ever surprised me as much as you, Theodora."

She meant it. Not Tar. Not Madame Despard. No one.

"Ah," said Theodora. There was something in the way that she delivered that monosyllable that set the stamp on what followed. Her accent remained the same but her intonation did not. There was muscle now in the arm that held the jolly hockey stick and there was astuteness in the mind that told it which way to swing. What she said next might once have been framed in apology and self-effacement. Now it rang with victory.

"Ah. You didn't think of me like that."

"No," said Catriona.

"You see," said Theodora smiling, "nobody ever thought of me as anything much. Just because I was plain. Have some lemonade. It's fresh."

There was a table with a canopy and a chair and a jug of fresh lemonade and two glasses.

"You first," said Catriona.

Theodora poured the lemonade into both glasses, drank from each, then offered Catriona her choice. Catriona took one.

Then she said, "Perhaps it's true. Perhaps you're right. You were plain but did no one see you were clever?"

Theodora shook her hair. "I was sent to a school where the girls were supposed to get married. Exams weren't supposed to matter."

"Yes," said Catriona.

"My," said Theodora. "You've been there. You *are* thorough. You're not the bimbo I thought you'd be."

"Gee thanks boss."

Theodora laughed. "I could have settled for less. Honestly I ought to have been grateful for it. Any man of my class poor enough and dull enough to take me on. But I saw Esmond and I wanted him. Wanted him more than anything in my whole life. You can understand that."

"No," said Catriona. "I've tried but I can't. I can't imagine wanting something to such – monstrous lengths."

Theodora turned her head and leaned back looking into the sun. You're an Amazon now, thought Catriona, but when you leave here and the tan fades . . .

"Monstrous? Am I a monster?"

"Yes," said Catriona. "Yes Theodora I think you are. Whatever had been done to you doesn't excuse what you did."

Theodora opened her eyes and looked at Catriona. "I wonder," she said. "Men wanted you and looked at you. And if they hadn't I wonder what you'd have done. We're very alike you know."

"We're all alike – the women in this – you, my mother, Jessie."

"Sorry," said Theodora. "Come again?"

You've picked up some of Esmond's mannerisms, thought Catriona. To use when? To use of course when the eventual Visitor comes to call and that happens to be me. I, who waited in fantasy for the Visitor to solve all, am now the Visitor arriving with the resolution.

"She's the one you only killed indirectly. But you had her killed all the same."

"Oh," said Theodora. "I'm sorry to hear that."

She sounded like Lady Bountiful regretting a delay in the opening of a village fête. Theodora caught a whiff of the anger running through Catriona and, as a good hostess, tried to smooth things over.

"But she was fearfully old."

"Fearfully."

"Honestly I don't think you should make a mock of me. I never did that with you."

"Did you not? Did you not?" There was, Catriona realised, a Scotsness to the turn of that verb, as if fiercely accurate

Jessie had reminded her of her roots and her duty. "Perhaps you didn't. But let us see what you *did*."

"All right," said Theodora. "I know you must be dying to explain it all to me. I know *I* should."

"You know," said Catriona, "you're a wonder Theodora. The great unnoticed undiscovered powerful woman."

"Gosh, I take that as a compliment."

There was no irony. She meant what she said. A part of her would always remain gawky, straightforward, polite, eager to share thoughts with a girlfriend.

As if to compound the thought Theodora said, "I'm waiting. Bated breath. Honestly."

"All right. But it's difficult for me."

Theodora looked attentively sympathetic. Catriona hurried on.

"I mean it's hard to separate what I know now from how and when I came to know it. Nothing really fell into place until Esmond died. And then I looked back and it could only be you. Maybe only *I* could have seen it. After all I was Esmond's lover too. And I was manipulated by Schmidt too and I had to do what you did – going along working things out bit by bit while the men pulled us this way and that."

"Girls together," said Theodora drinking her lemonade. She probably wanted Catriona to acknowledge a compliment. Catriona didn't.

Instead she said, "So it's easier if I take it bit by bit. But I'd better start by saying the obvious. Nothing makes sense if you didn't partially know things. If Schmidt hadn't tweaked you and teased you to keep you up to the mark – that's simply to say that you knew the general outlines of Despard's will. You all but told them to me when we first met, when I hadn't even heard the name Despard. Besides, Schmidt would have wanted to tell you enough to ensure that when the time came you delivered Esmond's vote on Schmidt's side."

"You put things so terribly well. I wish I'd had an education."

"Stick around," said Catriona. "I expect that Schmidt played on your fears. Perhaps he dropped my name. Perhaps he didn't need to. Because in a number of ways I suddenly appeared as someone whom Schmidt might be grooming."

"Let me move the umbrella a little. Otherwise you'll burn."

She moved the umbrella.

"Now it gets difficult for me," said Catriona. "I think my father might have explained it or rather he might in time have worked it out. But really it comes down to this. I don't know all the things you did over the years for Schmidt but I'm sure that you trusted him less and less. I speak now of a time before I come on the scene. Now I think – and I do believe this is pretty obvious – that you live increasingly in a state of terror. You don't know what Schmidt's up to. You don't know what he's liable to do. You have a dual terror. You don't want Esmond to find out what you've been doing, where the money's been coming from, so you can't afford to have Schmidt lose control of the Foundation. On the other hand you're going to be in his control for the rest of your life."

"Sorry," said friendly Theodora, "but aren't you missing something? I mean, it's all very fascinating and like a story book but where do Schmidt and I come in?"

"You didn't have enough money Theodora. You *bought* Esmond. One night somewhere at some dance or other in your own peculiar language you offered him a wonderful deal. Because after all you're the bright one. That was one of your sillier things – going on to me about Esmond's intelligence to throw me off. So one starlit night you hauled him on to a balcony and you let him know that you were immensely rich and you would give him a free rein. And don't ask me for evidence Theodora because otherwise he would never have married you. He wanted a rich wife who would let him play around and look the other way."

Theodora tipped her hat. She did it clumsily. It almost fell off.

"You mean a plain girl like me?"

Catriona fought down her anger. "I mean a clever woman who lied. You lied to get him and you lied about the terms of the agreement. Oh I don't mean a legal agreement. I mean the understanding that your class goes in for."

"Class," said Theodora.

"Yes. Because you didn't have the money you said you had. You were, I suspect, spending every penny of your capital. Of course the morality of it never bothered you, did it?"

"I had to have him," said Theodora.

"Simple as that?"

"Oh yes," said Theodora.

Afterwards that was what stuck firmest in Catriona's craw. She, Catriona, had never attempted to prise a man away from another woman. Theodora believed that the pretty and rich girls had an unfair advantage. It was therefore quite all right to lie. But Catriona had to go on. Moral recriminations could wait. These were negotiable, the facts were not, and only Theodora could confirm them.

"I suspect Schmidt came to you first. *He* wanted insurance. He wanted to buy up anyone who might have anything to do with the Foundation. But if you'd known you would have gone to him anyway. And so he provided the money you needed to go on being as rich as a plain wife needed to be to let Esmond live off her. You see Theodora, one thing I have checked is your expenditure. Cash for everything. School fees. Holidays. Clothes. Cash doesn't smell does it Theodora? And that was Schmidt's way. But it has a downside. Add up your legitimate income against your huge expenditure in cash. Where does the cash come from Theodora?"

Theodora rose. She dug into the bag by her chair side, pulled out a cigarette, lit it, inhaled deeply, blew out the smoke. And for the very first time she spoke to Catriona with something approaching animus.

"I'd forgotten you ran a bar. I suppose that makes you rather good at this accounting business."

"Yes," said Catriona softly. "A pity you were born into the wrong class. You could have covered up better. And while we're at it you smoked a little too professionally in Dublin for a woman who didn't know how to do it in my flat. Just another of your little lies. I suppose you smoked on the sly because Esmond didn't like it. You killed on the sly too but then he didn't live long enough to not like that."

"Would *you* like a cigarette?" said Theodora.

And Catriona wanted to cry out, well done, you don't rise to the bait; Esmond was right when he said that you were tough.

"No thank you."

"You know," said Theodora, "I don't see why you keep bringing up class."

"You killed for class Theodora. Not for lust or principle or even greed. You killed for the money to get the right sort of husband and send your children to the right schools and live in the right house."

Theodora blew out more smoke. She sat down and rested her strong brown forearms on the little table.

"I'm sorry to seem stupid Catriona but I can't see how I've killed anyone."

"Then I'll say it clearly."

"That would be nice," said Theodora.

"Very well. You came to see me in my flat. At the time I never thought to ask you *how* you knew about Esmond and me. But of course you knew about all his women and after a bit you pulled the plug. But you were on a fishing expedition with me. Because you knew that Schmidt feared Tar and you knew someone you thought was Tar was sitting in your usual collection point – Barrington Smythe's flat – demanding me as his daughter; and you knew that I was having an affaire with Esmond. So you fished. You named names to me and I must have seemed as innocent as I actually was. Then you saw on my table a book on the Spanish Civil War and you thought My God this girl is part of a conspiracy. She works for Schmidt. She's in my husband's bed. Yes?"

"If you like," said Theodora.

"Yet you still do not know the full terms of Despard's will. Schmidt has gone to ground. Although in any case I think he would always have contacted you, not the other way round. And anyway this Tar, whom Schmidt so fears, is a weak pathetic vessel so you lure him out and you kill him anyway."

Theodora started to laugh. Big laughs that shook her rib cage. "Darling you're a *hoot*. Why should I kill this chap? I mean presumably someone had to but why me?"

For a moment Catriona hesitated. Then she said, "Because Tar was a threat to you. Because Schmidt had talked to you about Tar. Because Tar – or Maxwell as he turned out to be – could only be in that flat because he knew the hippies used it and, although you'd never seen them face to face, they might just have picked up something about you. Because after all you'd used them to service Madame Despard, and take the photographs, and develop a separate little line in blackmail, and you wouldn't have wanted Schmidt to know about that. And surely the hippies knew about the American attempt on Madame Despard's life. They didn't have a name of course, but the money would have come from your sphere of operations. Perhaps even left in Barrington Smythe's flat."

"Baloney," said Theodora. She stretched the vowels like an upper class English girl reading the bubbles in an Archie comic. "Pure supposition."

"Yes," said Catriona. "Well inference actually, but let's proceed to the hard one. Bear with me if I imagine just once again. The mistake one makes – I mean about the other deaths – the mistake in ruling you out is twofold. First, nice Theodora Claremaurice would never do anything nasty. Second, how do you benefit? You don't benefit. The husband you loved is dead. Schmidt is dead. The Foundation has passed into my hands and you won't get a penny out of me. In the long run you're much worse off."

"In the long run I thought we were all dead."

"Some quicker than others, particularly when you're around. Anyway, look at it in a different way. Let me tell you exactly what happened. Jessie's death was an accident . . . "

"Was that the old one in Edinburgh?"

Catriona gripped the edge of the table to control her hands. She wanted to see Theodora's neck snapped till it lay on one side like Jessie's. She felt sick too but that passed. Theodora was asking politely if she felt all right. Perhaps a little more lemonade . . . ?

"That one. Schmidt must have told you that the Ambulance Brigade's members would inherit. So starting at the Spanish War Archive you went looking. There's evidence there Theodora. And the boys you paid to go over her place – they'll turn up eventually too."

"Eventually," said Theodora. "We're all dead eventually too. Like in the long run."

"But you didn't get what you were looking for and, until I told you about the voting membership in Dublin, you still didn't know what was *really* going on. You didn't know what would happen to you. Would you be exposed? Would Schmidt remain head of the Foundation? And if so would he keep up the payments? Would he blackmail you? So I told you. And you knew. But *you* knew something too didn't you? You knew I'd been with Esmond. And here I was suddenly the casting vote, the lover of your husband. And it really didn't matter any more did it? The whole damned thing. You just wanted to kill me. You'd come earlier to the hotel. You found Schmidt's note. You pocketed it. Why should he write to me, not you? It was a conspiracy wasn't it? You'd worked for him for years, running his errands and licking his Swiss boots. And I was swanning in, the centre of attention, taking away your husband too. So sod it, you thought. Sod everyone or whatever the genteel equivalent. You ripped up Schmidt's note and you followed me to the brothel.

"Once again, looking back, I was slow to understand. Only later you said you were a local girl. Everyone west of Dublin – every local – must have known about the police raid nonsense. You rang from a call box, you went round the back, you waited, you shot, you killed the wrong person."

Theodora sat again as she had sat in Catriona's flat. Hands together, attentively folded like a good little girl, lying incongruously in the V between her dark muscular thighs.

"The rest is obvious, though I have to go back one stage. You were starting to get your lines crossed. You were boosting Schmidt to Esmond while saying to me that you were afraid that Esmond was in cahoots with Schmidt. In effect that it was Esmond who was on Schmidt's purely cash payroll, not you. You were hedging too many bets Theodora. In case Schmidt lost you wanted to persuade me you were Ms Clean. At the same time you were trying your damnedest to get Esmond to vote for Schmidt *although you couldn't tell him why*. You couldn't say Darling, I've been on the take for years and if Schmidt doesn't go on running the Foundation I'll never be able to buy you another dozen pairs of silk socks. Except of course that finally you *had* to. After you made a mess of the shooting in the brothel, when you failed to kill either my mother or me, you had to tell Esmond some version of the truth. You told him why he had to vote for Schmidt. You told him you'd talked to me. And your world finally crumbled. He was weak and stupid. Oh he'd go along with you but you saw that minus money and plus potential scandal, he had no time for you. From then on in I think you probably wanted to kill the world. You came looking for me at Schmidt's lodge but that didn't quite work. Then you went back to Claremaurice and waited for the vote. If Schmidt had won you could have continued, though I think you'd already realised that for you to live, for you to be remotely free, you had to kill. After all you'd prepared it, just in case. Busboy explained it to me. He drew a picture in the sand. You had a gun ready out there and opened the windows and gave yourself cover. He said it was very good shooting."

"Actually," said Theodora, "the Tar person was an accident. I wanted you. Although I never disliked you. I was just angry. Spiteful. Probably why I missed. But I did get the men who'd been beastly to me. I couldn't win could I? Either way they had me. And I didn't want that. I wanted . . . " She stretched a hand into the Moroccan air and snapped up an insect as if it might be the word she sought.

"Power," said Catriona. "You had taken one terrible risk to get Esmond. Now in taking others and succeeding you realised your power. Look at the end result. Look at yourself now. You're powerful."

"You are not exactly," said Theodora, "what you were yourself."

It was true, but a bait to which Catriona could not afford to rise. "I didn't kill Maxwell. I didn't have Jessie killed. I didn't kill my father James Tar. I didn't kill Schmidt. Never mind all the rest. Never mind what you turned away from – the starving children and the desperate girls with their abortion money stolen. They are bad enough. But the others are direct and clear. You knew. You chose. And why? What's your excuse? What's your justification? Being plain? Being greedy? It's not enough Theodora."

Theodora leaned forward. She gripped her knees with her strong whitening knuckles. She looked out at Catriona from behind her tan with her old put-upon self.

"You don't know what it's like. You couldn't. You can't. You don't. To be made love to out of goodwill and good humour. To have him go to you for his pleasure."

"No I don't. And I don't know what it was like to kill him either."

Theodora leant forward. She put her head on her hands. "I loved him," she said. "And I couldn't hate you. It got too much for me."

Yes, thought Catriona. You did what you did. And perhaps if you hadn't I would still have despised you in my heart a little. Whereas now you have earned my respect for your own special kind of bad magnificence. After all, you did it yourself.

"Part of my problem in working out the thing was in simply

not believing you could do it. Not the person that I'd seen. Was it all acting?"

"Oh no." She sounded shocked. "I really loved being a wife and mother. That was my dream. But when I couldn't have it I discovered the rest of me. I never had to act at all. No more than when a girl like you pleases a man she is acting."

"That's different Theodora. Just like killing is different."

"No," said Theodora. "Honestly. Not when you get used to it. You see they all tell you that you can't move but they're fools really. Look at you. They may try to stop us from getting what we want but some ladies do."

Theodora's hair had dried. You want to be wet again. You want to be in another element. Perhaps killing does that for you.

"Besides," said Theodora. "I don't see what you can do. It's all quite convenient really."

"Perhaps," said Catriona. "I doubt that in the world that men run you will be charged. Except if I talk to the insurance companies."

"Sorr*ee*." The suffix was worried.

"You had very large policies on Esmond's life, didn't you? You benefited from a crime."

"No," said Theodora. "I don't think that will wash. The claims are very well spread. No. I don't think they would do anything at all unless – just possibly unless you wouldn't leave them alone."

Catriona nodded.

"Well," and Theodora stretched her athlete's body. "I'm sorry but I can't be blackmailed again. I'm really not good at it."

"No," said Catriona. "I wouldn't have expected that."

"And you're not much of a one for it either. Or for bribery."

"I don't know. Not now."

"So what then?"

"You killed my father. I want you to pay."

"I pay with every time my husband touched you."

"I may owe that to you. It's my father you owe. It's the others."

Theodora looked at Catriona as if trying to assess the needs of a different species. "I don't understand. I honestly don't."

"No," said Catriona. "I'm not sure I do myself."

Theodora looked up at the five o'clock distancing sun. "No," she said. "You'd get no support. If the worst came to the worst I'd just stay out of the country. But you'd be a terrible nuisance. Besides," and suddenly she seemed again to look both practically minded and helpless, "I've three little girls to bring up."

"Yes," said Catriona softly. "That's exactly what worried me."

And Theodora actually said it. "That's a *beastly* thing to say."

Catriona stood up. "My father was an assassin. You're a murderess. He may have been wrong but he killed for others. He believed in something. You kill only for yourself. I'm sorry because you're bigger than that – but it's the truth."

"I'm sorry." Theodora looked at Catriona with what seemed to be infinite wearied parental sadness. "I think I'm really just a very practical person . . . Well you know what I mean."

She was too polite to mention Catriona's murder to her face – too well bred to euphemise it. She was also something else – she was puzzled. Why had Catriona come like this in the first place? And why wasn't she frightened?

"What are you going to do Theodora?" Catriona pointed at the big strong brown hands. "Strangle me? Throw me in the pool and drown me?"

"I wish you wouldn't talk like that. You know I always liked you. You don't have to do anything – to tell anyone. I mean what good would it do? And then I don't have to do anything. Not a thing."

Catriona shook her head. "Oh but you will Theodora. It's a risk you can't afford to take. You could never be sure. I threaten you. And when you're threatened – you kill. When you want something – you lie. You might at least tell me the truth. Tell me what you're going to do with me?"

Theodora rose to her feet. "I think we'll take a trip to the desert. It's the best place. The desert's best. I shall make it painless. I won't leave you there alive."

"Just dead."

Theodora removed the gun from her beach bag. Then she hesitated. "Who have you told?"

"Him," said Catriona. "I told him."

The Consul stood in the entrance to the garden. He removed his hat and fanned himself.

"And he told them."

The Consul moved to one side. Twenty of the Blue People filed into the garden.

"Friends of Jimmy Tar," said Catriona. "Friends of my father. They want to take you into the desert. They agree with you. The desert's best."

Theodora was still. Perhaps – for she had always been resourceful – she thought for a moment of shooting her way out. If so she must have realised just as quickly how impossible that was. She looked down, then back up at Catriona.

"Perhaps I could have a few moments on my own?"

"Of course."

"I have a letter to write."

She walked up the steps into the house. Three minutes later they heard the single shot.

# 38

Catriona stood in the small graveyard at the back of the square ugly Presbyterian church. The March wind came in from the Firth of Forth, driving the cold mist before it. From the top of the hill you could see patches of Edinburgh – a spire here, a turret there – stuck up menacingly from the mist.

Of course even as she laid them down Catriona knew that they would quickly blow away. Why not, she thought – what would the dead do with flowers anyway? What was she here for herself? To do penance?

She stared down at the flat black stones that commemorated the lives of Mr and Mrs Lomax.

Behind her a male throat cleared. Robinson stood there, one hand thrust deep in the pocket of his British Warm, the other grasping flowers. She wasn't really surprised. He was always turning up.

"Did you have me followed?"

"Something like that," he stepped forward and laid the flowers beside hers. "But I thought you might come here eventually."

Catriona was quite glad to have someone to talk to.

"They didn't love me of course but they took care of me. And all I could do was dream of something else. I disowned them you know. In my mind. In my heart. They were entitled to something better."

"Don't make too much of it," said Robinson. "They're only parents. I hated mine."

And it came as a slight, distant, unimportant surprise that Robinson had possessed a childhood, a life that she hadn't known about.

"You know," she said, "we're alike – Theodora, Madame Despard, myself – we all had dreams about *doing*. Moving around, shaking things, putting the dreams into action. Didn't get us very far."

"It's cold," said Robinson. "I'll give you a lift. I told you once I like women who do things."

"But I think you're a – a swine."

"I thought I might be your swine."

She started to laugh.

He said, "The fact is Catriona that I'm up to your weight. Most men aren't. You're as strong as they come. Anyway think about it. Give it time."

She saw that he meant it. "You think that's what I want? Not another Esmond? An equal? Do you think that's what women really want?"

"Haven't the faintest. But I know what this woman could use."

"Oh do you. And what's that?"

Robinson grinned into the wind.

"A better class of visitor."

**ROSAMOND SMITH**

SOUL/MATE

Colin Asch was charming. When he came to stay with his uncle and aunt, he quickly became something of a social success. Women in particular were attracted to him: the little-boy-lost look, his sensitivity and idealism. They took him to their hearts and often to their beds.

No one understood that his only real pleasure was killing. Killing with a cold thoughtfulness and ingenuity. Killing again and again . . .

'Intelligently terrifying . . . Smith gives us a subtly observed, complicated monster' *The Independent*

'Rosamond Smith could easily become the world's Number One mystery writer' *Elmore Leonard*

'A powerful psychological thriller reminiscent of Patricia Highsmith' *Sunday Express*

'Tense stuff effectively rendered . . . creepy enough to stop you chatting up strangers for a while'
*Literary Review*

**HODDER AND STOUGHTON PAPERBACKS**

**MARC OLDEN**

# KISAENG

Park Song, aka the Laughing Boy, made money. Probably the finest counterfeiter in the world, his speciality was the US $100 bill.

Park Song also bought girls.

Manny Decker was a cop who investigated cops.

Corruption, brutality, links with organised crime: undercover work, dangerous and lonely. He liked it.

Tawny DaSilva was missing.

Daughter of the one love of Decker's life, she had set off for school and vanished.

Decker was about to head down into an international underworld of expensive vice and ruthless cruelty that would shock even him.

'No one has plumbed the secrets of the Orient with near the imagination' *Clive Cussler*

'Tough, realistic, sadistic and erotic, *Kisaeng* combines the traditions of Lustabader and Clavell, but outstrips them with sheer energy of narrative' *Fear*

**HODDER AND STOUGHTON PAPERBACKS**